MONTANA WOMEN

MONTANA WOMEN

TONI VOLK

SOHO

The author gratefully acknowledges a grant from
James A. Michener and the Copernicus Society of America.

Copyright © 1992 by Toni Volk

Published by
Soho Press, Inc.
853 Broadway
New York, NY 10003

Library of Congress Cataloging-in-Publication Data

Volk, Toni, 1944–
Montana women : a novel / Toni Volk.
p.   cm.
ISBN 0-939149-60-5 :
I. Title.
PS3572.03943M66   1992
813'.54—dc20   91-18737
                                                     CIP

Manufactured in the United States
10   9   8   7   6   5   4   3   2

Book design and composition by
The Sarabande Press

To
Gunther A. Byrd

MONTANA
WOMEN

CHAPTER

ONE

———◆———

1944

Their parents were dead, Harold and David were gone, and the world was at war. Some nights Etta woke up to all that with a smack, as though it were fresh news, fresh trouble. Then she'd want to get up and climb into bed with her sister Pearl and bawl. But loss, grief, or missing sex were things you didn't pass back and forth like that. No, in their family rupture and dissolution were worn privately, with discomfort, mortification even, like tight or stained undergarments.

So though she now lived with Pearl in the home left to them in a handwritten will, Etta kept the increasing weight of fear and feeling to herself. Pinched and out of sight. Of course Pearl did too.

Etta opened the door that said MONTANA TRIBUNE PUBLISHERS AND PRINTERS and poked her head into a large office where Pearl was tidying a desk. Etta watched her sort mail, thumb through papers, and straighten them.

"I'm here," she called.

"Okay," Pearl said and waved her to the bench along the wall. But Etta continued to stand in the doorway until Pearl lifted her coat from the oak rack beneath the clock and said good-bye to several men in ink-stained aprons still occupied there. She closed the door behind her and the men became blurred lumps through the milky, serrated glass. Pearl buttoned her coat.

"I thought we could have supper at the Falls Hotel to celebrate your birthday," Etta told her as they walked down the broad stairs to the first-floor lobby. Pearl was now twenty-five, Etta was twenty-four. They pulled their coats about them, though it was spring. A response, Etta guessed, to being vulnerable and alone.

Only when they were seated in the large dining room, had ordered a drink—Etta placed the order—and settled themselves sufficiently, did they free their arms from their coat sleeves and allow the coats to lie loosely about their shoulders.

"Why did you order sherry?"

"I don't know. Don't you like it?"

"I've never had it."

"Well, I read somewhere that it's a nice thing for women to drink."

"I'd rather have beer."

Etta expected that Pearl wouldn't drink it but she did. Pearl seemed to relax some and gazed about at the large room. It was rather dark and reminded Etta, except for the ruby broadloom carpet, of the library. It had the same sort of mahogany supporting posts and paneling and thick-legged tables. Even the chandeliers were similar, fussier of course, but similar.

"Remember on our birthdays when we were kids how Mother always got us the same thing like we were twins?" Pearl asked her.

"Yes. I hated that."

"I don't know why. You should have had to wait another year for everything. It was so irritating to beg and beg to get something and then to have you get it too.

"Don't blame me."

But Pearl wasn't blaming anybody. "Remember that year I wanted my birthday party at Gibson Park?" she asked.

"Yes, it rained."

4

"It was nice when we started out," Pearl said, signaling the waiter that they were ready to order. They had both decided on prime rib.

"When I got older I always wanted to have a beer bust there. Did you?" she asked, staring into her empty glass and twirling it between her hands.

"No," said Etta. She hated that park.

"Let's walk through there on our way home."

"It will be too dark," Etta said. She'd always felt uneasy there, even in daylight. In the summer large cottonwoods made long shadows and noise, almost a low moan, in the hot winds. The sun on the pond was like a bright mirror, too bright to look into without hurting your eyes. Winters, the park had a desolate feel and the winter winds still caused the bare trees to pitch and the sound then was more like cracking, like the trees were breaking up and ready to fall. She remembered trying to skate there on days like that, on ice always chipped and bumpy. There was an island on the pond with a stone ledge around it where they sat to rest or to take off their skates. Summers, large white swans circled the island out of reach of boys who tried to pelt them with rocks or firecrackers. The same boys hung around the island winters, rude and leering, often peeing in the fresh, clean snow, leaving jagged patterns of urine she and Pearl had to step around. Winos, too, came to drink from their sack-wrapped bottles and to sleep sitting against the tree trunks.

Men from all over the country passed through Gibson Park on their way west, stopping to take a side trip downtown to the bars on Second Avenue. From behind the park and along the river the men came, men on the move, silent, hungry-looking men, from freights that slowed to cross the Missouri, headed somewhere.

Once a man had come suddenly from behind a bush and held out his hand to Etta. She had stood there, transfixed by his hand, held there by fear or perhaps surprise and then, despite her curiosity, she ran to find her mother. She had often wondered

5

what the man had tried to say with that hand. Had it held a nickel? Had it said come? Had it asked that money be put there toward another pint of something? Or had that hand just wanted the lunch she held in her own hand?

She could still picture the man's face. It was expressionless, nondescript. That there was nothing about the face to describe made it memorable, evocative. Something about the man always made her feel anxious when she thought about him. Even now.

"I wonder where the swans go in winter," Pearl said.

"The what?"

"The big white swans."

"They probably go south."

"Or maybe the Park Department keeps them somewhere," Pearl said, staring at something behind Etta. "Did you know swans mate for life and if one dies the other remains alone?"

"You want dessert?" Etta asked.

Pearl shook her head. They'd both eaten everything on their plates, a habit they'd formed over the lean years of the Depression. They'd probably be too full to eat the birthday cake Etta had planned to serve when they got home.

"Let's walk up Central and stop at one of those bars," Pearl said.

Etta paid the check, helped Pearl on with her coat, and put on her own. Etta didn't like to admit to her older sister that she'd been in those places often with Harold, in fact, sort of liked them. "They're probably dirty," she told Pearl, knowing positively that no one swept or cleaned any of them with regularity.

"I don't care. I feel like something different."

Once on the street, they walked a couple of blocks and passed three likely spots before Pearl decided on one.

The counter and back bar were oak, dark and wrinkled looking from the layers of old varnish that coated them. On the walls were Charlie Russell paintings that made the prairie look reddish and pinkish and gold, colors Etta didn't think it deserved. The

prairie she knew was more the shade of wheat stubble, a faint
drab yellow, lifeless and ominously pervasive, spreading vast
distances impossible to estimate. Her father told her once that
Russell used to swap his sketches for drinks in bars like this,
sketches that later, after Russell died, became valuable.

They took seats at the bar. No one looked at them, yet Etta
knew everyone at some point would. They were out of place,
definitely out of place. Not so much because women couldn't go
into bars unescorted or because women who did were thought
less of. There was that, certainly. But it was more that they were
out of place because they sat up too straight; they didn't look
around in slow, sure appraisal like other women did to surmise
or presume possibilities here. And their clothes were too dull a
shade of anything, too maintained and sensible a cloth.

"Anyway, we have to have a beer now," Pearl said as if feeling
less sure of her idea.

Etta hoped the bartender wouldn't recognize her and want to
talk about Harold. But he only looked at her briefly and said
nothing.

Pearl examined the glasses he brought before pouring her beer.

"You think we should've gone to college?" she asked. Every
now and then, when Pearl got to mulling over the various dissat-
isfactions and disappointments of her life, she'd want to discuss
what she should have done.

"No," Etta told her.

"Why not?"

"We're not cut out to be teachers or nurses. So why bother?
You'd still work for a printer and I'd still have to keep books."
Etta decided not to mention her belief that their jobs and others
like them would be given back to men when they returned from
war—if they ever did, that is.

"We could've gone solely for the education."

"Why bother?" Etta believed you could educate yourself.

"We might have met a different kind of man."

7

"What kind?" Etta couldn't imagine a better man than Harold and decided to change the subject. "How are things at work?"

"Fine. Still, we're limited in some way," Pearl said, persisting. "You graduate from high school, go to college if you have money, or to work at Woolworth's if you don't."

"Yeah, well no one has money these days."

"Then if you don't get married, you eventually have to find something better than Woolworth's. And we did. So now what?"

"I don't know," Etta said. "Join the WACS and go to war, I guess." She decided it wasn't such a good idea to be in a bar drinking. Ever since David had been listed as missing in action, Pearl often became either morose or despondent. In a way she was having a harder time of things than Etta, who at least knew Harold was dead.

The bartender was grilling hamburgers now. He wore a butcher's apron and a visor that suggested that between customers he might be playing poker in the back. "Another beer?" he said to them and Etta recalled the hairy mole on his chin and that his name was Walt. She shook her head no. Somewhere along the line she and Pearl had exchanged roles. Etta now mothered the sister who used to mother her. When had that happened?

"Those guys at the table in the corner are staring at us," Pearl said when Walt turned back to the grill. It seemed to surprise her and she watched them through the mirror.

"Let's drink up and go," Etta said. As they collected their change and purses, one fellow from the group approached them. Like the others, his clothes were soiled by grease or oil and he had a few days' growth of beard. Mechanics, Etta guessed.

"You ladies care to join us?" he asked.

"No thanks, we're just leaving," Etta said, and she hurried Pearl out the door.

"A little sloppy and old, but kind of cute," Pearl said.

"You want to walk or take a cab?"

"Walk. I need the exercise."

It was a rare evening for spring—no wind or late-night chill. They walked slowly, stopping to look in store windows. They considered hats and dresses at the Mercantile and tennis rackets at the sporting goods store on the corner.

"Maybe we should take up tennis," Etta said. Pearl didn't answer. She wasn't paying attention. She was looking up the block after two women walking in the same direction east.

"There's Mavis and Darlene," she said. She was quiet for a block and Etta knew the two women had set her to thinking, to contemplating something about them she found a little frightening, a little mysterious—and infinitely interesting. Pearl loved to discuss the women and every story she and Etta had ever heard about the pair. The one everyone agreed on was that the women were mother and daughter and they had somehow fallen from a life of leisure and class because of *drugs*—something they shot into their arms—into a life of street roaming and bar visiting. Some even said prostitution but no one seemed willing to admit much knowledge on that. Yet there was a well-known whorehouse people said the two operated called Nine-Eighteen because of its address—918 First Street.

Speculation about who the women were before their descent fell into categories of class and distinction that varied with the preferences of the storyteller. There were a good twenty possibilities suggested, two of them common ones. The first was that the mother was once married to a rich rancher and they came from a nearby farming community—banished, no doubt, to the city. The other had the mother married to a rich doctor who had one of the big homes on Ninth Street and, of course, that made sense. She got her drugs from him.

"Or maybe the daughter was married to the doctor and got her mother started," suggested Pearl.

"I don't know," Etta said.

"Well, they look the same as they did when I was a kid. We get older and they stay the same."

9

It was a funny thing for Pearl to say, Etta thought, since the two women were always old as far as she was concerned. Yet Pearl was right. In that oldness they looked the same, though one was clearly the other's senior. One had black-gray hair—that would be Darlene—and the other one, Mavis, yellow-gray hair. No one really knew for sure just who was who, but it was taken for granted because of the first letters of their names, *M* and *D*, that Mavis was the mother, Darlene the daughter. In any event they looked alike—tall and thin with transparent faces, rather like onion skin pulled tight over large gray bones. The bone structure, though, was good. Then their hair, despite the color difference, had a matching fried quality. It was as though something had caused it to look singed. Yet there was something of beauty and glamor there too, shopworn and depreciated, but there all the same.

"Once I yelled something at them," Pearl admitted. "And they chased me."

"What did you yell?"

"Nothing really. 'Hey Mopey and Dopey.' Something like that."

"They chased you?"

"Yeah, for about a block but I ducked into the movie theatre with my bus fare and hid. I guess I thought they'd catch me and stick needles in my arm. I had to walk home then and got in trouble for being late."

"Well you were a brat."

"And you weren't, of course."

Etta put her arm through Pearl's and guided her to a cab parked in front of Al's News. "Let's go home and have cake."

The cab passed the mysterious old women, and Etta and Pearl watched them turn down the side street. "They're going home," Etta said.

"Yeah," Pearl answered. "To Nine-Eighteen."

CHAPTER

TWO

———————◆———————

"I don't want to baby-sit Leona's kids," Pearl told Etta.

"Why, did you have plans?"

"I was just making them." She was. She was considering suicide, as a matter of fact.

"Couldn't your plans wait? I won't leave them with you for long."

Couldn't your plans wait? Pearl hung up the phone in disgust.

This wouldn't be the first time that Pearl had taken care of the neighbor's boy but now there was also a baby. When their father got to carrying on, drunk and mean and on the fight, he'd go home to Leona, his wife, and start in. Once in a while the boy got it too. For all the attention Etta gave to the neighbors, nothing changed. This was one of the things about their life that annoyed Pearl, that nothing changed. Now if circumstances and conditions would start moving and surprising her, she'd consider sticking around just to watch. Possibly one of the changes she should manage herself before she died would be to thump Leona's old man on the head with something heavy. It didn't look like Leona ever would and, of course, Etta wouldn't. She believed in forgiveness.

Pearl put a bottle of burgundy to cool. She was no judge of wine and she knew it; in fact, she liked hers ice cold. But in all areas of her life, she did the best she could, keeping order, balancing her preferences with the rules, trying for the most part to plan the events of her life. Nothing was spontaneous anymore. She organized every little thing, made a big deal out of it. But getting rid of depression, she found, wasn't something you could make arrangements for. Hadn't she tried? She had been to three ministers, two doctors, and a psychiatrist. She had even joined a church group just to enlarge her social life. She had tried volunteer work, changing jobs, moving to her own place, moving back. She experimented with mineral baths and hot springs, changing her diet, vitamins and drinking.

In some measure the drinking was fun, that is, to the degree she had any recall beyond certain particulars. One night, for instance, she'd gone with Maize, a friend from work, to a bar where in a short time they were as much a part of the common foolery as anyone there. What occurred after she had danced with an ambulance driver from Black Eagle, her last memory, was an everlasting mystery and just as well.

Maize tried to tell her bits and pieces. "He borrowed the paperboy's wagon and hauled you up the street."

"Don't tell me any more!" Pearl had cried out, appalled.

Then there was the morning she awoke next to some stranger in her own bed and had to sneak him out of the house while Etta was in the shower. That ended drinking as a restorative; the guilt, however, remained. It was disconcerting to find she could be so riotous and unruly.

After that, she'd gone so far as to try prayer. Certainly Etta would never believe it but, yes, she'd tried prayer, knowing all the same that hers was merely one of millions of such pleas saturating the ether. It gave her, more than anything else, a sense of the extent of her problem.

It didn't occur to her to see a psychiatrist until one day she went over to Leona's. She decided to go over to see for herself what Etta had found to interest her there. To Pearl's amazement, she ended up confiding in this annoying woman so totally that Leona had eventually turned from what she was doing at the stove with a diagnosis. "Maybe you're having a nervous breakdown."

She said it calmly, matter-of-factly, with no emphasis at all. A nervous breakdown! Pearl tried to imagine her nerves, comparing them to cords and strings and tangled yarn. It was this image of knotted stringy stuff breaking off and falling around her feet that made her decide to see a psychiatrist. No doubt a nervous breakdown meant insanity—madness in some quantity, however small. And like immorality, madness was puzzling, disrespectful, and an inconvenience to nonsufferers. People did not like to hear of it. Finally she hadn't cared what it meant and walked in ready to confess anything that might absolve or deliver her. But she was not equipped that day for hindrance.

The receptionist had first of all avoided looking at her. While Pearl waited, the women straightened her blouse, fluffed a curl, and reapplied lipstick. Then she'd made a few entries into a notebook and then consulted a thick file of papers, obviously looking for something. Finally she turned to face Pearl. "Yes, I have an opening two weeks from Thursday," she said without a glance at any calendar. It was Monday.

Pearl was overwhelmed. She needed help now but she couldn't say that and fled the office. The next day she tried another doctor. Pearl had the same feelings of impatience, that any delay might make her change her mind, that she hadn't the time or the stamina to go for a long-term cure. Luckily, or unluckily, that one could see her the same afternoon.

Pearl didn't know what to blame her pain and anguish on and for that matter didn't care. She wanted relief, as immediate and permanent a thing as possible. At his request, she told the thin, balding psychiatrist all the dreams she could think of. She liked a painting on his wall of a lone steer searching the frozen plains for grass titled *Waiting for a Chinook*. But like too many things lately, it made her want to cry. So she stared at his license to practice and told him about her life: that her parents were dead; that she still lived in their house; that she had a sister who wasn't crazy and seemed happy; that as a child she had been caught masturbating by her mother, who cried and asked where she, a well-meaning mother, had gone wrong.

She didn't say it but her mother needn't have concerned herself. It wasn't something she did that often. There was a feeling after it she didn't like, a curious, perplexing feeling. Not that this was the only time she got this feeling, it could come over her anytime. And when it did she'd wonder, what is it? What do I want? Orange juice, a drink of water, Coca-Cola, chocolate? Or when she was older—a cigarette, a drink, sex, coffee? Often she'd ask other people about it. Do you ever get this feeling that you want something so bad you can taste it—it seemed to her the feeling was one she held in her mouth—yet can't put your finger on what?

"Well . . . ," some would say. Others said, "Yeah," in a tone that failed to convince her. And once in a while someone would cry out, "Exactly! I know exactly what you mean but I don't know what it is either." For some reason, Pearl thought the psychiatrist would be in the "Well" category and never brought it up. Instead she studied his shiny desk, bare but for a photo of Jane Russell, framed, glossy, autographed, and explained to him about David: that they had fallen in love; that against her own strong moral objections she had slept with him; that they had planned to get married after the war. But he didn't return, was missing in action, and a year later his mother received a picture of a baby girl in a white frock coat. The picture was sent by a French woman who wrote that the child was David's. His mother showed her the photograph. Pearl suspected that his mother never liked her but this was callous and meaner than Pearl deserved. Of course, this had been months before. The pain now, she explained to the doctor, was different. She guessed he hadn't believed her.

But there was no sense in going over all that again. Pearl went out to the kitchen. Would the kids be hungry when they got here or would they have had dinner? Maybe Etta would bring sandwiches or were they too young for that? She checked the refrigerator and cupboard. She had peanut butter and crackers, a quart of milk, and some maple syrup. If she had to she could make them pancakes.

Going back to the living room, she wondered if she should take up all the fragile things in the dining and living rooms, like the crystal vase Aunt Julia had left her. No, she decided; there was nothing in the house that hadn't needed breaking in the past thirty years.

Well if she did do *it,* she would leave everything in order. She'd finish her work at the office, clean out her desk, and leave instructions for a replacement. She would pay all her bills with one exception. The psychiatrist's. She would leave him the $24 she still owed him in twenty-four envelopes, one dollar in each, with instructions they be mailed out one by one each month. This would show him what esteem she held him in and how helpful it had been to have someone staring coldly, without a trace of recognizable human expression, and asking, "And how did you feel about that?" "Like hell," she had yelled once.

"He's only being objective," Etta told her at the time.

"Objective!" Pearl had cried. "I don't even think he's listening."

It occurred to her that perhaps the man reminded her of her father. There was something familiar about the way he looked at her, like her father had, without real attention, taking something about her into account with one glimpse and objecting to it, the objection clear, the reason not. How she'd hated that about her father—the way he looked at her. Even when his disapproval erupted as it did from time to time in sudden, jarring scenes, there seemed some larger intent on his part than the expression of mere anger.

One day he'd taken her to get ice cream. It had been a warm spring evening not unlike this night. Where Etta and her mother were, Pearl couldn't recall. Anyway, he'd let her choose from among the various flavors a hand-packed quart to take home. And while they waited in line there had been a cloudburst lasting maybe five minutes so that, when they came out of the ice cream parlor, the air was cool and smelled earthy and clean. She had felt such pleasure that night, walking beside him beneath the dripping cottonwoods, carrying the ice cream carefully, enjoying the streetlights' passing reflections in puddles of clean rain. But as was often the case with him, the pleasure was not to be relied on. When they entered the house, he spied her overdue library book on the hall table.

"Goddamn it!" he said or something like it. "I told you to take that back a week ago." Pearl could remember freezing, watching him as he threw the library book into the living room, where it landed spread open and torn on page 138. And a vase of lilacs had fallen to the floor too, and she could smell the limp and scattered blossoms as she dropped the ice cream, chocolate marble, and ran up the stairs.

Another time they had all gone camping and on the way her father had been in an exceptional mood, though she and Etta were bickering in the backseat.

"Girls," he said. "Let's play No Noise." This was a game they often played in the car, a game she always lost. The object of the game, besides general peace, was to succeed in not talking, no matter what. Laughing counted too and was usually the way their father, always game leader, got them and saved having to give either one the silver dollar he always put forth as an incentive.

So he proceeded good-naturedly to try to trick them. Mother had been the first to go out. She was easy. With Mother, you had only to get her day dreaming and then ask her a question. They had set up camp, however, before Etta broke down; Pearl didn't remember how that was accomplished. Anyway, for some reason Pearl had become obsessed with the game and when her father grew sick of it and called it off, declaring her the winner of the dollar, she still didn't talk. She couldn't. It was as though something had sealed shut inside her and no words would come. She knew she had let it go too far but she couldn't do anything about it. Finally, enraged, her father had torn apart the old pup tent she and Etta had always slept in on such outings and flung it in pieces into the woods. The forest, despite his rage as he kicked at the fire and banged on the hood of the car, seemed perfectly still until she herself broke its peace and her own silence and screamed.

And that was what she felt with the psychiatrist—open disapproval and impending rage. But on the surface he was disinterested; and though it annoyed her, it also reassured her. Could he be disinterested in a nervous breakdown?

"I'm not having a nervous breakdown," she told Leona the next chance she got when Etta wasn't around.

"Great. What's the problem then?"

"I think it's just boredom."

"Is that what he said?"

"Who?"

"The doctor."

But Pearl had quit seeing him. "Yes," she lied. Of course, it must have been boredom, even the doctor had it.

She remained depressed and sometimes belligerent, intolerant of other people's pain—hers was greater, or so she thought. Or else other people's problems made her despair more. She'd be unable to give comfort or receive it and became convinced that for some, there was no hope. Most people, she concluded, found life an endless arrangement of routines and duties. These duties, once simple and effortlessly done, now required extraordinary amounts of her energy and thought. And once she got started she couldn't stop. She'd work late into the evening, wrestling with long galley proofs in the dimming light, looking for manuscripts she had misplaced, and organizing all the typefaces that were always out of place. She found the effort depleting and wasteful. She had no enthusiasm. Who could get excited day in, day out, about ads for victory gardens or news of Hitler.

If she had had the energy, she would have tried moving or changing jobs again; she had no resources left for attracting a lover. But that mattered little since there were no men around anyway who weren't too old, maimed by war, or married.

And her prayer? Nothing. She felt absolutely nothing came of it. A brick wall might have served her better, absorbing the vibrations of her voice into its tiny unseen molecules, or maybe bouncing them back in disgust. But she felt nothing.

That was not all. There was more troubling her than profound tiredness and lack of hope. The general dismay she felt, her awe of peril in the world had grown into intractable anxiety that woke her mornings at about five o'clock. She tried to talk herself out of it, tried to simply withstand it. But every morning there it was again, stronger for her dread of it.

Pearl looked at the clock on the mantel but it had stopped. She guessed it was about 6:30. She decided to call Leona's and see what the holdup was. Pearl waited through ten rings and almost hung up, when George, Leona's husband, answered and yelled, "We're busy and don't call back," and slammed down the receiver. My God, she thought, there are worse things than dying.

Say she actually did *it*. There was certainly some pleasure here just in guessing everyone's response to such a thing. She liked to think old boyfriends might be surprised or that friends might try to calculate how long they'd been out of touch and feel sorry. But those she worked with would be the least amazed, the first to say, Well, she was moody, you know.

Say she actually did *it* tonight. Etta, always considerate, would feel terrible that she hadn't realized and been more help. She would think how insensitive, how rude of her to dump Leona's problems on Pearl the very evening she was busy getting ready to kill herself. Even so, Pearl shouldn't have to change the night just to accommodate Etta and Leona.

But how to do something like this was a problem. She wasn't one for violence and the thought of wounding or disfiguring herself was distasteful. After all, she only wanted relief, with as much dignity and discretion as possible.

Pills? She'd probably throw up and be embarrassed and suffer through an expensive ride in an ambulance — the guy from Black Eagle driving, no doubt, trying to remember where he'd seen her before. Then the neighborhood would talk for years, speculating and enhancing the smallest detail of her gaudy failure. The same for slashed wrists. Fail there and be left with glaring scars. How about driving her car off a cliff? Maybe not, she decided, recalling how long it had taken to save the money to buy it, how she'd skimped, how proud she'd been driving it home.

No, the simplest thing would be to attach a hose from the exhaust pipe to the inside of the car and let the engine run. Practical. It had a certain economy even. She could do it after the kids left. But she'd want to get it over with before it got dark. She hated fooling around in the garage after dark. Despite a large light bulb on the ceiling, she could never see in there and always had to get a flashlight.

Pearl sighed, went out to the kitchen, poured herself a glass of wine, and took it into the living room. Shortly, she heard commotion on the front porch. She put the wine just out of sight behind the lamp.

"Pearl, I really appreciate this," Etta said in greeting. "This time the police hauled George off and I'm trying to get Leona to press charges. And the poor dear, she's pregnant again."

It never failed — the poor dear this, the poor dear that. Just once Pearl wanted Etta to see that her own sister had problems too.

As usual Etta was late and out of breath. She had the baby in her arms and when she set it down it whimpered. She had to pull the boy's fingers from her skirt. "I won't be gone long," she told the children. "Jimmy, you remember Pearl, don't you?"

Etta went through the lumpy sack she carried. Distracted, disoriented, that was Etta. One of the things that never changed was the way Etta had of scattering herself about any room she was in. She scattered the contents of the sack around now—a bottle, diapers, toys, and books. She said she was only making the kids feel at home.

Jimmy, who was three, had his mother's tendency to talk a lot. He was bright, smiling, and Pearl had always liked him the times Etta brought him to the house. The baby was something else again. Pearl couldn't help staring at her and the baby stared right back. Pearl had no idea that a young child could look so serious, so suspicious. She was about a year old, pretty, and had small bruises on her right cheek that made Pearl wince.

"It's hot tonight," Etta said as she waved good-bye. Pearl started in on the mess in the front room while Jimmy asked her questions. He asked about everything in the room and china closet, about everything on the bookcase. He followed Pearl around as she picked things up and arranged them on the couch. The baby didn't move from where she sat on the floor, nor did she make a sound. Pearl carried the child to the kitchen and put her on a chair. Jimmy followed behind, chatting to Pearl as she got him milk and graham crackers. Pearl offered some to the baby. She refused the milk, but held the cracker tightly, silently.

"The baby doesn't talk," explained Jimmy. She seemed content to just hold the cracker and stare at Pearl.

Pearl decided it was too hot inside. "Let's go out on the front porch," she said. She picked up the baby, who now stiffened in her arms. Pearl hated to put her down on the porch floor and she knew the grass would be damp and full of mosquitoes. She held the child on her lap in the porch swing and Jimmy climbed up and sat beside them.

"What's your name?" she asked the baby.

"Her name is Shirley, but she doesn't know it," Jimmy said. It appeared he was right. The baby continued to stare at Pearl.

Pearl relaxed. She was exhausted, glad for the distraction. But she felt better, almost cheerful, just knowing she had an alternative, knowing she could put a bigger light bulb in the garage and all the rest. Poor baby, though. What choices did *she* have? Pearl sensed a whole life full of pain ahead for her.

It was a beautiful evening. The sun was just going down, and the horizon was red and pink. The lilacs that flanked the porch were fragrant after the unusually warm spring day. It was going to be a long, hot summer, Pearl knew, glad she'd miss the heat. The crickets were out in the huge cottonwood beside the porch. The tree's roots were bulging above the ground and beginning to thrust the porch upward at one end.

Jimmy tried to mimic the crickets, then continued his questioning.

"Why do they make that noise?" he asked. "And where do they sleep?"

Pearl answered him lazily. Even the baby seemed tired of all his energy. They swung slowly, watching the sky, fastening on the color and intensity of brilliance visible from where the house sat at the top of the hill. The porch overlooked a long street, narrow and lined on either side by trees. The street ran down the slope of hill into the sunset like a path, ending in reds and gold and fading blue. Pearl wished she had an ice-cold beer in the house.

Jimmy began to sing. Pearl couldn't identify the song but Jimmy sang it twice. When he started it a third time, the baby roused herself and appeared to take an interest in the singing. Her small voice was way off-key and she sang no words, but in a stunning, clear tone the child copied her brother. Her own small face remained serious as she concentrated on his.

It was unnerving. Pearl, who looked easily at those things both affronting and pitiable, could not stand to speculate on what life might require of this child. Yet for all the mean features of its life, this baby was trying to sing, like a crippled and caged sparrow might try to sing. Pearl wanted to object, to dispute the very effort. She wanted to protest that need everyone had, despite danger all around, to reach out in hope and longing. Instead she began to cry. Jimmy and the baby stopped singing to listen.

"What's the matter?" Jimmy asked timidly.

"I don't know," she said.

Jimmy patted her shoulder and the baby put her head on Pearl's chest, her chubby fingers clutching Pearl's neck. Pearl couldn't quit crying though she tried. The sound of it was ugly and intrusive in the quiet night and she was ashamed. Jimmy and the baby started crying with her as if perplexed, unable to cope any other way with her grief or for that matter, Pearl guessed, with their own.

The baby first, then Jimmy, cried themselves to sleep, still huddled against her. Pearl, too, was finally quiet. Only a crack of light remained on the horizon now and it illuminated a narrow line between earth and sky. It was hardly anything at all, just a brief, slight edge of gold that one might mistake for a place on which to stand or even walk.

It wasn't long after this that Pearl met Gordon Buckman. In the only instance of precognition she could ever remember having, she saw that he would change her life.

CHAPTER

THREE

Gordon Buckman hadn't been at his cousin's annual pig roast ten minutes when he noticed Pearl. An instinct told him this was the kind of girl you marry. She and her sister were standing over by the only tree in the yard. They were tall and dark and carried themselves with propriety and composure, so when he saw Pearl closer he was surprised that she didn't look so sure of herself after all. She had large, black eyes that waited for something, needed something, and that need, for whatever reason, softened him. Her sister Etta had the same extraordinary eyes, yet hers were sharp and impertinent, as if to say there was nothing they would not dare look at.

Curiously, the sister provoked feelings in him that he had to stop to analyze. Absurd as it was, he decided it was jealousy—he was jealous of this stranger's closeness to Pearl. The thought even crossed his mind that however close they were, it didn't matter, as they—he and the girl Pearl—would be living eighty miles away. All of this before he had spoken one word to either of them. What's more, it was then, looking at the two across the yard, that he knew he would patch it up with the old man, quit his job, and return to the ranch.

It was his friend Charlie who finally brought her across the lawn to him. "This guy who's been rudely staring at you has a name. Pearl, meet Gordon Buckman, known to most as Buck."

Buck found her easy to talk to and a good listener. She invited him to dinner.

The first time he went there, Etta wasn't home and he was grateful for that. He liked something about the house, an order, a solidness that went with what he saw in Pearl. They sat at the kitchen table and he liked that too. She hadn't tried to impress him with a tablecloth and china or the nonsense of candles. She served him chicken potpie on simple dishes and cold beer. She didn't jump up and down nervously, nor did she hurry to clear away the dirty dishes. She just sort of pushed them aside without interrupting what she was saying.

"So I decided if he didn't apologize I was going to quit."

"Did he?"

"Yes. 'Pearl,' he says," and she lowered her voice and raised her shoulders. "He's kind of fat, you see, and he says, 'I'm sorry I tried to kiss you and it won't happen again.' 'Okay,' I say and he walks me to his office door. And when I turn to go he pinches me. But not where you'd expect. On the arm. He pinches me on the arm."

"He's trying to reform," Buck said, and Pearl laughed.

The second time he was asked there, Etta was home. He felt inspected that night, as if Etta were looking through his skin to see what lay there. Pearl seemed aware of that too, not necessarily troubled by it, maybe even amused. That evening Etta cooked and they had a dainty sort of meal with unfamiliar names for things and a sauce on the meat. They sat in the dining room at one end of a large table and it was drafty there.

"Pearl tells me your father has a ranch," Etta said.

"That's right. East of here."

"You know, you never talk much about that," Pearl intervened, maybe to help the conversation.

"Not much to say. He has cattle and a few sheep and he farms a few acres." They smiled at him. "He runs yearlings but doesn't bother with cows and calves," he explained. "But instead of sending the yearlings back east like everyone else, he fattens them and sells them on the hoof to a meat packer," he added. He could see that none of this meant anything to them but they nodded politely.

"You don't ranch with your father?" Etta asked.

"No. Right now I drive a truck."

"Oh," she said.

"Try this jam," Pearl said and winked at him.

The conversation, what there was, went on like that. Buck ate less than he might have and picked up two hamburgers on the way home.

The last time he went there for dinner—more and more he declined Pearl's invitations and proposed something else—he didn't even get to eat. He and Pearl were in the kitchen. She was stirring gravy and Etta was setting the table in the dining room. They could hear voices from the house next door and Pearl became distracted as if those voices were all she could hear. He had never seen her nervous and he quit talking. When Etta came back into the kitchen she listened too, though no one said what the voices were all about. They were muffled and low but he could tell they were angry. Then everything was quiet for a time, and Etta and Pearl moved food from pots into serving dishes. In some relief, unspoken of course, they moved to the dining room and sat down to eat. Before everything had been passed a woman screamed. Etta said she'd see to it and got up. Buck followed after and Pearl ran alongside trying quickly to explain.

"It's Leona and George. Sometimes he gets drunk and violent. They have two kids and one on the way," he heard her say as he overtook Etta and entered the house. The two houses flanked one another so that the side porches that led to the kitchens faced each other. It was this side-porch door he entered.

"What's going on here?" he said to a man he presumed to be George who was shaking a very small woman.

"Who the hell are you?" the man bellowed.

Buck was conscious of Etta and Pearl behind him and Etta saying something. But he ignored them both. He grabbed the man by his arm and pushed him out the back door to the yard. They stumbled on the stairs and the man fell. Buck could smell newly turned earth in the garden and wondered if they'd been digging potatoes. The grass was slick with moisture and he sort of slid the man along the ground to the corner of the yard by the garage. He could hear him sputtering to catch his breath and crickets hammering loudly. For the moment all Buck's senses were more pronounced and his heart was pounding. For the moment he hated this man. It was as pure and luxurious a hate as he'd ever known. In this man he saw weakness, disgusting weakness, and for this he hated him.

"Listen, you son of a bitch," he told the guy, pulling him to his feet. "Stand up." Still holding onto the man, he groped along the garage wall for the water faucet. When he found it he turned it on full force and, still dragging the man along, followed the hose to its end. He stooped to pick up the nozzle. The man seemed to recognize the sound of running water and began to struggle but Buck held him by his hair with his left hand and squirted him thoroughly head to foot. The man finally dropped to his knees and bawled like a kid. Buck let him cry it out, and he soon fell asleep or passed out. Buck stripped him of his wet clothes, put George over his shoulder, and took him into the house. Etta was with the woman, and Pearl led the way upstairs to a bed where Buck deposited him.

"I'll stay with him overnight," he told Pearl. "You take the lady and kids next door."

Etta came up and looked into the bedroom suspiciously but

said nothing and left. Soon the house was quiet. He covered the man with a blanket and shut the door. He found another bedroom with a crib and a small bed in it. There were toys and clutter all about and a general feeling of vitality, as if a child might soon burst in the door. Buck took the pillow from the bed and went down to the living room, where he thought he might sleep. He used the bathroom, took off his boots, and lay down on the couch. He tried to picture what was happening next door. Pearl was probably calming the kids and Leona. Etta would be locating beds for everyone and cleaning up the dinner mess. Maybe they were eating the cake he'd seen on the buffet. He was hungry.

Buck had planned to tell Pearl that he'd gone back to the ranch. He thought they'd go for a ride after dinner and he'd tell her all about his day—that he'd spent most of it with his father in the country, that he wanted to take her there to visit sometime, and that he hoped she would like it. Buck wanted to explain how glad he was to be going back, explain how he never considered land something a man might miss. But he had. There was something about the challenge it presented, the contradiction land was— often providing and beneficent, then turning on you, untamed and formidable. The country could kill a man; he'd seen storms sweep across the Judiths and hit the prairie with a murderous force. He'd been in storms that he had to walk his horse in, or ones where he'd had to get out of his pickup every few feet to gauge the way because there was no visibility beyond his own hand. Storms like that could strike even on a spring day with no more warning than a black cloud. Sometimes they killed anything unlucky enough to be caught outside. He'd once found a sheepherder ten feet from the house after such a storm. The old man couldn't see the house, and if he'd cried for help, no one had heard. There was nothing to hear in that type of storm but wind. Buck figured the old boy probably walked through the blinding snow until he dropped, frozen or exhausted to death, never knowing how close he'd been to safety.

Buck was too hungry to sleep, and he got up to see what he could find. He helped himself to a beer and a leftover pork chop.

The next morning Buck woke about five. He poked around until he found coffee and eggs and made himself breakfast. He heard the newspaper hit the front porch and sat down with it to wait for George to get up. When he came downstairs, Buck poured him coffee and explained who he was.

"I've got to get to work," George said, backing out of the kitchen. "Sit down, George," Buck commanded. "First we're going to talk." George sat at the kitchen table and stared at the coffee.

"George," he said. "I understand that sometimes you get a bellyful and come home mean and cause problems here for the Mrs. and the kids. No one likes that, George, and it has to stop." Buck paused now, waiting for any signal that George had heard. George nodded, his eyes fixed on the floor.

"Now if things don't change," Buck said without even slightly raising his voice, "I'm going to come back here and personally break all your bones. Then I'm going to bury those bones in your own garden. You see how it is?" He waited for the slumping figure to nod again. "I'll be checking to see how well you're doing."

Having said what he'd stayed the night to say, he left the man still sitting there and went home.

"Did you threaten to kill George?" Etta asked him when she answered the door that evening.

"Aren't you going to say hello, how are you, come in?"

"Did you?"

"Not exactly," he said, still standing on the porch.

"Let me tell you," she said. "Might doesn't ever make right."

"We could argue that," he said, finally exasperated by the whole business of George and Leona. "But I don't know that your friend and her kids ought to have to wait around until you and I figure it out. Now is Pearl here?"

Etta said nothing more and motioned him inside. When Pearl appeared suddenly from the foyer he knew she'd heard. It was the way she looked at him and smiled that led him to believe that sisters or not, and close as they might be, Pearl was a woman who made up her own mind. If she wanted to marry him, despite anything Etta might say, she would.

"How about a movie?" he asked her.

"I can be ready in a few minutes."

"I can wait," he said and sat down.

Pearl went upstairs and he could hear Etta in the kitchen. He wished Etta liked him. It would make everything nicer. Easier. He couldn't see why she was so against him. Pearl said she wasn't but he felt it. Hey, I'm not going to hurt her, he wanted to go out to the kitchen and say. Not at all. In fact he felt good with Pearl, he wanted to take care of her, wanted to tell her things, things he had never wanted to tell anyone. Buck wanted to tell her about his dream, a recurring dream he'd had as a boy. The dream took place far away, as if in some other country, a dream so faint and vague he had to struggle to recall it, though there was the recognition that he knew it well. It was always of his mother running with him close to her breast, then putting him down, screaming at him to stay and not to move. Something like that. There were sprays of brilliant color, reds and blues and yellows, and a tremendous roar, then his mother disappearing into the sound. He could barely see her skirt rounding a corner, aglow in a reddish mist until it disappeared too.

He intended to tell Pearl that and the rest of it, about how when he was six or seven there had been a large prairie fire that threatened to take the barn and the feeding pens. Buck fought along with his father and the neighbors with shovels and dirt and wet blankets. He was overcome with feelings of grief and loneliness and terror when he looked into the fire, and he ran off and hid in the cool dark granary. That night his father told him how his mother had died. She must have carried Buck, just a baby, from their burning house and been killed when she went back in.

"What she went back into that house for, no one will ever know," Alma Peters told him when he was twelve. Alma was the neighbor who had found him.

"You were wide-eyed and alone, sitting in the ashes calling out for your mama," she said. "I always wondered what on earth made that woman go back into that fire."

That's what he wondered too, and he would ask Pearl. He would ask her what might be important enough to a woman to make her go back into a fire.

CHAPTER

FOUR

All Friday evening Pearl packed and unpacked a small overnight bag, considering and reconsidering what to take and what she might wear on the way. Buck was picking her up in the morning and driving her to the country to meet his father and to spend the weekend. That is, if the roads were good enough to drive on. Buck wanted to show her the ranch and drive her around the countryside.

"Saturday night we'll go into town for supper," he'd said earlier that week.

"But what if the roads get bad while I'm there?" she'd asked.

"Then you'll just have to stay," he said and kissed her.

"So you're going to meet Gordon's father," Etta said now.

"Etta, why do you call him Gordon?"

"That's his name, isn't it?"

"Yes, but you know everyone calls him Buck." Pearl thought Etta did that because she didn't like him and wanted to make sure Pearl knew it.

"What are you going to wear?"

"I don't know."

"How about those nice gabardine slacks?"

"Oh, I don't know," Pearl said. "Some older men don't like women to wear pants."

"He's a farmer, isn't he?"

"Yes."

"Well, he should like it then."

"Which blouse?"

"The blue." Etta sat down on the bed. "Pearl," she said. "I think Buck's going to propose."

"So do I."

"Is that what you want?"

"Yes."

"Just so you're sure," Etta said, frowning.

After ironing and folding several garments, Pearl settled on what Etta suggested. First of all, pale blue went well with her almost black hair and it was so cold out, pants made sense, at least to wear on the way down. She put in a white blouse and a navy blue cardigan sweater. And just in case pants wouldn't do, she included her favorite dress, a soft beige wool shirtwaist. What did women wear in small towns on Saturday nights anyway?

Pearl finally went to bed. In any case it wasn't what she was going to wear that would be remembered but what she was going to say. Pearl was pregnant.

She hadn't meant to get pregnant; that is, she hadn't intended to let things go so far that such a thing could happen. She'd wanted only to have some fun, to put her sorrow behind her and forget David. She hadn't meant to move Buck's hand that night either, that night they sat on a blanket leaning against a stump on the riverbank. They had cooked hot dogs over a fire and watched moonlight spray the river, first in slivers and ripples, then in a wide, lighted path from the bank where they sat to the other. In that watery light and the firelight before them, they had passed a bottle and sang songs about rivers, songs they knew parts of and others they made up as they went along. Within this context, she had relaxed against him, not drunk at all but overcome by a remarkable urge or maybe a hunch, a sense that all she had to do was pick a direction, any direction, however broad, leading somewhere—somewhere not meaning place, and direction not meaning choice. Direction now was any movement out of her own inertia. Any mistake she might make doing so was beside the point. Clearly she had nothing, absolutely nothing to lose. No matter what foolish thing she did, there was no more to be lost.

But had moving Buck's hand made her feel this or had feeling this made her move his hand? In either case, it seemed to her, one of them preceded the other, and the odd feeling had not occurred simultaneously with bringing his hand first to her breast and then to the bottom of her skirt, which had slipped up around her knees.

On the way home she had asked him what he thought about it—those events that followed.

"Do you still think I'm a nice girl?"

"Even nicer," he said, touching her hand.

"But do you still respect me?"

"Don't worry," he said. "I can tell you haven't been around much."

"How can you tell?" she said.

"Because I have."

"Oh," she said.

The next morning, Pearl was certain Etta suspected something had happened and didn't approve of whatever it was.

"Don't you want to hear about my date?" Pearl had asked—not that she was going to include details.

"No," Etta said. She was making something, coffee cake probably, or maybe popovers.

"Why not?"

"Just what is it about him that you like so much?" Etta said, ignoring her question.

Pearl stared at her. She hated when Etta detected confusion and then wanted to explore it.

"He doesn't chew with his mouth open," she said, but Etta wasn't in the mood for humor.

"Admit it. You haven't given this the least bit of thought."

"Yes, I have." But what she liked about him wouldn't make sense to Etta. She liked the way he looked at her sometimes, thoughtfully, actually taking her into consideration. And the way he sang along with the radio unself-consciously as though he were alone. Other things too, like the time she saw his shorts. He had bent over something—a flat tire, she thought—and his shirt had come up so that she could see the top of his shorts. White, clean shorts. And these shorts, being so white, made her like him. White shorts, of course, would not be something Etta could get her mind around.

"He's nice looking, he's . . ."

"In a flashy way."

"He's fun and he's nice," she said, ignoring Etta's comment.

"But what do you really know about him?"

"Not much, I guess," Pearl said, feeling leveled. Confrontation with Etta could do that.

"Why don't you like him?" Pearl asked her.

"I don't know. I just don't trust him."

"Because he threatened George?"

"Partly."

"Well, George hasn't beaten on Leona for weeks. Maybe you should be grateful."

Etta had turned from whatever she was stirring at the counter and waved the large spoon in the air. "But what happens the next time when this Buck isn't around? And George, now made to feel even more powerless and frustrated, adds this new anger to the old. What then?"

"God, I don't know," Pearl said. She was sick of Leona and George's problems. "How else do you deal with a bully?"

"All I know is one brute making another one behave can't be it."

"Buck is not a brute!"

Etta threw the spoon into the sink and sat down. "I know and I'm sorry. I just don't want you to get hurt again."

Later that afternoon they had played cards. They were out in the backyard with an old pinochle deck, a little bored after three games and lazily sipping cold beer.

"So what time is your date?"

"Eight."

"Want some dinner?"

"No, we'll probably pick up hamburgers."

Pearl had shuffled the cards. "Hey, tell my fortune," she said. When they were kids, Etta had invented a game with the cards. She assigned meaning and value to each card in the deck and if they drew two of something it signified a doubling of fortune or misfortune. Pearl didn't remember how Etta kept track of what each meant, perhaps she had a notebook or had memorized them. But Etta pretended to know the future and was so convincing that even their girlfriends liked to believe Etta held the mysteries of their lives in her worn-out deck.

"I can't remember how anymore," Etta said.

"Sure you can. The king of spades was authority, usually Daddy or that bastard principal, whatever his name was. Remember? And the jack of diamonds was danger in love."

Etta laughed.

"The queen of hearts was luck and money and if you drew it before an exam it meant you'd pass." Pearl shuffled again and drew a fortune hand of seven cards. Why seven, she'd forgotten.

"Come on, read them," she said, placing them facedown in front of Etta.

Etta picked up the cards and studied them. Pearl watched her,

35

reminded of the serious look Etta used to get on her face as a kid. Now she seemed confused.

"I can't do this anymore."

"Come on, tell me what I got."

"No."

"Then give them to me." Pearl grabbed for them but Etta held them in the air.

"They say leave this Gordon Buckman alone or you'll regret it."

"What?!"

"That's what they say—that Gordon Buckman will make a difference in any life he touches."

"Damn it, Etta. Give me those cards."

"No." Etta buried them in the deck as Pearl reached for them again.

"You're just afraid I'll fall for him and go away and leave you all alone."

"I hope that's it," Etta said. She'd marched off into the house with the deck and slammed the screen door.

That was at the end of the summer and Etta had had little else to say about Gordon Buckman since. And meanwhile, Pearl had carelessly allowed herself to get pregnant. Or had she done it on purpose?

The next morning Buck was twenty minutes early. "The roads are fine," he said, stamping off snow at the door. "Too damn cold to snow anymore." It was a theory he had that when the temperature dropped below a certain point it was too cold to snow.

It made her nervous for him to be early. She kept wondering what she was forgetting. He was rushing her and seemed nervous too. Buck's car was older than hers and she looked at it doubtfully. When he'd suggested the visit she'd told him it was silly to come all that way to get her and that she could drive her own car down. But he'd insisted.

"Should we take my car?" she asked him now.

"Hell no," he said. "Ready?"

Inside the car was a lap robe and she put it around her legs.

"Sit by me," he suggested, and she moved over.

The roads were dry and black against the hilly fields of snow, like ribbon tossed any old way across a white lumpy present. The starkness, sixty miles of it, was relieved now and then only by a solitary farmhouse or grain elevator or small town — sometimes as small as a post office, bar, and service station.

Buck was quiet and it was just as well. She needed to think. What should she say, she wondered. And did he even like children? Maybe he wasn't ready for that. After all, she wasn't positive he wanted her. She hoped his father would like her and that everything would go well. If it did she would tell him. If it didn't, well, she'd think of something else.

At the last town, they pulled off the highway onto a gravel road that wound another twenty miles around haystacks, fallen barns, more farmhouses, and a one-room schoolhouse. Smoke from the school's chimney rose white and straight up into the bright blue sky. There was no wind. Buck had a theory about that too, but for the moment she'd forgotten what it was.

"The teacher lives above the classroom," Buck explained. "There's probably twelve students in all who go there," he said.

"There's Charlie's place," he said and pointed over one hill to a thicket of trees and several buildings. "We're almost there." He smiled at her. "I hope you like it," he said. So did she, as she had a feeling it was about to become home.

"There it is," he said at the top of another hill. A barn, a house, a garage, an outhouse, a chicken coop, and corrals grew larger and more in need of paint and repair the closer they got. "My goodness," was all she could think to say.

37

"It's big," he said. "Needs some work but I'll get to that this spring. Charlie's going to help me."

There was something inviting about it all, the random grouping of buildings nested at the intersecting feet of several hills, a wide two-story house with a graceful porch and sloping roof at the highest point on the side of one hill, and below that, a large barn. Pennsylvania Dutch. With modifications, she decided when she saw the slanting addition that came off one of its ends and extended down to the ground. A shelter of some sort or windbreak, she guessed.

Buck drove up to the house through a pack of barking dogs. There didn't seem to be any distinction between barnyard and front yard, as no fence prevented a goat from standing on the porch or kept several sheep off the path leading to the back door. Buck yelled at the barking dogs and shooed away the sheep.

Inside, the house was cluttered with things, some of which she had to look at twice to identify: a part of a motor, an old butter churn—what was left of it—and some kind of wheel for sharpening tools.

"How do you do," she said, extending her hand to Buck's father, August. He was the picture of Buck—older, of course, and slightly shorter, but still a big man. His face was sunburnt and a day or so's growth of beard was almost as white as his thinning hair. He had hazel eyes that he narrowed when he smiled, and she could see that he had been an attractive man, in some ways still was. He certainly didn't seem too anxious to impress company— or had he expected any? He wore black wool pants, an undershirt, and brown suspenders.

Buck moved newspapers from an old captain's chair, the kind with short arms that could be found in the offices around most railroad depots. She sat down.

"So you're from the city?" August said to her when Buck left the room for another chair.

"Yes," she said. She had never thought of Great Falls as a city,

38

and his tone made her sure the admission had discredited her or otherwise diminished her value already.

"What's a city girl doing wearing pants?" he asked next.

"The style," she said and shrugged. Style somehow seemed not only frivolous but morally questionable when she reviewed it from his position across the table.

"Women wear pants all the time, Pa," Buck said, bringing in a ladder-back chair that was missing a rung. "You got some coffee made?" Buck asked and washed out a mug for her. It was bitter and strong and she guessed it had been boiling away there all morning.

"I was just about to start dinner," Buck's father said and got up.

"Can I help?" she asked and stood up too.

"No, you sit down. This ain't a woman's kitchen and it'd probably scare you to look around it much."

He was right. It was scary just watching him. First he took a big cast-iron frying pan that didn't look too clean down from where it hung on the sooty wall. From an old coffee can, he scooped out bacon grease that had to be rancid from sitting there on the back of that hot stove and dumped it into the pan. While that was heating up, he grated boiled potatoes onto a plate, then dumped them all into the deep grease that was now too hot. He then took pork chops from the icebox that had a color to them that made Pearl wonder how old they were. He spooned out more of the grease into another large pan and when it was smoking threw the meat in, which made grease pop and spatter all over the stove. He turned the potatoes with a rusty spatula and Pearl was sure she saw ashes from the cigarette in his mouth fall into the pan. Whether he noticed or not, he gave no sign, just turned the potatoes again and added salt and pepper. What on earth was she getting herself into here? The smell of bacon grease was making her sick.

On the positive side, if you could overlook the kitchen's disarray, it had its charm, scarred but nice nonetheless. If it were hers, she would simply cart away all the junk obscuring its nice features, paint and wallpaper and refinish the oak table and cupboard. The floors needed sanding and perhaps a braided rug. She would also cut down the bushes under the lovely bay window and open up the view. It was one of her worst habits—taking someone's house or kitchen or garden and changing it all around in her mind to suit herself, so that she never saw it the same way again. Sometimes she had the feeling her planning even changed those spaces for their occupants, that they sensed her disapproval or caught on to her mental overhaulings and became dissatisfied too. She really ought to stop, but it was something that happened without her thinking about it.

When the food was in front of her she could only pick at it. "I guess I had too much breakfast," she said. August didn't take any more notice of her than to glance at her plate when he got up to take a nap after he and Buck finished eating. At last Buck took the food away and she offered to help him wash the dishes, an unmatched assortment of china and glass plates, jelly glasses, and odd pots—three days' worth, at least.

"Come on, I'll show you around," Buck said when they were done. He flung the dish towel across his chair and took her hand. "Listen," he said, looking at her coat, "I'll get you an old jacket and some overalls." Her coat was a long camel hair with a fur collar and she saw what he meant. It was as out of place as she and her gabardine slacks were.

She waited in the living room while he went off upstairs. The shades on the windows were closed and she guessed the room didn't get much use. There was a picture on the mantel of a young blonde woman.

"Your mother?" she asked when Buck returned.

"Yes," he said. "She was pretty young here. Pa says it was taken long before I was born." Pearl wondered if the woman would have approved of her and welcomed her had she been here still.

40

Buck took her upstairs to a bedroom. "You can sleep here tonight and I'll be down the hall," he said, winking at her. He kissed her, then pointed to the clothes. He waited outside while she dressed. She pulled on long red underwear and over that a red plaid wool shirt and faded overalls.

At the back door she put on a parka-like wool jacket and an old pair of rubber boots that were too big for her until she put on another pair of wool socks. Buck gave her gloves and a wool cap and she was ready. She'd be lucky if she didn't get hives from all the wool.

Out in the frozen air, her nostrils kept sticking together when she breathed. Otherwise, in that apparel, she felt kind of gay, like a kid let out to play, free to get dirty or to climb fences or to let barbwire snag her clothes. Buck showed her the barn, the horses, the pens of cattle, and pointed out the outhouse. She used it twice and couldn't help wondering about the cost of indoor plumbing.

Later that afternoon, Buck drove her to the top of a hill in a pickup truck, to where they could see the white prairie like a large floor of irregular patterned linoleum between the top of the hill they were on and one off in the distance. "That's Square Butte," he said. He pointed out his father's acreage and told her how many sections there were and where their boundaries lay. Was that good? It didn't mean anything to her but he seemed proud of it. This was not the time to bring up her problem and she was sure he was trying to get around to saying something too. She thought for one brief moment he was about to propose and changed his mind. "You want to dress up and go to town?" he said instead.

It was all so exhausting. No, she didn't want to change or dress up. She didn't want to prepare herself in some big way only to have him let her down. She already looked kind of silly in what she had on and that went well with how she felt.

"Actually, I'd just as soon wear this," she said. That seemed to please him because he smiled and winked. "Then let's go in now and get something to eat." She laughed. He knew she was starved.

Should she, she wondered on the way to town, tell him her news even if he didn't propose? Whatever she did, she had to do it right away. She had already waited longer than she should have. It was because she couldn't have him marry her only for the baby and then throw it in her face someday—weren't women constantly warned about that? Or worse, hold it against the child. She'd rather go away somewhere to have it than have that happen. She could come back with it posing as a widow if she had to. War widows with children were turning up everywhere these days, and she had a second cousin in North Dakota who might help her. So would Etta, for that matter, if Pearl ever got around to confessing her problem to her.

In any case, lots of children had been raised without fathers. An invented father would do just as well; Pearl would make him a war hero or an accident victim if she had to but she would not force Buck into anything he didn't want to do. She might ask him to lend the child his name, though, because it was as much his fault as hers, after all, and any humiliation she might have to put up with she wanted to spare the child.

Buck pulled up in front of the Judith Hotel and Restaurant. The town was deserted. Only one car was parked on the street and it looked as if it had been there all winter. It was beginning to snow.

Buck opened her door and helped her out. "Watch that sidewalk," he said and guided her inside.

"Evening, Buck. What brings you out on such a cold night?" the man behind the bar said, looking not at Buck at all but at Pearl.

"I'm buying this lady supper. You got anything good to eat around here?"

"Sure do," the man said, giving his hand to Pearl. "Welcome, I'm Clark."

"How do you do," she said shaking his hand. "My name is Pearl."

"You've got to watch this fellow," Clark said, grinning at her. "He's slicker than you know what." He pulled out a chair for Pearl at a table. Above it was a war poster—a dead soldier, his parachute still on and limp around his body. HE'S DEAD BECAUSE SOMEONE TALKED, it said in bold orange letters. Pearl shivered.

"Give us two beers," Buck said.

"No thanks," Pearl said. "I think I'd like a Coke." She was hoping that it might settle her stomach.

"Honey," Buck said, helping her off with the big jacket, "what do you think of my old man?"

"He scares me to death."

For some reason Buck seemed to think that was funny and he laughed. "At least you're honest," he said finally.

"I don't think he likes me."

"Don't worry about that. He doesn't like anybody, least of all me."

"Then why did you go back to the ranch?"

"I don't know," he said.

"What's so funny over here?" Clark said, bringing their drinks and a menu.

"This is a funny lady," Buck said.

"So do you like the ranch?" he asked after Clark left.

"Oh yes," she said. "It's a wonderful place."

They looked at the menu. She had her choice of pan-fried steak, deep-fried chicken, or fried liver and onions. Was everything in the world fried? She chose the chicken and Buck ordered a steak.

"I was hoping you'd like it. In case you marry me."

"Is this a proposal?"

"I'm not too good at this kind of thing, am I?" He smiled and took her hand.

"There's one thing . . ."

"You don't want to!" He looked stricken.

"No," she said, "I do but . . ."

"But?"

"I'm pregnant."

"For chrissake," he said. His face fell a second time. "Why didn't you say something?" he asked gently. "Is that why you've been sick lately?"

She nodded.

"So we'll move up the wedding date."

"I want you to be sure about this," she said.

"I'm sure," he said and kissed her cheek. "Clark," he called out, "this woman's going to marry me. Bring us some champagne."

On the ride back to the ranch Pearl laid her head on Buck's lap in weariness. She felt the happiest she had in years—for all the plans they had made tonight, the hopes she had for this child, the relief she felt to have everything settled. All that agony for nothing, thank God. She had so much to be grateful for; the future for the first time held something in it for her. She was going to be married and have a child. She was going to give her child a home, a home on the range, she thought, and fell asleep.

The next morning Pearl smelled coffee and bacon. It was cold up in the bedroom—wasn't heat supposed to rise?—and she put the overalls and wool shirt back on over the underwear she'd slept in. She wondered if it was Buck or August in the kitchen or both. Would Buck come to get her so that together they could tell August the news or should she just go on down there where she could stand near the stove, warm up, and get coffee before it got too thick? At least she should go to the outhouse and down to the dining room where there was a mirror so she could see to comb her hair.

She had left the rubber boots at the back door, so Pearl went downstairs in the wool socks. In the dining room she pulled up a shade on the east window and sun lit the dusty room. The white hills were dazzling mounds of ice crystals and light and the sky was clear and blue. She wiped dust off the mirror over the buffet with her sleeve so she could see into it.

"Married?" she heard August say.

Buck's voice was barely audible and she pulled the shade back down. Why had he told August without her?

"She'll never adjust," August said in reply to something Buck said that she didn't catch.

"This is not the city," August said. Pearl's stomach was queasy again. She could smell something being fried in butter. She certainly didn't want to go out there now. But how was she to get the boots at the back door without going through the kitchen?

"She's pregnant, ain't she?" August said angrily. Pearl held her breath and listened.

"So that's it," August said.

"Yeah," she heard Buck say. She waited for more but nothing else was said. A chair scraped the floor, dishes were taken from a cupboard, the icebox was opened and shut, the fire in the stove popped. But Buck said nothing more. She went back upstairs to the bedroom and got under the covers. She breathed slowly and deeply, concentrating on controlling her stomach. I will not be sick, she said silently with each deep breath.

When Buck knocked on the door, she didn't answer.

"Pearl," he said opening the door. He hesitated, then came over and sat on the bed. "Honey, are you awake?" She moved from his touch.

"Why did you let your father think you're just doing me a favor?"

"You heard all that?" He sounded amazed.

"Or is that what's really going on?"

"God, no, I swear."

45

He put his head in his hands. He said nothing and neither did she. After several minutes he looked up at her.

"I just don't know how to talk to him," he said.

She turned away. Etta had seen something in those goddamn cards. Pearl had no doubt pulled doubles of both the jack of diamonds and king of spades or some other curse. But it wasn't going to make any difference; she was pregnant and that would be luck enough.

CHAPTER

FIVE

———————◆———————

Etta was nineteen when she met Harold one Thursday on her lunch break. She was walking across Central to the five-and-ten when a cab almost hit her. To her surprise the cab driver jumped out of the car and apologized.

Harold Blair had dark red curly hair and green eyes. He had a deep voice and talked in clipped sentences. When she got to know him better, she found herself breathing to the rhythm of his speech, so sometimes his habit of clipping off every other sentence gave her the sensation of running out of breath. Sometimes he ended what he was saying with a gesture that replaced the end of the sentence. "Would you care . . ." and he'd sweep his hand toward the car or the dance floor or the restaurant. Or he might say, "Oh, I just thought . . ." and shrug, leaving what he just thought to her imagination.

Etta felt irresistibly attached to this man who laughed gaily and smiled at her. She accompanied him fishing and hunting, walked the brush for him to scare up pheasants, or sat with him in a duck blind cold mornings drinking coffee, a finger or two of brandy in it always. She was crazy about him and didn't want to lose him.

When she got pregnant, she cried and carried on but didn't tell him because he had never proposed marriage or any future plans.

She asked an acquaintance for a name and address and went to a man called Doc who met her in a room behind an office on a side street in a questionable neighborhood.

After the abortion she bled a lot more than she had anticipated and felt lousy for several weeks. She said nothing to Harold even after she married him a year later. Except for her guilt, she was quite happy. While neither Harold nor Etta was extraordinary alone, they made an exceptional pair. They were both tall, her black hair and eyes did things for his ruddy complexion, and she could match him stride for stride on their long, fast-paced walks, an elegant thing to see. They were noticed everywhere they went, even on the street late at night. They were often known to get out of bed at midnight to go for a drink or a hamburger, always to some small place downtown, cutting a deck of cards with the barkeep to see who paid. They got a second glance anywhere, awesome on a stream at sunup in their hip boots, for instance, or rowing across Georgetown Lake at dusk.

When Harold was killed in a car wreck three years after they married, Etta was devastated. A large truck pulled out to pass a car on Gore Hill and hit Harold's cab. His only passenger lived. Etta grieved both for her loss of Harold and for the baby she had wanted and aborted, for the baby she had tried to have later and couldn't. Had she known Harold was going to die, she would never have had the abortion. But then how would she ever have known a thing like that?

About a year after Harold's death, an old woman came to Etta's door. She was a short, unsteady little woman with faded blue eyes and a fine hairnet over her wispy gray hair. She said her name was Helen Engle and that she simply must speak privately with Etta. Etta asked her to come in out of the cold.

"You don't remember who I am, do you?" she asked. Etta couldn't place her.

"I'm the one who was in the taxi when your husband was killed."

Etta sat down. She did recall that the last person to see Harold alive had called at the time or sent flowers or perhaps even come to the funeral and had shaken Etta's hand. Etta just didn't remember exactly.

"Well, you probably wonder what I want," the woman said as she took off her coat. "If you don't mind, I'll just sit down."

"I'm sorry," Etta said. "I don't know where my manners are."

"As I was saying, you must be wondering about me, so I'll come right to the point. You're grieving too long for Harold, holding him back, you might say."

"I beg your pardon."

"I say you're holding onto Harold and it's hard on him." The old woman shook her finger at Etta as she talked. Etta was astonished. The daring of this woman to speak of Harold as if he had just stepped out of the room to get coffee! For a minute she was too confused to think of showing the woman to the door.

"I have certain abilities, you see, and so Harold has been sending messages for you. I tried to ignore him but he's persistent. But I'm sure you know that. Anyway, finally I told him, 'All right, Harold, have it your way.'

"Are we alone?" the woman asked, looking around but not waiting for a reply. "I'm not in the habit of scaring people like this, but Harold insists." She stared at Etta. "I'll just rest now so the others can talk."

"Others?" Etta said.

"Shhh. They'll let you know when it's your turn. So don't be foolish and run off." She closed her eyes and settled back. "First a few words," she said. Etta watched in amazement. "I now lift beyond earth, to light, to truth, that the guiding ones may speak."

Etta wondered if she should pick up the woman in her arms and carry her to the front steps or whether she should call the police or Leona next door. She wished Pearl hadn't gone out.

Now the woman was silent, her mouth was open and her head

thrown back. Good Lord! She had come here to die! But no, she began to speak in a slow, careful voice, one with a strange rhythm Etta couldn't place.

"We are here in this time and we would welcome you. You have been grieving for a period and it has caused a wall of darkness to be almost suffocating you. You have judged yourself harshly for the abortion and that too is causing your soul harm. We send a message of love from your departed one and he asks that you end the time of sadness so that he is not distracted from his pathway. It is as though you have chains around his heart, pulling at him from your side. We would ask that you forgive yourself and forget the thing you call the mistake.

"You ones of Earth can never really do harm to one another, it is only your belief that would make it appear so. If you will look about you in the time to come, you will recognize the one you thought you destroyed. You will find opportunity to serve here, as though a mothering one. Know also that once the nightmare has served its purpose, it will go away.

"We see too that you are a soul of great beauty and goodness who has promised a life of service to others. We would ask that you question."

By now Etta was so flustered her voice squeaked and faltered. "Who are you? And where's Harold?" she whispered.

"We are your guiding ones. The one you speak of is in the vicinity, shall we say."

"What do you want?"

"Only to ask that you give up your guilt and sadness and surround yourself now with joy. We know you think this is a trick but if you would write atop the paper what we will tell you next, in the days to come you may substantiate what we say. It will be the proof you Earth ones do need so much of, do you see?"

"How do you know about the abortion?" she asked, shaking and searching the desk next to her chair for a pen. "No one knows about that."

"There is much that we know on this side, and much that we would share with you Earth ones, if you would give your permission. You see, we draw close to you many times but you are much occupied with the cares of Earth. Understand that the Earth is not all of life, nor is this Earth life your only life. You have lived many times."

"Why should I believe any of this?" Etta asked weakly, her heart pounding against her hand.

"Do as we say and you will believe."

Etta finally pulled a pencil from the desk but couldn't find any paper. She grabbed for the book on the coffee table, writing on the inside of the cover as the voice went on.

"Your Harold asks that you recall that first weekend you spent together at the place called Southern Cross when you first did trust him. Trust us now that way, he asks."

The voice went on to say that the diamond earring Harold had given her was in the basement on the floor under the shelves with the canning jars and that she had lost it on an errand there for pickled beets last October when the minister and his wife came for dinner. It said too that if she would not drink coffee and drinks of sweetness on an empty stomach her headaches would go away as this caused her blood sugar to rise and fall too quickly.

Then, the voice said, she should go to a certain undertaker and tell him that she had a message from the other side, that there is life after death. The undertaker, the voice explained, had placed a note in the pocket of a dead man that asked "If there is life after death, please let me know," and then had sealed the coffin for cremation. The voice told her the date of this note and where she might find the undertaker.

"It is time we depart," the voice said at last.

"But will I see you again?" Etta asked, at once aware how absurd it sounded.

"We cannot say. But if you would observe times of stillness

each day, we would speak directly to your heart. You might hear us in your thoughts or you might write atop the paper what we move your hand to say. But for now, go in peace, in love, in forgiveness. This speaking is ended."

"Wait," she said. "What about Harold?" But the old lady was silent.

"And you said something about a nightmare," Etta said, exasperated.

Now the old lady stretched and yawned. "Are you all right?" she asked Etta.

"No, I'm not," Etta said, ready to get to the bottom of things. "I want to know . . ."

"Oh, but you will, my dear." Abruptly she was up and had her coat on. Etta remembered now that the old woman had thrown the coat on the chair and then sat on it, caring nothing about wrinkling it.

"But I don't get it," Etta said. "How does . . ."

"I have to go. Have a nice evening," the old woman said, going out the door, disappearing as suddenly as she had come.

Etta stood in the foyer in disbelief, then went back to the front room for the notes she had made inside the book cover. What had the voice meant when it said the nightmare would go away once it served its purpose? Once in a while Etta would wake up screaming or crying but she never remembered why. This had gone on since she was a kid.

"Can't you remember anything?" Pearl would ask. She couldn't but Pearl never believed that. "You just want all the attention," Pearl would complain. But when it happened with Harold, he would hold her until she fell back to sleep. "It's okay if you don't remember," he'd say.

It wasn't until two weeks later that Etta went into the basement to look for the earring. She felt uneasy going down there, as if the voice of the old woman waited for her, perhaps a ghoulish body attached. She called to Pearl, who was bathing: "I'm going to the basement now." There was only silence and the sound of water behind the door so Etta yelled louder.

"I can't hear you. Leave me a note," Pearl shouted over the shower water. Etta thought it a good idea to give the exact location in case Pearl had to come in search of her so she wrote "I'm in the basement by the canning jars."

She took the flashlight with her because the small naked overhead bulb gave little light. When she found the earring she ran upstairs and banged on the bathroom door.

A few days later, Etta tried to call Helen Engle. But she couldn't find any Helen among the Engles she called. She tried Ingall, Engell, Ingle, Eagle, Angle, and even Angel. Etta worried that she had imagined it all and tried to find a trace of the woman about the living room and hall. But all she had was the scribbled notes on the book cover.

One Sunday after church, Etta stopped by the Reverend Vickery's office.

"Reverend Vickery," she said. "I wondered if we could talk." The kindly looking minister invited her to sit down.

"What I was wondering," she began cautiously, "was have you ever heard of a person going into a sort of trance and then a voice speaking through the person?"

"Well, uh, yes and no," he said, getting up quickly to shut the door. "Yes, now," he said taking his seat again. "I believe things of that nature are mentioned in the Bible. Unclean spirits, possession, you know. Jesus healed many who had unclean spirits."

"Yes, but I'm speaking more of a clean spirit," she said, amazed at herself, first of all for getting up at eight o'clock to make it to a boring service, and then for sitting here discussing a hallucination as if it were an infected tooth. "What I'm wondering," she said again, "is do you think the biblical accounts of angels are to be believed, that they really spoke to people and all?"

"Well, Mrs. Blair, I think we need to remember that those were dreams. If you recall, Joseph had a dream, Mary had a dream. The Bible is full of the miraculous. Why do you ask?"

"Oh, I just thought it would be nice if there were angels talking to folks nowadays."

"I doubt that, Mrs. Blair." Reverend Vickery smiled.

The next day Etta went to her doctor for a physical.

"You're in fine health," Dr. Harrison told her.

"Are you sure? You checked everything?"

"Of course. Why, you've been feeling good, haven't you?"

"Yes."

"Is there something you're not telling me?" He squinted at her over the bifocals that seemed ready to fall off the end of his nose.

"No, no."

"Good. And there's nothing I haven't told you. You're in good health, Etta."

Oh well, she thought, a tendency to hallucinate probably wouldn't show up at a physical anyway.

Etta did one more thing before making the effort to put the whole incident out of her mind. She yelled at Harold.

"Okay, Harold," she said. "If that's what you want, I'll let go. Damn it, go! And I wasn't hanging on, I was just missing you." Her feelings were hurt by the idea of being clingy and a burden to him, and she was angry. "And if you have anything more to say, don't send an old woman. Come yourself," she yelled across her dark bedroom.

She sucked in her breath at this, almost frightened now that she had just extended an invitation to a dead man.

*   *   *

Etta was certain she would forget the whole thing soon. She tried not to think of the old woman, or the funny accent; yet when she read her notes she could hear the strange intonation. Now and then she tried to find Helen Engle. Every time she saw a sign or an ad for palm readings or fortunes told, she went in expecting to see Helen. When she didn't, she would ask about her and stay through the reading to see if anything extraordinary would occur. But nothing did and no one as much as blinked at the name. Etta was getting quite a collection of fortunes. If all the things she was told came true, she would marry three times, have four children, and inherit money. Etta once stopped at a Gypsy camp that was located down by the river that summer. But all she accomplished was to give her coins and jewelry to the children who surrounded her.

One day Etta thought she saw Helen Engle in the Mercantile. She called out to the woman, but the woman disappeared into the elevator. Etta ran up a flight of stairs to catch it when it opened, but no woman resembling Helen in the least got out. Etta spent several hours searching each floor and the downtown streets that afternoon but nothing came of it.

Etta was becoming certain she had imagined the whole thing. But just in case, to be absolutely sure, she meditated early every morning. She entreated spirits to visit, sat with pen poised over paper, and listened carefully for a voice, a rustling of drapes, the movement of ghosts. She tried to keep her mind a blank, like a small blackboard, hoping some script would be written there, or that revelation, illumination might take place. Nothing ever did, but despite this, Etta found herself enjoying that quiet hour. She felt most happy and peaceful. Whether she ever proved to herself that an old woman had visited one night or not, she knew she had at last forgiven herself the abortion and was glad for that. What's more, her life was getting too busy to worry about all this. As if she really had promised to be of service to others, she ran about helping friends and neighbors, especially Leona and her new baby and, of course, Pearl. But the one thing that might have settled the matter once and for all, she couldn't do. She could not go to see the undertaker.

She knew something of this man. He was wealthy, he was prominent, he was little and pinched and severe looking and gave more money to the golf club than to the church. He was hardly one in her estimation to leave notes in the pockets of dead men. And what if she went to him? Would he admit to it even if it were true or would he say, "My dear lady, what can you be asking?" Then again, he might discuss it with his wife, and in a town like this, that's all it would take. Soon she'd have a reputation for being muddled or queer or spooky. Or worse than that, he might not know anything about it and then she would lose hope that there was something to it. For now she liked the whole idea of it. She feared the other possibility too, that he would admit to it and then she'd be in a worse position—confronted always with a startling unknown force operating in secret around her while everyone else went on uninformed. Knowing anything more, she felt, was too great a risk. The best thing to do now was keep busy.

For months now Pearl had been seeing a man she'd met through a friend at work. Etta found him charming at times but suspected he was too sure of himself for Pearl's own good. But he seemed to bring out some kind of humor in Pearl and so Etta tried not to mind him coming around. She was surprised, though, when they set a wedding date, after only six months or so of scattered evenings out and a few dinners in.

For months before and after the wedding, the house buzzed with activity. Pearl and Etta scrubbed and cleaned and inventoried a houseful of furniture, dishes, silver, photos, and their childhood keepsakes. Some of the things would be given away, some would stay, and many would go to the ranch where Pearl and Gordon Buckman were going to live. Every time he left the house, Gordon took home a load. That was his name, Gordon, but no one called him that.

"Buck," he said the first time he met her, tipping a large cowboy hat. "Just call me Buck."

The several times Etta saw Reverend Vickery during this time, he inquired quietly about her health, then avoided her—not an easy thing to accomplish as they went through the items to be given to the church or during the small wedding held in the front room. The wedding itself was unremarkable, but Etta thought the large, uneasy ranch hands slinking about the white-laced card tables that held tea cakes and punch gave a momentous quality to the reception.

Etta certainly was not one to count months on her fingers but when Pearl announced a baby on the way not long after the wedding, Etta was worried. She wished they'd waited a while, just until the war was over, until the world in general achieved some kind of order again. But Pearl was happy about the pregnancy and spoke of the blessing of the back injury that had kept Buck out of the war in the first place. It was time to forget the ugliness in the world and get on with life, she said. Etta didn't argue, and often spent her weekends at the ranch, helping Pearl clean and paint and decorate the nursery or sew layette sets and diapers of soft white flannel.

The day Pearl went into labor, American pilots dropped a bomb on Hiroshima. Etta sat in the waiting room of the hospital with Buck all that night. From the nurse's station a radio could be heard. Buck ran out finally to get an evening paper. They read it in silence. At last Etta sighed. She said she didn't see how this immoral act was any solution to the world's problems.

"What else could they do?" Buck asked her. They fell silent again. The news of the bombing had reduced the joy of birth to a quiet vigil.

When the nurse came out to say it was an eight-pound, one-half-ounce girl, Etta cried, feeling it to be as much her accomplishment as theirs. Buck smiled at her and said shyly that he'd thought all along it would be a girl.

The baby would be examined and bathed and sent to the nursery, the nurse explained. The mother was asleep, tired from the long labor and the ether. They waited again.

When the nurse returned, she directed them to a glass window down the corridor. They spoke through a small window to request that Baby Girl Buckman be brought up front. A little red face with black shiny hair was all they could make out. The child was rolled up in cloth like a ham in butcher paper. Dear God, Etta prayed in silence, may this child grow up free in a world without bombs, in a world without war.

The nurse told them they could see Pearl now for a few minutes. Pearl was jubilant but exhausted, proud, and unaware of any news but hers. "I want to name her Katherine," she said, "but we can call her Katie." Buck kissed her cheek.

"You know, it was so strange," she said of the delivery. "All of a sudden there was just this feeling of . . . I can't explain —just a squishy feeling and she popped right out," she said in tired wonder, nodding off, not noticing Etta and Buck's embarrassment.

Etta went home. It had been a long night and she went right to bed. When she got up, she turned on the radio and found the morning paper in the hedge. The headline said, YANKS DROP ATOMIC BOMB ON JAPS. "Untold damage was done Sunday by the bomb President Truman described as having 2,000 times the blast power of the British 'Grand Slam,'" Etta read, then turned the page to the inside. She found Vital Statistics. BORN it said in bold typeface. But there was no Buckman baby listed yet. Of course not, she was just born; she'd be in the evening paper. But under DEATHS, also in bold, a name caught her eye. Helen Engle, seventy-six, 1004 Sixth Avenue North. Etta was so surprised she stuck her finger in her coffee and almost spilled it looking for something to write the address on. She found the obituary, which described Miss Engle as a former teacher of mathematics who had retired in 1934. She was survived by a brother, Earl.

Etta dressed quickly, intending to go immediately to see if this was her Helen Engle. She felt a keen sense of disappointment. She wanted the old lady she remembered alive. She had a list of questions compiled over the months and hoped Helen Engle could answer them. The one most on her mind now was about what the voice had said about Earth ones not being able to hurt each other. In view of all the soldiers killed, all the Jews killed, and now the bomb, she had to know how that could be.

She drove quickly to the address. It wasn't more than ten blocks away, a small, modest white frame house. Etta didn't know what she was going to say when someone came to the door. She rang three times and at last an old man answered. Yes, he said, he was Helen's brother. He didn't resemble the woman she remembered in the slightest and she looked about the foyer for clues.

"Are you Mrs. Blair?" he inquired.

"Yes," she said, at once alert—as if in danger. "How on earth did you know?"

"I didn't," he said. "But the day before Helen died—that would be Saturday," he explained slowly, as if that had a lot to do with it, "she said you would come and to give you this." He handed her a small sealed envelope that she took from him in astonishment. She hesitated to open it in front of the man and her hands shook. She tore at the envelope and pulled out the note. In the darkness of the hallway, Etta could barely make out its contents. "Dear Mrs. Blair," she read. "They meant the night-mare about the child. By the way, I'm glad you found your earring." In a larger script beneath, it was signed "Helen Engle."

What child? She didn't remember anything about a child.

"Did you know Helen long?" she heard the old man ask.

"No," she said. "Mr. Engle," she asked, "is this it? I mean is this all? Didn't she say anything else?"

"No, no," he said. "That's all. She did say, 'Earl, pick me out a nice pine casket with no frills.' She was that way, you know."

"Thrifty?" it finally occurred to Etta to say.

"No, not that. Pine," he said. "She liked pine."

"I've got to go," Etta said, the envelope in one hand, the note in the other.

"Nice to meet you," he said. "Watch that step now. Say, Mrs. Blair," he called from the door as she ran down the walk. "I added a few frills anyway. Couldn't help it. You'll see," Etta heard him say as she got in the car. "Come to the funeral and you'll see."

Etta stopped the car at the corner, undecided. She wasn't sure now which way to go.

CHAPTER
SIX

After Etta left the hospital, Buck brought out the gift he had been saving to give Pearl when the child was born. It was a sapphire ring that had belonged to his mother and one of the few things that had survived the fire she died in. That was only because she had put it in a safety-deposit box at the bank along with the deed to the land, a promissory note, an ancient family Bible, and two poems she had written as a young girl.

"It's beautiful," Pearl said. "Someday I'll give this ring to the baby." She had tears in her eyes. "To Katherine," she said. "To Katie," she said, trying out that name too.

"Well, sweetheart, I better go and let you rest," he said and kissed her good-bye. "Don't forget I won't be back until the day after tomorrow. The auction in Lewistown, remember?"

"All right," she said and smiled.

Buck's car was the only one in the hospital visitor parking lot. The sun was just coming up and he wondered where he might find a place open for breakfast. He also would need to get gas, which was rationed now. But he wasn't in that big a hurry; there was no auction in Lewistown that day. He had lied about that. He was really going home to see to the home improvements he planned to surprise Pearl with. After all these years he was having the plumbing finally put into the bathroom and he wanted it finished before she came home from the hospital. That gave him about a week. He knew how pleased she'd be to have it done now that the baby had arrived.

A couple of months before she had asked if it was possible to do it right away. "If it's a problem of money, I have a little that I inherited from my folks," she said.

"No," he'd said. "When it's time to do it, I'll pay for it."

A few days later he'd brought up the issue to his father, who'd built the house more than thirty years before. The house had been almost completed when the original farmhouse burned to the ground and his mother was killed. After that, his father lost interest in the new house and didn't bother to plumb the bathroom, though there was running water in the kitchen and back shed, where they showered with water heated by a coal stove and kept in a holding tank. The back shed was also where Buck put the first washing machine the house ever had. For years Alma Peters, Charlie's mother, had done their wash. When Pearl moved in she insisted on doing it and he bought the washer.

"What do you think about finishing that bathroom, Pa?" he said one day when Pearl was out working in the garden.

"Probably a good idea. Women need those kind of things," his father said, as if there was a whole list of items men could do without.

He knew his father liked Pearl by how easily he agreed. Buck thought it was because she surprised his father; she even surprised him. Pearl was a natural-born farm girl and took to gardening, feeding, cow milking, to animals, even to the prospect of the coming harvest. She grabbed onto all of it, took hold of each new thing as if it was another missing piece she had just restored to its place in some rare collection of experience. Nothing gave Buck more pleasure than watching Pearl work around the place in his huge overalls and shirts she'd had to wear while she was pregnant, accompanying him everywhere, even on the tractor. She wanted to see just how seeding and haying were done, she said.

One day he took her down to Charlie's and let her pick out a foal from six Charlie had. He enjoyed her excitement and was glad he had thought of it. She had chosen a black colt; its mother was one of Charlie's best mares. He watched her stroke it gently as she informed it matter-of-factly of its responsibilities and new position in the household. "And by the time you're big enough to hold me, I'll have had the baby," she said. She named the colt Baby's Boy because, she explained, when the baby was old enough she would let it have the horse.

Already now, the baby had one coal black colt and a blue sapphire ring.

Buck made two more stops before he got home, one for cigars and one to let Alma and Charlie know the news. He noticed when he drove into Charlie's that the gold star the Navy had given to Alma was in the front window. She'd received it when her other son, Charlie's younger brother Matthew, was killed at Guadalcanal.

Alma hugged him gingerly — it was not her custom — and gave him a blanket she had crocheted for the baby. "Put this in the bassinet to surprise Pearl," she said.

"You'll celebrate with me tonight, won't you?" he asked Charlie.

"Sure. Meet you in town about six."

"At the Mint," Buck said.

"A girl, huh?" was all his father said. While not interested particularly in the fact that he was now a grandfather, he was clearly absorbed in what the two plumbers from Lewistown were doing in the bathroom and he'd watched them all day.

"I'm going to meet Charlie in town tonight," Buck told him. "Do you want to come along?"

"I prefer to drink and dine at home," he said, puffing on the cigar Buck had given him. "Worst damn cigar I ever smoked," he said, but Buck noticed he didn't put it out.

It was 6:30 before Charlie arrived at the bar. By then Buck had already given out the rest of the box of cigars and bought the house a drink. He was just ordering a steak sandwich from the café next door when Charlie came in.

"Make that two," Charlie told Gladys, the waitress who was taking orders at a window in the common wall between the two enterprises.

"Jesus," Buck told him. "Everyone's wild tonight."

"Celebrating the baby, huh?"

"Yeah, and the bombing. They say the war will be over soon."

"That's good," Charlie said, without looking pleased.

"What's wrong?" Buck asked, finishing his beer.

"There's something sad about it," said Charlie. He held up two fingers to request drinks.

"About what?"

"How easy it is to kill an entire population."

"They asked for it."

The bell rang at the window and Buck got up to get their food. "I'll get this," he said to Charlie and pushed away the money Charlie tried to hand him.

Up at the window, people in the café yelled their congratulations to Buck.

"What'd Morty say?" Buck asked Gladys over the noise of both bar and café.

"He wants to know what you named it," she said.

"Tell him Katherine."

"Katherine," she yelled to the cook at the grill behind her.

"The whole damn town's out to supper tonight," Buck said.

"Yeah, too hot to cook," she said and handed him the ketchup. "Say, you going to be around a while?"

"Sure."

64

"We get off pretty soon."

"Good," he said. "I'll buy you a drink. Tell Morty that means him too."

When he got back to the bar Charlie was still discussing the bombing. "One of these days," he said, "the Japs will drop one on us."

"Nah," said Chester, who owned both the bar and café. "We're the only ones who know how to make those things. It's all secret."

"It is now," Charlie said.

Everyone in the place had an opinion, and Buck guessed most of the patrons had been in there all afternoon. Many of them had sons or brothers in one or more of the armed services. Chester's boy was an Air Force pilot who'd won a silver star, and his wife, Mabel, kept a picture of the boy in his uniform on the mirror over the bar. Mabel was almost ten years older than Chester and not quite sixty. It was rumored she had once had an affair with August years ago but no one could say how many. Buck could not picture his father with Mabel—or with any woman, for that matter.

"Charlie," Mabel said now. "Look at it this way. The killing will stop, and our boys can come home because of that bomb."

"And we can have sugar and eggs again," said Parker Edwards. Parker Edwards was a veteran of the Spanish-American War who thought that fact alone should keep him from being inconvenienced or deprived by any further warfare. Others could, of course. It was their turn, he said.

"And your mother can stop saving bacon grease," Buck said to Charlie. Throughout the war, Alma had diligently saved lard for making glycerin for ammunition. She stockpiled it in milk cans in the chicken coop and camouflaged the cans with straw, adding more grease furtively as though enemy troops were in foxholes across the creek.

But what Buck didn't say, what no one said, was that while

65

some soldiers, like Mabel's son, would come home, others, like Charlie's brother, would not.

"So you're a papa," Gladys said loudly to Buck as she entered the bar. She then came up behind him and poked him in the ribs.

"Hi," Buck said. "Chester, Gladys here needs a drink."

"Hello, Charlie," Gladys said and Charlie nodded.

"Gladys, how about some music?" Chester said and handed her some coins. Buck watched her walk to the jukebox. She had a way of swaying from side to side when she moved. She punched in some numbers and the machine lit up and started to play.

"Like that?" she asked him when she got back. Buck wasn't sure whether she meant the song or the way she walked. "Sit down," Buck said, getting up to give her his stool. The bar was full.

"No," she said. "Let's go sit at a table."

"Okay," he said. "But where's Morty?"

"He's coming."

Mabel brought their drinks over to the table. "How's your old man these days?" Mabel asked Buck.

"Good," he told her and handed her a five. There were a lot of people in the bar now who Buck didn't know. Maybe from Lewistown, he guessed, because he'd seen several Fergus County plates on the cars outside.

"How's everything with you, Buck?" Gladys asked.

"Fine."

"And married life?"

"Good."

"Got tied down fast, didn't you? Then like that," she said and snapped her fingers, "a kid."

"That's right."

"And you're happy?"

"That's right," he said again. Gladys could be insistent when she was in the mood to be and it looked like this was one of those times.

"So what are our chances for a little fun?"

"Not too good."

"Never again?" she said.

"Nope."

"Mind if I join you?" Charlie said and sat down without waiting for an answer. Gladys frowned at him and got up to play more music. When she got back Charlie was explaining the problem he was having with an old combine he'd bought secondhand and was trying to fix before harvest started.

"You better get the old man to look at it," Buck told him.

"All right," said Charlie. "I don't give that crop more than two more weeks."

"I'll see you later," Gladys said, obviously not interested in the conversation.

But an hour or so later she was back. "Here I am," she said. Gladys was not bad looking when she didn't pout.

"We see that," Charlie said, not sounding too pleased.

"What's taking Morty so long?" Buck asked her.

"He went home to get his wife."

"When's Pearl getting out of the hospital?" Charlie asked him.

"Next week. They keep them in there seven days."

"When my sister had a baby, she was in ten days," Gladys said. Charlie ignored her. "So how's it feel to be a father?"

"Damn good," Buck said. "Wait till you see this kid. Blackest hair I ever saw. Pearl says she's going to be blonde though."

"How does she know?" asked Gladys.

"Because her eyebrows and eyelashes are light."

"Nah, you can't tell by that," Gladys said.

"Buck, I'm going home," Charlie said. "How about you?"

"I promised Morty a drink."

"Well," Charlie said, getting up. "Give Pearl my regards."

"I'll do that," Buck said. "And don't forget to come by to try out the new facilities."

"New facilities?" said Gladys.

"Yeah, Buck got a new pink toilet," Charlie said.

"What's with him?" Gladys asked after he left.

"Who, Charlie?"

"He's so serious. And he acts like I'm going to poison you."
Buck laughed. "Charlie's Charlie."

"Ever since he came back wounded from wherever he was."

"Okinawa."

"Anyway, he's no fun. But you are," she said and smiled.

"Here comes Morty," Buck said and waved to him and his
wife, Doris.

"Congratulations, Buck," Doris said. "I hear it's a girl."

"Thanks, Doris. Sit down." Gladys moved her chair closer to
Buck's to make room for another chair.

"Where's my cigar?" Morty asked.

"It's coming," Buck said and motioned to Mabel. She didn't
have to ask what Morty and Doris wanted to drink and Buck
guessed that they, like most people at the Mint, had drunk the
same thing all their lives. "Add a cigar to that," he said.

"So what are you up to, Gladys?" Doris asked.

"Not a damn thing," Gladys said, pouting. "This town's
dead."

Mabel returned with their drinks and a cigar she had tied pink
ribbon around.

"There you go," Buck said, handing Morty the cigar. He could
feel Gladys's knee touch his and he moved his leg over as far as he
could.

"This one's on the house," Mabel said.

Someone turned up the jukebox, and Buck, because Gladys's
leg was annoying him, went up to the bar and asked Mabel to
dance. "I'd be delighted to," she said and took his hand.

"Buck, did I tell you I'm a grandmother again?"

"You sure did. Your daughter-in-law had another boy, you
said."

"Yes, and now his daddy can come home from war."

"Can I cut in?" Chester asked, tapping Buck on the shoulder.

"You bet, Grandpa," Buck said.

"I'll dance with you, Buck," Gladys said and put her hands on his shoulders. Gladys danced the same way she walked, her bottom swaying from side to side, one hip alternately higher than the other one in the process. It was too hot to be dancing and everyone sat down after the song ended. Morty and Doris were arguing about Morty's teeth.

"A good dentist can save the ones you got, right?" Doris asked Gladys.

"I'm just going to go get them all pulled and get new white ones," said Morty. His teeth were stained tobacco brown, about the color of his eyes.

"Then your teeth will match your hair instead of your eyeballs," Buck said.

"A person's always better off keeping their own teeth," Doris said.

"Let's dance," Gladys said to Buck. By now Buck was a little drunk, and though it was cooling off he was still hot. He felt Gladys's hand on his knee. He got up with her, felt her dress damp against her back as he held her, saw slight perspiration on her face as she looked up at him. She was a fleshier woman than Pearl, and Buck recalled the fact now.

"Loosen up," she said. "Charlie's gone." She pulled herself in closer and he could feel her breasts against him.

"You make it difficult, Gladys."

"I try to," she said.

"You said it yourself. I'm tied down."

"I'm not asking to be adopted," she said. "I just want you to come out and play tonight." The song ended and she pulled away. Before they had sat down again another slow record dropped into place in the huge glass jukebox. "One more," she said and led him back to the dance floor. She resumed her favorite position for slow dancing, both arms about his neck and her cheek on his shoulder. It didn't feel that bad; actually it felt good to have her there. She'd been his friend and other things off and on for a long time.

They danced like that for at least three more songs. Buck wondered who was watching him and who was too drunk to notice. Gladys was quiet, content to barely move to the music. Finally she looked up at him.

"Are you weakening?" she asked and blew into his ear.

"Not quite," he said. The one thing about Gladys he'd always liked was that even though she wouldn't take no for an answer sometimes, she never tried to make a habit out of him.

"But almost?" she asked.

"Almost," he said and took a deep breath of her perfume.

CHAPTER

SEVEN

———◆———

The day Pearl came home from the hospital there was a strong wind, so despite the heat she had to cover the baby to keep it from smothering in dust. Buck helped her into the house, then made two more trips back to the car for groceries and baby supplies and gifts, which he stacked and balanced guardedly in his arms. The wind continued blowing the rest of the day and all that night so that the screen door banged from time to time, disturbing Pearl's sleep. The baby, she'd remind herself and peek into the bassinet beside the bed. When it made the slightest noise or movement she would wake again, startled and alarmed, unsure what was required of her.

Pearl was always tired. The baby cried often and sometimes wouldn't stop, though she tried everything she knew to soothe it. She'd diaper it again and again, feed it, rock it, or pace with it on her shoulder, frantically patting its back with each tiny cry.

"It's this lousy canned stuff," Etta said when she got there a few days later. "Why aren't you breast feeding?" Pearl didn't know. It hadn't occurred to her. She recalled only that after the birth, they bound her breasts with cloth and said she'd dry up soon and to go to sleep.

"I swear people have forgotten what breasts are for," Etta said, testing the milk from the bottle on her forearm.

Etta was never entirely satisfied with anything that concerned the baby, as though she had been appointed its guardian and was uncertain whether to trust them with it. Buck said it drove him crazy but Pearl didn't mind. She liked Etta puttering in the kitchen or sitting with her long legs crossed beside the cradle, singing or chatting, rattle in hand. It was nice to have another woman around, especially Etta, who knew her so well, who listened, and understood exactly what she meant when she explained things and sometimes when she didn't. With Etta there they could get away once in a while, if only to shop for groceries and hardware, or sometimes for dinner at the café in town or for guitar music at one of the bars.

If not for Etta, Pearl and the baby could have gone for months without seeing a female. All the neighbors, besides living miles away, were bachelors or old men or busy wives who stayed home with children. Often weeks went by without anyone coming at all. There would only be Buck's father around then. And usually he got the only company who came and he hoarded the visitor down at the bunkhouse, where he preferred to live.

Buck refused at first to believe that. "Why won't he live with us?" he asked her for weeks, unable to comprehend why the old man should abandon the house he'd built and lived in for thirty years. August only said, "What the hell, I built the bunkhouse too and that's where I want to stay."

Pearl was relieved. She was always nervous around the man. She was certain he didn't like her and felt the struggle to please him like constant uneasiness. Often she had to work with him and as hard as she tried, things went wrong. One morning when Buck was sick, she'd gotten up at dawn to drive the old man while he fed. He'd stood on the back of the hay rack, pitching hay as she drove the tractor across the field. Whether she hit a bump or not she didn't know but suddenly she heard a sharp whistle behind her. She had knocked August off the hay rack and she could see him brushing snow off his legs and back, his breath circling his face in the brilliant winter air.

It was Katie who got on with him. To Pearl's amazement, when Katie grew to crawl and then to walk, she would climb up his legs onto his lap. The first few times Pearl held her breath for fear the old man would toss her off onto the floor. But he allowed Katie to nestle next to his chest, explore his shirt pockets, and even tug on his beard, white and stiff as wire. August seemed comfortable with the child, continuing his conversations as if she weren't there, focusing on her now and then only when he was about to emphasize a point, his white eyebrows arching over cheeks weathered and permanently tan.

Despite missing Etta and her own clumsiness with August, Pearl liked her new life. There was first of all Katie, a beautiful, smiling child who now ran at the faintest noise to the window to call to her father, her grandfather, or to cows or dogs or sheep, pointing and naming everything in sight all the way to the horizon.

Then there was the landscape itself of soft rolling hills, hills that spun color and shadows in the earliest morning light, then did it all again in different and deeper shades at dusk. She watched the hills constantly at these hours and had the sense sometimes that it was the hills, and not the light, that moved like slow, rising waves.

Pearl loved the smell of the countryside—alfalfa and new-mown hay, sweet clover and fresh rolled barley. Sounds from the prairie comforted her; they were reliable and she counted on them: wind, meadowlarks, the low hymn of crickets. Even the sound of cows chewing in the feedlot was a steadying influence and evoked some deep peace she was thankful for. The silence that fell with the winter snow calmed her and even vicious blizzards made heaping curves out of formerly hard angles.

Pearl liked fixing elaborate breakfasts, hearty dinners. She

---

didn't mind cleaning or baking, enjoyed wearing old house-dresses and Levi's and gave Etta all the clothes and high heels she was once required to wear to work. She spent long hours with Katie walking the trails made by cattle, picking berries or wild-flowers, or reading from faded picture books full of fairies and kings.

It was only Buck that perplexed her. And his father. And that secret place they lived in, a world remote and unapproachable. Sometimes she came around a corner too fast and unannounced and would hear their voices, ugly and profane—for men's ears only. As soon as she was noticed, the tone, the laughter would become civilized again. Recognizable. She resented that aloofness, that withholding of something from her. She tried to understand Buck and she tried to make friends with August.

The day Buck took the last of the lambs to the stock auction, she waited dinner. But as was often the case, he didn't show up, so she and Katie went ahead without him. She bathed Katie and read to her. After she put her to bed, Pearl sat on the porch to watch the sun go down. She could hear August and his best friend, Norman, a man who had been crippled and blinded in one eye by lightning ten years before. He was a man who now ran for cover at the first indication of an electrical storm. He watched the animals for signs. "There," he'd say. "See how quiet? The birds have taken cover." Or he'd say, "That herd's huddling together. A storm's coming." And sure enough, in a few hours it would be storming.

Norman was well known for the large potatoes he grew and shared with everyone on Squatter Creek. They were the largest potatoes Pearl had ever seen; some were as big as squashes because, as Norman said, he knew the right time of the moon to plant. He'd brought her some earlier that day.

Pearl listened to their voices, faint but for the laughter—gay, distinct laughter that made her feel lonely. After Katie was asleep, she cut two pieces of raisin pie and walked across the yard to the bunkhouse where August spent most evenings now. She knocked at the door timidly, remembering her own father and how she felt knocking at the door to his garage years before, wanting then as now to disrupt something she knew was happening within. What she had hoped to find in that garage she didn't know. But the walls were only covered with strange-shaped objects and tools. Nothing to suggest the reason her father spent hours there or locked it, why he brought nothing from it, absolutely nothing to suggest activity had taken place.

She knocked louder, chilled now by the cooling night air. The door swung open before her. The two men stood awkwardly as if caught by surprise. The room was pleasant in a primitive way — saddles and bridles and ragged horse blankets hung from an exposed beam and a ceiling of old planks formed an A above it. The walls were unpainted wood, seasoned a dark brown by woodsmoke of many years. A small stove hissed warmly.

"No, I can't stay," she said, declining a chair and putting the pie on the table.

"Buck home yet?" August asked.

"No, he probably got hung up somewhere," she said. She sensed that they all knew where that would be, one of the three bars that constituted the greater area of business activity in the closest town, Winslow. As if she had an appointment elsewhere, she nodded and backed out of the room, reluctant to go, leaving voices behind her, now hushed and secretive.

She was almost asleep when Buck came in. She heard him splash water in the sink, flush the toilet, then drop his boots noisily beside the bed. She smelled the odor of alcohol and smoke on the clothes he threw down.

"How was the auction?" she asked.

"Not too bad. Got a fair price on all but the two bum lambs."

Pearl wanted to ask him why he hadn't come home for supper, why he liked sitting at a bar talking to other men so much. She allowed him to pull her close. It was these times she felt most perplexed, these times she missed other men she'd known or things about other men she'd known—their habit of talking to her or dancing with her, or just sitting with her until intimacy charged the two of them like a slow current. Even when she had first known Buck, there was something of that, a nearness, a proximity. But now he withheld something, turned to her with some physical need and that was all, leaving her empty and wanting or sore and dry in some deep place inside.

The next morning Buck said he had to go to town again and Pearl decided to go with him. There were things she needed at the store, but mostly she needed to get out. Once in a great while she felt this way. Usually she was more than content with the way things were, not with Buck exactly—he confused her, disappointed her. But she was content with things in general.

By the time he was ready to go, she had changed her mind.

"You go ahead," she told him because Katie was coughing and perhaps a little feverish. Pearl had checked her every half hour or so that morning.

"What's wrong with my girl?" he asked Katie and leaned over the couch where she lay to kiss her. "You want me to stay home?" he asked Pearl.

"Oh no," she said. "Katie needs cough syrup. Don't forget to get it," she told him three times before he left.

As the day went by Katie's temperature rose even higher. Now Pearl checked it by thermometer and swabbed the toddler's small head and chest with cool rags to bring the fever down. Katie whimpered restlessly in her arms, sometimes coughing until she cried. Pearl spent most of the afternoon rocking her, trying to sing calmly and reassuringly, trying not to cry herself. Why doesn't he come, she wondered, positive the medicine would make a difference. Katie was worn out from coughing. Pearl bathed her in the kitchen sink in tepid water and wrapped her in cool towels. Though she was afraid of giving Katie a chill, she felt she must bring the temperature down.

Pearl tried calling Etta. Maybe some of Etta's prayer stuff would help. When there was no answer she decided to try tracking down Buck. By now he'd be at a bar if he were still in town.

Pearl held Katie in her arms and the phone between her ear and shoulder and dialed the Mint Bar. She waited while the bartender called out, "Anyone seen Buckman?"

"Nope, not tonight," he told her.

"Well, if he comes in, please ask him to call home," she said. She was aware how desperate she sounded. She was calling the next bar, the Dutchman, when she heard August at the door.

"What's going on?" he asked.

"I'm trying to find Buck," she said.

"Calling the bars?"

She nodded and hung up the phone.

"If women knew what's good for them they'd never call bars looking for their men!" he said angrily. "What's wrong with the kid?"

"She's sick," Pearl said and burst into tears. How dare he think she'd bother to look for Buck if not for Katie. She ran with the baby into the bedroom and slammed the door. She lay on the bed waiting for August to go out the back. Oh, God, she cried, please help me, my baby's going to die. She felt broken now, by helplessness and panic, by anger. She propped herself up on pillows, putting Katie across her chest, exhausted and dozing with the jerking rhythm of Katie's wheezing.

Pearl awakened later to dogs barking and the sound of Buck's pickup. The baby slept beside her now, the fever broken at last, her breath cool and steady. Pearl felt lighthearted, relieved and grateful. Then she thought she heard a second vehicle. If Buck had brought someone home from the bar for breakfast— sometimes he did that—she was going to throw a fit the likes of which Squatter Creek had never seen. She went to the window. There was Buck getting out of his pickup in the moonlight that

77

flooded the yard. He staggered beside the fence, using it for support. How he ever drove in that condition she didn't know. Coming up the lane behind him was August in the big truck. His headlights caused lumpy shadows of Buck and the dogs to float across the gravel.

The old man must have gone into town after him! As amazing as that was to her, and it was truly amazing, she knew nothing was needed now.

"You sons-a-bitches," she yelled at them through the window.

CHAPTER

EIGHT

1949

It was Buck, of all people, who saw that Etta was odd. He could tell, it seemed to her, right away. Once he told her she was the oddest person he'd ever met. That time he had caught her flicking at the air around Katie—there was a reason for that.

Etta could see the space around people.

That is, three times in her life she'd seen it: a particular air that for some reason showed up visible and distinguishable from other air, not unlike sunbeams that sometimes show up like streamers falling from a window. Of course there were no linear rays here, what she saw followed the curves of the body, enveloping it like casing on a sausage. The first time, she saw it around Rae Jean Pannage in the fourth grade. Rae Jean had been in the middle of a piano solo in front of the class and toward the end, Rae Jean started shining. Just as people often said—so and so lit up, or so and so glowed—that was exactly what Etta saw Rae Jean do. Rae Jean lit up and glowed. Etta watched her the whole time she stood by the piano and then as she walked to her seat behind Etta's desk and even when she sat down, until the teacher told Etta to turn around and pay attention to the next soloist. But that one didn't light up, and Etta followed Rae Jean around the school all that day and for the next year too, watching to see the phenomenon again but she never did. Finally Rae Jean moved with her family to Cincinnati.

Then years later Etta saw it around Pearl, not the glow exactly but the space, but this time it was all muddied up and had a compacted look of weight to it that worried Etta. At last she realized what caused that. Pearl was extremely depressed.

The last time she noticed it was around Katie, who was sleeping on the couch one afternoon because she hadn't been feeling well. Her long hair lay damp around her face, and her face was moist too and pink—the way a sleeping child's face often flushes. The air around her glimmered in soft pastels but for one area near her stomach, which was dark like the shade of a bruise. It seemed to be a denser kind and not moving like the rest of the space. Etta suspected it was a different temperature, maybe even colder—it had a cold look. And she knew if she were to give it a push, sort of flick it out, Katie would not be sick. She just knew that and that's what she was doing, snapping briskly at the air near Katie's stomach when Buck came in.

"What's going on?" he said.

"Oh, hi," she said. He had surprised her and broken into her concentration but she had indeed cleaned away the purple-brown, bruise-looking stuff. It turned out to be warm instead of cold.

"What are you doing?" he demanded.

"She's so hot," Etta said and, feeling foolish, fanned Katie some more.

"Etta, you're the oddest person alive," he said and sat down to keep an eye on her. But it was precisely as she'd thought. Katie's ailment left promptly and the rest of the day she romped about the house energetically. Pearl even remarked on her sudden recovery.

Etta would have explained what she'd seen to Pearl as Pearl was so accustomed to the unconventional where Etta was concerned that she no longer regarded it as spectacular or even curious. Perhaps she never had. But Buck wouldn't see it that way, he would know it for what it was, something weird. What he didn't know was that besides being eccentric herself, queer things happened to her and, often as not, the people she met were unusual too.

Yet none of this impaired the way most people viewed her. They considered her ordinary, adjusted, and capable, boringly so, to the extent that they tended to rely heavily upon her opinions, made her the caretaker for their secrets, the mediator for their quarrels. They even jockeyed for her attention with the silliest of perplexities. Especially Leona, calling her over late at night to ask something as trivial as: "Etta, how do you tell a six-year-old she has to get her shots?"

"Say 'You have to get your shots'," Etta told her, yawning.

One time Etta asked Pearl for her opinion. "Describe me," she said.

"Well, you're tall . . ."

"Not that way. As a person with certain traits or lacking certain traits."

"Let's see. You're a person who can take charge. A doer. Ummmm, solid and stable." That's how she put it, solid and stable. Probably everyone, with the exception of Buck, of course, thought Etta was solid and stable too. Except for other odd people and they were able to pick her out of a crowd.

Edgar, though, was a different story. Edgar, whom she had dated more than six months now, saw neither strength nor strangeness. What did he see? Perfection that was bound to fail him soon, that's what. She had reasoned all this out—the oddness Buck saw, the common plodding Pearl saw, the dream Edgar envisioned—all of it, for days. It was this she wanted Edgar to understand before she sent him off to Seattle without her and it was this they had argued about over lunch.

When Edgar dropped her back at the office, she shook off her raincoat and took off her sweater. It would be a good time to clean out Mr. Robbins' files, Etta decided, and she unlocked his office with the key that hung on a hook nearby. He had taken his wife out to the country to look at some property he was thinking of buying. The files, like the rest of Mr. Robbin's office, were a mess. His desk alone was so heaped with piles of paper and manuals and catalogs that had she sat in the chair in front of him there, she wouldn't have been able to tell what tie he wore.

She sat down in the chair. It was a flowered chintz that looked out of place in this bare office, a room adorned only by clutter and the chair. Perhaps she wouldn't even be able to see his chin. Etta kicked off her wet shoes and put her feet up on the desk, after first pushing aside a pile of paper with her toes. It was Friday afternoon, the dreary close of a miserable, rainy week. The sky was gray and heavy though it had stopped pouring. Still it drizzled relentlessly and she had gone out in the dark, chilling showers to tell Edgar why she couldn't marry him and move to Seattle, where he had a bright future with a company that made airplanes. Would she ever go through the rainy season after this without thinking of Edgar?

First of all, she told him once they had placed their order, there was something peculiar about her, and she expanded on that, too broadly perhaps, because it only intrigued him. Finally she had to be more specific. "Here's an example," she said. One day she had taken the bus downtown because she had a terrible tooth-ache and just wasn't up to driving. She had called in sick that morning and made an emergency dental appointment for one o'clock. The bus was fairly crowded and she had to make her way, in great pain, past the front seats behind the driver where packages and canes and large feet blocked the aisle. She found a window seat toward the back. Before many more stops, a middle-aged man got on and came directly over to her. And though there were plenty of seats as well as other passengers to choose from, he had rushed over and sat down beside her as though meeting an appointment.

"Are you sick?" he said.

"Toothache," she told him, holding her chin in her right hand.

"I'm a chiropractor," he said as if that had critical implications. Had she missed a valuable detail? She switched hands to hold her jaw. Why a conversationalist this morning of all days?

"Let me see your hand, please," he said.

"I beg your pardon," she said, sitting up straight and looking, really looking, at the man for the first time. He had on brown slacks and a tweed sport jacket and carried a briefcase. From all appearances, he might have been a salesman. Were there samples in the case? His face was pale, his skin the porous, flat-textured type, and probably soft, she guessed. His eyes were circled by pouches that made her wonder if he weren't very sad.

"Your hand, please," he said again.

Being the odd person she was, she obediently passed it over. (At this point in her story Edgar had let out his breath rather quickly but said nothing.)

"Now I'll just press on this nerve here," the man said, "and hold it for one minute." He looked at his watch as if timing it and held her right ring finger or perhaps the middle one, near the knuckle if she recalled correctly, and simply pressed rather hard.

"Now then," he said. "This will stop the pain long enough for you to get the problem taken care of."

"Well, what happened?" Edgar asked her.

"I suppose I thanked him," she said. Or had she thought to? She didn't remember everything, only that the pain stopped, that she had shopped a little and when the pain didn't return she went to the drugstore, used the phone to cancel the dental appointment, and had a chocolate soda. There was no sense in wasting a day off. The pain never did come back and it had now been a couple of years since.

She recalled nothing else about the man except how he'd talked on and on. "Now, the feet are full of nerve endings too. You can control the body by manipulation of the feet if you know what you're doing. As a matter of fact," he'd said, "I've known pregnant women to go into labor with the right touch in the right place." He paused briefly to look into her eyes, maybe to gauge the shock value of his words. "That's why I never work on the feet of a pregnant woman. You can cause an abortion with little more than pressure here and there. Why, I know a fellow up in Havre who makes his living doing that—abortions. They say folks come from miles around. Perfectly safe, I'd say."

Was it true? My goodness, she had thought, remembering her own unhappy experience, half listening as he talked away. (The memory of her own unhappy experience she omitted in her story to Edgar.) The man was still talking as he reached around her to pull the stop cord and as he walked out the back door to the street. She thought she saw his mouth still moving when the bus pulled away.

Certainly the man was bizarre, Edgar agreed, but it didn't mean Etta was. Edgar didn't seem to understand that things like that only happened to her. Pearl, now, could've sent the man away with one dirty look. In fact, he wouldn't have approached her in the first place because Pearl wasn't odd.

Then there was the time, she told Edgar, that another strange man came into the office, said his name was Gillespie, Arthur Gillespie, and that he had an appointment with Mr. Robbins.

"Mr. Robbins will be right back," she told him and asked him to take a seat. Etta had then gone back to her problem, how to figure the depreciation on the warehouse Mr. Robbins had purchased last year. He always stuck her with the taxes and she hated that.

"Excuse me," the man said. "Just figure how much of the purchase price was for land and how much was for the building—the county tax office will have that ratio. Then divide the cost of the building by the number of years allowed for this type of structure and you have your depreciation for last year. If improvements were made, add those costs to the price before dividing. And if you didn't own the building the entire year, divide the depreciation by twelve, then multiply that sum by the number of months you did have it.

She must have looked at him with astonishment or alarm or annoyance because he said, "I'm sorry, I peeked at your desk when you got up for coffee." But at that moment Herman Jones, who also worked in the office, came in with a question and by the time she'd finished finding Jones a file, Arthur Gillespie was gone.

"Where did Mr. Gillespie go?" she asked Jones. "You know, the man sitting right there," she said when Jones looked blank.

"I didn't notice anyone," Jones said. "The office has been empty all morning." No, she'd insisted, he had an appointment with Mr. Robbins. But as it turned out, he didn't, and Mr. Robbins couldn't place an Arthur Gillespie, nor could he be found in the files or on the appointment calendar, and come to think of it, she had not left her desk for coffee either.

"Well, that wasn't so unusual," Edgar said.

"Yes, but what if I imagined him?" she asked Edgar over her club sandwich. While he thought that over she went on to the next reason.

"You'll come to expect clean, matching socks, pressed pants, and dinner at six, I know it," she said. "And I don't think I'm that kind of woman anymore." Etta had adopted patterns the last few years and might have lost her knack for cooperation.

"We'll get a housekeeper," he said.

However, Etta thought she had even gone beyond some invisible point of need, past some basic principle of compromise necessary for marriage. She could neither take care of a man nor let one take care of her.

But stronger than all other concerns was this one: Etta's parents and Harold, by dying, had deserted her, and all she really had left was Katie and Pearl. She could hardly go off to Seattle now and desert them.

Edgar argued that one.

"Etta, I've heard you say time and again that you must develop deeper connections with other people, that you live on the margins of your sister's life."

That was true. She saw herself as sort of a friendly dog waiting around for the leftovers of Pearl and Katie's life—table scraps to suggest the banquet she had missed. Sometimes Etta resented it. Besides being odd, at times she was an angry person who felt life had been brutish to take away more than half her loved ones— she alternated between blaming them and blaming life—and then leave the remaining two entangled like hired hands in some wasted farm life several hours away from her.

"And you're not crazy about your job," Edgar said.

That was also true. She'd even told Edgar how she'd argued with Mr. Robbins sitting right here in the green chintz chair. She had gotten irate while doing the payroll—not her job anymore— for Jones. Jones, she explained to Edgar, had been given her job as bookkeeper when he returned from the war. That she understood; a veteran had priorities. But when she found out Mr. Robbins paid him more than he paid her, though she'd always done twice the work he had, and even now did most of it because Jones preferred delivering lumber, she got mad.

"I could understand him making more if he'd worked here longer," she'd told Mr. Robbins. "Or if he had a family to support. But no." Here she had pounded the arm of the chair. "He's single!"

"Now, Etta," he'd said. "There's no cause for alarm. It has always been the company's policy to pay men more, probably because until the war they were our only employees. It was something my father did." That was the way Mr. Robbins always explained things he could change but wouldn't.

"I've set up a nice pension for you, dear," Mr. Robbins said, trying to distract her.

She'd thought of quitting but as Pearl pointed out, she'd just have to start all over and then probably find the same problem everywhere else anyway. At least here, more so since that day, she had sort of an unspoken control over things. It was as if Mr. Robbins, too preoccupied with piling clutter and disorganizing anything anyone arranged, let all management slide over to her. Etta worked out a polite business relationship with Herman Jones. Otherwise, Jones avoided her.

"And you're dying to travel," Edgar pointed out next. "You've said so yourself." She was learning one thing from all this: Edgar listened to her and remembered what she said, particularly if it supported his point of view. He reminded her that she had always longed to leave Great Falls, that the town was clutter on otherwise clean landscape, misplaced, something wind might have dropped on the prairie floor. Well, those were his words, not exactly the way she had put it. She had even told him, he said, that she had the most pressing urge at times to go home, but that she didn't know where that was, only that it was not here.

He was right. Etta spent long hours deliberating its location. Moreover, for someone who never went anywhere to speak of, and whose life was fixed, she reflected heavily on travel and how other people lived. Not wealthy people or ones who were famous. No, she took to guessing, for example, the destinations of vagrants who hopped on and off freight cars on the edges of town, and to contemplating the lives they might lead. What would it be like, she asked herself, to ride the trains, to live no place in particular, to eat around small campfires, to dip into strange concoctions under the cover of darkness? Then to move on to the big cities, sleeping in doorways, as she had seen one man do right down the street. The man's head lay flat on the doorstep, his right hand holding its edge as it might a pillow, the left clutching the last of some beverage, desperately acquired, no doubt. She had stared.

Sometimes it was someone she knew who aroused such thoughts. Like Baylor Evans, her neighbor. Every day he had met the 5:15 train from Minneapolis. Every spring he had found the first wild buttercup and carried its blossom tenderly back to town. What might a man like that have had in mind? And what dreams had gone on without him? When he died alone, Etta wondered how that might have felt to him.

It was typical of Etta to ponder such things and others, such as what it was like to be a man. And, as one, to have sex with a woman. Was it nicer? Maybe, she guessed, as men seemed never to tire of it, never to falter in their pursuit of it, never to view it as she sometimes did, as an intrusion now and then lacking some artistic quality, or maybe simply joy. Sometimes sex even made her feel sad. Worse than that, sometimes it scared her. Not always, but sometimes. It even had with Harold. Why was that? It was a subject she'd like to bring up sometime — but to whom? To Pearl? No, she couldn't.

That attitude of hers toward sex, by the way, was another reason not to marry Edgar but she never got around to saying so, for they had argued through lunch and she had said at the end that nothing mattered but that she had this allegiance to a dream — despite any propensity for seamy abstractions — a dream of family, of children filling a house, of holidays around a crowded table, of gay events and milestones, celebrations of the landmarks in a happy life. And that she was too damaged by the abortion to bear children was all the more reason, however illogical, to stay here alone to take what she could get of the bones and leftovers of Pearl's life. And no, she said finally, she would not allow him to give up the job in Seattle. Absolutely not.

So that was lunch. Had she done the right thing?

Etta put her shoes back on. They felt mushy and cold. If she didn't start on the files now she'd be here late trying to finish up. She planned to put everything more than two years old into a box for storage. She wanted to separate personnel from customer and supplier files. Then she would clean out all Mr. Robbins's odds and ends, and what was not utter garbage, she would put together under "miscellaneous."

There were newspaper clippings about the lumber industry everywhere. An article about warping, for instance, might be filed with *T* for trouble or under *P* for production, depending on which aspect of the article had left the latest impression on Mr.

Robbins. Or an article he loved about an award given for quality lumber could be found sometimes under *A* for award and other times under *E* for excellence or *G* for goals. How could he read these faded things another time, she wondered. She tossed several into a box to send home with him.

Then there would be house plans and old photos, hardware catalogs, and competitors' ads. She might find old correspondence, unpaid bills, or a customer's obituary, five years old, all jammed in the cabinet tightly but not neatly. It was easier to recall which things a file had been placed between than to locate it by alphabetical order. Toole or Tucker, she knew, could be found between a protruding manila envelope containing God knows what and several frayed pages of a magazine that featured table saws.

Etta lifted out a stack of files, then another, and put them on the floor. She might just as well sit there to go through them. She was still on the floor when Jones came in, files spread around her, her shoes off again, and a cup of coffee nearby.

"Mr. Robbins," she heard Jones call.

"No, it's me," she said.

He came around the desk where he could see her.

"Where's Mr. Robbins?" he asked. He appeared agitated.

"Fort Shaw," she said. "What's wrong?"

"Everything," he said and sat down on the floor too. This was an unusual thing for Jones to do. He was not a casual man. He had a lunch sack in his hand and he put that on the floor beside him, then moved it in front of him between his legs. He was slightly shorter than Etta and about her age, a nervous sort, hardly the type Etta could picture aggressive enough to have been to war or to have wrestled away her job. He looked even more frail there before her with his legs crossed awkwardly and his arms enfolding his chest.

"I need to talk to someone," he said. Yet he didn't go on. Etta waited, wondering if she shouldn't say something to hurry him. She would never finish with him sitting there.

"I stole one thousand, five hundred and forty-seven dollars," he said at last.

"You did what?" she said. Surely he was joking.

"From Mr. Robbins. Out of the safe," he said.

"Oh, my," she said.

"It took me a while," he explained, waving the brown sack. "A couple of years. A little one time, a little more another."

"Why tell me?" she asked. After all, the man could hardly be counted on to say good morning to her.

"I didn't mean to," he said. "I came to tell Mr. Robbins and when he wasn't here, well, I had to tell someone.

"But I'm giving it back," he said. "I don't want it. It's all here." He waved the sack again. "You've made a mess," he said, staring at her piles as if just now noticing.

"Yes," she said. Her legs were stiff, and her left foot was numb.

"So here," he said, handing her the money.

"Oh, just put it in the safe."

"Of course." He got up then and stood over her. "Could you open it for me?" he asked. "I'm too nervous," he added when she hesitated.

"Oh, all right," she said. "Pull me up." He took her hand and she stepped over a pile of files. "Let's see," she said, leaning over the safe Mr. Robbins kept in the closet. "Six forward, eighteen back . . ." She turned the knob easily, quickly at first, then moved it one complete last round forward and a slight distance backward slowly until it clicked. Everyone around the lumberyard knew the combination to the safe. They might as well leave it open. Inside there were random piles of money, insurance papers, a deed to the property, Mr. Robbins's business license, and more odds and ends he was saving.

"You put it in," Jones said, thrusting the sack at her. This time she took it.

"What are you doing?" he asked when she took the money out of the bag.

90

"We don't need that," she said and handed him the sack.

"Of course not," he said.

She placed the money as she guessed Mr. Robbins might have. A handful crosswise on two other handfuls, another leaning against all that and one beside—a tossed-in effect. Was this how Mr. Robbins managed to make it look so messy?

Somehow the little additional money made no impact on what was already there. Everything still looked the same. Mr. Robbins always kept large sums for payroll and deliveries of the new merchandise he sold in addition to lumber. The rest might have been savings. He didn't trust banks, he said often, not since the stock market crash.

"There," she said, closing the safe and smiling.

"Well, I guess I'll wait for Mr. Robbins," Jones said uncertainly, glancing at the chintz chair.

"To confess?" she asked. He nodded sheepishly. His eyes were on her wet shoes.

"I wouldn't," she said. He looked up at her as if the words had brought him out of a faint. He started to say something but she waved her hand authoritatively and he backed down. He was so thin.

"I just think that—what I mean is," she said, "you changed your mind, you put it back. There's no sense running a thing like this into the ground." She wondered if he'd kept the money hidden in his house or put it into a bank. Had he earned interest?

Jones appeared doubtful.

"Mr. Robbins is so sloppy, he'll never notice the difference," she said.

"I never expected this from you, Etta," Jones said. "That is, to understand and all."

Well, it was a surprise to her too. "Oh, I thought of doing the same thing once," she said.

"Stealing money?" This appeared to confound him and he sat down in the chintz chair. She returned to the floor by her piles.

"Oh yes," she said. "Well it would be easy, as you know. Mr. Robbins is nervous about having so much. He's very careless with it, doesn't keep track of it even when you give him the exact figures," she said, pointing to the account books. "He's quite happy to get rid of it any chance he gets, except when it comes to my salary," she said. "Maybe I thought he owed it to me."

Jones nodded. "But you never took any?" he asked.

"No," she said, crumpling an old envelope with an unidentified telephone number on it and tossing it into the wastebasket.

"Why not?"

Etta laughed. "Because about that time my sister reminded me that if something were to happen to her I was to raise my niece. How would that be for her, I wondered—her only aunt, maybe her new mother, off to Bermuda. That's where I thought I'd go. Or worse, what if I were caught and sent to jail?"

"I see," he said and relaxed into the chair a bit. They were both silent then and Etta picked up where she'd left off, Cartwright next to Carter, then Custer. She could be done by 5:30.

"Well," he said after several minutes had passed. "I think you're right. I guess I'll go now."

"Listen, Etta," he said at the door. "I heard you say your roof was leaking. I'll be glad to come by tomorrow and fix that for you."

"Why thank you, Jones," she said. "But I've this terrible need to drive out to my sister's in the morning."

"Oh," he said. He looked hurt and frail again.

"But if you really don't mind fixing it, come by tonight for dinner and I'll give you a house key."

"That's fine," he said, smiling.

"See you about seven," she said and placed Donavan underneath Darby.

CHAPTER

NINE

They were just on the last curve on Benchland Hill and the sun was low, about to set. It wasn't until here, no matter how far he'd driven, that Buck considered himself home. He liked the view best when coming around the corner before dropping down the hill. He could see almost everything he owned; that is, everything he would someday own. He could see the abandoned schoolhouse at the T of the road coming in from Winslow. He could locate Charlie's place, Johnson's, the old Clapshaw homestead, abandoned also, and the green snake of the creek as it twisted through the flat, and not so flat, belly of the land. He liked the chopped-up yet ordered look of things and how roads below had corners to them and how neatly square and chipped out the wheat and hay fields were against the rounded, swelling hills of pastureland. Man had taken control here.

"Pa, you're not singing," Katie said.

"Old man river," he joined in loudly, and Katie clapped. The three of them, Buck, Charlie, and Katie, had sung every song they knew on the way in from Lewistown but this was her favorite and they were on maybe its sixth round. They had been in town all day, picking up parts, vet supplies, and tools. They had looked at new machinery and new pickups and later filled up the truck with sacks of chicken feed for Alma and beet pulp for Buck. They had stopped for lunch and later for pie and coffee.

Somewhere between stops they'd gone three places shopping for Katie. Buck had bought her jeans, black cowboy boots with white stitching, and red tennis shoes that Pearl wouldn't like because she worried that Katie would step on a rusty nail or a rattlesnake. The boots and jeans had been easy, but when it came to the tennis shoes, Katie insisted on red. The lady at the first store showed her navy blue and then white ones. "No, red," Katie said.

"How about these black ones?" Charlie asked at the next store.

"Those are boys'," she said.

"Jesus, but you're fussy for a four-year-old," he'd said.

"Better fussy than not give a damn," she said seriously, her chin jutting forward.

"Who says?"

"Grandpa."

"Well, one more store then," he said winking at Buck, who was really enjoying this.

"Doggone it if women don't know what they want from birth," he told Charlie.

Katie was pretty and she had this stubborn streak Buck kind of liked. Good-natured but just spunky enough to show a little personality for a kid. Pearl said he spoiled her but he didn't think so. She never really made demands. Buck just got a kick out of her, the way she said things that sounded just like Pearl or Alma or his old man, or the way she entered a room, quietly but with some energetic quality that made you look up. He liked to watch her from the window when she walked down to the barn. He'd be damned if it wasn't a little strut she had, a little cocky even. He'd have to remember that when she got older—that if she walked that way then, it was natural for her and not put on.

Charlie liked her too and never got impatient with her. She was on his lap now, one elbow out the window. The sound of their voices in the warm dusk was pleasant. They stopped at Charlie's and unloaded the feed.

"Better get on home," Buck said. "Pearl will be worried."

"Good night, Katie-did," Charlie said, picking her up and putting her through the open window of the pickup.

"Night, Charlie," she said.

"See you Sunday," Buck told him and made a U-turn in the yard around Charlie's two dogs, who were lying unperturbed in the road. Sunday, he and Pearl, her sister and Charlie were going to the rodeo in Geraldine. He wasn't crazy about the idea of Etta coming along but there wasn't much he could do about it. Just so she didn't end up liking Charlie and marrying him—which was probably just what Pearl had in mind. The thought of her ever living down the road from them was a prospect he didn't care for one bit.

"Pa, don't forget the mail," Katie said at the bottom of the lane.

"Your ma or grandpa probably got it by now."

"No," she said. "They never get it."

She was right. The mail was still there. There was a *Tribune*, a postcard from Etta saying she'd drive down Saturday, and a package the size of a shoebox. It had a letter taped to it and was addressed to August Buckman. The postmark was Anamosa, Iowa. Only one person he knew had ever been to Iowa. He distracted Katie with the postcard, hoping she hadn't noticed the package. He left it in the mailbox.

"That's all?" she said.

"That's it," he said. "Why, expecting something?"

"No one writes to me," she said, the tone of her voice suggesting that he was dumb not to have noticed. He laughed.

*   *   *

95

Later, while Katie took her bath and Pearl did dishes, Buck walked back down to the mailbox. He took the package to the barn and lit a lantern. Just as he thought, the package had to do with his mother.

"Dear August," the letter said. "I am Martina Gray, daughter of Hilda Porter. You may recall Claire speaking of my mother, as the two corresponded regularly after Claire's family moved west, up until the time of Claire's tragic death. Though they were only second cousins, they were close childhood friends. In any case, I came across these letters the other day; apparently Mother tucked them away years ago, and I thought you might like to have them. If you have any of my mother's, I'd appreciate your sending them on to me. Mother has been dead a year now and mercifully passed after many years of crippling arthritis . . . ."

Buck didn't read the rest. He hid the box, still unopened, behind some sacks of feed. He didn't want his father to find it. He felt they were his.

He went back to the house, pausing as he did at the screen door. There was a new hole in it and he stuffed his handkerchief in it to keep out flies and mosquitoes. He'd fix that tomorrow.

"You're in a good mood," Pearl said in the kitchen, her back to him, reaching up to put something in the cupboard.

"How can you tell?" he said, kissing her on the back of her neck.

"I could hear you out there whistling." She turned and smiled.

"Katie in bed?" he asked.

"Yes. She just conked out. You must have had quite a day."

"One hell of a day," he said, moving his mouth down to her right breast. There was the fresh smell to her shirt of clean laundry dried in the sun.

Buck woke earlier than usual and sat on the back porch with a mug of coffee and smoked. The air was already warm, though daybreak was no more than a thin line of gray across the top of the hills. A scorcher, he predicted, but a good day anyway. This morning Buck would learn more than he'd ever known about his mother, the woman his father never talked about.

Once he'd asked Alma about her. "Was she pretty?"

"Well, yes," Alma had said, sifting flour or cornmeal into a bowl at the kitchen table.

"What was she like?"

"She was a good cook . . . ," she said, pausing. "And a real seamstress."

"But what was she like?"

"Like I said," Alma said, now adding milk and eggs to the bowl. "She liked to sew. Made me a dress once. Real nice."

That was about all he could get out of her. Or was that all Alma knew? It had exasperated him. He wanted to know what his mother had thought about things, though he couldn't say what things exactly. He wanted to know whether she was nice or funny or happy and what she felt deeply about and whether or not she had loved him, her son. Those kinds of things, important things that might tell him something about himself, about the part that was not like August and never would be.

All he'd ever had of her, his mother, the young woman called Claire, was what he created of her. At twelve, he believed she went back into the fire to get his favorite toy, something soft and homemade, something he couldn't sleep without. At twenty, he imagined her going in after the payment on the entire year's crop, money desperately needed for survival the following year.

At thirty, he decided she'd gone, troubled and unhappy, back in to kill herself because by now he thought of her as mysterious, perhaps sad and unhappy with August. She had become like Buck, someone who wanted more out of life, a tortured person, sensitive to what was missing or inadequate. But now an imagined mother wasn't enough. He wanted to know the real one.

The sun was up now and he heard Pearl in the kitchen and

soon smelled side pork frying. He grabbed his work gloves and went down toward the barn to turn on the water in the tanks and do the feeding.

Everyone at breakfast had a certain joy. Pearl, because Etta was coming and because, he liked to think, she had enjoyed making love to him the night before. Probably too, she was happy because he hadn't been out drinking in months. Katie, of course, was happy about the trip yesterday, about Etta coming, and about new red tennis shoes. And he had his letters, which he would sneak down by the creek to the shade to read later, leisurely and alone.

Even August was in a good mood and wandered over, as he rarely did, for morning coffee. He had to prefer either Buck's or Pearl's to his own, though he'd never admit that.

"Do you like my new shoes?" Katie asked August.

"Aren't they a little bright?"

"I like them bright."

"Well, your ma's right. You shouldn't wear them around the place. But they'll be just fine to wear to town," he added when she frowned.

"How about some breakfast, August?" Pearl asked.

"No thanks. I already ate. Did I see you out in the dark this morning?" he asked Buck.

"That was me," Buck said cheerfully. No matter what time he got up, he could be sure August had gotten up earlier and was at the window waiting for sunrise. He expected August to add something sarcastic like "Just getting home?" Or "Up all night?" But he said nothing more.

Before the old man left, Pearl asked him for dinner.

"My sister's coming," she said. "We'd like to have you too."

"I'll see if I can make it," he said as if he had a thousand things to do. Buck smiled at Pearl, who looked annoyed.

"Where you going, Pa?" Katie asked him when he got up from the table a few minutes later.

"I'm going to check some fence down by the creek."

"Can I come?"

"Not this time, gorgeous. Can't be worried about you falling in the creek today."

Pearl looked at him suspiciously, or maybe just curiously. She knew the creek was shallow now, in fact, almost dry.

"You can help me get ready for Aunt Etta," she told Katie.

Buck grabbed an old picnic blanket kept behind the seat of the pickup and the box of letters he'd taken from the barn. He could see every pebble in the creek bed and the shallow water ran lazily and without much sound. The few trees along this section of the creek, almost on Charlie's land, were wind bent into crippled shapes that made sparse shade for flies and birds and for the grasshoppers beneath them that jumped in the dying grass along the edges of the dried-out banks.

The letters had no particular order to them and he arranged them by year and month of postmark. The first one was dated November 1911.

"Dear Hilda," he read. "Winter is here and it has been snowing for three days. It's a dry, powdery kind of snow that you can shake off if you fall in it . . . ."

Buck skipped to the next one.

"I remember sitting down on the riverbank on that path that comes off the main road. You know, where it winds downhill from the church and then turns left at the bottom. Well, there I was on a stump waiting for you and the river was high and moving fast. It was spring and the trees had leafed out all beautiful and green . . ."

Apparently she hadn't met August yet. Buck looked for a later one.

"I have a new customer who seems quite wealthy. She ordered twelve summer dresses, mind you. The problem is she is quite cantankerous and hard to fit as she has little patience for the time it takes to be measured and fitted properly. And at this she requires extra time as she is of a roly-poly build that . . . ."

"Jesus," Buck said aloud. Was this all? Just schoolgirl letters? Some of them had drawings in them, simple, awkward sketches of dresses, coats, hats. Most of them were dated between 1911 and 1913. There were only a couple during the years she would have been married and pregnant. But there was nothing he could find so far about either August or him.

One was a Christmas card dated December 1916, but it had nothing more to it than a usual greeting. "Merry Christmas to you all and best wishes for the coming year," she had written across the bottom.

The last letter written was marked April 1917—just months before the fire. The dates on his mother's gravestone were August 4, 1896–July 22, 1917. He tore it open.

"The house," his mother had written, "will be completed this summer. It has a sunken living room according to plan and all the fireplaces will be marble. The banister for the large open staircase is polished oak that August had imported from back east, and the front porch has pillars like you find on those southern plantations . . ."

Buck couldn't read on. The house that she referred to had a cement stoop out the front door that no one ever used. There were no fireplaces, no banisters on the narrow, closed staircase, and the only thing sunken about the living room was the way it sagged.

Buck stayed a little longer at the creek, swatting off flies that continued to land on him. The sun had taken over his shade and it was hot. He gathered up the letters finally, not bothering to put them back into their envelopes. One by one, he tore them into pieces and threw them toward the creek. Some pieces made it and floated on downstream in the shallow water or stuck to bare rocks. Others were carried by a breeze Buck hadn't noticed before and littered the banks or lower branches of the bushes.

When they were all torn and thrown, he got up, not bothering to take the blanket, and got into the pickup, which was hot now too. He drove back to the road but instead of going to Charlie's as he'd planned, or back home, he headed for town.

The next morning he could remember little about the rest of the day and evening before. Only that he'd stopped at one of the bars, run into Gladys, and hadn't gone home.

That Gladys was in town had not struck him as unusual.

"Buck!" she'd said. "Surprised to see me?"

"No," he said.

"Didn't you know I got married and moved to Glasgow?"

"Oh, yeah. Some fly-boy, right?"

"A sergeant."

Buck turned his back on her.

"You want to come out back and see my pickup?" she asked. "We put a topper on it."

"No."

"Come on."

"Leave me alone," he'd told her.

But apparently she hadn't because that's where he woke up, cramped and stiff, Sunday morning—in a small homemade outfit on the back of a pickup at the edge of town. Gladys, barely visible above the sheet that covered her, was still asleep.

Buck found his clothes and shoes, then hunched over beneath the low ceiling by the canvas flap and got dressed. He closed the flap behind him and walked across town to look for his truck. He was ready now to go home.

CHAPTER
TEN

———◆———

Saturday night after a good deal of discussion—argument actually—Pearl convinced Etta that the three of them should proceed to the rodeo as planned whether Buck came home or not. It was 10:30.

"He's off on a toot," she said. "Probably an all-night poker game."

"How can you be so sure?"

Pearl ignored the question. "I'm going tomorrow, even if you and Charlie don't."

"All right then," Etta said. "Katie will enjoy it."

"We're not taking her." Pearl said firmly.

"Why not?"

"It'll be too hot for her. And I want to enjoy myself without having to make a dozen trips to the bathroom and hot dog stand."

"I'll do that," Etta said.

"No you won't. This time you and Charlie are going to have some fun."

"What's that supposed to mean?"

"You know. Have fun, get married, move next door."

Etta laughed. "He's not my type."

"You don't even know him."

"But I know that." If anything, he was Pearl's type. He would have been much more sensible a choice for her than Buck but Etta didn't say that. But it was so obvious. Pearl was even better friends with him than Buck was. Not surprising, because in her opinion, friendship would not be something Buck would be good at. Good God, but she disliked that man.

In the morning, they took Katie down to Charlie's. His mother was going to babysit. Charlie, of course, asked where Buck was.

"Anybody's guess," Pearl said. She was angry but determined to have fun anyway. That was typical of her.

Charlie only nodded and got into Etta's car.

Reluctant as she was, Etta soon caught the spirit of the occasion. There was something contagious about Pearl's attitude, a sense of abandonment she filled the air with, that became, as the day wore on, exhilarating. A rodeo was a new experience for Etta and she soon forgot that her white dress was getting dusty in the dirty, hot air, that she should stay out of the burning sun, and that it was against her usual better judgment to drink so much beer.

Etta watched one event after another with dismay—calf roping, bronco riding, barrel racing. She expected that at any moment someone would be killed—trampled under thudding hooves, or squashed beneath the massive flanks of a falling bull. She sipped the cold beer nervously, fascinated by the energy of the crowd and the alarming suddenness with which everything happened. Gates swung open to release animals and contestants—great bulls, frightened calves, bucking stallions and lanky riders with hats in hand. Once a cowboy flew over the side of his horse and hung there upside down. His boot had caught in the stirrup and he was dragged a good six feet before being rescued by other men on horses and a rodeo clown who pulled away a cinch or something from the rearing bronco's belly. Etta and the crowd sat back down, relieved. It was all so swift and violent.

Unexpectedly, Etta got drunk, and not surprisingly, so did Pearl and Charlie. Not falling-down drunk or tired drunk or satiated drunk, but the energetic kind that made them want to keep on going, to eat everything in sight, and as it turned out, to dance. Etta hated to dance.

After the rodeo, they went to a bar in downtown Geraldine. Etta was as bad as anyone there and they were all bad in her opinion. To her surprise, she not only danced with everyone but sang songs too, arm in arm between Charlie and Pearl. And when someone—a fellow she had danced with earlier—drove a motorcycle into the bar through the crowd and stopped at her stool, she good-humoredly got on behind him for a swing around town.

The ride was longer than a swing, though. He drove through town to its edge, off onto a graveled road and then through a field. It was cool and sobering to speed through darkness behind some stranger, but perhaps not quite sobering enough. When the unidentified driver stopped suddenly and led her to a bed of grass under a tree, she did not protest. She was sufficiently drunk to enjoy his voice in the quiet night.

"You're beautiful," he said. "What's your name?"

"Dorothea," she told him for the fun of it.

"I'm Clifford," he said. "And you, pretty lady, excite me." He kissed her then and slipped his hand under her shirt to her breast. She felt the heat of her sunburn against his skin, and she relaxed into the soft damp grass.

When Clifford deposited her, wind blown and ragged, back at the bar, she was ready to resume normal behavior. But it was another hour before she could persuade Pearl to go home, and Charlie, she noticed, kept his eye on Pearl. By now Etta was feeling a little dizzy and went to the restroom, which turned out to be an outhouse behind the bar.

On her way back in, along the boardwalk between outhouse and bar, she heard two men talking in the dark.

"So which sister's married to Buckman?"

"I don't know."

"Don't matter. Either one can out-party old Bucko any day."

That comment did it.

"Let's go," she insisted when she was back inside and Charlie agreed.

"One more song," Pearl said, but they took her arms to guide her out the door.

"Wait—my beer!" she said.

"You're taking it?" Etta asked. There were at least four or five cans lined up where she had sat, some opened.

"Damned right," Pearl said, grabbing them off the bar. "Sorry," she said, happily waving to her audience, who booed Etta and Charlie.

Pearl sang from the backseat, Charlie drove, and Etta thought, worried, analyzed, and prayed in the front. She tried to figure out what had happened, and at what point she should have done something to avoid it. Had she gone nuts? It certainly appeared so. How could she act like that, like some whore? And at her age. This was something she might have done at seventeen—in fact, she had, as she recalled.

Good God, how it must have looked—returning to that bar all rumpled and half-dressed. How would she explain that to Pearl or had Pearl even noticed? Pearl had gone crazy too. All three of them had. And now, how would they explain the late hour to Alma when they picked up Katie? Lord Almighty.

It began to rain halfway home and then, soon enough, to pour. When they turned off the main road onto the gravel, there was no visibility beyond the dim headlights. But Charlie kept on going. Etta prayed to God to kindly overlook their sins of the day and get them home safely. Pearl, quiet finally, must have fallen asleep.

To Etta's relief, Charlie pulled into his lane and yard. It had stopped raining and a light went on in the house.

"Listen," Charlie said, getting out of the car. "Come on in. I'll make you breakfast and then drive you home."

The three of them, hanging onto each other in the dark, made their way across the yard, stumbling once on a sleeping dog, who yelped and woke up all the other dogs.

"Shut up," Charlie yelled, and the barking became low whimpers in the night.

Inside Alma appeared at the kitchen door, shaking her head in disapproval. "I never thought I'd see the day. Shame on you, Charlie. You too, Pearl. Why you all look terrible. What happened to her?" She pointed to Etta.

"You know how Etta is. She got us drunk and wouldn't bring us home," Pearl said seriously. For some reason that struck Etta as funny and she laughed. Evidently, she was not as sober as she'd thought. Alma looked shocked. There was something about Pearl's straight face and Alma's disapproval that was humorous.

Charlie laughed too. Pearl looked smug.

"You drunks better eat something," Alma said and got out eggs and a pan.

Alma sat down with them while they ate and wanted to hear all about the rodeo. She told them everything Katie had said during the day that was in her opinion remarkable. She said that Buck had come up about six o'clock that evening to pick up Katie and wanted to know when Pearl and Charlie were expected.

"'They didn't say but I'd guess earlier than you ever get home,' I told him. But I was wrong there."

After a second cup of coffee, they were ready to go.

"I can drive two miles," Etta said. "We'll be all right."

"You sure?" Charlie said.

"I'll drive," Pearl said. "The lane will be muddy and you'll never get over the hill. I'm not in the mood to drive off into the dam tonight."

"No, I can do it," Etta said and got into the driver's side, determined now. She thought Pearl was still drunk.

"Etta," Charlie said through the car window. "Remember that once in a while everyone has to blow off a little steam. Don't be so hard on yourself." His words caught her by surprise and once more she felt ashamed of herself.

Pearl started singing again before they were even out of the yard and kept it up the rest of the way until they reached the entrance to their own lane.

"Stop," Pearl said. "I'll guide you from here. What you have to do is back up and get a good running start, gun it up the hill and keep it from sloshing off the edge of the road. But don't slow down or you'll get stuck. It'll be slicker than shit, as they say around here. You ready?"

Oh God, Etta prayed. Here goes. She accelerated to the floor, shot up the first part of the hill, then hesitated at the corner as they came to the dam.

"Gas!" Pearl cried.

The car ricocheted past the dam and over the top of the hill. Etta let out her breath and pulled up ten feet parallel to the feedlot.

"That was easy," she said, quite pleased.

She had no more gotten the words out when the car, remaining in its parallel position, slid sideways down the hill into the feeding-pen fence.

They both laughed now. Sliding sideways in deep mud had been a curious sensation.

"You'll have to get out my side," she told Pearl as she pulled herself out uphill. The car was at a definite tilt. She held several beers for Pearl, who had not forgotten them and had handed them to Etta through the window.

"You're crazy," Etta told her. She put the beers down on top of the hood and helped Pearl out the awkward angle by pulling her with her right hand.

The car door fell shut behind them; the mud was to their ankles. Pearl grabbed the beer.

A noise made them turn toward the bunkhouse, where August stood staring at them, their predicament clearly exposed by the dripping yard light on their left.

This was not funny, Etta decided. This was not Alma's mild disapproval. She felt outrage emanating from the old man. But obviously Pearl either didn't pick up on that fact or didn't care.

"Pretty good driving for a city slicker, huh, August?" she yelled, shaking her right fist, still wrapped around the top and bottom of two cans of beer. "Rotten parking, though," she said, laughing, and led the way into the house.

Now Etta felt the exhaustion. It was 4:00 A.M. She was sunburned and sore, the air was muggy from the rain, and the room too hot to sleep in even under the open window.

Please forgive me, Etta prayed, worried that this day had revealed something of her true character at last—a brazen, drunken, irresponsible one. Never, ever again, I promise, she added, hoping that it was all a fluke and circumstantial, a good lesson maybe. Or had it been a warning of things to come? Heaven help her, she would reform now.

It was just too bad though, she decided, that it had all been so much fun.

CHAPTER
ELEVEN

———————

Katie finished her breakfast and waited for her grandfather to finish his.

"Grandpa," she said. "You want to hunt mushrooms?"

"Not today. We have to go to Charlie's."

"Again?"

"This is the last day."

"Can we hunt tomorrow?"

"Maybe," he said. "If I'm up to it."

Katie watched him eat. He lifted the food as if it was heavy, his hand shaking with the weight. Sometimes the food fell from the fork back onto the plate and once it missed the plate and table entirely and disappeared from view. After that he squinted at the remains and pushed away the plate.

"You two ready?" her mother asked. She was putting potato salad and fried chicken into a box.

"Go on ahead," her grandfather said. "I can drive Katie down."

"No, I'm in no hurry," she said. "I'll just finish these dishes."

When they got there, her mother took the food to the house and Katie and her grandfather watched from the fence. Her father and Charlie and some other men were branding and vaccinating calves, after first crimping their testicles and horns. Katie could see her mother now beyond the pens, herding large cattle into chutes. Katie didn't see how she got the big animals to do what she wanted. They were cows Charlie had just bought and he had to change the brand on them to his.

The smell of seared hide filled the air, and blood and pieces of horn made ripples in the dirt where they fell. She didn't like to watch.

"It don't hurt them none," her grandfather said.

"Then why do they cry?"

"Just ornery," he said.

"I'm going to the house," she told him.

Inside, Alma was rolling out pie dough. She was talking to another old woman but motioned Katie to come in.

"This here's Katie," she told the woman. "Buck's girl."

"Katie, you want to peel me some carrots?" She got Katie a peeler and went back to what she was saying. "So I told him, 'Charlie, you ought to marry some nice girl before you get too old.' You know all he does when he's not working is read."

"What about that one from Coffee Creek he was seeing?" the woman asked.

"Nah, nothing ever came of that."

Katie had peeled the last carrot and arranged them all in the pot provided her when her mother came in the door.

"They finished up yet?" Alma asked, pointing with a floured finger to where Pearl could find soap and a clean towel.

"The calves are done. They'll get to the cows after dinner," Pearl said as she washed up. Her mother's jeans were now dirty and her shirt stained by a brown smear down its front that Katie guessed was dried blood.

"How's August?" Alma asked.

"Not too well."

"He's getting old," the woman said. "Like the rest of us."

"Well, I wish he'd get to feeling good. I'd like him to take a look at the Buick," Alma said.

Katie's grandfather liked to work on things. Sometimes she helped him. When he worked on any of the vehicles around the place, she either sat up on its wide fender or squatted on the ground beside where he lay beneath it and handed him tools he taught her the names of. He taught her other names too.

"This is a fuel pump; that's the carburetor," he would explain, and she'd repeat the names after him: fuel pump, carburetor, radiator, battery. "Here's the spark plugs; don't drop them," he'd said a few days before, handing the old ones to her as she sat leaning over the engine of the cattle truck. "If you want something to run, you got to take care of it." He wiped his hands and took a hand-rolled cigarette from his breast pocket. He liked to roll a few ahead of time and keep them in a tin box in his pocket. "You have to keep your ears tuned to how a thing runs. Listen," he said and started the motor. "For chrissake, don't fall in," he yelled over the noise of the engine, then came back to where she sat. "You can tell what the problem is if you got good ears." Satisfied then, he'd turned off the engine.

Whenever they would get into the pickup to go to town or to check cattle in some distant field he'd open the door on the driver's side and boost her up. "Which one's the brake?" he'd ask.

"This one," she'd say.

"And that?"

"The clutch," and she'd move over so he could get in.

Sometimes he'd let her shift for him, indicating the right moment by a nod of his head. "You can hear when it's time to shift if you listen," he said often.

"It won't be long until Katie will be driving," he announced once at dinner.

"For God's sake," her mother said. "Let the child start school first."

But since he got sick they didn't spend as much time in the garage, and now when they went somewhere her father or mother wanted to drive them. He didn't talk so much anymore either and sometimes they just sat on the hill in the sun or waited on the creek bank for fish to jump or gophers to pop up out of holes.

Katie helped her mother set Alma's large dining-room table, then watched out the window for the men to come up to the house. When she saw them coming she ran to open the door.

"How's my girl?" Charlie said and swung her up to the ceiling.

"Charlie," she cried. "You're all dirty!"

"So I am," he said and put her down. The men took turns at the sink, talking as they washed, dripping water on the floor and counter, leaving smudges on the white towels Alma had stacked nearby.

Her grandfather felt good today. When they all sat down, he laughed and talked too.

"What do you think, August? Old John's wife is pregnant again," someone said.

"Is that so?" a man across the table said, looking at old John, who wasn't much younger than August.

"Get the right equipment together," her grandfather said, "and those things happen. That is, if the equipment works," he added and everyone laughed.

After they were all finished Katie followed the men outside. She sat with her grandfather against the barn where the sun warmed them and made her drowsy. She closed her eyes and listened to the sounds—men yelled and the branding chute closed tight and noisily around the cows that bellowed when the hot iron struck. She winced as each cow threw itself against the sides of the metal chute and she waited each time for the rack to give way or fall over. Finally there was the sound of hooves thudding across the ground when a cow was released and soon enough another one was brought up front.

When she woke up, her cheek was scratched from lying across her grandfather's wool shirt. He took her by the hand and they walked up to the house, where the men had already gone again to eat. The men were sitting on the porch waiting for supper, drinking beer and smoking in the falling sun. Her father and Charlie were tuning up guitars and when they saw her Charlie sang, "Katie with the big black eyes is the only girl for me."

The next morning Katie worried that her grandfather was sick again because he didn't come down to the house for breakfast. She was certain also that her mother was mad about something. She hadn't talked or smiled once through the meal and didn't put out butter or the syrup she usually heated and poured into a little pitcher. Her father seemed not to notice her mother at all and directed his attention to Katie.

"Katie, be a sweetheart and get me the jelly," he said. "And the butter." He was cheerful all morning and kissed Katie on the cheek when he sat down to eat and, afterward, gave her a quarter for her bank.

"So are you rich yet?" he asked, flipping the coin in the air before making it disappear and reappear behind his ear.

"Just about," she said. Her bank was almost full.

He put out his cigarette, took a final sip of coffee, and got up to get his coat. He was going to town. Katie knew by the way he was dressed, in good boots and pressed pants.

"Buck," her mother said at last. "If you're not home in time to feed, the stock won't get fed."

"The hell you say," he said, adjusting his hat in the mirror by the door. "That a fact?"

"Yes," her mother said, biting her lower lip. "I'm not going to do it."

"Fine," he said. "Let them starve." He walked out the door and didn't bother to close it. They could hear him whistling until her mother slammed the door shut.

Katie cleared away the dishes and stood on the stool her father had made her, rinsing and stacking the plates in the sink while her mother strained the morning milk. Katie took the leftover pancakes out to the dogs and put out milk for the cats. Her mother remained quiet as they made beds and folded laundry.

"Can I go down to Grandpa's?" Katie asked.

"May I," corrected her mother. "After lunch. If you get your room picked up by then."

"Make sure he's not napping," her mother told her when she prepared to go. "And take these," she said and handed Katie a bag of cookies. Katie yelled and pushed at the three dogs, who barked and jumped at her. "Get down," she hollered. They followed behind her to the bunkhouse and waited while she listened for sounds of her grandfather. She could hear a fire in the stove and the creak of his rocker and she knocked.

"Come on in," he said. "You want to play cards?"

"Sure," she said and put the cookies on the table.

"What will it be today. Old maid or poker?"

"Grandpa," she said, "Mama says I can't play poker anymore."

"Oh well, old maid then."

The old man helped himself to coffee that he poured from a pot on top of the small potbelly stove and smoked cigarettes he kept in a cigar box on the table. He won all but two of the games. "Hey, you cheated," he said when she won. "Grandpa," she said, "I don't cheat." She was getting tired of playing.

She watched him take thin papers from one end of the cigar box. He laid out one at a time, then tapped out tobacco from a pouch he also kept in the box. He rolled each one neatly and licked the paper, then stacked them up at the front of the box, saving out a few for the tin box he put in his pocket. He closed the lid and blew any spilled tobacco onto the floor.

"It's almost time to feed," he said. He got up and looked out the window at the house. "Your pa's not home yet so I guess your ma will be out soon."

"Mama's not going to feed today," Katie told him.

"Who says?"

"She did."

"She told you that?"

"She told Pa."

"What'd he say?"

"He said, 'Let them starve.'"

"Aw, she'll do it."

"No, sir."

"Sure she will. Women are soft."

"She's mad."

"Well then, we'll have to do it," he said.

"Okay."

"Look there," he said pointing out the window.

Katie got up to see what he was looking at. It was her mother in her old jacket with a scarf around her head going to the barn.

"See?" he said. "Women are soft."

CHAPTER
TWELVE

———————◆———————

"The old man's getting ready to die, I just know it," Buck said often now when he watched his father's slow, clumsy movements to the barn through the window.

"How can you talk like that?" Pearl asked, shuddering.

"He just gets older and older. Day after day, dying a little more."

"Buck, I can't stand this talk," Pearl said. She'd noticed the deterioration too, even worried for fear the old man would be alone with Katie at some point and choose to die then, collapsing perhaps in the barn where the two often went to feed the animals, or in the pickup he refused to quit driving, maybe causing an accident by his dying that would kill Katie too. She thought about the possibilities constantly but couldn't bring them up to Buck. She had only asked him to keep August off the tractor. "For God's sake, do that," she told him. "Use any excuse."

Pearl tried to discourage Katie from spending so much time with the old man, tried to keep her busy and distracted with visits to town or baking the things Katie liked—brownies, gingerbread, or roll-out cookies. "You can even crack the eggs," she'd tell Katie, motioning her to the wooden stool she kept in the kitchen. "You can even have a milkshake," she'd say when Katie balked at getting into the car.

Katie and her grandfather had a strange relationship. Pearl had always thought that. "Like some old couple married fifty years," Buck described it once. Exactly. Why hadn't she recognized it? Like the Mathers who lived down the block when she and Etta were growing up. They tottered around town silently, seeming to lean on each other though Pearl never once saw the two frail bodies touch. You just got that feeling when you watched them, and that maybe they never had to speak, just thought out messages that the other could pick up and nod to. That was Katie and August. Two silent figures teetering around the ranch, on their way to the water troughs or the barn or to dinner, always ten minutes behind the time Pearl placed hot food on the table, even though she was careful to put it out only when she saw them nearing the porch. Still they found things to delay them, the removal of muddy boots, the discovery of some new thing, a burr on the cat's head, a tangled rope, a broken zipper.

It worried Pearl to think of Katie constantly so near impending death, as if it were an entity that might think of the child as an appendage to August and to be taken in the course of things. Or that by her insistence on being near him, her energy might diminish and fade too. Or August himself, Pearl feared, might take something of Katie with him, out of love and ignorance, like her attention, her enthusiasm. There was so much she gave to the old man. "Baloney," Etta said. "Katie loves him and he'll die a happier man for it."

In the six years she'd been at the ranch, Pearl still hadn't made friends with August. Oh, he was more used to her, more thoughtful of her, he sometimes even looked at her as if there was something about her he understood and it made her avert her eyes shyly. Some years ago he'd gone as far as to pass her the bottle of whiskey he always got out after any job that required hired hands or the neighbors' help. As usual, the bottle had gone from one dirty man's hand to another, a ritual of patience she'd observed time and again as interloper. Her help was wanted, needed even, to herd cattle, to shear sheep, for this, for that. Then when the task was completed, she was dismissed to the kitchen or nursery while men congratulated and rewarded themselves in this manner. That's how it was, unquestionably a man's ritual, fraternal, mysterious, unexplained.

So the bottle went around the circle or down the line or across the table until that day August held it out to her. She was startled but accepted it. Pearl first knew whiskey by its haphazard inclusion over the years of her childhood in holiday eggnog—small teaspoonsful to each drink, if brandy or rum was not available; failing that, whiskey, barley corn whiskey, as her father judged it after the "short snort test" he always made. She knew it later mixed with coke in the backseat of someone's car or at parties in some field. As an adult she drank it only rarely, diluted with coffee and cream. Whiskey was not something she considered an award.

She who regarded whiskey thus, notwithstanding its appeal among men, took the longest, largest sip from August's bottle that she could. It raised her status with haying and branding crews after that and no man hesitated to pass it to her now. They all saw that change, all except Buck. Or maybe he saw it too well. Maybe in his eyes, she'd gone over to the other side, to August's side, that part that stood in opposition to him always, that place of stability and composure that looked and saw a weak son, a failing man, a needy spirit.

"My own father hates me," he'd often say. "The son of a bitch hates me."

"He doesn't hate you. He just worries about you," Pearl said. Buck saw no connection between his absences from the ranch or his hangovers and reason for August to worry. Other men were often as irresponsible as Buck, that was true. There was more going on here, though, something in Buck's countenance that made the others unsure, something Buck knew about and was sorry for too. It was something like that—nothing Pearl could put her finger on, but it made August worry, her worry, and Buck himself worry. Even Katie wore a dazed expression lately, a far-off look of thought and concern, bearing it even in the controlled movement of her body, now tempered with a dawdle to match her grandfather's. Did they all wonder, with August gone, who would be in charge?

Pearl decided to send Katie to Etta's until it was all over. August had given up his walks now, his condition worsening with a rapidity that astonished them all; but still he insisted on sleeping in the bunkhouse. There was nothing more medical science could do once the body got a certain age, they were told by a doctor from Lewistown.

"Keep him comfortable. Let him eat what he wants," the doctor said. "If he wants to smoke, let him. If he wants a drink, well and good." He was so old himself, Pearl suspected he might have been repeating something told to his own family that morning.

August never admitted to pain, just moved delicately as if something inside hurt or refused any longer to work. Otherwise, he showed none of the signs of senility Pearl feared, such as bedwetting or craziness or loss of short-term memory. He suffered as far as she could tell only from nightmares and often he woke them with screams or cursing. Buck said he thought the old man was reliving a wild past in his dreams. He'd heard, not from August, of course, but from others who knew, that August had once rustled cattle, or had at least been pretty chummy with some well-known thieves. Someone had even told Buck about a hanging once, reportedly of a black man, maybe one of the cowpunchers who had once driven cattle up into Montana territory. August and his friends were said to have hung the man without trial from a balcony beam that Buck could still point out to Pearl at the Judith Hotel. The crime? The storytellers weren't sure but perhaps he stole a horse. Or maybe that was just an excuse to take the cattle. Anyway, Buck loved to tell these stories, and he told them as though his father were a legend and already dead.

"Did you ever ask your father if the stories are true?" Pearl said to Buck.

"Hell no," he said.

"Why not?"

"Jesus," he said. "You go ask him."

No. Pearl wasn't about to do that. Yet she knew as well as she knew anything that August would answer truthfully. Damn, the man was going to die and take all that with him. Her questions would be left to the philanthropy of local oral histories, stories enlarged by speculation, by bourbon, and by fifty years of telling.

Pearl decided it was necessary, whether August liked it or not, to move him into the house to Katie's room. Pearl wasn't happy about this; she didn't want him dying there. Nor did she want Katie returning from Etta's to his absence and the smell of decomposition that even now Pearl detected, or worse, to a spirit waiting there to say good-bye. These thoughts and others kept her awake and alert to any sound from the bunkhouse.

"Will you stop all this," Etta said when she came to get Katie. "How do we know it's not more pleasant to die than to be born?"

Pearl decided she just wouldn't answer. She wasn't in the mood for a philosophical discussion of death.

"After all, Socrates said that to fear death was the pretense of wisdom," Etta said.

"What's that supposed to mean?" Pearl asked, exasperated. Anything odd that Etta believed she put into the mouth of some expert. She had the queerest notions sometimes. Every year she grew more strange, more attracted to bizarre religions and beliefs, extracting a bit here, a bit there, jumbling and fitting it all together until it suited her.

"Then when she thinks it all fits, she tries to push it on me," Pearl told Buck after Etta left.

"Ignore her," he said. "Or she'll be wanting to do a séance after the old man dies. What she needs is a man."

Pearl doubted that. She guessed that Etta probably had all the men she wanted, not that Etta ever said much about it. Buck was probably right about the séance, though.

The old man didn't seem to mind moving to Katie's room and didn't ask where she was, as though knowing it appropriate to spare her. Pearl sensed too that the room comforted him, the soft blues and purples of teddy bears and curtains, of ruffled pillows and bright toys. Something of Katie was there—in the morning sun on her dollhouse, in the bathrobe she forgot that hung unevenly from a hook, in the faded sweatshirt on the doorknob of her closet, the pair of outgrown cowboy boots limp in the corner. There was even a faint smell of her, rather like fresh air and grass stains, pleasant and clean.

"It won't be long now," August told her the morning he died. Of course it was morning. Everything eventful happened to Pearl in the morning. Mornings stood out like exclamation points in her life—her wedding, Katie's birth, her parents' deaths, now this.

"Don't talk like that," she said, not knowing what else on earth to say.

"Listen to me," he said and beckoned her closer with an insistent, knotty finger. "You and Katie take care of my boy."

"You know we will."

"You get what I'm saying? In some ways he's worthless, but you and the kid are good for him."

"Oh August," she said awkwardly. "Someday you'll be real proud of Buck." She bent forward and kissed him on the forehead.

"Woman," he said loudly as if sound might protect him from her. "Don't be slobbering on me. Let a man die in peace."

Pearl backed away automatically like a slap had stung her cheek.

"You old bastard," she said and knew for the moment she meant it.

"That's better," he said.

After the funeral Buck was joyful. His cheer was not flaunted, of course not. But there it was all the same, seeping out cracks in his grief, spreading across his voice and causing a noticeable expansion of his chest as if some internal swelling were taking place. Pearl understood. August's concern and disapproval of his son had done things to Buck over the years. Now maybe Buck would at last be free to realize something of himself. She hoped that was possible for all their sakes.

But for herself, Pearl felt loss keenly. Not for a friend, they had never achieved that, but for an ally, one who always kept things from getting too far out of hand, an ally who said there were limits to what anyone had to take. With August around, she had felt safe, even from his son. Silly as that sounded in the discussions she had with herself, she agreed to it and mourned.

CHAPTER
THIRTEEN

Katie had been at Etta's for a long time now. Every morning Aunt Etta came to her room and sat on her bed talking to her until she was wide awake. Then Aunt Etta made breakfast, except on Sundays when they went to a big hotel and had waffles.

Katie wasn't sure how long it had been. First her mother had started suggesting that she go there and then one day told her that Aunt Etta was coming to pick her up.

"I don't want to go," Katie told her.

"You like Aunt Etta, don't you?" her mother asked.

"Yes."

"It's just while grandpa's sick."

"Are you coming too?"

"No, but I'll come to get you soon."

Evidently her father knew all about it too because he yelled in the door to her, "Katie, come see the new lambs before Etta gets here." She stepped off the back porch onto his shoulders and rode there, bouncing down the path past the barn to a small shed no larger than a chicken coop. It was a shelter for the mothers of calves, colts, and lambs. Her father put her down at its door and opened it. It was warm inside and smelled of straw and birth, of oats and dung. There beside the tired mother were two black-faced lambs, weak and wobbling but on their feet.

"By the time you get back, they'll be running and hopping," her father said.

"Pa," she asked, hugging the lamb closest to her. "Can you come with me?"

"No, sweetheart, I have to stay here. Listen," he said. "I think I hear Etta in her new car. You'll be the first one to ride in it. Now be a good girl and go say good-bye to your grandpa."

When she got to the bunkhouse her grandfather was at the door.

"I have to go," she said.

"So I hear."

"Get better, Grandpa."

"If I can, I will," he said and lifted her up.

"You're giving me a whisker burn, Grandpa."

"It's good for you. Puts hair on your nose."

"I don't want hair on my nose."

"Oh well then, I'd better not do it." He put her down and leaned awkwardly to kiss the top of her head.

"Good-bye, Grandpa," she said and walked to the car where everyone waited.

"Good-bye," he called. "Don't let your aunt turn you into one of those town brats."

"She won't. She doesn't like brats," Katie said and waved.

"Do you like my new car?" her aunt asked her when they turned off the highway into Great Falls.

"Sure, Grandpa says Fords are good."

"He does?"

"Yeah. He says about as good as Chevys."

"My goodness, but he's taught you a lot of things."

"Yes, about trucks too. See there's a Kenworth," she said and pointed to one parked in front of the grain elevators. "Hey, there's a Dodge half-ton. Did you see it?"

"Sorry, I missed it," Etta said. They were near the courthouse now.

"There's two Fords like this one, only brown and blue," Katie said. "And a Packard and a Nash and a Buick just like Alma Peters'."

"So what kind of car does your grandfather like best?"

"I don't know."

Etta pulled over to the curb and parked. "Your mother says you need shoes, so let's stop here."

"School shoes?"

"No, play shoes."

"When I go back, I'm starting first grade."

"I know," Etta said.

Etta showed Katie around her neighborhood and introduced her to the kids in the family next door. Jenny was Katie's age, Shirley was eight, and Jimmy would soon be twelve. The parents invited Katie and her aunt to dinner and they walked across the lawn that evening with ice cream cups that Katie had never seen before. She was reluctant to give them up but her aunt said they could get more. While the parents, George and Leona, made drinks, the kids took Katie out front to play until time to eat. Later Leona gave Katie the leftover cups to take home because she said she didn't want three kids fighting over two cups.

The next day Etta asked Katie why she didn't go outside and play with Jenny and Shirley.

"I don't want to," she explained.

"Why not?"

"They make fun of me."

"They do?" Etta seemed surprised.

"Yes, they say, Don't you know how to jump rope? Don't you know how to roller skate? Don't you know nothing?"

"Anything. Don't you know anything," Etta said.

"How come Mama didn't teach me how?"

"She taught you to ride a horse, didn't she?"

"No, Pa did."

Etta was thoughtful. "I suppose it's because you don't have sidewalks."

Katie slumped further into the chair. "I don't know how to play hopscotch or jacks either."

"I do," Etta said and brightened. "After lunch we'll walk to Kress's and buy chalk and jacks and a jump rope."

"And skates?"

"Well I'll buy them but I'm not too good at that."

When they got home from shopping they sat on the kitchen linoleum to play jacks. Aunt Etta looked uncomfortable but explained it was only because her legs were long and stiff. "We'll start with babies and eggs in the basket," she said. It seemed impossible to pick up jacks and catch a ball at the same time but Aunt Etta said just to keep at it and it would come.

The next morning they tried hopscotch. Etta found two chains in her jewelry box, then showed Katie how to draw all the squares. First Jenny then Shirley came over and watched. "Can we play too?" Jenny said.

"Ask Katie," Etta said, hopping over the squares with the chains in them.

After lunch Shirley knocked on the door. "Can Katie come to Gibson Park with us this afternoon, Mrs. Blair?" she asked.

"Is your mother taking you?"

"No, my father."

"Your father?" Etta looked puzzled.

"Can I?" Katie asked.

"Maybe I should come along," Etta said. She seemed to be thinking.

"I'll be good," Katie said.

"Oh, I know that, honey," Etta said and smiled. "I just thought he might need help."

"I'll help him," Katie said.

"Go ahead," Etta said finally.

Jenny and Shirley's father pushed them on the swings and merry-go-round. He carried a large sack full of stale bread and put it off to the side by their sweaters. When they were too dizzy to do any more they walked by the flowers to the pond. There were six brown ducks and two large swans that swam over to eat bread out of their hands.

"They were so pretty," Katie told Etta later. "And they didn't hiss at all like geese do."

"Well that goose at the ranch only does that when she has babies."

"I know," Katie said. "Why don't the swans have babies?"

"I don't know, I suppose sometimes they do."

"Then where were they?" Katie had asked. But Aunt Etta didn't know that either.

One morning Shirley brought tea out to her backyard. Actually it was root beer Kool-Aid that they pretended was tea and she had some crackers that became cake.

"Now it's time to go to the doctor," she said after they finished the tea and cake. She ushered Jenny and Katie into the garage, where it was dark and a little damp.

"It's cold in here," Katie said.

"Here's a blanket. Lie down now, the doctor's coming. Jenny, you be the nurse. Pull her pants down and I'll get the thermometer."

"I don't want to play," Katie said.

"It's okay. It's not a real thermometer," Shirley said, holding up a Popsicle stick. "I just lay it on your weewee and it doesn't hurt at all." By now Jenny was pulling at her pants and Katie pushed her away. She had a funny feeling in her stomach and between her legs. She wanted to play, yet she didn't want to.

"Okay, I'll do Jenny first," Shirley said, and Jenny pulled down her pants. Katie watched while Shirley touched Jenny with the Popsicle stick first in front and then, after directing her to turn over, on her backside.

"Is this bad?" Katie asked.

"Yes," said Shirley. "So don't tell."

Katie watched in silence until she heard her aunt calling her from the next yard. "I have to go," she told them.

That afternoon Katie sat on the porch in the swing. "Hey," Etta said when she came around the front to move the hose. "Aren't you going to play with the kids?"

"No," she said.

"They're not making fun of you again, are they?"

"No."

"Is anything wrong?"

"No."

"Well, you don't look too happy. Listen, I can hear them out back. They're running through the hose. Don't you want to join them?"

"No," she said. "Aunt Etta, do you want to play jacks? You can see how good I am at ups and ups."

"All right," Etta said. "I'll get a golf ball and we'll play on the sidewalk. This porch gives me slivers."

They played until it was time to start dinner. Katie helped Aunt Etta make a salad and broil hamburgers. They were almost finished eating when the phone rang. Katie could tell by her aunt's voice that it was her mother and that something was wrong. "Oh, dear," she heard Etta say. "When? . . . How's Buck? . . . You okay?"

"My grandpa's dead, isn't he?" Katie asked when Aunt Etta returned to the table and sat down.

"Yes."

"I'll never see him again, will I?"

"No, honey, you won't."

Katie knew about death. She'd seen lots of dead things—her cat, lambs, cows, and once a horse. Things didn't move when they were dead, and her father took them away. He dragged the horse over the snow like a sled with the truck and she watched until they topped the hill and she could no longer see them. He wouldn't let her ride along and she suspected that all the dead things were over that hill.

"Katie, honey," her aunt said and came over to her chair and knelt there. "You see, we all die. And it's a hard thing to understand."

"Why do we?"

"I don't know. No one knows."

Katie tried to think what it might be like to be dead.

"I don't think Grandpa will like it," she said finally. But her aunt didn't answer. She hugged Katie and kissed her cheek, then got up and found their sweaters.

"Let's walk to the park and feed the swans before it gets dark," she said.

"We don't have any old bread," Katie said.

"We'll take new then."

The park was full of families finishing picnics under the trees or playing baseball on a large field near the railroad tracks. Katie watched a small child throw bread into the water and laugh when the ducks dove for it or quacked. Finally her mother picked her up and they disappeared. Couples walked by holding hands and other mothers yelled for kids and whistled for dogs. "Let's go get an ice cream cone," Aunt Etta said when they had fed the last of their bread to the swans.

They walked slowly with the cones and Katie tried to keep hers from dripping. "Will I go home now?" she asked her aunt.

"Next week."

"I'll only be to ups and half-ups by then."

"It's okay. When you're ready I'll drive out there and teach you downs and downs."

That night Katie had a terrible dream and when she screamed, Aunt Etta came running into her room. "What's wrong?" her aunt asked and got under the covers with her.

Katie told her the dream, that her father had tied a rope to Grandpa's leg and pulled him through the snow to the hill.

"No, honey. It doesn't work that way for people. Your grandpa will have a special place where everyone can bring him flowers. That's where his body will be. But his love, that will stay with you."

"With me?"

"Yes. When you need that love, you just think about him and he'll be there with you."

"He'll be there with me?"

"Sure," Etta said.

Katie tried to imagine it. Oh, no, she thought. Maybe he'd been there this morning in the garage. Maybe he'd be there every time that she was bad.

"How do you know that's how it works?" she asked.

"I don't for sure," Etta said, more serious than Katie had ever known her to be. "But I'm almost positive."

"Oh," Katie said. She didn't know what to think about it.

"Aunt Etta," she said finally. "You want to sleep with me tonight?"

"I'd love to," her aunt said. "I'll go get my pillow."

One lucky thing, Katie decided, he'd be too dead to tell on her.

CHAPTER
FOURTEEN

Etta had looked forward to Katie staying with her. She had been so pleased she found herself acting foolishly. For example, she volunteered to go to the ranch to get her. That was imprudent enough, given the condition of her car. Or it should have been. But no, she'd gone on daringly and bought a new car to do it in!

"You already bought it?" Rusty, a fellow she'd been seeing for several months, asked when she called to tell him.

"Why not?" she said.

"Well, I guess I thought you'd have me help with that. You know these car dealers. They drive a hard bargain."

Etta suspected that. No doubt she'd been overcharged and she didn't feel like giving the details so Rusty could point that out. He imagined himself to be an expert at most things.

"A Ford, huh?" he said.

"Yes, dark red."

"Red, huh?"

"Yeah, a two-door."

"Un huh."

"I'll take you for a ride after work, if you want."

"Great," he said, his voice brightening a little.

But even after an hour on the highway, Rusty was still doubtful. "So what made you do it?"

"It was time," she said. That, she knew, sounded ridiculous to him. She wasn't about to admit to him that she wanted it mostly for this one trip to the ranch. He would have said that she'd only needed to make repairs and get a tune-up on the old car. Or that he could drive her. Or that Greyhound now serviced that area.

His opposition to her extravagance, real or imagined, made it all the more pleasurable.

Rusty was even less thrilled to hear that Katie was coming for a visit.

"Well, that's nice," he said, kissing Etta's neck. They had picked up a chicken at the store and Etta was frying it at the stove.

"So when's she due?" he asked her later as they sat in the porch swing. They had taken their coffee and desert to the front porch.

"Thursday."

"Hmmmm," he said and swung lazily. "How long will she stay?"

"Oh, I don't know. Maybe a month or so."

"A month!" he said and almost spilled his coffee.

"Yes," Etta said and explained about August being sick.

"So what does that have to do with the kid?"

"Well, she's real attached to him, and my sister isn't crazy about her seeing him die."

"We all die," he said as if that explained something. Etta didn't know how to respond.

"I'm looking forward to it," Etta said. "I'm going to drive down to get her." As soon as she said it she was sorry. Predictably, Rusty wanted to come along.

"But you said Thursday," he said.

"Right," she said. "I'm taking it off."

"How about waiting for the weekend and I'll come along?"

The idea of taking him out with her to get Katie didn't appeal to her at all. "I can't," she said.

"Why not?"

"I've already arranged to start my vacation on Thursday . . . and they're expecting me."

"You're taking your vacation for this?"

"Of course. She's only six."

"Well, get a sitter."

"I am the sitter."

Rusty had quit swinging and said no more. Etta could feel him sulking in the dark.

"Want a nightcap?" Etta asked him later that night.

"Okay." Now he was at the kitchen table watching her put away the dishes.

"Some things are real disappointing," he said, stirring his drink.

"What things?"

"Having a kid here and all. It certainly cramps my style," he said.

"Your style?"

"You know. Staying over and all."

"It's not forever."

"Still, I'm not real happy about it."

Etta wiped her hands on the dish towel and hung it over a hook on the wall. She sighed. She didn't feel like pacifying him. She wanted to go to bed. But he went on.

"A month's a long time."

"Why are you acting like such a baby?" she asked.

"I am not acting like a baby. You're the one that's putting everyone else before me."

"Not everyone," she said. "My niece."

"See! You admit it."

"Go home, Rusty. I want to get some sleep."

"Every time I want to discuss something, you want me to leave."

"I'm tired."

"Fine," he said. "But if you can't discuss this . . ."

"I'll discuss it tomorrow," she said interrupting. She opened the back door for him.

"Maybe I won't call tomorrow."

"All right," she said.

"Look, Etta. What you don't see is that a lot can happen in a month."

"Like what?"

"I could meet someone else."

"Suit yourself."

"If that's what you want, fine. I'll go out with other women while you play nursemaid."

"Do that," she said.

"Okay, then. I'll call you when what's-her-name goes home."

"Her name is Katie and don't bother," she said, closing the door on him.

Etta had found everyone at the ranch nervous and absentminded. Even Katie. The child was puzzled because she had to go to Etta's and not too happy about it either. She knew something was going on, that it involved her grandfather's illness, and that it wasn't good. Katie was reluctant to leave him, and Etta had never seen her so sad and serious.

Once she got Katie to town, Etta did everything to cheer her up. She took her to movies, tried to involve her with the kids next door, and played games with her. But instead of enjoying the games, Katie worried and complained about how much better the other kids played.

"They don't know how to do half the things you know how to do," Etta told her.

"Like what?" Katie asked.

"Like what you do around the ranch."

"Nobody cares about those things," Katie said and slumped into a chair.

Etta showed her how to use a camera and Katie took pictures around the yard and at the park. When they got them developed, Katie groaned. "They didn't turn out good at all," she said.

"They're fine for first pictures. You'll get the hang of it," said Etta. Actually, they were pretty good. Katie had a nice sense of composition.

"Hey, look at you," Etta said, showing her the ones she had taken of Katie. "You look just like your mother did. Look, I'll show you." Etta rummaged through a desk drawer full of photos until she found some of Pearl at about the same age.

"I look like you too," Katie said, now studying a photo of Pearl and Etta squinting into the sun. They looked gangly. Etta was missing teeth while Pearl's teeth looked too big for her mouth.

"Did you live here?"

"Yes, see that's the back porch there."

Katie was interested. She wanted to see more and Etta directed her to the desk. When Etta came back later, Katie was still looking at pictures. She had them spread all around her in categories. Ones of Pearl, of Etta, of both, ones of holidays, summer vacations, people she wanted identified, and so on.

When Katie went out to play with the kids next door, Etta started to put them all away. Then she changed her mind. Some of these pictures she hadn't seen for years and she found herself studying them too. She thought she should write down any information she could remember about them.

Pearl's friend Dottie—about 12 years old, she wrote on one, Etta's tenth birthday, she wrote on another, after counting the candles on the cake she was blowing out in the picture. She had to use a magnifying glass.

Pearl, mad about something—about eight, she wrote. No, she wasn't mad, she was just sad, Etta decided, looking again. In fact, Pearl looked sad in most of these pictures. As she recalled it, Pearl was as sad then as Katie was now.

Etta put the pictures away and went out to start dinner.

Katie hadn't said much when August died. She was quiet and went inward to grieve. Etta knew she didn't quite understand. Etta did her best to reassure her, especially when she became concerned that August would be dragged like dead livestock to some place on the ranch. Katie even dreamed about it and woke up screaming.

Etta rushed into Katie's room and found her sobbing. She tried to comfort her as Katie described her dream. Etta was amazed at how detailed it was. Katie knew the color of August's shirt, that the snow was dirty and packed down with tire tracks, that chain, instead of rope had been used. Etta couldn't help comparing it to the nightmare she still had from time to time. It had never revealed a detail. She awoke just like Katie but without knowing why. It was as much a mystery now as the first time it happened, perhaps around Katie's age.

That night she slept with Katie and the child was much calmer in the morning.

"Did Mama sleep here when she was a little girl?" she asked.

"Yes, she did."

"Did you too?"

"For a while. Then I had to move."

"Why?"

"So your mother could have her own room. So I could too." At the time, Etta had thrown a fit. She did not want to sleep alone, even though she was ten.

"I don't want my own room," she'd cried.

"You can't always sleep with your sister," Father said.

"It's okay," Pearl had intervened.

"What the hell is the point in having a three-bedroom house?"

he yelled at their mother, who as Etta recalled never had too much to add to these discussions. "Grow up," he said. "Both of you."

Etta had surrendered sadly then—she was never a match for Father. Pearl, as usual, wouldn't give in so easily. Just to irritate him or maybe out of sympathy, Pearl always let Etta play in her room or sleep with her when Etta woke up from a nightmare.

"So when I had bad dreams, I slept in here with your mother," she told Katie.

"I like this room best," Katie said.

"So do I," Etta said.

Tuesday, Buck came for Katie. Etta had gotten all of Katie's things together and put them in the foyer. Etta had made her a red denim bag to put her toys in. It contained jacks, a jump rope, chalk, hopscotch chains, a puzzle, several books, and Etta didn't know what all. She'd also bought Katie some school clothes, shoes, and a cream-colored monkey with a black face. The monkey sat leaning on the red bag on top of Katie's suitcase.

"I'm so sorry about your father," Etta told Buck at the door. He looked tired and fragile somehow. For once Etta felt herself softening toward him and she kissed his cheek in a rare show of affection and concern.

"Thanks, Etta," he said and came inside. "Everything's ready to go, huh," he said, picking up the monkey. "Where's Katie?"

"She went to a movie with the neighbor kids. We didn't expect you until late this afternoon. Where's Pearl?"

"Charlie's mother's sick. So Pearl went over to help out."

There was an awkward pause now. She and Buck had never been very comfortable around each other. "Come on in the kitchen. I was just making fudge for Katie to take home."

He put the monkey down and followed her.

"How about a beer?" she said.

Buck sat at the table. He was in a good mood and became quite animated, telling her news of Pearl and Charlie. But when he talked about his father, he became serious and lowered his voice. It was odd to hear him talk about his boyhood. She had never expected Buck to be so candid, not with her.

"So after the hired man left, Pa took to cooking himself. The food wasn't great but it was a hell of a lot better than the hired man's."

The fudge was cooling now and Pearl got out two more beers and joined him at the table. "He did all right, raising you by himself like he did," Etta said.

"I guess so. It couldn't have been easy for him. I was a handful."

Etta smiled at that. "I'll bet you were."

"Yeah," he said and grinned sheepishly. "But the old man was tough."

Etta could just imagine. She had found August cold and intimidating. She had always marveled at how easily Pearl got on with him. "Funny thing, but since Katie's been here, I've been thinking a lot about my own father," she said. "You know he could be real mean."

"So I've heard."

"I think he was meanest to Pearl. Those two clashed. You couldn't leave them alone ten minutes without an uproar." Etta got out a bag of potato chips from the cupboard and handed them to Buck.

"I suppose because she was the oldest. The oldest have it the worst."

"No, the only kid has it the worst," Buck said.

"Or the best," she said and they laughed. She went to the refrigerator for more beer.

"You know that scar Pearl has on her shoulder?"

Buck nodded. "Didn't she get it when her bike fell on her?"

"Not her bike. Mine. And it didn't really fall. Father got mad and pushed it off the worktable and Pearl was sitting on the floor a few feet away and it hit her."

Pearl had ridden the bike that day and had a wreck with it. She had bent the wheel and fender. She had taken the bike to the backyard and was trying to bend it back into shape with some kitchen tools, or maybe she borrowed some. Etta couldn't remember. But whatever the case, they weren't Father's tools because those were always locked up.

So then when Father came home he said he'd fix it and he put it up on the worktable. Etta had watched from the garage door as he sat on a stool beside the table and worked. The chain was off and several spokes were missing. Others were twisted.

Pearl was on her knees on the floor over a pan of water. She was trying to find the hole in the inner tube. She was explaining that the tire had gone flat, that she was on a hill, that a car was coming, and so on. And Father was interrogating her: Why were you giving Dottie a ride? Where was her bike? Didn't you notice the tire was low? When did you fill it last? He went on and on like that and Pearl tried to keep up with him. Finally she said that she hadn't checked the tires because it was Etta's bike or something to that effect. It was then that Father went berserk.

Etta had wanted to run but she just stood in the doorway, watching as the argument escalated and her father pushed the bike from the table. It went flying and landed on Pearl.

Etta couldn't believe how emotional she was as she related the story to Buck. It was as though she were right there in that doorway again.

"And I always blamed myself for that," she said, tears now running down her face.

"It wasn't your fault," Buck said. He was standing at the table in front of her now and he patted her shoulder.

"But I begged her to trade bikes for the day," Etta said, crying. "I always got her in trouble. I always wanted all the attention." Etta was crying hard now, and Buck leaned over to hold her.

When he stood up straight again, he touched her head and sort of smoothed her hair, maybe in the same way he touched Katie's head or smoothed her hair—maybe in the same way Etta's father had touched her head.

At least that's what it seemed like when Etta tried to figure it out later.

What happened next was a catastrophe. For a minute Etta was back in that garage. She was hysterical. She screamed and slapped Buck across the face. Naturally, he drew back in surprise.

"Goddamn it!" he said. "You're crazy!"

She was shocked herself and didn't know what to say. She simply stared at him in amazement. About that time, Katie came bursting in the back door all wound up about the movie.

Somehow Etta got through the next several minutes. She pretended to listen as Katie described the movie plot, she packed up the fudge, she saw Katie to the car, she said good-bye, and she watched them drive away. Katie held the monkey and waved from the front seat, but Buck, Etta's furious and somewhat humiliated brother-in-law, kept his eyes straight ahead.

Then Etta went back into the house and wept.

CHAPTER

FIFTEEN

1953

In the several years immediately succeeding August's death, most of the old-timers in the area died too. Three, all from Squatter Creek and the ones Pearl knew best, went in a five-month period the next year.

The man called old John was buried in March by his son, young John. Norman, August's friend of many years, went in June, and Alma, Charlie's mother, in July.

Pearl missed Norman, who after August died used to show up twice a week for dinner or supper, still managing to drive an old '42 pickup that had lost most of its paint to rust and its fenders to collisions of one sort or another.

When Buck wasn't around, Norman sometimes talked about the past. "Now I ain't one to tell tales on the dead," he'd begin by way of introduction to the story on his mind.

"Tell me about August," she asked him once.

"A straight shooter, that one," he said. "Got himself into a few scrapes like the rest of us, but a straight shooter. His word was good." That was the extent of what he'd had to say about August.

"Did you know Buck's mother?" she'd asked.

"Nope, never did. Those years I was in Great Falls trying to make a living off a little business I had there, a bar down on the south side. It's all torn down now," he'd said, shaking his head.

"Had a lot of trouble there in those years. The building was owned by an old fart run out of Canada. That man screwed me over more than once. Why that fellow was so crooked they buried him straight down."

"Straight down?" Pearl asked.

"Hell, yes!" he yelled, pounding the table. "Face first. And so many people hated him, they had to close the casket so people couldn't spit on him."

"My God," Pearl said.

"I killed a man once," Norman told her not long before he died. "Suppose I'll go to hell for it, but couldn't be helped. This couple, you see, were sitting at the bar arguing. She was a sweet-looking little thing and he was almost twice her size. I told them it was late, that I was closing the place up but they kept on arguing. Then this guy started to push the lady around and I told him to stop but he wouldn't. So I took out this gun I kept under the bar and told him again. And the man went crazy, knocked everything off the bar, then ran around behind where I was and pulled a knife. When he grabbed for the gun, I shot him."

"What happened?"

"Got off. Self-defense. The funny thing, though, the woman disappeared sometime during all this. No one ever knew who she was." Norman sighed and stirred his coffee. "Suppose I'll go to hell for it," he said again.

"I doubt it," Pearl told him, as if she knew what rules applied to going to hell or not. "It could have happened to anyone," she said softly.

Norman was almost totally crippled by then and the patch over his blinded eye had begun to hang loose over his shrunken face. But he drove the old pickup anyway, even the day before the night he died in his sleep.

But the death hardest on everyone was Alma's. Pearl thought Buck felt almost as bad as Charlie. "Alma was the closest thing to a mother I ever had," he said.

It was a dry, windy summer, and the day of the funeral was probably the hottest one of the year. The graveyard was as parched as any wheatfield around, and the grass brown and dead. The spindly wind-bent trees were near dead too, and sagebrush had gathered in stacks along the graveyard's fence. The words of the preacher could hardly be heard in the wind, and there was a lady there Pearl didn't know whose hat blew off and skipped the fence and flew on across the prairie out of sight. Then something happened to the rope holding the coffin as they lowered it and one end fell into the hole, leaving the other end of the coffin up against the side.

Then there was some problem trying to wedge it in, and Buck and Charlie had laid down on the ground to pull up the fallen side so the other side would fit. They stood up after a shocking thud of placement, their suits dirty, Katie between them holding their hands, the three obviously upset by this unexpected accident.

Charlie didn't come around too much after the funeral, and Katie asked about him. It worried Pearl too. But a few months later, he stopped in. By then harvest was over and Buck was out doing the summer fallowing. Katie was at school.

Pearl made Charlie coffee. "So how are things?" she asked. He looked thin and tired.

"It's like this," he said. "The house is quiet, I'm restless as hell, and I can't help thinking there's more to life than this. I want to get married, Pearl, and I want to have kids. Fill the house with activity, with life," he added. "I never felt the loneliness before when Ma was around. You know what I mean," he said.

"I know," she said, not really knowing what else to say.

"So that's what I have in mind to do."

"Is there a girl, Charlie? Someone special?"

"Not yet. But I'll find one," he said and finished his coffee.

"Good luck," she told him when he left.

"Thanks. You've been a good friend and I appreciate that," he said. "Buck's a lucky man to have you and Katie."

"Thanks," she said and smiled at him.

Buck laughed when she told him. "He's crazy. You can't just put an ad in the paper for a woman or go out and find one just like that."

But Charlie did seem to have a plan in mind. Though they hardly saw him all fall, they passed him on the road to town several times.

"You're dressed fit to kill," Buck said once.

"You look real nice," Katie told him through the window. "Where are you going?"

"To dinner," he said, grinning.

Winter was early, and Etta's visits were becoming as scarce as Charlie's. With Alma and Norman dead and Charlie off on a woman hunt, Pearl felt isolated. She thought Katie and Buck did too. And though Etta called often enough, all she talked about was Leona, Leona's kids, and Leona's husband, George.

"So what's new with Leona?" Pearl would ask, more to keep her on the line than because of any real interest. Why Etta made such a project out of her next-door neighbors Pearl didn't know.

"Well she has a part-time job at the gas company and she likes that."

"How about the kids?"

"Well, Jimmy got into trouble at school a couple of times, but that's been straightened out. The girls are fine. They spend a lot of time at the house when Leona's working but that's okay." Pearl guessed that was why Etta hadn't been around to visit.

"And George?"

"He's been doing pretty good lately. Keeping out of trouble, going to AA."

Every call was a variation of this conversation.

* * *

Both Etta and Charlie were able to come for Christmas despite heavy snow and bad roads. "How's it coming?" Pearl whispered to Charlie Christmas Eve. He knew what she meant. "No one yet," he said.

Before Etta left for home the day after Christmas, Pearl brought up the isolation she felt. She might not have made it that clear.

"Well, I'm just plain bored," is how she put it. "I'm talking to the cows now, it's so bad."

"Pearl, why don't you drive to Great Falls? It'd be good for you and Katie to get away."

"But then think how Buck would feel out here all alone."

"Tell him to come too."

"But who'd do the feeding?"

"Ask Charlie."

"Maybe," she said. "I'll see."

But as it happened, Pearl never did get to Etta's the entire winter. It turned unusually cold after New Year's and they lost livestock to it. Buck needed more help all month than he ever had. In February, half the herd was ailing, and every day Pearl was out with Buck rounding up steer for penicillin shots or helping build shelters or chopping holes in ice that had formed over the night in the water tanks. They drove blocks of salt out to pastures and to the new shelters and then, when almost out of alfalfa, hauled grain out in the back of the truck to supplement the feed.

One morning, they woke up to snow so deep the school bus wasn't running and their own truck couldn't make it over the hill. They made Katie stay inside. "Leave the water running in all the taps," Buck told her. "And every hour or so, run hot water down them."

They then spent the morning constructing a sled of sorts and pulled it full of hay behind the Caterpillar to a pasture several miles from the house. They found three dead cattle frozen stiff inside the shelter they had made. The other cattle huddled nearby, their eyes heavy with frost and almost shut.

"We have to herd them closer to the house or they'll all be dead soon," Buck said.

"How?" Without the pickup or dogs, it would be impossible.

"Can you drive this?"

"I think so," she said. "But it's been a while."

He showed her how to move the gears that made the large machine turn.

"That's all there is to it," he said. "Push 'em home. I'll watch the sides and run down strays."

Pearl was freezing. Her hat kept slipping up, the scarf around her face was frozen, and so were her gloves. She could no longer feel her feet. But she was more worried about Buck, who had to fight the deep snow with every step and sometimes run from one side to the other, yelling and waving to keep strays moving with the others. Some looked ready to just lie down and die.

It was slow moving through the deep snow for the cattle too, and by now the sun was at that point in the sky on a winter day when what temperature there is falls, and everything — the snow, the white sky, the air — has a bluish cast to it, the blue of intense and penetrating cold.

When they were at last near the barn, she heard Buck yelling at her. She turned. He was grinning. "Do you remember how to stop it?"

"God no!" she said.

"That lever on your right. Pull it slowly," he hollered.

Her hand was so stiff she couldn't feel the lever, but soon the thing stopped a few feet short of the fence and a pen of cattle on full feed.

They herded the cattle the rest of the way on foot into one side of the barn, then closed off all the feed that fell automatically into troughs from the huge piles of grain above.

"What about what's still there?" she asked. The last thing she wanted now was this bunch to bloat on grain they weren't used to.

"There's not much and it won't hurt them. Might warm them up some," he said. "Let's go inside."

They could see Katie at the window, her breath making a clear spot in the frost. She was probably worried, they'd been out all day.

But she'd managed to keep the fire going in the woodstove, had made herself a sandwich for lunch, and had listened to the radio much of the day.

"Schools are closed in ten counties," she said.

Buck made Pearl take a bath in cool water.

"You don't want to warm up too fast," he said. He brought her a warm drink of whiskey and water and a blanket to wrap in. He heated some stew for them and they ate sitting around the stove.

Buck was worried the water pipes would freeze overnight, though they were insulated. He stoked up the fire when they went to bed and left water running.

In spite of that, the next morning the pipes were frozen. Charlie came over to help, and he and Buck had to go under the house with an acetylene torch and a space heater to slowly thaw them out. Pearl kept water boiling in several pots to pour down the pipes. It didn't seem to help.

"It could be worse," Buck said. "If the pipes had frozen yesterday, we'd have had a real mess."

"God help us," she said. "One crisis at a time."

"Let's just hope the cold breaks before lambing," she heard Buck tell Charlie.

Pearl didn't have much chance to talk to Charlie, but he'd hardly have had any luck finding a wife in this weather, she decided.

The next morning, Pearl looked forward to staying inside but a heifer on full feed was in labor with a calf. It had never happened before that Pearl knew.

"How could it be pregnant?" she asked. There wasn't a bull on the place.

"We must have bought it that way. That's the trouble with buying heifers. Let's move her outside where we can see."

"But I thought cows had calves in the spring."

"It won't be full term," he said, closing the barn door. "And'll probably be stillborn. The nitrogen in the feed does that." He tied the animal to the fence.

"I don't think this is normal," Pearl said. She could see the calf's hooves as the mother strained to give birth.

"She's in trouble," he said. He worked with the cow for some time, trying to help pull out the calf.

"Go get the pickup," he said.

"Why?"

"Just back it up right here," he said.

Pearl finally got the truck started and backed down from the garage to where Buck motioned her.

"We'll have to pull it," he told her when she got out. He was fastening a rope around the hooves. "Drive slowly and I'll tell you when to stop."

"Do we have to do it this way?" It seemed brutal to her.

"You want to save its life, don't you?"

"Yes."

"It's the only way."

Pearl got in and followed his signals in the mirror.

"Stop," he shouted.

The calf was dead and probably had been for days and the mother almost. They practically carried the poor thing back to the barn.

* * *

Miraculously, the animal survived the winter. They all did. It finally warmed up not long before lambing and the whole countryside was one mess of mud and dirty melting snow. It rained often that spring and farmers looked forward to good crops and a drought-free summer. There was every reason for optimism, Buck said. And that seemed true for everyone.

By early June, Charlie had a steady girl, and before harvest was over, he was married.

CHAPTER

SIXTEEN

It was still dark when Buck got up. As usual, Pearl had already gone to the kitchen to make coffee. He dressed for warmth and splashed some water on his face to wake up. The bathroom was cold.

He carried his boots down the hall to the living room. Pearl and Katie were sitting in the horsehair chair with the large squarish arms. There was a floor lamp behind them and its light encircled them gently. Katie was reading in the cadence of the storyteller, her voice low and affected. It almost made Buck start to see them this way; it was a picture he wanted to lift reverently from the light to carry in his pocket or move across the room and hang on the wall. They looked up at him in the doorway and smiled, their faces glowing with the softness of the light. There was something pinkish about it all, enfolded as they were in the huge maroon chair.

Buck couldn't smile back. Response was all at once frozen in feelings, strong feelings that reminded him both of hunger and desolation. He did love them, though they might not think so. He went on into the kitchen and stood in the dark at the window and gulped his first cup of coffee. Soon there was light at the horizon, faint and unpromising of anything remarkable about the day. He put on his boots and his coat and went out to feed.

Buck turned on the water to the tanks in the feedlot, then backed up beneath the bin he had built in the loft in the southern corner of the barn. He pulled out the slat boards on the chute and let the grain fall down into the truck and fill to the third line of the box he had devised to measure grain. When full to this line, the load approximated sixty buckets of feed. He still didn't believe he and his father had actually measured out buckets by shovel from a pile in the truck—his father had insisted there was no other way. It had bothered Buck's back to bend to that awkward angle but now he just drove to the pasture where the steers being prepped for full feed were and simply lifted up another slat board and scooped out the grain. The cattle would always lope toward him when they heard the truck. It took him thirty minutes total.

Next he checked the tanks and turned off the water. He threw down hay to the cattle in the feeding pens and to the sheep that roamed the place obnoxiously, leaving dung and patches of soiled wool everywhere. Buck preferred to work with cattle over other things. Farming he hated, all of it—summer fallowing, seeding, harvest. His father had always said there was nothing like putting seed into ground that would one day be their bread. Buck disagreed; all aspects of farming were hot, dusty, tedious. But sheep were worse. He didn't like sheep dip or shearing or wool and he resented the way one sheep took the lead; its slightest turn right or left and the others turned suddenly in unison, mocking every movement, even breaking out in a startled run if the lead sheep indicated that. There was no doubt that if people were the same—and weren't they?—his father would have instinctively been one of those lead sheep.

Cattle he regarded differently. They were more independent of each other. He liked to buy stock from cattlemen he knew from the Missouri River breaks, badlands where cattle seldom saw a man. Free to graze unattended, they became fierce and reckless. He bought cattle there from the Bailey brothers that had never been branded and that he had trouble containing in any corral. He got one once that jumped out of the feedlot regularly and he spent hours at a time rounding it up. He often wondered how the Baileys had ever crimped that one or got it into a truck. He'd finally had to shoot it, unbranded, in the head and butcher it right there in the feedlot. Certainly cattle were decidedly more interesting than anything else around the place, but not quite interesting enough.

All time on the ranch, past and future, was related; each year flat and familiar, surviving the one before. Had he wanted to tell someone what he'd be doing ten years from the day, he could have. Just bring him a calendar and he'd fill it in, day after day, year after year, with events too ordinary and alike to have any singular features but the ones he imposed. And after a slow death from days like this, he would surely be buried beside his father in that parched and barren graveyard outside of town.

It was light now, clear and bright and cold. Buck pulled up his collar and headed for the house. Inside it was warm and he washed up. Katie was already at the table and he leaned down to hug her, ready now to face their demands on him, those things that emptied him, tortured him, obligated him. His family looked to him for something they had found in his father. They searched unknowingly for his father's strength and he couldn't fault them for that. His father was a man always certain of things, one who never questioned his own abilities or opinions. It was what he admired most about his father and what he liked least. Had Buck had more of that quality and his father less, things might have been different.

Buck would have understood a father who had lain awake nights in fear of what he couldn't do, what he couldn't provide, what he couldn't be. He could have loved a man who knew what it was to walk some infertile field, and having recognized something of himself there, cried. Or one who knew how it was to drink to still a craving, persistent and unidentified.

Pearl brought out biscuits and gravy, side pork and eggs.

"We're baking a cake for the party tonight, Pa," Katie said.

"What party?"

"The shivaree for Charlie and Maggie," Pearl said and passed him the gravy.

"You're going through with that? I told you Charlie hates that kind of stuff."

"Well maybe his wife doesn't. Anyway, try to stop Anne Johnson when she starts planning."

"Anne Johnson? For crying out loud." Buck didn't mind these get-togethers so much when old John Bergman's wife thought them up. She was always good for a keg and everyone brought a bottle.

"Yeah," Katie said. "And when they're asleep we'll sing outside the window and wake them up for the party."

Buck couldn't help smiling at her. His daughter's hair was illumined by sunlight as if her head was what drew it into the window from the sky.

"Too bad Alma didn't live to see Charlie finally married," Pearl said.

And to such a good-looker. Buck didn't see how Charlie did it.

"We're taking them a wedding present too," Katie said.

"Oh yeah? What's it going to be?"

"We don't know. We have to buy it."

"That's right," said Pearl. "So that means you have to hurry if you're going to pick up poles today. If you get back by noon, we can go to town."

Christ, he'd forgotten all about the fence posts. He didn't know how Pearl kept track of all these things. No wonder she always thought he was irresponsible. But that wasn't it. He never minded hard work; he just couldn't handle all that routine, those boring details that had to be looked after in the same way every day. He actually admired the way Pearl submitted to order, even to disorder. The fact that this would be his second trip for poles

was disorderly. Pearl had a patience with delay and postpone-
ment that he never had. If he went for posts, he wanted them
ready. He didn't want to drive forty miles to find the post man
gone to Billings. That's what had happened last week, and his
irritation had been so intense, he'd actually kicked open the
man's gate and left it. Where he was begrudging, Pearl was
yielding; she leaned into systems and procedures, she let them
accumulate and form some corresponding wholeness that ful-
filled and satisfied her.

Why wasn't it that way for him? Why did he have to go off at
predictable intervals in search of diversion, any distraction that
might amuse or detain him? It was one of the great mysteries of
his life, that others could be so pleased with things and he so
malcontent. He was often stricken by demands and longings so
overpowering they could make him forget any other thing he
might be doing. It was what precipitated any unwarranted trip
into town. He never asked Pearl to understand because he didn't.

"Can I go with you to get poles this time?" Katie asked.

"Hey, what about the cake?" Pearl said.

"I don't feel like baking. Can I, Pa?"

Buck looked at Pearl. It was a decision she would be in charge
of.

"Oh, go ahead," Pearl said. "Just be back by noon."

Buck hadn't driven ten minutes when Katie told him she had to
go to the bathroom.

"Damn it, Katie. We just left the house." He pulled off the
gravel into a field. When did an eight-year-old quit acting like
she was three? He waited, offended, while Katie—in slow
motion—opened the door and climbed carefully down from the
pickup, disappeared, and finally climbed carefully back in.

Katie was subdued for the next twenty minutes of the ride and
Buck felt ashamed to have complained.

"How did Charlie find a wife?" she asked abruptly.

"I suppose he met her someplace."

"What place?"

"Oh, probably church."

Katie laughed. "Everyone knows Charlie won't go to church," she said. Buck smiled and twisted his face to mimic Alma. "Sure, I'll lend you the money. The day Charlie goes to church," he said, altering his voice to a squeak. Katie laughed again. Buck liked the way she laughed, it sort of rolled out, softly, deeply.

"How did you find Ma?"

Buck had to stop to think. He couldn't remember meeting her, and when he thought about it, it was as if he had always known her, yet he divided his life into halves—before Pearl, after Pearl.

"Probably at church," Katie said and smiled at him. It was unlikely Buck would get to church any oftener than Charlie.

"We're here," he said and pulled up to the gate, wondering what Ben Jackson had thought last week when he got home to an open gate.

Ben came out to the pickup with his kids following him, a girl about the size of Katie, the boy taller. Ben kicked at the barking dogs and led the way to the house.

"Come on in," he said and held first the door to a large square room full of newspapers, egg cartons, and firewood and then the door to the kitchen.

The kids took Katie off somewhere and Ben's wife poured coffee. She sat down at the table beside Ben. Like a smaller version of him, she had rosy cheeks, a round face, and sandy hair. The Jacksons looked like Hutterites to Buck, Hutterites without the dark clothes. Ben favored the younger males of the sect, before beards covered their pinkish chins. His wife pushed a platter of cinnamon rolls to him and waved away a fly that had survived the autumn chill.

"How many poles you want?" Ben asked.

Buck got out the sketch of the new pens he wanted to build, the length and width in feet scribbled and crossed out and scribbled again in the margin. The kids were back in the kitchen and they crowded around the drawing.

"I figure about eighty," he said, passing Ben the paper.

"You want some milk?" Mrs. Jackson said as she handed Katie and her own children each a roll.

"We're going outside," the boy said. The boy resembled the parents. Buck watched him zip his jacket, a dark blue wool that accented the pink of his skin. The girl, on the other hand, had an olive, sallow complexion that made her look unrelated.

"Outside where?" Buck said to the boy.

"We want to show Katie the new kittens in the barn," he said.

"Keep your cap on," Buck said to Katie as he knew Pearl would. Katie always pulled off the caps Pearl knitted for her, complaining they were too hot. She usually left them somewhere—the school bus, the barn, the yard. Pearl often identified pieces of caps that might remain after a dog or lamb had chewed them. "That was the yarn I got on sale" or "That was the one I made for good," she'd say. But she kept knitting Katie new ones.

"You adding some new cattle or just repairing old pens?" Ben asked once the kids went out.

"A little of both," Buck explained. "You got to keep expanding these days if you want to stay ahead."

"It's the truth. A fella can hardly make it off the land anymore. Might just as well move to town and get a job. If I'd had any brains, I'd have gone to college."

Buck poured himself more coffee from the pot on the table. He'd tried college when he was younger. But he was too impatient to plod through course after course that took him nowhere. He'd seen the slowness of it all. To look forward to four years of that slowness did things to him. He could hardly sit still in classes and sometimes getting drunk was the only way to wind down to the pace the rest of the students moved at. After quitting school, before he'd met Pearl, he'd tried other things. He worked for the stockyards in Great Falls, for the meat company, and had driven a truck for a big transporter. He'd hoped for action, immediacy, results. At first he liked driving a truck, the sense of movement, of getting somewhere. But there was always the return and he'd be back to where he started.

Buck could do anything for a while, months even. Then everything in him stopped and no mental force could will him back. It was only the relief after he'd quit that saw him through these failures—the times his father avoided looking at him, his eyes elsewhere, disappointed and accusing, focused on something in the distance.

"But this is the best life for children, honey," Ben's wife said, smiling.

"I'm not saying there aren't compensations," Ben said. "If you can survive to enjoy them."

"I never want to move the kids to town," she said and then suddenly turned toward the door. Buck guessed she heard what he heard, yelling or screaming from somewhere outside. He got up and ran out, certain that something was wrong with Katie. It was a feeling he had in his stomach that told him something had happened to her and that it was his fault.

He could see the boy running from the barn toward the house and when the boy saw Buck coming, he motioned and ran back the way he had come. Buck followed as fast as he could and jumped the fence to where Katie lay. When he got close he could see she was bleeding around her eyes, her right arm and her clothes were bloody too, and parts of her jacket and pants were torn away.

"The cattle spooked and ran over her," the girl cried.

Buck picked her up carefully. He was sure she had a broken arm and cracked ribs and maybe she'd lost an eye or was dying. Ben opened the gate for him, then the door to a late-model car.

Buck told Ben to speed up until he hit the first bump. After that he said nothing. He thought Katie was unconscious, yet she said things. "Pa," she said a couple of times and other things he either couldn't hear or that made no sense to him. He was grateful for her every breath and offered any deal to life, to God, to the devil if that would do. There was nothing he wouldn't agree to to spare her life. Make it one more mile, he chanted randomly to himself, one more mile. Forty miles seemed interminable. How would he keep her from breaking into pieces or bleeding to death? Though the blood had dried by now, he was afraid to guess the extent of her injuries. He resisted moving even slightly lest her back or neck be broken.

Buck was finally able to see the lights of Lewistown. When they got to the emergency room, Ben ran in and two men followed him back out with a stretcher. Buck was reluctant to surrender her but they seemed not to notice. They were efficient and impersonal as if she were just another load of cargo to unload without breaking.

Inside, a nurse asked him questions that he answered with his eyes on the swinging doors Katie had disappeared behind.

"I want to be with her," he said. The nurse nodded and directed him to a bathroom to clean up. "You don't want to scare her with all that blood," she said.

When Buck was allowed in finally, another nurse was scrubbing on Katie's cheek, at a deep wound below her eye. The nurse held something that reminded him of a toothbrush.

"She can't feel it," the nurse explained when he gasped. He felt nauseous and thought the woman would never stop scrubbing. He himself could puncture the belly of a bloating animal to release pressure or make a slit in the throat of some choking calf to make a new entrance for air. He could crimp off a bull calf's balls or put a hot iron to its hide without stopping to spit. But this was making him feel faint and he knew if that nurse didn't quit soon he would knock her to the floor.

"Mr. Buckman, is it?" a man in white said from the door. "If you could wait outside, I'll stitch her up and take some X-rays."

"What's wrong with her?" Buck said.

"She's okay. Might have a cracked rib and I think a broken wrist. Then she's got some bad cuts and they were opened up quite a while."

Buck felt like an accusation had been made.

"It was a long ride," Buck said. He was relieved yet worried some unfixable damage had been done to her face. "Will she be scarred?"

"She's young. She'll heal."

"Do a good job," Buck said and left the room.

Ben was out in the waiting room. Buck had forgotten all about the man, this person whom he'd gone to on a simple errand, and whose children Katie had had the rotten luck to meet. A meeting unfortunate and ill timed. What the hell could he say to such a stranger?

"You want to call your wife?" the man said.

Oh God. Another detail he'd forgotten. He had to let Pearl know. By one o'clock she'd have been angry because they were late. By now she'd be worried sick. And later she'd know he was to blame because there were no accidents except the one that happened to you when you were born. The rest she'd say were somebody's fault. Yet Pearl wouldn't think that it was his fault because he'd taken Katie with him or because he hadn't stayed with her. It would be his fault because his irresponsibility in general, his inability to take care, wasn't something he could prevent from affecting others and Pearl knew it. And for that she would hate him someday.

Buck fumbled in his pockets for a cigarette.

"The phone's down the hall," Ben Jackson said and handed him a dime.

CHAPTER

SEVENTEEN

1957

One day Pearl woke up to the truth. It arrived early one morning with the sharp chill of a late autumn dawn. There it was, truth, clear and cold. After all these years, for no immediate reason that she could think of, she was seeing what she had neglected to see from the beginning.

Buck fooled around on her and probably always had.

It was as simple as that. She hadn't caught him, no one told on him, there wasn't even a recent hint. She just woke up and knew.

What did it take, she asked herself all week long, for some people to figure things out? Was she stupid? She didn't know if she was angrier with herself or him. It was as if in some silent agreement she had been party to all of it, cooperative, amenable, participating by her very failure to see.

Her mind ran from one bit of testimony to another—the time Buck and his cousin's wife came out of the barn with such silly looks on their faces, the evening she thought she saw the same woman's hand on Buck's knee under Pearl's own dining table, and all those times Buck never showed up and she believed he was at one of the bars with the guys. There was that time at the Winslow rodeo when she thought it odd when some woman leaned toward Buck, exchanging as serious a look as Pearl had ever seen passing between strangers. Well that's what she had thought, that they were strangers. One glaring past incident after another came somewhere out of her memory to trouble her.

She would never be so gullible again. It was becoming easy to interpret facial expressions, turns of the head, hurried phone calls, choice of clothing, even smells. Especially smells. How he smelled when he left, how he smelled when he returned. It was all obvious when you were ready to see.

She still hadn't told him she knew and she wouldn't until the day she left. That day she would throw out everything she'd discovered as if it was a physical thing, maybe a huge tapestry, ugly for its provocative colors—the red of blood, the purple of bruises, the mustard color of poison mushrooms, the orangeness of a dying leaf. She imagined herself walking out the door, turning for a last look, and seeing him wrapped and tangled in it like a circus tent had collapsed on him.

At least that was how she had felt when she was still indignant, when her anger was still feeding her energy.

Had she ever loved Buck? She didn't know. Nevertheless, she had agreed to an alliance that she had respected and worked at. How unfair his infidelity was, how insulting. He was no prize, undependable for the most part, sure to drink too much always. Yet she had kept to the bargain she thought they'd made. She managed his home, took care of his child, his dying father, his premature lambs, his sickly calves, even ironed the shirts other women put their shoulders to on some sweaty dance floor. None of this enough to keep him faithful.

If he didn't want her, who in the world would?

Pearl's hopes of the marriage becoming any better were gone and hopes of there being something of substance available for Katie were gone. There was even the fear that Katie might have inherited one or more of her father's moral frailties. Never mind that it wasn't apparent now. Couldn't stuff like that be hanging around clean, pure cells, ready to grow under certain conditions into some genetic monster? She'd been so careless to pick him for Katie's father.

"You've got to decide what you want," Etta told her. They went on long walks on the hills every weekend when Etta came down. They'd wait until Buck was busy or Katie was off horseback riding or studying and they'd walk until they were tired and then sit down to discuss things.

"Come and live with me," Etta said. "It's your house too, you know. Think about it. Katie wouldn't have to ride that damn school bus every day. She'd have friends in the neighborhood, wouldn't be so shy and withdrawn. You could get a job and meet new people, have a little fun. Think it over," she urged.

Pearl wasn't ready to leave yet, though she couldn't have told Etta why. It was as though a great paralysis, a huge tiredness commanded her. If sometimes she couldn't move a leg off the couch to go start dinner or an arm to turn on the shower, how could she move a household, a child, a life? She wished for the return of anger.

Pearl talked it over with Maggie, who now came to visit regularly with her toddler and new baby. Was she disillusioning this young mother by crying on her shoulder all the time? What was it doing to her, Pearl wondered, late at night. But Charlie, though quirky, was solid, and Maggie seemed to appreciate that. She'd never have the problems with Charlie that Pearl was having. More likely, she was just boring Maggie to death. The whole subject—her suspicions, her feelings, her preoccupation with injustice—absorbed all Pearl's attention. She enjoyed sarcasm toward Buck like she had never enjoyed it before, not clearly overt but not exactly subtle either. He'd sometimes turn to her, puzzled by some bitter comment.

One afternoon at a farm auction during a break for dinner—a potluck—everyone was discussing the morning sales or the value of items to be offered later. The hostesses were sisters and, owing to their father's recent death, the new owners of all the machinery, tools, and household items there. They strutted among the tables with coffee and lemonade. Their hustle lost momentum, though, around Buck, and Pearl saw that they understood his appreciation for their assets other than property.

"I'm bidding on that forklift," Buck told the group at their table.

"And which sister?" Pearl couldn't help asking, though unintentionally louder than she meant to, which made Buck and the man on the other side of him look up at her. They both wore the same expression—uncertainty—and she smiled at them pleasantly to confuse them further.

Didn't he get it, she wondered. Didn't he see she knew? He had to. Buck was many things, but he wasn't dumb. She always suspected that a lot of his problems were caused by an intelligence he either allowed no outlet for or that his life didn't require the use of.

Etta kept getting mad at her. "Pearl, you're wallowing in a pit and you like it. There's nothing anyone can do about that but you."

Then the next time she'd say, "Pearl, tell him everything you suspect and see what he says. Tell him you won't put up with it." Another time she told her, "You have two choices—leave and don't look back or forgive him and stay. But if you stay you have to forget all this."

But more and more Etta was saying she didn't want to discuss it. "When you're ready to deal with it, let me know. Until then, I don't want to know what you think he did last night or last week!"

It was easy for Etta to talk. She'd always been on her own. She'd never been dependent on anyone, not since she was fifteen. Even when she was with Harold, she'd worked, then after he was killed, she got insurance money and pension checks each month. What did she know about supporting a child or finding a job after all these years? It was bad enough she didn't have Buck to talk to about this. That was the strangest thing about it—she was used to telling him everything and missed that. That was loss enough, but to have Etta abandon her too was disabling. After all, she'd only asked her to listen.

Etta didn't seem to need a man, either. She was still slim and attractive, yet she never used it to any advantage. For Pearl, a man was required, though she wasn't sure why. It was just one of those things she could not possibly imagine—going through life lonely and divorced. But what man would want her? Her hair was thinning and limp, and she felt overweight, lumpish, and defective. Every year while Buck grew in some way better look-ing, she was becoming the matron. She hated Buck most for putting her in this predicament. Had she known, she would have stayed on top of things, insisted on living in town so she could work, kept a foot in the social stream, so that relating to others, men others in particular, wouldn't have become so disquieting an experience. Or she just might have had a few affairs too. She'd never have worn herself out this way, on his ranch, on his life.

Pearl wasn't prepared to start over. What's more, if she left, Buck would probably forget to cut the wheat or take the cattle to market. Or he'd spend all the profit on women. So that even though he'd be willing to help her and Katie financially, she was sure that without her there wouldn't be any money.

She told all this to Maggie, who listened wide-eyed when she wasn't chasing kids. She was always running to pull the baby out of something—the toilet, the toilet paper, the ashtrays—and two-year-old Patrick off the bookcase or the back of the couch, where he liked to climb.

It was hard to concentrate. Pearl would just get to a juicy detail or be in tears when Maggie would bob up from her coffee to extract the baby's fingers from a drawer. What did Pearl care if the baby got into the drawer, or got water or toilet paper all over the bathroom. She didn't care if he plugged the toilet. Just sit

down, Maggie, she wanted to say, and listen to my heart breaking. Of course, she never said things like that.

Then after Maggie gathered up the two kids and all the toys
they never touched, Pearl would lie down, exhausted from the
frenzy of Maggie's visit. "I'm sorry," Maggie would say as she
went out the door. "I feel so bad for you. You're going through so
much."

Pearl had to assume Maggie told Charlie. Didn't wives tell
husbands stuff like that? But he never acted like he knew, just
teased Katie as usual and asked her along on errands or for
horseback rides on the weekends. And if he took the boys somewhere he included Katie too.

One day Pearl was home alone and Charlie came to borrow the
post-hole digger. Pearl walked out to the garage with him.

"Pearl," he said, turning to her unexpectedly. "When you get
sick of this, you'll go for something better."

At first she didn't comprehend. When she did, she felt angry.
She'd had it with everyone and their easy, arrogant solutions to
her problems.

"Goddamn it, Charlie. If I could make myself feel better, I
would. If I could make myself prettier, I would. If I had the
confidence to leave and go find a job or another life, believe me,
I'd do it today!"

Having said all that, she was afraid she was going to cry.

"Hey," he said. "I'm not criticizing. If I weren't married, I'd be
the first to try . . ."

"Try what?"

"To pull you out of here."

She was astonished. She lifted her head to see if he were
ridiculing her or laughing. But he looked straight at her, maybe
looking at her for something too. Then he stepped forward,
kissed her on the cheek, and turned and walked out of the garage,
whistling tunelessly like he always did with Katie or his sons.

She didn't believe it. Charlie hadn't so much as glanced in her direction that she could recall. Charlie had never even smiled at her indecently, or winked at her, or stared. Men were the strangest people on earth. There was no way to ever tell what they were thinking. They just went around doing what they wanted. Whether or not it was stunning or surprising, they didn't seem to care.

She watched him swing the post-hole digger into the back of his truck and get into the cab. Without looking back once, he drove away. Without a thought about leaving her jarred and startled, he just drove away.

Take it all back, she wanted to yell at him, and leave me in peace.

CHAPTER

EIGHTEEN

Thursday, after lunch, Katie's teacher introduced Clifford's mother, Mrs. Bumgardner, to the class, even though everyone already knew her. She came every year to talk kids into joining 4-H. She brought exhibits from the county fair—articles of clothing kids had made, a selection of preserves that no one cared to sample, tomato plants, cabbages, and once a single ear of corn. No prizewinners among them. Just throwaways, the stuff kids left and didn't want to see again, uncollected, spoiled fruits of failed effort.

But this time Mrs. Bumgardner passed out cookies and talked about raising animals. She showed a picture of the Charolais bull calf that had won all the prizes at the last fair.

"This is for girls too," Mrs. Bumgardner said. "How about you, Katie?"

"Well . . . ," Katie said.

"It's not as difficult as you might think. Your father can help you. He can't do the work, of course. But he can advise you."

"Can your mother advise you?" Katie asked shyly, knowing Mama, not Pa, was the one who might like this sort of thing.

The class laughed. Mrs. Bumgardner looked puzzled.

"Mothers help with sewing and baking, stupid," Clifford Bumgardner said.

"My mother doesn't sew," Katie said.

"Clifford," Mrs. Bumgardner said sharply. "Apologize to Katie. Mothers can advise about animals too." She looked doubtful even as she said it.

Katie was embarrassed. She had called attention to herself. She had revealed something about her family, though she wasn't sure what. She suspected that other mothers were alike somehow, but not like hers.

"How about it, Katie?" Mrs. Bumgardner persisted. Everyone waited for her answer.

"I don't think so," Katie said, staring at the floor. She could hear the boys in the back snickering.

"Well, talk it over with your parents before you decide for sure," Mrs. Bumgardner said, smiling kindly.

"Well, thank you for coming, Mrs. Bumgardner," her teacher intervened. "You can leave the forms at the table by the door."

Katie noticed that after school, three girls picked up forms.

When Katie got home, the morning milk was still sitting out on the counter and no one seemed to be home. Disgusting, she thought, looking at the yellow skin that had settled at the top.

She changed clothes and went outside. She heard the auger in the barn, but the pickup was gone. Mama or Pa, either one, would be unloading barley, and the other off in the pickup somewhere.

Katie filled a bucket with oats from a seed sack in the granary. It was too full and very heavy, and she carried it carefully with both hands, trying not to spill it. But her father, coming around the corner of the barn, ran right into her and knocked her down. Katie started to laugh because it struck her funny. With the auger going, they hadn't heard each other. But she sobered when she saw his face.

"Goddamn it," he said. "Pay attention to what you're doing."

"It was your fault," she screamed daringly, but he didn't even turn, just headed back to the auger, not even caring that she had sassed him.

Katie kicked the bucket and left the spilled grain where it had fallen. Geese and sheep now gathered to fight over it. "I hope you all bloat and die," she said, shooing them out of her way.

She went back to the granary and dumped more grain into another bucket—not so much this time—and carried it to the fence along the east side of the horse pasture. She poured the oats on the ground and banged the empty bucket against the fence. Five horses loped across the field at the sound and gathered around the small piles she had made. Katie took down a halter she kept on the gatepost and slipped it on a large roan gelding. When he was finished eating, she led him to the barn to saddle him. She was a little afraid of the horse but decided to take him anyway.

It took her some time to get the saddle on him and then to pull the cinch securely around his large belly. She led him finally to the fence because he was easier to mount there. She had devised a system. With her right foot on the lowest rung of the fence, she could easily step into the stirrup with her left foot and swing her right leg over the horse's broad back.

It was chilly even though there was no wind. She guided the horse across the creek to the top of the hill and stopped to look down at the house. She saw that the pickup was back, and that Aunt Etta was there too. Aunt Etta's car was a bright spot of red among the dusty, faded vehicles and pieces of equipment near the garage. Besides rusted-out parts to a combine and an old tractor, there was a grain truck, an old Chevy on blocks, and a jeep that didn't run.

Aunt Etta was driving out often lately, and as Katie well knew, there was some reason, unexplained, for the frequency of these visits. There would be no chance to bring up 4-H if she stayed. When she came, Pa went into town, Mama and Aunt Etta drank coffee and discussed any number of boring things, and when they thought Katie was asleep, they talked about Pa.

Katie gave the horse the lead down the hill. At the bottom, she let him trot along a narrow gully, directing him to the flat prairie floor where she would run him until he sweated, until she sweated. The horse knew what was expected, and without prompting, began to gallop. Except for his hooves hitting the cold earth, there was no sound. The whole countryside was silent, and Katie finally began to relax and to move with the horse.

Some miles later, Katie pulled in the reins, turned the horse right, and led him up a cow path that traversed a high, flat butte. At the top she dismounted and let him graze on what was left of the dried grass. She zipped up her jacket and sat against a boulder out of the wind. No matter how still things were below, up here there was always wind. But here she came anyway, in all weather, to think. Somehow life had become something about which she had to think. It did not just unfold as it once had, simply, predictably, or even unpredictably. Now it was a matter requiring careful thought. It had become, she feared, hazardous.

She saw in everything a capacity for breakage and collapse—the barn looked ready to fall down, half the time anything electrical or mechanical wouldn't work, and everything needed paint and repair. The plainest household ceremonies were abandoned these days—opening drapes, turning on the radio, bringing in the mail, and the house was strangely dark and quiet. Her mother took long walks alone or with Aunt Etta, returning silently, too preoccupied to care that she'd forgotten to turn on the oven and that the chicken or roast was still cold. There was little conversation at dinner anymore. Yet suddenly, late at night, her parents would begin to talk. Their voices would wake her up, suddenly on some track, running insistently and without effect over the arid, undefended regions of their lives.

They forgot her. Twice they neglected to wake her up for school and she missed the bus. Her mother, without apology or explanation, simply drove her into town. And her father was drinking more too, and kept bottles handy to the barn and garage. Sometimes the drinking put him in a good mood, but more often he became distracted, withdrawn, or angry for no reason. Then he'd go into town, banging furniture and doors as he left, in a great show of noise, clanking and barreling down the lane in that beat-up truck, as if commotion made him feel better.

But the grievances were all privately owned and maintained. No charges or admissions were ever made beyond general complaints or melancholy. "What's wrong, Pa?" she'd asked him one day. She had run to the house for another pail; they were cleaning chickens in the garage. When she returned he was just standing there, staring at the dead chicken on the butcher block.

He just turned and looked at her in bewilderment.

"Oh, Katie," he said as if she'd just returned from an errand of twenty years. "Can you finish up here?"

"I can't split chickens," she'd said to his departing back. But he hadn't answered; he'd just gotten into the pickup and driven off. In frustration she had gone inside with several dead chickens and plopped them down on the counter. Her mother was talking on the phone.

"Katie, what on earth?" her mother said, her hand over the earpiece.

"I can't finish these by myself!"

"Good God, must you be so dramatic? Where's your father?"

"Gone. He just left in the middle of it."

"I'll have to call you back," Pearl said into the phone. "Everything's a drama around here. One big deal after another." And to Katie she said, "Take those smelly chickens back to the garage, I'll be out in a minute."

Katie sighed. It was time to go. The sun was low in the sky now. It would be a moonless night and they would have trouble in the dark. She got up and patted the horse, giving him a carrot from her pocket. He nuzzled her back, and she hugged his large neck.

She mounted, this time using the boulder the way she had used the fence, and rode slowly back down the trail. At the bottom, she spurred him and he reluctantly loped.

"Come on," she urged him. The sun was almost to the ridge of hills west of the dam, and the night promised to be cloudy and cold. The horse picked up speed, maybe understanding the need to get home before dark.

Katie was unprepared when the gelding, spooked by something, reared suddenly. A rattler this time of year? she wondered as she flew through the air. She landed in sagebrush and rolled across the rocky ground, unaware of pain until she tried to get up. Her right leg, her back, and both elbows hurt. Her ankles, despite boots, felt bruised from the spurs that were now bent and hanging loosely around her heels. The horse had run off.

"Come back here," she yelled at him. "You son of a bitch. Come back here." She could still see him.

"Come back or I'll kill you!" she screamed. She really would, she decided, and burst into tears. As soon as she got back, she would shoot him, hunt him down and shoot him.

Katie unbuckled the spurs and threw them. She got up and started walking, slowly because she hurt everywhere, then faster. The pain became heat and she walked as fast as she could, then ran toward the setting sun. She stumbled going up the hill above the house and fell to her knees. She got back up and ran down the other side, wading furiously through the creek, not bothering to cross over the boards ten yards to her left, not caring that her boots and pant legs were wet or that she was miserably cold. She ran across the field behind the house, going over and over in her mind what she would do. The guns were in the garage. Ammunition in a wooden box on the shelf. In detail she remembered what her father had taught her. And if she could knock a tin can off a fence, she could hit a horse.

When she got to the garage, she almost tripped over something on the ground. It was an empty bottle and she kicked it out of her way, climbed on the workbench, and got down the hunting rifle from the gun rack. The cartridges felt cold in her hand, and she loaded them one by one. She walked deliberately, carefully, to the pasture. The sun was almost behind the hills, and what light was left reflected on the water in the dam and in the large metal trough where the horses, now large shadows in the dusk, were drinking. She got on one knee, using the bottom rung of the fence to support the barrel of the gun. The thing was heavy on her shoulder, cold against her cheek, and she aimed with care at the large roan still wearing the saddle.

This, she thought with wonder as she pulled the trigger, is what it is to be crazy.

The impact when she fired threw her to the ground, but she knew she had done it. She had killed the horse. She saw him fall to the ground.

"Katie! What in the hell!" she heard her father yell.

"Oh, no," she cried. "I killed the wrong one." She saw it now, an innocent mare struggling with death, looking at her across the pasture, wondering why it had been struck down.

"It's the wrong one," she sobbed. "The wrong one."

"Katie, stop it," her father said. He took the gun and pulled her toward the house. "Stop it, just stop it," he said. She felt feverish now as though she had caught fire and were burning. "It's all right," he said. "It's all right."

"I killed the wrong one," she repeated, trying to make him understand.

"You didn't kill anything," he said. "Did you hear me? You didn't kill anything."

"But I saw it," she said, barely able to talk now. She felt that she was passing up and behind her body, floating above a fire in her head.

"No, honey. You didn't kill anything. You missed," she heard him say from what seemed a great distance.

When she came to, she realized her father was carrying her toward the house, and that her entire body was in pain.

"Mama, where's Mama?" she cried.

"She'll be home soon," he said.

"Don't tell her," she said and began to cry. "Please, don't tell her." Katie knew with sudden clarity that though her father might understand this, her mother never would. Not as long as she lived.

He put her down on the porch steps and sat beside her. "I won't tell," he said. "I promise." He wiped the hair from her face—a rare and generous gesture that made her cry harder.

"That's enough now," he said. "I expect she'll be home soon."

I expect she'll be home soon.

It was the way he said it, the way his hand moved helplessly to his brow, the way he looked away from her to the dark horizon at the edge of the road—these things, for reasons she couldn't have explained, told her that her father expected nothing.

They watched the darkened road together. They watched it at the point where it sloped around the corner and made the slightest of entrances into their lives.

CHAPTER

NINETEEN

It was Christmas Eve day and there was a bright glare from the sun on the snow. Etta put the presents into the car and ran back to the house for her sunglasses. The sky was deep blue and cloudless. Actually there were clouds but they lay on the ground. Indeed, the clouds were more like fog and they overhung the road and fields, just a few feet deep, gently rolling in the wind along with blowing, drifting snow. It was a remarkable phenomenon and all the way from the Air Force base to the top of Belt Hill she rode through lawless, foaming waves, pure white and blinding against the blue, bright sky. She had never seen anything like it in her life and didn't expect to again—a rare combination of conditions that produced an ethereal hypnotic sort of enchantment that affected her with slight euphoria and loss of equilibrium.

When she dropped down Belt Hill, the fog was gone. She accelerated to make up for lost time as she wanted to get to the ranch before lunch.

That afternoon, Etta supervised the baking and Pearl the cooking. They prepared for both Christmas Eve and Christmas day dinners. They baked dinner rolls, cinnamon rolls, pumpkin and mincemeat pies. She helped Pearl pare vegetables for dinner, cut up onions and celery for turkey stuffing, and dry and cube the bread. They made chip dips and hors d'oeuvres, rolled out sugar cookies and iced them, and washed cooking and baking utensils continuously.

The house was a mess. Katie wrapped packages between the various batches of cookies and where there wasn't dough there was paper or tape. Buck wandered in and out of the kitchen, gay and interested in the activity, often sampling food or nipping from a bottle of whiskey on the counter.

"You girls are going to a lot of trouble for so few guests," he said.

"But they're special guests," Katie said, smiling up at him.

"You're the one who's special," he said and kissed her cheek.

By five o'clock it was dark and Katie offered to do the feeding. Etta asked if she might tag along. She put on a pair of Pearl's jeans and boots and bundled up in an old jacket, hat, and gloves.

It was a stunning night and snow fell softly in thick flakes that made Etta want to stick out her tongue to catch some or lie on her back in the new, clean snow and make angels like a child would. Katie seemed not to notice anything about the weather and was rather businesslike, filling Etta in on the intricacies and larger details of operating a feedlot.

"You see, these animals aren't ready for full feed yet," Katie told her. "You have to build them up to that so the nitrogen in the feed doesn't burn out their stomachs. For example," she said seriously, "let's say a pregnant heifer accidentally gets in the feedlot—sometimes they come that way when we buy heifers—we usually have only steers and no bulls," she said, explaining thoroughly. "So if that happens they always miscarry because the feed's too strong."

"Oh," was all Etta could think to say. She helped Katie fill buckets and dump them into the feeders. The steers stood in a circular row, bumping each other and volleying for room all around where Etta and Katie stood on a large mound of grain in the center of the homemade wooden troughs. They sat down, Katie to see that all went well, and Etta in appreciation of the beauty and stillness of the night. Still, that is, with the exception of cattle chewing, a sound magic and ancient and one Etta liked to imagine at the manger scene some other distant Christmas Eve.

"I love this," Etta said.

"What's so great about watching cows eat?" Katie asked, frankly practical and surprised by such sentiment.

They could see lights now making a path around and over the hills, miles off, and at last nearing and pulling in their lane. "Maggie and Charlie," Katie cried. They put the buckets away and turned off the water and walked arm in arm to the house.

Inside, the table was spread with food and dishes. Maggie had brought the ingredients for Tom and Jerrys and a ham from Charlie's hogs that he had smoked and cured. Pearl had made au gratin potatoes, baked beans, a tossed salad, and a spinach casserole. Etta arranged cheese, deviled eggs, and crackers on a red platter. Maggie filled Santa Claus mugs with Tom-and-Jerry mix, and Buck added the rum and brandy. Charlie helped himself to eggs and cream from the icebox and made Katie and his sons, Pat and Joey, some eggnog. "Maybe a bit of rum in Katie's," Etta heard him tease. When everyone had a drink, they toasted.

"To us," Buck offered.

"To another wonderful year," Maggie said and touched her mug to his.

"Amen," Charlie said and added his.

"Merry Christmas," sang the boys, prompted by Katie, who stood between them.

They all took a seat at the dining table and Pearl asked Etta to say grace. With the exception of that prayer, the meal was a boisterous one; the spirit of the holiday or alcohol had excited everyone. When they were through, Buck and Charlie cleared the table.

"We'll do the dishes," Charlie said.

"Who's 'we'?" Buck teased.

"And you two cowboys can help," Charlie told the boys, who were running wildly around the house. Pearl sat at the piano and played Christmas hymns. It was an old player piano that their father had had delivered by tow barge from Minneapolis via the Missouri River when they were kids and, years later, it was delivered to the ranch by cattle truck. When the men returned, Charlie sat at the piano with Pearl.

"I didn't know you played, Charlie," Etta said when he struck a few chords. "Well I do," he said and played "Silent Night." Everyone stood around the piano and soon they were all singing.

There was something about Charlie that Etta liked. It was that he was present but unnoticed for who knows how long. Then belatedly you saw that he had grown on you, that you had acquired a taste for him, and that he was addictive.

Maggie, on the other hand, was at once noticeable and appealing. She had light eyes, not quite green, and light hair, not quite blonde. Her complexion was fair and without fault. There was a quality about her, perhaps style, but also a fragility that left her exposed and woundable. A child, Etta thought.

When Etta returned from the bathroom in the middle of "Away in a Manger," she was almost certain she saw Buck's hand briefly drop below an imaginary line of compromise beneath Maggie's waist. She had to allow, however, in consequence of her general dislike for Buck and three Tom and Jerrys, for error. Moreover, she had a sucker's predilection for thinking her loved ones were at all moments cherished and unthreatened.

In spite of this, Etta was taken by surprise that spring, when in celebration of Pearl's birthday, she went again to the ranch and Pearl told her the news: Buck was having an affair with Maggie, Charlie had left accordingly, and she, Pearl, was considering doing the same.

"It's the meanest thing he's ever done," Pearl said, getting out two beers from the icebox. "Do you believe it? His friend all these years. And Maggie, well, she wasn't my best friend—you're my best friend—but I thought she was close. It's so disgusting."

"Are you sure?" Etta asked. Not that she couldn't believe it, but it was a rather clumsy business mixing it up with old friends. Up to now, Buck had settled on single women, or widows, or married ones whose husbands strayed conveniently too. Well as far as they knew that was the case. Were Buck and Maggie in love? Not that Etta would excuse them for that or Buck for being more discriminating in times past, nor was she discounting what Pearl suffered in the course of these swindles.

"I'm sure," Pearl said. "I caught them necking in the pickup."

"Where were the kids?"

"With Charlie, I guess. That's another thing that gets me. I probably was babysitting half the time they were together." Pearl banged her bottle of beer on the table.

"So where were they?"

"Here's what happened. Katie told me the brown gelding needed exercise, right? So I rode him around and then tied him up down by the creek. I was just sitting there and I thought I heard the pickup so I walked over the hill. When I saw it was Buck's I went over and there they were in a fast clinch."

"My God, what'd you do?"

"I was going to walk away but I was furious. I banged on the hood and they jumped apart. Maggie rolled down the window and I said 'My, does Charlie know too, or is this our secret?' You should have seen the looks on their faces. Then Maggie started crying and I walked off."

"What did Buck say?"

"He spent the rest of the week justifying himself. He said there was only that one time and that it would never happen again."

"How did Charlie find out?"

"I guess Maggie was afraid I'd say something so she told him herself."

"How about Katie?"

"I don't think she knows. I sure hope not. What kid needs to know her father's an ass?"

"You better not drink anymore or she'll wonder what's going on," Etta said. Katie would be getting off the school bus any moment and would question their drinking. Pearl, as a rule, took an occasional drink but never in the afternoon and certainly not beer. She hardly ever drank it anymore because she said it was fattening.

"Oh, Etta, what am I going to do?" she cried and Etta held her in her arms. Etta couldn't help thinking of their own father. Not that he was anything like Buck. And certainly his fidelity to Mother had never been an issue. He was loyal to the end. When she died, he died.

Dying was the thing Etta faulted him for most. It took her years to forgive him that. She had been prepared for her mother's death; she was always in poor health and not much was done for cancer in those days. But for her father to follow her within the year was an infraction of their rights. It was an injury she blamed him for, to misplace them, to grieve over what was allowed, to prioritize his loss over theirs.

"He didn't choose to die," Pearl had said at the time. "For God's sake, Etta. The man had a heart attack." Etta still believed that he had chosen and when she forgave him, it was for not choosing them.

"You can't let these things get to you," Pearl had said. But these things did get to you. They would get to Katie. Her estimation of this one man, her father, would determine the men she would meet and the woman she would become—just as her and Pearl's feelings about their father had divined the life they had led.

"So then yesterday," Pearl said, "Charlie left."

"What a mess," Etta said, thinking of Maggie and her sons. She wiped at Pearl's tears with a tissue she took from her purse.

"Etta," Pearl said raising her beer bottle. "A toast. To my birthday."

CHAPTER

TWENTY

───────◆───────

The trip to Billings began happily enough. Both Pearl and Etta were in good spirits. Pearl felt good as soon as she got even a few miles away from the ranch. Some pressure was off. But then Etta had to put it back on. She began by worrying and sighing. Pearl could tell by the way she was driving that she was worrying. She would slow down, then she'd speed up, slow down, speed up. She drove the way other women churned butter. Following that, finally, was commentary.

"I think Katie really wanted to come," she said after an hour of choppy driving and those sighs.

"We've been through all that." Pearl turned on the radio, hoping Etta would just worry and not talk. But she found herself waiting impatiently for Etta's next comment, which came a half-hour later with the weather report.

"I don't feel good about leaving her with Buck."

"Jesus Christ, he's her father."

"What's happened to you? That place has changed you."

"What place?"

"That ranch."

"Jesus, Etta. I've been there more than a dozen years. Is this something you've just noticed?"

"See what I mean. You talk like an old hired man."

"Well, sometimes you annoy me. You always know what's good for everyone."

"I just know leaving Katie with a drunk doesn't make sense."

"You think leaving him alone is any better? Then he'd really . . . ." Pearl didn't finish what she was saying. She was horrified. Etta was right in some way. She'd left Katie there to babysit, to keep him out of trouble, to keep him home.

"You left her there to keep him away from Maggie."

Etta really was psychic. Now she was reading her mind. "The hell I did," Pearl said angrily. She couldn't think of a defense.

"There you go again."

"What?"

"Swearing."

Pearl turned off the radio. They had lost the weather report to static. She sat back sullenly.

"And what if he did?" Etta asked.

"What if he did what?" Etta was getting on her nerves.

"Went to Maggie's."

Pearl couldn't think of an answer to that.

"In fact, I wish he would," Etta said. "I wish he'd run off with her."

"That's the lowest thing you've ever said," she told Etta.

"Well, I'm sick of hearing about him. He just makes your life miserable."

"At least I have someone." It was mean and Etta showed that on her face. All the same, thank the Lord, it silenced her.

Pearl was too irritated to take it back or to be sorry. She knew she was overreacting, but she'd be damned if meanness wasn't the only way to handle Etta sometimes.

They drove the remainder of the trip in silence.

At the hotel, they carried their own bags to the elevator, staring past the bellboy who'd offered help. Once in their room,

Pearl collapsed on the bed. She felt sick and tired of something. Everything.

"Are you hungry?" Etta asked her softly.

"Etta," Pearl said, sitting up. "Why did we come?"

Etta sat down beside her. "You wanted to get away so you could think. We were going to have fun, relax, get some perspective." She got up then and looked out the window.

"You wanted to come to a decision about your marriage. Oh, Pearl, I don't mean to be so hard on you. I'm just worried about you."

"I know and I'm sorry," Pearl said. She was. She didn't need to turn on her only ally in the world. She just couldn't help it sometimes.

"I'm sorry too."

"You don't think Buck would really run off with Maggie and leave all the kids, do you?" Pearl asked suddenly.

"No, Buck's not that bad and neither is Maggie."

"They'll be all right then?"

"Sure."

"You know Buck can be real good with Katie. Gentle and sweet," Pearl said. At least he used to be able to. How long had it been? she wondered.

"I know," Etta said. "Let's go get some dinner."

After peeking into the hotel dining room, which was cold and empty, they drove around town. Etta told her to choose a place and Pearl decided on a supper club next to a well-lighted theatre. There was something nice about all the neon.

Pearl wasn't really hungry and picked at her food. Etta tried to cheer her up.

"Tomorrow, we'll go shopping and have a nice lunch. Do you still want to get a haircut? Leona's cousin gave me the name of a marvelous hairdresser here."

Pearl nodded without enthusiasm, though she indeed liked the idea of a marvelous hairdresser. She ought to try something new and outrageous.

Pearl had wine, Etta had tea.

When Pearl ordered her second glass, Etta said nothing. But the third was just too much.

"Drinking is no answer," Etta said when Pearl waved to the waiter again.

"I know," Pearl said and ordered it anyway.

Etta seemed resigned to keeping peace and said no more about it. She went on with ideas for the next few days and Pearl tried to forget her irritation and relax. There was no sense in letting Etta provoke her. Pearl could be in a perfectly good mood and Etta could ruin it. She always could, even when they were kids. Etta had a way of looking over her shoulder and whether she said anything or not, she would be critical. She had a way of project-ing it instead of saying it. Once she had reached out to touch something Pearl had just put in place on her dresser. Pearl just knew she was going to move it over a fraction of an inch just to make the point that Pearl hadn't got it perfect. Pearl had been so annoyed she'd struck her. In retaliation, Etta had kicked her in the leg and then they'd fallen on each other in a tangle of vicious clawing and hair pulling. And their mother, hearing the noise, had run to the door and burst into tears, which stopped them at once—that is, once they noticed her. Mother was always sad-dened and mystified by how swiftly, how enthusiastically, they could turn a simple birthday party, for example, or quiet game into a brawl. It not only seemed to terrify Mother, it paralyzed her. So for that reason, with the same rapidity they had hated each other the moment before, they now made up just to make Mother recover the ability to act. Then for a time they'd manage to keep the more serious quarreling out of view of Mother—but sometimes they'd be back at it within the hour.

Pearl pushed away her drink. She decided to call home as soon as they got back to the hotel. She'd gotten to thinking about Buck again. Surely, he wouldn't run off and leave Katie alone.

They were finished now and waited for their check. "Pearl," Etta said. "How about letting Katie come stay with me this summer. And you take the time to work it out with Buck and make up your mind."

Pearl was startled. "I don't know. I don't think Buck would go for it either." It was likely Katie wouldn't even want to, but she thought it heartless to say so.

"Well, think about it, okay?"

"All right," Pearl promised. All at once she could see how lonely Etta might be and what a solitary life she must have had all these years. It was funny she'd never thought this before. But really, who did Etta have? She had Leona's troubles next door and Pearl's troubles a few hours away. It made her sad to realize so late the truth of this.

"This might be harder on Katie than you think."

"What?" Pearl hadn't been paying any attention.

"I said this might all be harder on Katie than it is on you and Buck."

"For chrissakes, I said I'd think about it!"

Pearl regretted at once snapping at Etta like that and she couldn't look at her. She wished Etta would just kick her on the shins under the table. But no, she would look hurt. She would have already managed to assume Mother's position in the doorway. Just the thought of that made Pearl want to cry.

CHAPTER

TWENTY ONE

Katie knew a bad idea when she heard one. Staying home with her father over Easter vacation was one of the worst and she told him so. Naturally she phrased it in his terms. "I hate hauling cattle," she said; it was the thing next to branding and dehorning she hated most around there.

"I need your help," he said. "Hell, I'll even take you to a movie." Katie had looked across the dinner table at her mother, hoping for support. Her mother only shrugged, her attention elsewhere.

"Come on. Spend some time with your old man for a change." Katie had sighed. She didn't know how to tell him she didn't like spending time with him anymore.

So she stayed. The morning her mother left, Katie fixed breakfast. But her mother was too rushed to eat it and her father wasn't hungry. Katie cleared the table and threw the uneaten food to the dogs. She washed the dishes slowly, intent on her view of the lane as it swung around the horse pasture, though she knew no one was expected. She was still disappointed that she hadn't gone along. Her mother and aunt were driving to Billings to shop over the long weekend. That, and Charlie, were on her mind. When her father brought in the milk, she strained it and poured it still warm into jugs, careful to seal and shake it and put it into the refrigerator before a skim could settle.

"You know," she told her father, "if Charlie knew he was going to leave like that, you'd think he'd have come said good-bye."

Buck emptied the coffeepot and sat at the table. It was rickety and practically leaned against the sill of the window cut purposely low by his own father years ago so the old man could sit in a rocker and push wood into the stove with his foot, free then, as he put it, to drink coffee and watch the sun rise on the just and the unjust of the whole of Judith Basin County.

Once the sun was up there was little to see except the road. Her father watched it now.

"Forget Charlie," he said finally. He got up to look for his tobacco pouch and after a noisy search of drawers and cupboards, finally took tobacco from a can in the refrigerator and rolled a cigarette. Then he took out more tobacco and patted it into a square of gauzy material, the kind they used for filtering milk, and tied it with a string he found in a drawer. He put it in his coat pocket and went outside to roll grain.

Katie browned a small beef roast and put it in the oven. Then she picked up in the house and got her jacket. She drove the truck down to the barn where she could hear the auger feeding barley and beet pulp into a large bin. Buck saw her and came over.

"I'm going down to Maggie's with the milk," she told him.

"Take it easy on the gravel, will you?"

When Katie got to Maggie's she found her busy cleaning. She had made a pile of things she wanted to throw out, mostly egg cartons too ragged to use again and canning jars with cracks or chipped lids. She was nervous and frail, Katie thought, but pretty too. She had on old slippers and a loose house coat. Its pockets were bulging with stuff; she emptied some into the garbage and put some on the counter. Without Charlie around, Katie felt awkward here, realizing how little she knew Maggie even though she'd been their only babysitter for the boys.

"Hot chocolate?" Maggie asked. She got out cocoa and milk

and also some eggs for Katie to take home. The kids hung onto Katie, they were restless and irritable. Maggie had little to say. Katie wished she could ask her about Charlie and where he went. Her own guess was that he'd headed for Missoula or Spokane, that country west of the Continental Divide he had always talked about. Why he went was what she really wanted to know. There was so much she didn't understand about this kind of thing, like how he could desert them just like that. But she knew better than to ask Maggie about it.

Did it have something to do with what Katie had overheard at Arlo's Hardware a few days earlier? Mrs. Meyers, an old lady who lived in town, had hunched over the notched and grooved counter toward Millie Hart, the clerk, explaining what she'd heard about a thing . . . a thing Maggie was having that was bound to infuriate Charlie. "And he's not an easy one to rile either," Mrs. Meyers had said with a little whistle, intended, perhaps, for emphasis. Katie would have heard more had she not dropped the pound of ten-penny nails Arlo had weighed out for her in back.

"Come help me, Katie," yelled Joey. She was glad to have something to do, realizing that she was staring at Maggie. She followed Pat through the house to the bathroom and untangled Joey from overall straps that were wound around his leg. She helped him wash up and noticed something unmistakably familiar on the shelf. Her father's tobacco pouch. It was soft and dark brown, an old thing her grandfather had made from a hide he'd tanned and softened and even sewn himself. He had put a miniature of his brand on it, the same brand her father used now. She felt it with her finger, a lazy H, a bar, an upright S.

Katie could hear the boys calling to her now and she took the pouch out to the kitchen.

"Pa's tobacco pouch was in the bathroom," she said looking at Maggie.

"Oh," Maggie said, puzzled herself. "He must have left it the other day when he fixed the toilet."

"Mom, Mom," Joey shrieked, pulling on Maggie's dress. "Tell him it's mine."

"I had it first," Pat countered loudly, practically lying across the scarred old wagon they were fighting over as if to hold it to his breast.

Katie waited for Maggie to settle the quarrel; the boys' whining was getting on her nerves. But Maggie just stood there staring at the wagon and suddenly Katie knew what it was to be all alone and to long for something. For what she didn't know. She told Maggie she had to go.

"You forgot the eggs," Maggie called to her. "And the pouch," the boys yelled from the porch as she started the pickup.

Katie drove slowly along the rutted lane past the only trees on the creek, then onto the smooth gravel county road that led to their own lane a few miles away. She stopped on top of the hill and parked. Here the land dropped sharply, clifflike, a place where Indians once drove buffalo to their death. She and Charlie used to ride here and once they'd stopped nearby to look over the broad sweep of plain below.

"This whole area was settled by honyockers," Charlie told her then.

"Honyockers?"

"That's what my old man was," he said. "And your grandpa. They came here with everything they had. Didn't know how to farm, didn't know the land, didn't know spit. Brought everything—family, furniture, livestock.

"Some like my old man rented whole boxcars from the railroad. In the end, though, we had to eat the stock and burn the furniture for firewood." He'd patted his horse and twisted his dirty hat to a more favored position on his head. "The railroad folks told everyone they could turn this land into a garden. And, of course, that wasn't true so people left." Charlie spit on the ground. "But not before they dug up most of the grass and let the topsoil blow to kingdom come."

"But people are still here," she said.

"Yeah," he said. "Some stayed. The ones that liked wind and drought."

"And rocks," she said. There were rocks everywhere on both wheat fields and pasture lands.

"And the goddamn rocks," he'd said and laughed. His laugh was deep and infectious as though there were dimensions to joy apparent only to him, dimensions he was willing to share but not disclose.

"Well I'm not going to stay here," she said.

"And where might you be off to?"

"Seattle," she had said.

The wind rocked the pickup now and whistled on across the haunted prairie. The immenseness, the horrifying vastness of nothing she could see made her want to cry. Katie couldn't remember hating anything like she hated this view and this wind.

She drove on finally and stopped at the mailbox, throwing the bundle of letters, magazines and newspapers across the dirty, tattered seat. It was almost noon and she hurried, remembering the roast.

By the time her father came in, she was stirring gravy and mashing potatoes. They ate quietly, reading the mail and the papers.

"Want to help me this afternoon?" he asked. "I'm going to fix the line of fence north of the dam."

He napped on the couch for half an hour, as was his custom, and she did the dishes as usual, the radio on and no one listening.

The wind was cold and Katie pulled her wool hat down over her ears. Her hands and feet felt numb despite the gloves and boots she wore. They parked above the dam excavated some years before to catch rain and runoff from melting snow. Here the cattle cooled themselves in summer, stirring up sediment that clouded the water, and here they drank the year round when it wasn't frozen.

Katie supported posts while her father pounded them, each blow of the sledgehammer vibrating through her. She could smell the creosote that would keep the posts from rotting out below the soil. She held the wire stretchers taut against the rusty wire. Buck twisted new knots. Then they walked the fence line searching for breaks and weak spots, leaning into the wind that pulled at their jackets and beat on their faces. She was glad when he motioned toward the pickup.

"Let's go over to the Trail Head for supper," he suggested. Buck stopped at the house long enough to run inside for a six-pack. The cab had warmed up and the sips he gave her of the cold beer tasted good.

The Trail Head Inn was cheery and warm. It was an old log structure built as a trading post for those Easterners who had once followed the Missouri River to areas near the Badlands on their way to settle in places like Winslow and Stanford.

"Hey, what brings you two out on such a cold night?" asked John Turner, the bartender.

"Pearl's off to Billings with her sister," Buck said. "And I was just starting to cook when I remembered that your hamburgers ain't all bad."

"Hell, you just remembered you don't know how to cook. So how's everything?"

"Just fine," her father said. He sat down at the bar. "We're going to have fun. Ain't that so, Katie?" He motioned her to sit beside him.

Turner stared at her. This scrutiny made her uncomfortable and she mumbled something about their plans to see a movie in Great Falls the next night.

"No kidding," Turner said, grinning at her, which made her more self-conscious.

Buck took tobacco from the now dirty gauze bag and rolled a

cigarette. His big fingers stumbled clumsily with the un-accustomed string. Katie got up and walked over to the jukebox.

"I heard Charlie up and left. What do you suppose that's all about?"

"Who knows," her father answered.

"And how's Maggie?" Turner asked next. Katie returned to the counter and sat down.

"Good, good," Buck answered. Katie watched his face for guilt or pleasure. "She's thinking of leasing out the place."

"Haven't seen her since Charlie left," Turner said, wiping the bar with a dirty rag. "Some guy, that Charlie," he added, thereby beginning a round of Charlie stories. It seemed to Katie that all anyone could talk about these days was Charlie.

"He was kind of an odd one I always thought," Turner said, placing hamburgers and hashbrowns in front of them. He handed Katie the ketchup.

"A cheap son-of-a-bitch," her father said. Katie frowned at him.

"He certainly never spent anything on clothes," Turner added. "I swear he wore the same hat all his life."

"Hell, yes. And when it got hot, he'd squash that old thing up and put it in the jockey box. Then when it got cold, he'd bang the goddamn thing out on the dashboard and put it back on."

The men laughed, as though all style themselves. Turner handed her father another can of beer.

"Always gave you lousy whiskey," her father said. "Once I asked him, 'Charlie, what is this crap you're serving?' and he says, 'Hell, you old bastard, you can't tell the King's whiskey from the cheap stuff.' And I says, 'Charlie, that's where you're wrong. Even my dog don't like this crap.'"

Turner nodded as though he'd had the same experience. The two men went on, taking turns with the stories, and she was all but forgotten.

"You know what he did once?" Turner said confidentially, though there was no one else in the bar. "You know that field of barley Charlie has south of his place, the one in Fergus County?" He grinned and pounded out his cigarette as he talked. "Well, there's a dirt road that runs through it. A county access road and it goes to some fields that Barney Johnson owns.

"Anyway, I'll be damned if once that son-of-a-bitch didn't dig it up and plant barley on it."

"He dug up the road?"

"Hell, yes, and Barney complains, see, so the county commissioner sends someone out from Lewistown to look into things. But all Charlie says is to tell old man Johnson that if he wants to ruin good barley then to just drive across it."

Even Katie thought this was pretty funny. She could picture Charlie chewing his tobacco and spitting while the man from Lewistown tried to bawl him out.

"Why did he have to go?" she said suddenly. She didn't mean to say it and they both turned to her like an alarm had gone off.

"You never know what troubles a man sometimes," Turner said kindly, looking off toward the wall in a way that made Katie think he knew a lot about it. "Anyway, it's nothing for a nice kid like you to worry about."

"Hell, no," Buck said. "It's no one's business."

Buck finished another beer, his food, and a cup of coffee. Turner had left them to wait on the people who had come in, a group Buck nodded to, a group Katie could feel staring at them.

"We're going to the big city tomorrow," Buck told Turner as he paid the bill. He always called Great Falls the big city.

"Taking up a load of fat cattle, aye?"

"That's right, me and my partner here." They said good-bye to Turner and nodded to the group, who stared again.

"Nice seeing you, Buck," a woman wearing several large

pieces of turquoise jewelry said to him. She winked then and he smiled.

Who was that? Katie wondered.

"Ted Michaelson's wife," her father said, as though he'd heard the question.

CHAPTER
TWENTY TWO

After he was certain that Katie had gone to sleep, Buck put on his jacket and hat and drove down to Maggie's.

"Honey, I'm so glad you came," Maggie said, shutting the door behind him. "It's been an awful day," she said, kissing his face and neck.

"Hey, calm down," he said. "What's wrong?"

"Joey keeps crying for Charlie. The toilet's backed up again. My car wouldn't start. And I miss you." She began to cry.

"Come on," he said, guiding her into the bedroom. "Everything will be all right. Just relax," he told her, massaging her back. Her skin was soft, young. There was something lean and needy about Maggie, something physically irresistible.

"Honey," she said after he had made love to her. She was barely touching the back of his neck with long, gentle strokes of her fingertips. It was so soothing to him he was touched somehow.

"Ummm," he said, not wanting to talk, just to sleep.

"Are you listening?"

"Uh huh."

"Are you going to marry me?" she asked, now feeling his earlobe.

"Sweetheart," he said. "I thought we agreed to take our time."

"You haven't told Pearl yet, have you?"

"Told her what?"

"That you love me."

Buck was silent. He sat up, the mood he'd been in gone. No, he hadn't told Pearl. It was not something he could explain to Maggie but he was attached to Pearl. He liked her. He wasn't ready to give her up. Something in him needed her, even if whatever it was he needed wasn't enough.

Buck dressed, a little annoyed now by the whole predicament he found himself in. He hadn't prepared for this to go so far. And it wouldn't have if that goddamned Charlie hadn't left. Everyone took affairs so seriously. They could never see them as the diversions they should be. You didn't have to break up homes over them.

He went to the kitchen and got out what was left of Charlie's whiskey. Maggie followed him.

"Don't drink, honey," she said. "Come back to bed and talk to me."

Ignoring her, he sat at the kitchen table. She hesitated, pulled her robe tight, and sat down too.

"I know you don't want to hurt Pearl. I didn't want to hurt Charlie either. But it can't go on like this."

He filled his glass.

"Don't you want ice?" she said and went to the refrigerator.

Buck had nothing to say. He was being pulled apart by women. The two of them, Maggie and Pearl, had hold of his balls and were yanking.

He refilled his glass. Now, because Maggie was alone, he was obligated in some way. He couldn't abandon her. He wasn't a complete asshole.

"But almost," he said aloud.

"What?" Maggie asked.

"Nothing," he said.

She put some ice in his glass and brought him some water that she ended up drinking herself.

"It could be so good for us," she said shyly.

He looked at her. She was so little, so collapsible, it scared him.

"Cheer up," he said. "I'll take a look at your car."

He went out to his pickup and got jumper cables and started Maggie's car. He left it running and went to the garage for a plumber's snake that he knew Charlie kept there. He took the snake to the house and then ran it down the toilet, twisting it until the toilet flushed easily.

"Do you think the septic tank's full?" Maggie asked.

"Couldn't be," he said, recalling that he had helped Charlie put in a new one just before Alma died. "This one should last another ten years at least."

"You better not put any more paper down it, though," he said when he was done. "Tomorrow I'll bring down some stuff to flush out the pipes and keep the bacteria working. I better get going."

"You have to go?" she said.

"You know I do. Katie's alone."

"Why didn't she go with Pearl?"

That same voice. He didn't answer, didn't feel he had to. The truth was he'd wanted Katie to stay. She was good for him. Or maybe he just wanted an excuse to go home where it was peaceful, where Maggie couldn't work on him and break him down.

"I'm sorry," she said. "Will I see you tomorrow?"

"We're hauling cattle tomorrow."

"Tomorrow night then?"

"Sure," he said, feeling suddenly sorry for her. She was simply helpless sometimes.

"Try not to worry," he said, holding her gently before he left. "I promise I'll take care of you." He'd said it, and while it satisfied her, he already regretted it.

He'd forgotten that Maggie's car was still running. It was almost out of gas and he turned it off. Well, that would be the next crisis; she'd run out of gas and call him. Buck slammed the door of the pickup and sat there in the dark. Maggie had turned off the lights in the kitchen. He had lived this scene before many times, sitting here in the dark watching the lights in this house go out. When? With Charlie, as kids, drinking beer after a ball game probably. He just couldn't remember. Only it was Charlie's mother Alma putting out the kerosene lamps then. Jesus, if Alma were alive she'd whale on him good. He started the pickup, not wanting to even consider what Alma would do. He was guilty as hell.

He couldn't shake the irritation he felt. Maggie, so whiny sometimes. Women threw themselves at you with everything they had—tough as nails, he'd think. But then it turned out they had more they needed from you than they ever planned to give back. It was never enough to love them or reassure them. They wanted inside and to own something there. All of them did it. Pearl too. Her unforgiving silence one minute and biting sarcasm the next was driving him away. Even Alma, long dead, seemed to be demanding something of him from her grave. He imagined her looking at him as she had when he was a kid, a shrewd look that said you were no more than a piece of shit. Sometimes women just pissed him off.

The irony of it all was that Charlie turned out to be the lucky one. He was out of it.

CHAPTER
TWENTY THREE

———————◆———————

It was dawn when they climbed the fence into the feedlot. Buck had already decided which animals looked the most ready and together they moved in and separated them one by one from the others. Katie was always amazed at how easily he approached large cattle, maneuvering them effortlessly with waving arms and expertly timed commands. War whoops were probably more what they were. But she was terrified that they might run her down because they, too, were afraid; that and their size made them clumsy. She held a long stick in her hand as if it could hold them back. She felt the warmth of their large bodies as they passed, brushing her with shedding hair that hadn't been shiny since the day their mothers licked them dry. This hair, Angus black or Hereford red for the most part, was matted with waste, waste that got so deep in the feedlot it had to be shoveled out with a Caterpillar each spring and piled in high mounds to dry.

Katie shook her stick furiously at the last of the load, a nervous Hereford steer that started to turn in the narrow chute and run back toward her. She screamed and jumped up on the fence, hoping her legs were high enough to keep from getting crushed. Buck came up behind her, laughing, and the steer went back through the chute and up the ramp to the truck.

"You always forget that they're more afraid of you than you are of them," he said.

Katie was hot and tired from the running and the fear. The sun was bright by now and she knew in a few weeks the mound of waste from the feedlot would steam with an odor so penetrating no one for miles around would hang out laundry. And it wouldn't stop smelling until the hot, dry winds of summer had beaten out all the moisture, until nothing was left but dark, rich loam—just what the soil needed but never got because of the difficulty and expense of spreading the stuff.

"Hey, Katie! You coming?"

Her father was already in the truck and impatient to start the eighty-mile drive to Great Falls. They drove in silence down the lane, then the eighteen miles of gravel to the narrow highway that was always crowded with semis and grain trucks.

"We'll be able to take the yearlings up to the mountains next month," he said, breaking the silence. "You'll like that."

This was the one job Katie looked forward to; she loved the mountains. The year before there had still been a lot of snow, but Neihart Creek was running and the grass was up. They had driven the calves on horseback over the ridge not too far from Kings Hill, where they skied sometimes. They ambled for hours, the air fresh with still wet pine and tiny purple flowers. When they were done her father had mixed hot water and whiskey in large mugs, hers weak but still able to make her shoulders tingle. They stayed overnight in a little cabin with a drafty outhouse. Charlie and Maggie had come, too, but because of the kids, had gone home right after dinner. Pa had continued drinking long after they had gone and typically there had been a fight.

"You always drink until there's none left," Mama had said.

"Don't be a bitch," he'd answered.

"Sure quiet today," Buck said then, interrupting Katie's thoughts.

"I was just thinking," she said. "Do you suppose Maggie will still come with us now that Charlie's gone?"

"Naw," he said. "I doubt she'd be too interested in that."

"Why not?" Katie asked. But he was frowning at something up ahead. They were coming down Bootleg Hill and a jack-knifed semi in the right lane made him concentrate on slowing the truck without causing the load to shift. Katie was aware now of the cattle moving behind the cab, a rolling, noisy movement as they pawed the truck bed and rocked the sides of the bulging stock rack. All she could think about were the horror stories she knew about shifting loads coming through truck cabs and was relieved when he was able to slow down and pass the semi.

The sun was now glaring on the small hills of farmland and pasture, still frozen with snow and barren of color except for the bluish tint of sagebrush that stuck out in ragged clumps. Soon they could see Great Falls. They passed the Air Force base and the tract homes that had sprung up everywhere east of town on more of the same pasture.

She helped unload the cattle at the packing plant. They bawled and balked the same way they did when taken from their mothers, sensing now the greater loss as they moved in a tight huddle into the old brick building. Katie waited for her father by the holding pens, transfixed by the flow of waste coming out a chute on the side of the building into a large dumpster. Her stomach tightened at the combination of odors, of death and scorching hide and hair, of hot blood and chemicals.

"They'll grade high," he said with pride when he came out of the building. They returned to the truck hurriedly. It was almost noon and he wanted to cross town to get a load of feed supplement before the traffic got heavy.

Katie sat up behind the cab on the top board of the stock rack and watched as her father and another man loaded large sacks of beet pulp into the back end of the cattle truck. The manure left by the cattle was all getting pushed to the end below her and she climbed back down. She got in the cab while her father paid the man.

"Let's go over to The Stockman's," he said at the filling station while they waited for gas.

"We're awful dirty," Katie said, inspecting their clothes for mud and manure.

"But not too dirty for a movie, right?" His tone was the same one he used for her mother. His words, in fact, would be the same too. Katie knew that she had now become, by some wrinkle in the family fabric, the one he yelled at instead of Mama.

"Can we get a sandwich first?" Katie could hear her stomach growling.

"We'll eat later. I want to catch Hank before he takes off."

But Hank was behind the bar when they arrived, waiting on a beer distributor who bought the house a round. Seated at the bar were an old man who stared into his glass and Hank's wife, Helen, who was chatting nonstop to a man fixing the pinball machine.

Hank greeted them and without asking Buck what he wanted to drink, drew him a beer. Katie always needed time to adjust, not only to the dimness but to the tavern odor. She remembered the smell, remembered it as a young child peering into the cool, dark bars as she trailed behind her mother down some street, passing doors open and inviting on a hot summer day. But the smell—smoky, stale, and a little sour—always made her turn back to the heat of the street to catch up to her mother.

"Are we still going fishing?" Hank asked Buck.

"You bet. Let's avoid the jetbutts and go the weekend after opening. There's a spot up in the Judiths I want to try."

Katie paid close attention as the two men planned. Hank

would bring bourbon and something to chase it with. Her father would tie flies and bring bacon, steaks, and Mama's homemade bread. They'd take Buck's pickup, Hank would buy the gas. They relished their anticipation as they would the trip. The real enjoyment would come in retrospect, next year, perhaps, in this bar or another.

Hank's wife came over now and sat down on the other side of Buck, tossing her curly hair as she settled herself, arranging her cigarettes, ashtray, and drink, pointing out to him how an ash had melted a hole in her good pants. She wore a western-style shirt, satin with stitching around the yoke. Hank wore a similar shirt and shiny pants cut to fit over his clean tan boots. Katie remembered that Charlie called it the Nashville look once and Pa had laughed.

Helen and Buck were now engrossed in a conversation Katie couldn't hear; Hank ran across the street to the bank to deposit cash from the night before. Katie listened to the music, holding her glass at the top when she sipped so the pop, her third, wouldn't get too warm.

"Aren't you young to be in here?" the old man two seats to her right asked her.

"Yeah," she said. "I'm just waiting for my father."

"Easter vacation, huh?" he said. "What's your name?"

Encouraged by his friendliness, Katie answered his questions, the ones he didn't answer himself.

"Why do people live in this god-awful country anyway? Damned if I know," he said and began to explain why he'd left Montana once and gone to California. He was barely audible, as if it didn't matter if she heard and as though he'd told it a hundred times before. He seemed to reminisce for his own sake, to get clear on some ambiguity contained there in that singular and consequential event.

Katie felt annoyed. Her father and Helen always had too much to talk about and none of it ever included her. Besides, she was starved. Hank returned and smiled at her and brought her over some beer nuts.

"So why are you here?" Katie asked the old man. When he looked startled by the question, she added, "You know, here in Montana instead of California."

"Oh," he said. "I came back."

"How come?"

"I don't know." He seemed confused.

"Helen's going to make a burger run," Buck announced to everyone. It was almost four and some of the early shift from the smelter were coming in.

"Pa, can't we go?" Katie said. "If we don't hurry, we'll miss the previews." She was feeling sick from all the pop.

"Tell you what, honey," Buck said, getting up from the stool to put his arm around her. "In a little while we'll all go over to Eddie's Club and get a steak. We can go to the movie later." He patted her shoulder. "So don't be a nag now." He turned back to Helen then.

"Katie gets crabby when she's hungry."

"Then feed her," Helen said.

"You're the one who was going for food," he said, annoyed.

The bar was filling up now. Hank was busy with the orders coming in—two Luckys, three Olys and a shot, a pitcher of light. The barmaid had peroxide streaks in her hair and was wearing a short outfit that reminded Katie of the baton twirlers who led the parade to the fairgrounds each summer when the county fair opened. Katie watched her tap her foot absentmindedly to the music while she waited for the orders.

Katie realized the old man was talking to her. "Pardon?"

"I said I came back because I thought things would be better." He said it seemingly unaware of any time passing since her question of twenty minutes ago. "I figured my wife had missed me." He stared at the line of beers in front of him. "Thought I'd get a better job."

Katie stared at his beers too. Why did Hank bring him another one every time someone ordered a round when he already had three?

"I thought things would get better," he said again, looking directly at her now. There was something about his eyes that made Katie feel like crying.

"Did they?"

"Nope. Never did. My wife found some miner from Butte and moved away. Couldn't get another job with the railroad and had to go to work at the zinc plant."

"Why didn't you leave again?" she asked.

"By then I was too tired."

"Too tired?"

"Yes. Too damn tired."

The old man appeared exhausted now. They sat in silence, staring again. He had forgotten her.

Katie wished she had thought to bring her English book. She had some sentences to diagram by Monday. She tried to think how to rewrite the letter for Social Studies her teacher had told her to do over. She had written "Dear Mr. Khrushchev, Do you really hate America? If so, why? Is there something bad about us I don't know about?" Her teacher didn't like it and said to stick to questions about agricultural reform.

Now Buck was talking to Hank and she heard him order her some more beer nuts. Apparently Helen heard him too.

"Give the kid some money to go get a hamburger," she said, dropping off dirty glasses at the bar.

"If she can be patient for a few more minutes, I'll go with her," he told Helen.

"She's been patient, you old fart," Helen said.

"There's a place down the block," Hank said. "She'll be all right."

"Oh what the hell," her father said. "Get me something too." He took money out of his pocket and handed Katie a twenty.

"Wear your old man's coat," Helen said, looking at her windbreaker. "It's damn cold." Without a word to Buck, Helen pulled his jacket off the back of his bar stool.

"Jesus, woman," he said to Helen. "How do you put up with her?" he asked Hank.

Katie walked a couple of blocks to a café and ordered two cheeseburgers and fries to go. While she waited, she watched a group of girls about her age laughing over some photographs they passed back and forth. How nice it would be to live in a town and have friends down the street.

Katie sat down to eat. She wanted to warm up before walking back in the cold wind. She put her father's sandwich inside her jacket to keep it warm. If only she could persuade him to go home. The thing was that by now he probably wouldn't be able to drive.

Katie was in no hurry and picked at her fries, making designs on them with ketchup. When Mama wasn't around, her father had absolutely no sense. The waitress came by and Katie ordered a piece of apple pie though she was full. She inspected the contents of her father's pockets: matches, the receipt from the meat packers, the keys to the truck. She ate half of the pie and began scratching her initials on the table with the keys. When the waitress glared at her, she put the keys away and went to pay.

There were no empty seats at the bar when Katie got back and the old man was gone. Buck was laughing loudly about something and she put his sandwich on the bar.

"Thanks, honey," he said. "Want you to meet some folks." He pushed her towards the people he'd been talking to.

"This is my kid," he said and put his arm around her. "She's one hell of a cowhand." He patted Katie on the butt and she moved away from him, annoyed. But he didn't seem to notice. "Should have seen this little lady today with the meanest, fattest sons-a-bitching cattle you ever saw. She can push 'em around like nobody's business."

Katie listened, fascinated yet horrified to hear this version of the day's events. She had been altered, made to fit.

"Let's go, Pa," she said.

"What's the matter?"

"I want to go home."

He laughed. "I'm just going to tell them this one story I heard and then we'll go. He turned back to his new friends. "Just like her ma, always bitchy when she wants to go." Katie groaned and went to the restroom.

"And hell if Charlie didn't plant barley on it," Katie heard him say when she returned. He went on talking but Katie couldn't hear him.

"Katie," he yelled, turning to her. "What the hell's the name of that fool calf that used to follow Charlie around?"

"Course, that ain't nothing compared to how Katie followed Charlie around," he added. "Ain't that right, Katie?" He smiled. "Come on, tell these folks the name of that fool calf."

"I didn't follow Charlie around. He asked me," she said. The comparison made her sick, and it was all she could do to keep from crying.

The calf was one Katie had seen Charlie pull from its dying mother. It was a sorry-looking thing, a runt too wet and shivering even to stand or bleat. Charlie wrapped it in an old blanket, braced it between his legs and suckled it with rags dipped in warm milk. The heifer followed him around any chance it got, even when it was grown.

"Katie's mad now," her father said laughing. She turned her back on him.

"I'm sorry," he said. "Promise, I'll just eat this sandwich and we'll go."

He put out his cigarette, picked up the sandwich and turned to his friends. Absentmindedly Katie stared at his change and at the tobacco pouch beside it. The pouch! She picked it up and looked at it, as if seeing it for the first time. She put it in her pocket and walked out the back door.

Katie stood in the cold darkness for some time, trying to make sense of it all. She figured he must have gotten the pouch back from Maggie last night after she had gone to bed. Yet all day long he'd used that silly gauze thing. And to think that once she had wanted that pouch more than she wanted anything. She had even asked her grandfather if she could have it.

"What the hell for?" he'd asked loudly as if she couldn't hear him.

It was just the right size to carry little stuff in, like the arrowheads she found where the mushrooms grew or the small rocks she liked to paint faces on.

"Marbles," she told him.

"As soon as I'm done with it, it's yours." But after he died her father began using it and she said nothing.

Katie was shivering but she continued to stand there. Finally it occurred to her what to do. She climbed up the side of the stock rack on the truck, her shoes searching for places between the slats. She could dimly see the sacks of supplement piled behind the cab and she knew that the weight of the sacks had squashed all the manure to this end. Its stench plus the ammonia smell of urine was lifted to her nose every few seconds by the wind. She took the keys and money out of the coat pocket and put them into one in her jeans. Next, she threw the old tobacco pouch as hard as she could into the manure, then took off her father's jacket and dropped it in too.

The next thing Katie knew, she was in the truck headed toward the highway. She had never driven this big of a truck before and she had to sit on the edge of the seat close to the steering wheel. She felt excited. But that soon turned to worry when she realized she did not have enough gas to make it home. The road was almost deserted. So far she'd seen only two other vehicles, both going in the opposite direction toward town. The night seemed unusually dark and she guessed that it was cloudy. Katie dared not take her eyes from the road to study the sky though because it was only her concentration, her will to stay on the road, that kept her from tumbling off onto either side into the ditch. Her hands were stiff and stuck to two sweaty portions of the steering wheel. She was exhausted.

Katie ran out of gas east of Raynesford and, relieved, loosened her grip on the wheel and coasted over onto the shoulder. She tried to sleep. Her stomach growled and she was cold. A vehicle passed and shook the truck. Her mind went from one image to another: a cop tapping on the window wanting to know what in the hell a kid was doing out alone on the highway in a cattle truck; then it was her father, sad and puzzled, asking her why she had thrown his stuff into the cow shit; then just as quickly it was Mama demanding to know what all was going on here.

None of it was real. It was stuff she dreamed or maybe imagined. Only the cold was real, the cold and her father now banging on the window were real, the cold and her father and the sun coming up over the hills—these things were real.

She unlocked the door and it swung open.

"What in God's name do you think you're doing?" her father yelled. He pulled her out of the truck and slapped her across the face. It crossed her mind that slaps stung more when the skin was cold. Or did they? She searched her memory for comparisons, leisurely, as if thought and motion had slowed now.

Her father let go of her as suddenly as he had taken hold of her and she went sprawling across the gravel of the shoulder bed, the sensation of slow motion gone.

"Take it easy there. You're going to hurt her." It was Hank. He pulled her to her feet and brushed her off. She could smell liquor on his breath.

"The goddamn thing's out of gas!" her father yelled. He was now trying to start the truck.

"Calm down. We'll go get some," Hank told him.

Her father was still furious, and he slammed the truck door. He got into Hank's car and slammed that door too. Hank opened the back door for her and nodded at her to get in.

No one said another word. She was stiff, and now her leg was bleeding from being scraped across the gravel. She marveled that though her leg was cut, her pants had not torn. She was shaking from the cold and could not warm up, though the sun coming through the window felt good to her. Her father did not acknowledge her presence except to twice turn and look at her in disgust. And though otherwise he moved only to light one cigarette after another, he seemed to be bouncing up and down on the seat in agitation.

Katie cracked the window despite the cold. She could have headed west instead of home. She should have filled up with gas first thing and then gotten on the road to Spokane. She should have gone to find Charlie. That's what she should've done. And when she found him she could have asked him all the questions on her mind: Are you okay? Is it true about Maggie and Pa? Is that why you left? Will you ever come back? Did I follow you around like Pa says or did you want me there?

"How about some breakfast?" Hank said now and pulled into the truck stop at Raynesford.

CHAPTER
TWENTY FOUR

Pearl called late one night not long after the trip to Billings with unexpected news. "I've been thinking," she said. "If you still want Katie to come for the summer, it's okay."

"Of course I do," Etta said, not daring to ask why the change of heart. They talked briefly; Pearl sounded worried or tired.

"So it's all right with Katie?" Etta asked her.

"I guess so. I didn't expect her to agree but she did."

Etta suspected something had happened. Pearl, however, was not going to say what. She had stopped confiding in Etta. But this time, Etta didn't care. Katie was coming for the summer; it didn't matter why.

But then a week later, Pearl called back. "Listen," she said. "Katie is driving me nuts. She either stays cooped up in her room, or she stomps around the house complaining about everything."

"How come?"

"I don't know. She and Buck must have gotten into a fight while we were gone. They've hardly said a word to each other. You were right, we should have taken her with us."

"She'll be okay."

"I hope so." There was a pause then and Pearl sighed. "Listen, are you sure you can handle her? She can be a brat, you know."

"I'm sure." Now Etta paused, knowing her next question might irritate Pearl. "Are you sure you don't want to come too?"

"I'm sure," Pearl said decisively.

Etta spent the end of April and most of May fixing up the house. She painted her parents' old room for Katie, had the floors sanded, and bought an area rug and matching spread. She had the chimney cleaned, the screen door repaired, and the hedges trimmed.

Pleased by the improvements, she then bought a mirror for the hallway and a new runner for the staircase. She even spent a day in the attic. She went through everything — a trunk of old clothes, old receipts in a tin box, a basket of buttons. She hauled a fan with a bent blade and an old broken sewing machine out to the garbage.

Etta found boxes of pictures — of Harold; some of her and Pearl as skinny, gawky kids; Katie as a baby, a toddler, a preschooler; old boyfriends, and even one of Buck taken in the backyard. There were more — Leona's kids at various ages and all Katie's school pictures too — and Etta mounted them in a scrapbook she bought at the dime store, writing a note under each with names and probable dates. But instead of putting the finished scrapbook on the coffee table as planned, she put it in a box back in the attic. She found it depressed her for some reason.

The next day Etta was still depressed. She called in sick and wandered around the house in her bathrobe. She sat on the couch and leafed through old magazines. Then she went out to the kitchen to look for something to eat. But what she found either didn't appeal to her or looked too old to still be edible. Finally she got a Fudgsicle out of the icebox and took it to the bathroom to eat in the tub while she soaked.

When the water got chilly, Etta dried off and went to her room to dress. She looked through the closet for some time and, unable to decide on what to wear, slammed the closet door in disgust and put her robe back on. She went back downstairs and got the mail. There were no letters, just a magazine with an article explaining how to turn a front porch into a sunroom and she sat down with that. Etta turned on the radio. She flipped back and forth across the various stations but there was more talk than music and then she accidentally knocked the radio off the table. Etta thought it was probably broken because now all she got was static. She unplugged it but didn't bother picking it up; instead, she threw the magazine with the article on porches into a nearby wastebasket.

By now it was about four o'clock. Suddenly the idea of dropping the radio amused her. It had been the only act of consequence thus far that day. Etta decided the next should be to take herself out to dinner. She liked the idea.

She went back up to her bedroom to dress. This time she opened the closet with her eyes shut and swung her hand back and forth in front of her neatly hanging clothes. On the count of ten, she let it fall. And what her fingers first touched, in this case a green pleated skirt, she pulled out. She found a sweater to match in the bureau and dressed. Etta spent more time than usual on her hair and makeup as if preparing for something special. By the time she got into her car, she was humming.

Etta had two places in mind—Vito's on the west side or Barney's downtown. She flipped a coin, knowing indecision now might throw her back into depression. Tails. She headed downtown.

Etta asked for a booth. Apparently it was too early for most diners, because the place was empty. She looked over the menu and the waitress went to get her a glass of wine.

"How about the veal and dumplings?" the waitress said when she returned to find that Etta still hadn't made up her mind.

"Fine," Etta said. "And a pot of tea."

Etta congratulated herself for coming up with such a good

idea and thought next she might take herself to a movie. She even smiled at a man walking toward her who'd just come in. Then she realized she knew him.

"Etta! Do you remember me?"

"Wally Evans. I sure do."

"How long has it been?"

"A few years," he said. "I've been living in Havre."

"Yes, I think I heard that," she said.

"But I'll be back for good next month."

"Business brings you home, huh?"

He nodded. He stood there, maybe unsure what to do next. "Are you with someone?"

"No," she said.

"Mind if I join you?"

"Please do," she said, glad for the company. Glad for his company, for she remembered him fondly. At one time she'd had a crush on him. She even went out with him once. She might have been fifteen or sixteen. She tried to remember why they hadn't ever really gotten together.

"So tell me," he said. "Are you married?"

"Widowed," she said.

"Sorry," he said.

"Well it's been quite a while now. How about you?"

"Divorced."

"You were married to Phyllis Brand," she blurted out. The name had just come to her.

"Right," he said. "But let's talk about you." He signaled the waitress. "When I knew you, you were working after school at that hat shop on Central."

"Molly's Millinery," Etta said and laughed. "And you worked down the block at the sporting-goods store."

"And on Saturdays you always ate at that lunch counter on the corner."

"How did you know?"

"Because I used to watch you walk in there every Saturday morning."

"For heaven's sake," Etta said. It was true. She always went early so she could get the corner table by the window.

The waitress came over now and he declined the menu. "I'll have whatever she's having," he said and turned back to Etta.

"Even after I was married, I used to think about you."

"No kidding," Etta said and smiled shyly. For some reason, she felt foolish. Maybe because he was so nice looking. He had the oddest shade of hazel eyes and perhaps—she debated this—a perfect chin.

"Say," he said. "I know this is short notice and all, but there's a great film at the Civic. You interested?"

"I'd love to," she said.

They were early for the movie and Etta suggested a walk. It was balmy and they strolled several blocks and even walked through the train depot. There was no one there but an old man sweeping up and Etta led the way back outside. They still had a half-hour to wait when they got to the theatre. They took seats upstairs in the loges.

"I remember our date," he said seriously. "It was one of those perfect evenings."

"Oh yeah?" she said. "What did we do?"

"We went to a ball game."

"Yes," she said. "Your friend Eddy was playing shortstop."

"Right. Then we went to that place by the park and had sodas."

"The White Spot," she said.

"Then we walked back to the park," he said and touched her shoulder lightly. "Remember, we sat by the pond?"

Etta felt a little uncomfortable now. Yes, she remembered that. And that they had made out. They had, in fact, ended up wrestling around on the grass behind some benches, sort of arguing their way through a very unsatisfying bit of lovemaking, as she recalled. A picture came to mind of his jeans and her skirt all tangled up and damp with dew. She had felt foolish then too. She had gone home satisfied for other reasons nonetheless. She was in love. But he'd never asked her out again. Etta blushed, recalling her confusion.

"Let's go there just for fun sometime."

Etta must have looked doubtful or surprised because he quickly amended the comment. "Don't get me wrong," he said. "I just thought it would be nice to sit by the pond. I hear there's flower beds all around there now."

She relaxed again but said nothing.

"You know I really had a thing for you in those days." He took her hand. Etta remembered now what she'd liked about him. He had this boyish smile that was disarming. Once he'd come into the shop to pick up a package for his mother and had put on some hats to amuse her while he waited for a hatbox to be brought up from storage. He had smiled at her from under a bright red felt tam the way he was smiling at her now.

"I used to hang around on the corner after work hoping to catch you walking home."

She laughed. Sometimes he'd have a little bag of peanuts or gumdrops and he would fill her hand while he talked, never eating any himself. And often he'd walk backward up the street, talking to her as he did. "That fool boy's going to walk into a store window if he don't watch where he's going," Miss Molly had commented once.

"Then I finally got the nerve to ask you out."

"I never thought of you as shy," Etta said.

"Just with you," he said. "I always heard John Potter talking about you and thought you'd never go out with me."

"John Potter?"

"Yeah, you remember. He worked at the gas station on Fifth." Etta had a faint memory of someone tall with a short, thick neck.

"He talked about you all the time."

"He did?"

"Yeah. I suppose he had a thing for you too."

Etta smiled at the thought of someone she couldn't even recall having liked her. She looked over at Wally. Funny, she thought, this morning she was depressed and now she felt grateful just to be alive. She smiled at that thought too.

"What are you smiling about?" he asked.

"Nothing really," she said.

"Anyway," he said. "I should have married you and had a fling with Phyllis. You know, instead of the other way around," he added.

"The other way around?"

"Yeah, you know. I shouldn't have worried about all that nice girl crap."

"All what nice girl crap?"

"You know, all that stuff about marrying a nice girl."

Etta was dumbfounded. Wally went on nervously. "Now, I've upset you. Hey, I'm sorry. I didn't mean anything."

"That's why you never asked me out again? Because I wasn't a *nice* girl?"

"Etta, I didn't mean that. Of course, you were nice. But you know how guys were in those days."

"No, how were guys?"

"What I mean is I should never have listened to John Potter."

"John Potter! What's this got to do with John Potter?"

"Well, you know. He was always going on about you."

"What about me?"

"You know, about your reputation."

Etta was silent.

"Let's not talk about this anymore. I've upset you and I'm sorry."

Etta felt numb. She thought Wally said something about popcorn and she shook her head and he got up. She remained sitting there. The lights blinked and went out. Music started. Heavy velvet curtains parted at center stage and swung rapidly to the sides, not at all the graceful way she'd seen these curtains open before.

There were several previews or maybe a newsreel and the movie might have started. She must have sat there for some time—or maybe no time passed—before it occurred to her to get up and go home. She wasn't even aware of passing through the lobby on the way out and would not have noticed whether Wally Evans stood in a line for popcorn or not. The next thing she knew she was in bed with a magazine as if she'd never left bed the whole day.

But sometime during the night, she awoke able to recall the cut of the suit Mamie Eisenhower had worn in the newsreel, every store window she'd seen on her way to the car, and that she had dropped her house keys on the back porch. And what's more, she thought over everything she could have said to Wally Evans.

She could have said, "How is it that two people, male and female, can get together in certain ways that change her and not him?" No. "How come what we did made me not nice and you . . ." No. "Why is it that what I did with you gave me a reputation while you just . . ." No. "How does it work that I had a reputation while you merely had a fling?"

Etta spent the rest of the night constructing and reconstructing what she might have said. That and trying to remember who in the hell John Potter was.

The next day, Etta told her boss she was taking the summer off.

"You mean you're asking if you can?" he said.

"Right, I'm asking if I may," she said.

"Sure," he said. "Take a trip around the world. Get married. Live it up."

She ignored the sarcasm. "Well, no," she said. "My niece is going to stay with me."

"I thought she was a teenager."

"She is."

"And you can't have her stay with you and still come to work?"

"I could, but I don't want to."

"Well make sure Beatrice can fill in," he said.

Etta was restless and spent the morning organizing her desk. She called Beatrice, who now came in on Tuesdays and Thursdays, and arranged for her to work full-time over the summer.

"This will be great," Beatrice said. "I won't have to stay home and listen to the kids fighting all summer." Etta hung up, puzzled. She couldn't imagine preferring this boring office to a yard full of kids.

Since she was tired and nothing much was going on, Etta decided to go home right after lunch. She told her boss her plans. He just looked at her. She ignored him and got her purse and sweater. She thought he started to say something so she paused in the doorway. But he only continued to stare at her with a funny look on his face. He probably wanted to fire her, she thought, and didn't have the nerve. Finally she waved to him and closed the door behind her.

When Etta got home, she was still restless and decided to do some yard work. She raked up all the dead winter grass around the house and sprinkled grass seed in areas that had become paths to the garage or alley and in shady spots where snow had lain all winter, melting finally into muddy holes.

"The fertilizer is coming tomorrow," she told Jenny, who had wandered over after school. Jenny was now watering the new seed for her.

"Do you remember Katie?" Etta asked her when they were through. Katie hadn't really seen much of Jenny and her family the last several years.

"Sure, your niece."

"Well, she's coming to stay the summer. Do you think you could show her around? Maybe introduce her to other kids?"

"Sure."

Etta smiled at her. They were standing on Etta's porch steps now. Jenny was growing up. She was a nice kid and Etta was fond of her.

"I forgot. I came over to tell you that Mom wants you to come for dinner."

"All right. Thanks. Tell her I'll be over about six."

She watched Jenny cut across to her yard, kicking at a ragged baseball that they had found in the hedge. In Jenny, in that whole family, Etta saw hope. There had been a stubborn reluctance over the years to give in to trouble and it had paid off. Leona and those kids had put up with more from George than they should ever have had to, but slowly, surely, it had changed him. And if he could change, anyone could.

Etta sat down on the porch swing, her mind still on George and Leona. It was as though Leona, Pearl too, by daring the possibility of misery, had learned how to get life by the throat and shake it. In some courageous way, they both had refused to be intimidated.

It was Etta who, fearing change or doing anything wrong, did nothing. She had avoided all conflict, had taken no risks. And she never got excited, really excited, about anything anymore. The last several years she'd lost interest in most things, things like her job, the house, traveling, dating.

She used to enjoy dating; she'd even liked having a steady boyfriend. Well, for a time. That is, until a peculiar moment when something always repulsed her. She'd go happily along, enjoying some guy's company, not planning marriage exactly but at least looking as far down the road as a fishing trip the next summer or an upcoming holiday. But then the guy would touch her a certain way, or have some silly look on his face, or perhaps criticize her for something. She was never certain what it was that made her turn away to remember that she had letters to write, laundry to do, a lawn to mow—a life to get on with that now, for sudden and unknown reasons, would no longer include this man, this stranger (at this point, no matter how well she'd known him, he became a stranger), and the sooner he left, the better. He would be confused, of course, and then angry.

"Why did you do this to me?" a boyfriend once asked her.

"Do what?"

"Lead me on?"

Had she? She didn't know. In fact, she didn't know what that meant—leading him on. But it suggested paths, routes, crosswalks, someone at her heels.

My God. It was incredible what an insignificant and uneventful life she had. She had clothed herself in the merest rags of experience, protecting herself with a philosophy that shut out encounter. She had reasoned her way into safety that allowed no exposure to anything without guarantees. It was why the scrapbook had saddened her. Her own history had become a collection of prints, the sum of the number of recordings of small moments in other people's lives.

As her mother used to say, it was a rude awakening.

CHAPTER

TWENTY FIVE

Aunt Etta said this was to be Katie's room for now, that the next-door neighbor Jenny, if Katie recalled, was the same age, and that everything that looked for the moment like hell in her life was bound to turn out fine—the last reference, no doubt, to Katie's parents and why she was there.

Katie unpacked her things, several pairs of jeans and sweatshirts, T-shirts and shorts, a swimming suit Mama said she would need. The room was exactly to her liking. She'd napped there before when she was younger, had even stored toys in the window-seat box. It was a nice place to sit because the trees practically came through the window, rustling ever so slightly against the screen. She preferred the nestling of trees to the view of wide space she was accustomed to. Katie liked the blue-gray color of the walls, the light airy feeling there, the pine floors that shone.

"Katie," Aunt Etta called from the staircase. "Dinner is ready, dear."

They sat primly and formally at the table: teacups, no mugs; china, no Melmac. Katie could tell there would be no loud discussions at the table, no gossip, no arguing.

Aunt Etta said a brief grace and urged her to begin.

"Your Aunt Etta," Katie's father had reminded her on the way there, "is weird—one of those religious fanatics. But," he said, "I don't suppose it'll hurt you any."

Since Easter vacation her father had acted as if she, too, were strange, he might even have felt she got it from Etta. It wasn't that he held anything against her, forgiveness or not was never a question with Pa. It was more that some things he understood, others he didn't.

The next day they had breakfast on the screened porch. Tea rolls and bacon, fresh strawberries. As if by prior arrangement, Jenny from next door joined them and asked Katie if she would like to go swimming. Katie agreed to meet her later and was immediately sorry. She went to her room and dug out the swimsuit. It was a ragged, dingy thing she hadn't worn in some time. It was too small. Katie felt as if she'd run up against something very complicated, a world she was unprepared for.

"Katie," Aunt Etta said, peering from the doorway at the sorry-looking suit. "That will never fit. We'll go shopping."

Aunt Etta was definitely a proper sort, yet there was a quality of savvy about her that surprised Katie. She knew exactly which suit Katie wanted. It was blue and had two narrow red stripes on the left side.

"Makes you look nice and slim," Aunt Etta said, as if Katie could have looked otherwise.

"Too flat," Katie said, wiggling the bodice that could stand by itself. In fact, she could suck in her chest to make the top of the suit stand away from her body several inches.

"Plenty of time to fill out," Aunt Etta said. "Plenty of time." On the way home she began the first of the little talks she would give Katie from time to time all summer.

"Katie, you do know why your mother let you come here, don't you? She loves you and feels you're too isolated out there and that you're missing out. She wants you to meet kids your own age, do things kids do. You see that, don't you?"

"Yes," Katie said, knowing that the real reason she was there was that she had frightened her father when she took the truck—though he hadn't told her mother about it—and these days everything she did disturbed her mother. They no longer knew what to do with her, what to say to her. Not that adults ever knew what to say. It was pretty obvious that when they told each other anything, it was carefully selected and didn't have to be true. Just as well, she guessed. Sometimes it worked to her advantage.

Katie and Jenny walked all the way to the pool. Jenny was talkative and questioning, pointing out places of interest all the way.

"Will you miss your parents?" she asked.

"I guess," Katie said. It occurred to her she was missing them already.

"How come you're staying here anyway?"

"My parents are having trouble."

"Fighting too much?"

"Yeah."

"Getting a divorce?"

"Maybe," Katie said without adding any details, like she thought her father was a drunk and chased other women. Or that Mama was always depressed and spent a lot of time in bed as though to save all her strength for their fights.

"Paris Gibson Junior High," Jenny said, pointing ahead to the right. The school was huge and imposing, a stone castle-looking affair on one side joined conspicuously to a newer brick structure on the other. Katie couldn't imagine going to school there.

"Here's where we eat," Jenny said next, guiding her into Mel's Donuts on Fourteenth Street.

It was a long way to walk to go swimming—all the way across town to the westside. They changed in a big steamy locker room and laid their towels on hot cement beside the pool. All around, people were eating lumpy dough-covered hot dogs on sticks. Katie observed Jenny chatting to kids she knew, and it gave Katie a sense of what she had been missing, the feeling that she was in charge of anything. Guiding a tractor over a hill was one thing, making a friend quite another. And now it would be a while before she drove anything. She'd had to promise not to drive any vehicle as long as she was at Aunt Etta's. You'd have thought she was going to steal a car or something.

Jenny was about Katie's height and weight, short and skinny. She had green eyes and sandy hair that made Katie think of a shampoo ad. She was a true social being and Katie marveled at her self-confidence, her ease of movement among the towels and oil-slick bodies strewn everywhere. Katie tried to keep up with the conversations — clues, she felt, to something.

"Where are you from?" asked a tall, slender boy.

"Winslow," Katie said.

"Visiting Jenny?"

"No, my aunt. Next door to Jenny." The boy helped himself to a corner of her towel. He had green-gray eyes and was already tan.

"You want a pop?" he asked. The boy alternated sitting on Katie's towel and one that belonged to a girl named Sandy who sat ten towels down on her left. Every now and then the boy did a jackknife from the high dive, then came back to sit down again. On the way home he and a friend caught up to Katie and Jenny. His name was Billy, his friend's name was Roger.

A few nights later Billy kissed Katie under the lilac bushes in Aunt Etta's yard. She imagined that Jenny and Roger were doing the same sort of thing in the porch swing. Katie wasn't that impressed with the business of kissing, and while it was a warm, soft feeling on her mouth, she couldn't imagine why such a big deal was made of it. She liked having his arms around her and her head on his shoulder but after a while it became awkward and her neck got stiff in that position. She hesitated to move and supposed he did, too. Katie guessed that this kind of thing got better as it went along.

Jenny slept over that night and they lay in bed with Almond Hersheys. Jenny took her time eating hers. She ate around the almonds dramatically. "What do you think it's like to do it?" she asked.

"Do what?" Katie said, though she knew perfectly well what Jenny was getting at.

"You know."

"Uhmmmm," Katie said, stalling. After all, she was just adjusting to kissing.

"Betty Bain's big sister says the guy lies on top to put it in."

"Sounds impossible," Katie said, trying to imagine how that could be.

"There's probably more to it we don't know," Jenny said, crunching the last almond.

Katie still couldn't give up her habit of waking early, and she was startled by the sounds of milkmen and sirens, the absence of others—roosters, dogs, cattle. She waited anxiously in the window seat for the days to begin. Aunt Etta awakened about eight, the neighborhood on the whole about nine. She tried to read from the volumes of Nancy Drew and Hardy Boys on the shelves, baby stuff she didn't like anymore.

Every morning Jenny either called or came over. She'd want help with the lawn, help with the laundry, help making cookies, sandwiches, or beds. And she didn't like to run errands by herself either and would insist on Katie's company. Sometimes Katie thought that if Jenny hadn't always been there making the overtures she'd have sat all day in the window seat. Billy and Roger were over at least once a day, too, and it made Aunt Etta nervous. "A girl doesn't want to grow up too fast," she'd warn

Jenny and Katie after the boys left, as though already detecting growth.

Toward the end of the summer Aunt Etta decided to drive to the ranch to talk to Mama.

"We need to make some decisions about the school year," she told Katie at breakfast.

It made her feel panicky—more things happening that she couldn't do anything about. Not that she knew what to do about them anyway. She pictured Aunt Etta saying that Katie had better go home, she was growing up too fast here and her parents saying, no, she gets into too much trouble at the ranch.

"Katie, dear, are you listening?" Aunt Etta asked. "I said I'm going to ask if you can stay the school year. You'd like that, wouldn't you?"

"And go to Paris Gibson?" Katie still couldn't imagine it.

"Yes," Etta said. "Now, while I'm gone please do your work. I've arranged for you to stay at Jenny's tonight in case I'm late."

Katie kept busy all afternoon; she watered the garden and hedges, folded laundry, washed the dishes, and tried not to worry. She even cleaned her room. That is, she pushed everything on the floor into the closet. Her room was the only place in Aunt Etta's house that got messy, and whether she noticed at all Katie didn't know. She never said. Katie worked until Jenny called to ask if she wanted to go get a hamburger with her and her brother.

Jim's car was black, though he planned to paint it baby blue with red pinstripes and a flame. It was an old car with running boards and a funny smell to it that was rather nice. It had stiff gray upholstery that prickled their bare legs and its four doors all opened from the middle. And if his girl friend Patricia hadn't come along, they would have gotten to sit in the front.

Patricia sat close to Jim and from time to time he kissed her while they waited at the window of the drive-in for their order. Katie noticed they both appeared to think kissing was quite marvelous.

"See that place?" Jenny said, pointing through the open window. "It's haunted!"

"How do you know?" Katie asked, studying the old weathered-looking house for any indication. It was pretty ordinary except for a sign that hung lopsided nearly to the ground. The house was across the highway and back away from the road. There was nothing else on that side of Tenth Avenue but sand and prairie and sagebrush.

"That's the Tumbleweed Tavern," Jenny said. "Last year the police came and closed it down."

"Let's go look," Katie suggested.

"You better stay away from there," Jim said from the front seat, all at once listening to their conversation.

"That's a ba-a-a-d place," Patricia added, not taking her eyes off Jim.

When Jim dropped them off, they got bikes and flashlights out of the garage and headed for the old tavern. By the time they got there, it was almost dusk and the wind was coming up.

"Who's that?" Katie asked Jenny, pointing to a grotesque looking woman hard to focus on because she was walking west of them in the glare of sundown. There was something alarming about the way her dress flew around her body in the wind and scarves or rags did the same about her head. Katie counted nine goats following her.

"That's just the old goat lady," Jenny said. "She lives in the dunes out here somewhere with those goats."

They left the bikes and walked the rest of the way because the sand drifts that had collected on the road were hard to ride through. When they got to the porch, they could see the marks where a padlock had been, and scars where the wood had ripped. The door was ajar.

Katie could feel an aching in her stomach moving slowly up into her throat. Her hands felt slippery on the flashlight. They stopped to listen. Only the whisper of sand lifting into the wind across the prairie was audible from their position in the doorway. Jenny called in "Yoo-hoo, anybody here?" Her voice resonated through the old place. "I don't want to go in," she said.

"Me neither," said Katie, but they both stepped inside and moved slowly to the middle of the large room. The fading light from the windows revealed a bar, empty now of bottles and glass and bright mirror.

"Look here," Jenny whispered. She held up a rusty bar tray that said, GREAT FALLS SELECT, FINE BEER. A jukebox stood in one corner, its glass smashed and scattered about the floor. There was a fireplace, its hearth blackened by flames that must have regularly licked up and out around the stones. But there were no tables left to prove patrons ever sat there, noisy and laughing the way Katie imagined they once had. To the left was a staircase and the two of them stood staring at it.

"Probably an office up there," Katie said.

"You think we should go up?" Jenny asked.

"I don't know. You don't suppose some old bums are hiding up there, do you?"

They stepped cautiously up each stair. Jenny held onto Katie's arm tightly, throwing her off balance. At the top of the stairs was a wide hall with six doors. One opened into a bathroom. Everything in it looked rusty, and it had a musty smell of urine and antiseptic. The other rooms were empty except for bedsprings, stripped of mattresses or coverings, that marked the near center of each floor. Jenny finally let go of Katie's arm.

The light from the west room windows was the last of the day, and it lay in folds of pinks and purple across the horizon. Their flashlights on the walls cast shadows across the metal springs onto the floor. The walls were bare but for a square of white above the light switch in one room. Jenny shone the flashlight there; it was a sign and in large letters said, PLEASE DO NOT THROW RUBBERS ON THE FLOOR.

The words had a magic quality, as if they said, Quiet please, someone is dying here, or Stop, something of importance is taking place. Katie knew rubbers as those things Winslow town boys threw bloated with water at girls getting off the school bus. And, like all the other kids probably had in that decent Catholic town, she envisioned the proximity of rubbers to sex and sin.

"Jesus," Jenny said. They stood there in silence, transfixed by the mystery of the world in which they had just intruded, one barely bordering anything they knew. They were listening, Katie guessed, as though memories were lingering there in the stillness, memories they could pick up with their brains the way a radio picked up sound waves. Not just memories, but the nature itself of remarkable nights, raucous lives. But all they heard through the broken panes of window was the eerie sound of goat bells murmuring across the sand.

"The goat lady," Katie said.

Many an evening she must have walked the goats by that place, must have heard the music, the same music Jenny or Aunt Etta might have heard from their porches on hot nights of summers past. The goat lady must have seen the lights refracting red across the sand, barely visible from Tenth Avenue. She might even have paused to wonder about the sporty coupes and station wagons parked near the porch, cars that might have just that day hauled Brownie troops and groceries or someone's grandma. Katie wondered what stories the old woman could tell them of all that.

When the thing brushed their legs, they screamed in unison and ran down the stairs and out the door. When they'd pedaled a fair distance, Katie looked back at the tavern, glowing now with a reddish light in the setting sun. She could just make out silhouettes at the horizon bobbing up and down in swift movement away from the place. The old lady and her goats—probably frightened by their screams. They pedaled hard down the old road and across the highway, slowing only when they got to neighborhoods and sidewalks.

"It must have been a cat," Katie told Jenny. Now assured of safety, she was amused by the visit and escape they had just made. But Jenny wouldn't answer and Katie knew her fright had turned to anger. She wouldn't talk even when they got home. The house was hot but they sat at the kitchen table anyway instead of on the porch.

Katie wished she had thought to take that sign. She wasn't sure why she found it so astounding. The contradiction, she guessed. She had never thought of prostitutes as the type to fuss over a floor like Aunt Etta would or to bother to say please.

Jenny got out fudgesicles and they sucked them in silence beneath a glaring light. A moth banged itself against the glass shade. That and crickets through the screen were the only other noise.

Lying in her big poster bed later, Jenny finally talked. "Do you suppose our fathers ever go to places like that?"

"For crying out loud, Jenny," Katie said.

"Well, do you?"

"Of course not," Katie said, wondering too.

CHAPTER
TWENTY SIX

———————◆———————

Leaving Buck wasn't as simple as Charlie had made it look when he walked out on Maggie. So Pearl hung on. She hung on without anything to clutch and no fingerholds left.

She had done this all summer, that is, until the day Maggie's oldest boy called for help. Pearl had just done the feeding and brought in the milk.

"Mama's sick," he said. "Can you come?"

"What's wrong?"

"I don't know," he said, and she could tell he was frightened and perhaps in tears.

"I'll be right there," she said and hung up, puzzled. Where was Buck? She had just assumed that when Buck left the night before in a rage, he had gone to Maggie's.

When she got there, the boys were still in their pajamas and Maggie was in bed. Maggie was too thin and pale despite a fever. Her hair was damp and hung lifeless about her face. She was barely conscious, and Pearl wondered if Maggie knew she was there.

"Has she been throwing up?" she asked Pat, glancing at the plastic bucket beside the bed.

"Not today," he said. "Last night. Mostly she sleeps."

"How long has she been sick?"

"Yesterday and today," he said.

Pearl thought of taking her temperature but didn't want to go through everything looking for a thermometer. It shouldn't matter, as it was obviously high. She put Maggie into a clean nightgown and swabbed her face and neck with a cool washcloth.

"We'll let her sleep now," she told the boys, who had been watching silently. Pearl sent them to get dressed and she made breakfast. After cleaning up the kitchen, she checked Maggie. She was cooler and still slept.

Pearl went out to feed the chickens. She took the boys with her and they found her a bucket and told her how much. They gathered eggs and fed and watered the hogs. There was nothing much in the way of livestock around here anymore, and the neighbors over the hill did Maggie's farming.

Maggie was still asleep and Pearl did the laundry, hung it out, vacuumed, and made lunch. She let the boys help her. She felt their worry.

"Will she be okay?" Joey asked.

"Sure. She's probably got the flu."

"What's that?"

"It's germs," Pat said.

"Yes, probably a virus," Pearl said.

"What's that?" Joey asked again.

"Well," she said, "like Pat said, germs."

Germs now seemed an acceptable answer and Joey didn't ask anything more.

"We'll make some soup," she said and got out vegetables. "When your mother wakes up, it will be ready."

Maggie didn't wake up until late that afternoon and Pearl knew her fever was broken. Pearl had cleaned the boys' room, changed their sheets, and brought in the clean laundry, still wondering where Buck was.

She took Maggie a tray. The boys had picked flowers from the garden, folded a napkin, and arranged utensils. She added hot vegetable broth, a piece of dry toast, and a cup of tea.

"Pearl," Maggie said, "thank you for coming."

"Do you like the flowers?" Joey asked. Both boys were beaming from the side of the bed.

"I love them," Maggie said, smiling.

She could only eat a few bites and fell back to sleep. The boys, despite feeling relieved, were disappointed. They were irritable now and restless and Pearl sent them out to get the mail.

"A letter from Daddy," Pat said, waving it in the air. He had started to open it already but Pearl told him not to.

"Let's wait for your mother," she said.

"No, now, come on," he said. "Please."

"No—later," she said and put the letter on top of the refrigerator. She noticed the postmark was Idaho. The boys were starting to argue now and Pearl sent them out to play. She was feeling irritable now too, and looked for something to keep her busy. The house was hot.

Maggie woke up again and went to the bathroom. Pearl changed her sheets and got out another clean nightgown. She asked Maggie if she could eat a little Jell-O. Maggie said no, she had a terrible headache. Pearl got her aspirin and water and called the boys in to bathe. After their baths, they put on clean pajamas and sat on the bed with Maggie to listen to the radio. Pearl sat in a chair beside the bed. Exhausted from worry and the heat, the kids soon fell asleep.

Pearl put them in their own beds. When she got back, Maggie was asleep. She felt a little feverish, and Pearl put a cool rag on her forehead, turned off the radio and light, and made up a bed on the couch.

In the morning, the sound of Maggie and the boys in the kitchen woke her up. She put on her clothes and went out. Maggie had made coffee.

"You shouldn't be up," Pearl told her.

"But I feel better, and I'm so stiff and sore I had to get out of bed."

Maggie still didn't look very healthy and she had no color in her cheeks. And she was weak. She sat at the table and let Pearl make her oatmeal and a soft-boiled egg. The boys, Pearl noticed, were back to normal—energetic, hungry, and picking at each other. After breakfast, she sent them out to play.

"I really appreciate your staying over," Maggie said. She looked as if she was about to cry. Pearl guessed how awkward she must feel to be dependent on and grateful to the wife of her lover, who, by the way, was still conspicuously missing.

"Forget it," she said. "You should go back to bed now."

Pearl went outside and fed the chickens and hogs, then rounded up the boys and took them with her to do her own feeding and milking. There was no sign of Buck. There was still yesterday's milk on the counter, now sour. There wasn't much of it, the cow was almost dry. By the weekend, Pearl would be buying milk in town.

The boys were halfway over the hill by the time she was done putting away the new milk, and she yelled at them to come back to the house.

That night, after making Maggie and the boys dinner, she went home. She thought Maggie would be all right now, though she was still weak. But Pearl didn't feel well herself.

She was in bed when she heard Buck come in. She heard the screen door, the refrigerator door, then his footsteps in the hall. She felt as if she now had Maggie's fever and that her hearing was oddly acute.

"What are you doing in bed so early?" he said. She noticed he had on new clothes.

"Maggie's sick. You better go down there and check on her."

Buck almost started. He was caught off guard and did not hide first surprise, then guilt. Pearl felt sorry for him.

"Go ahead," she said. She was going to be sick and didn't want to in front of him. "Take the boys some milk," she said and went to the bathroom.

That night and the next day, having caught whatever Maggie had had, Pearl slept and woke, slept and woke, over and over, recalling vague, nonsensical dreams. She knew also that Buck was there taking care of her. Finally she woke up feeling refreshed and clear, clear about everything.

Leaving Buck was not her problem. In some sense, they had accomplished separation long ago. What Pearl was having trouble with was trying to identify herself, trying to reassemble who she was, who she could be. She was trying to establish how much of this life she had become, how much of it she could own and take. Because sharing Buck's life had changed her and the near-hysterical small-town girl she had been, a girl who in moving eighty miles away might have been going to China.

But if those miles had in some respects narrowed her experience, they had also expanded and elevated it. There was about this place an unlimited sense of room. Earth had a way here—earth that was flat and earth that was not—of rolling endlessly beneath an omniscient ceiling of sky. In that way, room had been made for her. And in that new exposure to space, her own dimensions had increased to fill it; she was able to locate herself, to affirm her own presence here. She had become, for the first time, effective, and had then taken advantage of Buck's own failure or refusal to be. She understood that now. The more irresponsible he became, the less he managed, the more she was able to take on. Over the years there was nothing she hadn't learned how to do. It might take her more effort, for example, to chase a sick cow she was too small to sit on into a helpless position in the branding chute. But once she got it there and calmed it, she could give it shots, puncture its bloated belly, give it a tracheotomy or whatever it needed to live. As it became more common over the years to find Buck at some bar, it became more common to find Pearl at the barn or grain elevator or on the tractor. And others, even Buck's father when he was alive, had known it, and this too contributed to her own estimation—that she, Pearl, had worth.

Not that she'd taken over, not at all. It just turned out that need that ever be the case, she could have. She could have.

And this was what she held onto now, a confidence she'd earned here and an identity with place. All the summers of hay fields and dusty harvests, the springs of muddy cowshit and bellowing calves, year after year of wind cutting its own path through prairie, these things had become the substance of her life. How would she fit a now enlarged self back into a town of fifty thousand, a town no longer home to her?

Nonetheless, the experience with Maggie, seeing her sick like that, then getting sick herself, had freed her. She couldn't say why. She just knew she had to go, that she wanted to go. So when she heard Etta's car coming up the lane that very afternoon, weak as she was, she went outside to meet her, grateful that help had come.

CHAPTER
TWENTY SEVEN

Aunt Etta returned from the ranch the next morning. She was vague. Nothing was actually definite, she said, but she had left Katie's parents in the middle of making plans. She was a bit apprehensive and distracted all day. Finally, just before dinner, she told Katie she would work on it. Katie didn't ask her what that meant; she knew. That meant Aunt Etta would pray about it. Katie had noticed she did that sort of thing a lot.

The first time Katie had seen her working on something, Katie had come downstairs to squeeze some orange juice. It was early, about seven, the time she usually sat in the window seat thinking Aunt Etta was still asleep. But there she was sitting in a chair, her hands on its arms, a do-not-disturb look on her face that made Katie retreat quietly to her room.

When they were setting the table for dinner, Aunt Etta told her she wanted to explain some things, so Katie wouldn't get the wrong idea.

"Oh, it's all right with me if you pray, Aunt Etta," Katie said to avoid the explanation.

"Thank you, dear," Etta said, smiling. "But I want to explain how I go about it so you'll understand prayer is not manipulation.

"You see, one must never pray for a certain outcome. In this case, for a marriage to heal or a marriage to break up, or for you to stay or go back. You ask only for the best outcome for everyone involved—even the so-called enemy."

Katie figured Pa must be the so-called enemy here. She nodded, glad that Aunt Etta was done with the subject now and pouring tea. Prayer or not, Mama and Pa were coming to town in the morning, presumably with a decision.

After dinner, Jenny and Katie met Roger and Billy on Central Avenue. Katie liked Billy and enjoyed the things they did. She was even beginning to think kissing had possibilities. They had decided to go swimming at the Smelter Hill pool, and she and Billy now walked a half a block or so behind their friends toward the smelter. The employee pool, Billy explained, was only for big shots. Roger, who knew these things, had told him. What's more, he said, Roger's father had worked there for twelve years and had never so much as gotten a toe wet in the employee pool.

They caught up to the other two and walked across to Black Eagle on the old Fifteenth Street bridge, now deserted and closed to traffic. Tall, imposing girders of a half-finished new bridge shone in the lapping waves of the river, waves they could see beneath them through gaps between old bridge beams. On the other side they followed the river east, climbed the hill, then the fence with the notice, ANACONDA COMPANY—NO TRESPASSING.

There didn't appear to be anyone around to care that they were there but Roger cautioned them not to make noise. They dove and swam, rather like beavers, silent but for an occasional loud slap of water. Not more than half an hour passed before there were voices and lights searching the pool. But by then, they had climbed over the edge, then down the hill, scrambling into the bushes where they had hidden their clothes in four neat piles. But they couldn't find them, and Katie and Jenny huddled there to wait while the boys located them. The mosquitoes were unmerciful in the warm, damp grass, and Jenny soon began to cry. Katie put her arms around her, as much to shield as to comfort, despite her own fear and misery.

After some time, the boys returned. The guards had taken their clothes, they said, so they finally had to come out of hiding to ask for them back. Grateful for the clothes, for a warning and no calls to parents, they walked home, humbled sufficiently by hundreds of swollen bites that covered any skin their swim suits hadn't. The boys left them at the corner of Twentieth and Katie said good night to Jenny in the yard.

She quietly hunted for cotton balls and witch hazel, careful not to wake Aunt Etta. She was glad Jenny hadn't slept over, she wanted to be alone. Her parents would be here in the morning.

When they arrived, Aunt Etta and Katie were standing in the yard, nervous, expectant. A few leaves were already dying on the bushes or blowing around the yard. An early fall, Aunt Etta predicted. It seemed to take hours between the time Pa pulled in the drive and the time they got out of the pickup. Mama hugged Katie, Pa mussed her hair, holding one hand on her shoulder and away from him as though she were something he was examining and trying to get in focus.

They sat on the porch. Aunt Etta brought Pa a beer, and Mama asked for lemonade. Katie thought her mother looked pale, as if she hadn't had any sun in weeks. Aunt Etta asked her if she wanted to lie down and Mama said no, she was fine. They spent a few more minutes remarking on things like the heat and Katie's mosquito bites and then got right down to it. Mama had decided to move there with Aunt Etta and Katie. Pa could have visitation privileges. In fact, they wanted Katie to go down with him for a few days and help get some things. That way Mama could rest. Aunt Etta didn't seem to think too much of the idea from what Katie could tell by her face but she said nothing.

Katie was surprised by all this though there was no reason she should have been. She knew some changes were bound to happen. She felt neither gladness nor displeasure with the news, just surprise.

A few hours later Katie and her father were in the pickup headed for the ranch. He slowed down every time he passed his usual stops and glanced at the bars. There was one at Belt, another at Raynesford, another at Stanford. Mama had instructed him that under no circumstances was he to stop for a drink. He had a couple of beers anyway. A six-pack was at his side.

Her father didn't say much. He asked her how she liked things and whether she had made any friends. She told him about Jenny.

"Get along okay with your aunt Etta?"

"Sure, she's great," she said.

He didn't say anything more until they got to the gravel county road. He pulled over so she could drive.

"Missed that, haven't you?"

Katie smiled.

Finally they came to their lane and climbed the top of the hill; he waited while she opened the gate. She had an almost aerial view of the place. It looked so foreign, so changed, yet there was something here she recognized. The barn looked shabby and ready to fall down, the house needed painting, and the machinery and old vehicles all around gave the place a junkyard look. Her stomach knotted up just looking at it pressed there vulnerably between slight mounds of hill, hills too small to protect the place from wind or the sheep from coyotes. Parched and sunburnt grass was the only vegetation around the house.

Inside, the shades were drawn against the heat and the air felt rancid and lifeless. Katie turned on some fans. Her father got out a cold beer and she went to her room. She had posters all around the walls, her attempt to bring in color and to mask a shabby job of plastering. She took down two that were falling off the wall — a circus poster and one that said JC ANNUAL CATTLE STAMPEDE with a cowboy sailing across the back of a bucking bronco.

She didn't know where to begin. Much of what looked okay here wouldn't fit at Aunt Etta's. She went through her drawers. Most of her clothes were too small or too ugly. Katie didn't want any of them, especially her T-shirts. She remembered one morning at breakfast months before. Pa had commented that soon she'd be poking holes in all her shirts. The look on his face confused her, she felt ashamed. Not that she didn't want full woman's breasts, it was just that her body was changing haphazardly, no design, no warning. Sometimes she dreamed she'd gone to school and forgotten her cardigan and there were her tiny, pointy breasts exposed and poking out like Pa said, obscenely, from her rib cage through her shirt.

She threw everything into piles—give away and throw away. She came across a picture of Charlie sitting on a horse. She was embarrassed just thinking how she had worshipped the poor guy. It was humiliating to have been so immature.

Her father was standing in the door now.

"Quite a mess you made," he said and grinned. Katie had a feeling that he was unsure how to talk to her and felt he had to grin after everything he said, to reassure her of something. "We ought to eat a little dinner, don't you think?"

They ate lunch meat in sandwiches piled high with tomatoes and horseradish and lettuce. Her father drank beer and she drank cola, an unusual thing to find in the refrigerator. There was no milk, and Katie wondered about that, then realized the cow must be dry. Or maybe it was dead, for all she knew or cared—after all those years of straining milk and then lugging it down to Maggie's, sometimes spilling it and forgetting about it until it soured in the sun and made the car or pickup stink. Then her mother would scream at her to go clean it up.

Katie was curious to know what happened to Maggie, if Pa ever saw her anymore, or if she ever heard from Charlie. She wondered but not enough to ask. She still wasn't sure how much of all that her parents ever figured out she knew.

"What's Mama taking to Aunt Etta's?"

"Aw," he said. "As it turns out, your ma doesn't want to take much. This could be temporary, you know."

She didn't know. For some reason that depressed her and she knew she was glad about Mama's decision and didn't want there to be a possibility of living back here.

Katie felt like a guest and didn't clean up any more than to clear the table and stack things in the sink. She worked in her room some more or rather she looked through all the junk she had collected as a kid—stamps, arrowheads, petrified rocks, 4-H ribbons, old photos. She saved one photo of her parents standing beside a '46 pickup.

Katie joined her father on the porch after a while. He, too, had been digging through some old things and brought out his guitar. She hadn't heard him play it in years and they sat on the swing while he picked and tuned and hummed. Finally he played some folk songs and Katie sang along. The dogs were puzzled by the music and stirred slightly on the porch.

"That's nice, Pa."

"Ain't no Eddy Arnold," he said.

The sun was almost down, and the hills changed colors and tones rapidly, brilliantly, until black suddenly descended like a venetian blind closing. It was getting late and she went to the bathroom to wash up. He continued to play.

"Going to bed, Pa?" she asked, sticking her head out the screen door.

"Think I'll just finish this beer," he said. She noticed he had a bottle of bourbon, too. She shut off her light and turned on the bathroom light to divert all the bugs and moths in there. Most of the windows in the house needed new screens.

It was several hours later when she awoke. First she felt hot, constrained, pressed down, as if she were wrapped in thick ropes. It was a nightmare but she couldn't quite wake up. She felt so heavy, so groggy, so far away yet something kept pulling at her. First it seemed she was being dragged along, then pushed. And there was a great weight smothering her and she had to struggle to breathe. She was suffocating, about to die. Then suddenly she was wide awake.

"Pa!" she screamed. "Don't, don't!"

She could smell a bitter mixture of alcohol and sweat, greasy hair and aftershave. She twisted and jerked from under his chest and heard him cry out.

"Oh, baby, I'm sorry, I'm sorry," he said.

Katie ran through the house and outside. When she got to the road by the barn she heard the lambs get up in alarm and the geese flutter several times and then settle back again.

It was a cloudless night and she sat out of sight in a hiding place she knew on the hill, sick to her stomach, wishing she were safe at Aunt Etta's. She could hear her father calling her name, looking for her in the yard with a flashlight that bobbed in the dark and twice fell from his hand as he stumbled drunkenly. "Come back," he said. "I won't hurt you."

In some new clarity that came from looking down at her life in the dark like that she saw that she was not only afraid of Pa but of everything else too—life, people, herself. She waited there long after her father had gone back into the house.

Katie was exhausted. Finally, after she was certain he would not come back out again to look for her, she went to the barn. She could hardly see and had to feel her way along a wall lined with hay bales. She threw off a top layer of dirty straw from an old pile of it in the corner and lay down. Not much remained of her torn nightgown and she tried to cover herself with loose straw from the stack. But the night air was cool and she trembled with cold, unable to keep out the dampness and shame that now penetrated her thin shelter of straw and courage.

* * *

Katie was stiff and sore when she awoke and still felt nauseated. She was no longer afraid. Fear had been replaced by a dull ache of something worse. She went up to the house. Her father was passed out on the couch and the dogs were whining to go out. Katie took a shower and got dressed, brushed her teeth several times. She sat on a chair across from him to wait, lifeless and resigned. He woke up finally, puffy and old.

"I'm ready to go now," she said.

He went into the bathroom to clean up. Now Katie waited on the porch.

"Got your stuff?" he asked.

"All I want."

He nodded.

It was the longest ride of her life. The road hadn't ever been so dusty or the fields so dry. When they went through town he asked if she wanted breakfast. Katie told him no.

They stopped at Raynesford at the bar. Her father went in to get a cold beer and he brought her out a pop. It seemed to settle her stomach. Still they didn't speak.

Fifty more miles and no matter how fast her father drove, the air in the pickup didn't move.

Katie was grateful to reach Great Falls, glad to get to Aunt Etta's cool neighborhood of trees and green grass. As if clairvoyant, Aunt Etta was on the porch waiting for her, but she wanted her mother.

Aunt Etta ran down the steps while Katie climbed out of the pickup. "Where's Mama?" Katie asked.

"Honey, she's lying down." Aunt Etta grabbed Katie and held her and for the first time in months, Katie cried.

"Don't worry about your mother," Etta said, stroking Katie's hair. "She'll be fine."

Her father never got out of the pickup and Katie wasn't sure how long he sat there before driving off.

CHAPTER

TWENTY EIGHT

1960

Pearl missed the country. She missed great expanses of land and sky, the soft contours of hill that in twilight looked like bunched and crumpled velvet. When she sat on the porch at Etta's, she felt closed in by the nearness of houses and trees and hedge that in summer kept her in gloomy shade and in winter reminded her of decay and the passage of time.

But moving to town had its compensations. Pearl enjoyed seeing Katie leave for school with friends, just as she and Etta once had. On Squatter Creek, Katie had been the first one to get on the school bus at seven and the last to get off at four, a long day. No, Katie was happier in town and busy learning the social graces of adolescence, if there was anything graceful in that. To Pearl's relief, Katie had become less quiet, less private.

Pearl was sure Etta liked having Katie around. Etta never complained about supervising or feeding the teenagers who dropped by, nor did she mind picking up after the bluster and clutter they left behind them. That too relieved Pearl. She'd worried about how Etta would react to all the changes she and Katie were sure to occasion. Could she adjust, Pearl had wondered, to a teenager or to Pearl's moods or slowly acquired sloppy habits? She, who had once treated order as an absolute, now cared little for methods and systems or the conditions of the house. She hoped, however, to snap out of it soon.

There were forgotten pleasures to living in town. Pearl appreciated as much as anything having a store on the corner, a market six blocks away, and a library nearby. It was good to walk around the neighborhood, to go with Etta or Katie or Leona for ice cream as she had once done with Etta and her father as a child. He used to walk between them, holding their hands. Sometimes Mother would join them and then they would walk two and two, adult and child, one pair following the other and their cat following all. The cat, Bean, had always tagged after the girls, waited inconspicuously outside while they attended to shopping or school, then appeared appropriately as they began the walk home, faithful and attentive as any dog.

And for her part, Pearl liked divorce. She hadn't expected that. She enjoyed the freedom of light meals or no meals, of coming and going, of having those about her coming and going without it threatening her well-being (Buck had hardly ever left the house without her wondering: What woman now?). Nor did Pearl miss having to get home to milk or to feed or to fill the water tanks. It was as if there had been a rope at her waist at all times that allowed her to go no farther than six hours or forty miles away, unless she had to get the noon meal too, which reduced all that, with some exceptions, to nothing. By some means, these conditions had neither confined Buck nor impeded him. He regularly did what the day or hour suggested. A crisp fall day might mean hunting, a lazy summer morning could indicate fishing. Rainy days were certain to result in drinking—though any day, for reasons not clear, could mean drinking.

Most of all, Pearl liked having her own money. That was something she had always hated, asking Buck for money. She would write every check to the grocer for five to ten dollars over the amount—sums spent on groceries were somehow correct and expected. This way she avoided either having to ask for a few dollars or explaining checks not so favored as ones for food. She then used half for pocket spending and saved the other. She explained her system to Maggie once, thinking it would be useful information for a young wife to have. Later she discovered that, to the contrary, Maggie thought it corrupt and indecent of her and tattled to Buck. To his credit, he had laughed and given Pearl a settled rate each week. Now Pearl handed out her own money—to Katie, the milkman, the grocer. She had a job.

There weren't many places she didn't apply. First for daytime work, then after nothing came of it, for night shifts. She was finally hired at Pagliacci's.

"Have you ever waited tables?" Beto, the owner, asked.

"No," she said.

"So why should I hire you?" Beto was large, barrel chested, and probably hairy from what she could see of his neck and chest. He was missing the top button off his shirt. It was too early for the supper club to have opened, but all the employees were there and Pearl was sure every one of them could hear. She was tired of interviews of this sort, actually of interviews in general, and in a tone that made that clear told him her qualifications.

"I work hard, I'm punctual, I can get along with others, and I'm honest."

"You always cheerful?" he asked.

"Not always," she said.

"A third of the time?"

"More or less." This was going badly. Worse even than usual.

"Less, I hope. This place is not known for cheer, or for atmosphere, or for employee socials. It's known for the finest steak in the country, the best ravioli west of Chicago, for stiff drinks and fast service. Got it? Fast service. Now go get an apron and I'll show you the right way to core lettuce."

Beto bullied everyone and was never cheerful himself. "Go wash that greasy crap off your face," Pearl heard him tell another waitress named Rita. Or "Move your ass," he often snarled at everyone. But he loaned Harry, the bartender, money, paid Rita's kids' dental bills, and threw out anyone who mistreated his waitresses—that privilege he would not share. He let everyone take home unsold specials and day-old bread. After a particularly trying night—and there were many—he'd make everyone a drink.

Pearl knew he liked Etta—he said in a brawl he'd want her on his side—and Katie—Pearl had caught him smiling in her direction. He encouraged both to come for dinner at least once a week. He liked to think working mothers could still see their families when they worked for him. He told Pearl to eat up. "Damn," he said. "Skinny, runty waitresses are bad for business. Not only that, they don't have any stamina."

On Pearl's break she either wouldn't eat or had only a small salad or a cup of minestrone. She was not about to trade her new slenderness for stamina, though she doubted carrying added poundage around could result in endurance anyway. Pearl only admitted to herself that she left work exhausted, her feet swollen and inflamed by pain, her back aching from heavy trays and the buckets of ice and chicken she carried from the walk-in cooler.

Each day of her new career began by clocking in. Then she made salad dressings—Thousand Island, Italian, and French. She mixed them in five-gallon containers that required her to bend into a position not unlike milking a cow in order to stir the mixtures completely. She cored and tore a crate of lettuce, brought up cases of tomato sauce, salad dressing ingredients, and spaghetti from the basement, and inventoried the supplies of chicken, steak, and homemade ravioli in the giant cold walk-in. She replaced condiments and piled baskets with breadsticks, Italian bread, and pats of butter, arranged flowers and set tables. All this before the front door was ever unlocked. By the time customers were allowed in—there was often a waiting line— Pearl was sweaty and tired, needing a clean uniform and a break.

She hated working nights, getting yelled at, and customers irritable with hunger or sometimes too much to drink. Occasionally men were rude and suggestive but often the women who accompanied them were worse. Weekends were always the worst. One Saturday night, she had trouble with a certain couple. Pearl noticed them when they came in because they seemed to her to be mismatched. He was portly and short; she was tall and smartly dressed and walked as though in appreciation, or perhaps in celebration, of the value of her clothes. The man was indifferent to everything but the menu and the rings he wore and fondled with pink, puffy hands while ordering. But not three minutes later Pearl heard the woman say loudly, "Bert, if you don't stop drooling over that slut, I'm going home." "Do that," Pearl heard the man answer even louder. Who the man was drooling over Pearl didn't know; he was hardly—in her estimation—a man women might fight over.

"I think it's time you both went home," said Beto, who was helping out a busboy at the next booth. He handed them their coats and led them to the door.

Nonetheless, tips were generous and the only reason Pearl didn't quit.

One night Pearl came around the corner of the dining room with a tray of food and there was the hostess seating Buck and some woman. Pearl just stood there in the doorway holding the tray, flabbergasted. It never occurred to her that he could intrude himself on her life like this. Didn't he ever go anywhere, for God's sake, without a woman?

"I'll deliver that," Beto said crisply, trying to assess the situation and taking the tray from her.

"Table five," she said and fled.

She stood in the back of the kitchen, paralyzed and angry, even though she guessed Buck didn't know she worked here. He hadn't even been to the house to see Katie since Pearl moved to town. And that was at least six months ago.

"Pearl," Beto yelled when he came back to the kitchen. "Add up all those checks in the office and see if we balance this week. Evelyn, cover Pearl's tables for a while." When she was done—it took her several hours—Buck was gone.

Another time, not more than a month later, she was clearing a table and someone grabbed her around the waist. Shocked, she almost knocked an armful of dirty dishes to the floor.

"For crying out loud," she said when she saw who it was. "Charlie, of all people. Where have you been all this time?" She hugged him and kissed his cheek. "You're a sight," she said, appraising him. "God, it's good to see you."

She was hovering over him, she told herself as he ate. She bought him dinner; that is, she would not give him a bill. Charlie waited for her to get off her shift and they walked arm in arm down the street to get a drink. They sat in a booth at the end of a large barroom.

"Pearl, you look good," he said, taking her hand. "I heard you and Buck split up."

"Yes," she said, smiling. "Have you seen Maggie and the kids?"

"Yeah, the boys spent a couple months with me before Christmas. They're growing up. How's Katie?"

"She's fine. You know she always thought so much of you. Missed you like crazy when you left."

"Yeah," he said. "I missed her too."

"So tell me what you've been doing all this time."

"Odd jobs mostly. Logging, mining, that kind of thing. In Idaho and Wyoming. Even spent two months in Alaska. I had a crazy urge to travel, I guess."

"What now?"

"I'll try to stay in one place at least part of the year for the boys."

"No more ranching?"

"No more ranching. The place is leased out and Maggie gets

the income. Someday the boys will have it and can do what they want with it."

Charlie had an intenseness, a seriousness about him that led Pearl to suspect that he was puzzling something, or adding numbers in his head, or otherwise preoccupied. That notion was shattered when he smiled at something she said, or when he laughed his dear, glad laugh that led her to surmise, quite wrongly again, that he didn't take life seriously.

"Pearl," he said suddenly. "Come home with me tonight. To the motel, I mean—hardly home."

Pearl was surprised, yet she wasn't. But what would she tell Katie and Etta?

As if anticipating that worry he said, "Call Katie and tell her you're going to help out an old friend tonight and that's true."

"All right," she agreed and smiled.

In the morning Pearl woke up to rose walls of a dark 1940 shade, drapes of the same taste in decorating, and a worn matching spread. She was disoriented.

Charlie! she remembered. But where was he? How awful he was to leave her alone and wondering what end of town she was in. She showered, though the stall was drafty and small and smelled of wet cement. Pearl had just finished dressing and was combing her hair—she would not go home looking fallen and distraught—when she heard the door.

"Breakfast is served," Charlie called into the bathroom. He carried a tray with two metal dome lids and a pot of coffee. He spread a blanket on the floor and placed the tray in the center. They sat down, side by side, and leaned against the foot of the bed. He had brought eggs, bacon, hash browns, biscuits, and jam.

"Where'd you get this food?" she asked, delighted.

"I had to pay off the cook across the street for trusting me with his dishes."

"And here I thought you deserted me," she said. He only smiled and poured her coffee.

"Pearl," he said. "I probably won't be around for a while. But when I come back, will you see me?"

"Sure," she said.

"Have me to supper."

"Okay."

"Don't tell Katie. I'll surprise her."

She agreed. She wouldn't even tell Katie she'd seen him in case he never came back.

"I'll call you at work then," he said as they prepared to leave. He took what remained on the tray across the street. "I'll be right back," he told her and she leaned against her car to wait. It was a marvelous warm blue and golden morning and the sun was making slush and puddles of the winter snow. A chinook, she thought. The ever-loved and awaited chinook.

When he came back, he kissed her good-bye. "I like you," he said. "I really like you," he said and kissed her again.

It was only after her period came twenty-two days later that Pearl could recall that night with Charlie with peace or pleasure. If you dance, you pay the fiddler—Rita's favorite saying and that law of casuistry meant for women—kept going through her head. Women were the ones struck and punished indiscriminately for sex, the ones scorned or embarrassed or abandoned. They who benefited least from sex, who lost most by it, were the ones who knew its artless humdrum if married, its unspoken shame if not.

Anxiety had tortured her all twenty-two days, despite the fact that Charlie had stopped at the drugstore for prophylactics— safety she knew, more often than not, to be as thin and reliable as the men who wore them.

CHAPTER
TWENTY NINE

———————◆———————

It used to be Charlie, before he left, who really appreciated Buck's coffee. God knows, he drank enough of it. Years of mornings he and Charlie had sat at the kitchen table, calculating ratios of barley to beet pulp, or designing new corrals and loading pens or not talking business at all, just talking. Buck, as folks around had taken to calling him when he was a boy, would let the water boil, pull it off the fire, then sprinkle coffee grounds on top. After they'd rolled and simmered just one minute, Buck took the pot off the fire, cracked an egg and put that in, never minding if small pieces of shell went in also. When everything settled, he poured it, strong, clear, bracing. Pearl hadn't liked cleaning all that mess from the bottom of the pot and said he just wasted eggs. That is, before she left too.

But these days Buck didn't bother with the eggs anyway and today the coffee simmered too long. He poured a cup and took it with him to shower. After he'd used all the hot water, he dried his lean body and shaved carefully. He was looking healthy and Katie would see that. It was important that she see something new, something good about him if he were to make up to her for all those years of silent snarling because he was hung over or moody or otherwise unavailable. He knew his faults.

Buck tried to iron one of the two clean shirts he found hanging in the closet. The iron baffled him; he made a mess, scorched one part near the pocket, pressed in many of the wrinkles, and burned his hand. He wanted to get to town before the stores closed to buy Katie a present and so finally settled on wearing the other shirt wrinkled. When he was ready to go, he took his silver belly hat out of its box and adjusted it in the mirror. He was a man who kept two good hats, preferably Stetson, one silver or tan, the other a quality straw. He was careful at the first sign of deterioration to replace either and wear the old one around the feedlot where he could now allow anything to happen to it. Buck looked good in a hat. A hat set off his cheekbones and his strong chin. And tonight he would look his best.

Buck didn't take the time to eat. He wasn't that hungry and knew he should hurry. He had to stop in Winslow to buy the gift—what it would be he didn't know—pick up a spare tire, and get up to Great Falls before six. It was his plan to go directly to Etta's when he got there and ask Katie to dinner. He intended this to be a new beginning for them, something special and father-daughter. Buck missed her terribly, he even missed Pearl. And he'd changed, of that he was sure.

Buck estimated that it had been over a year. He hadn't had a drink, not a real drink to speak of, in over a year—not since that night. He had gone over that night a thousand times. Always it was the same. He hated himself for that night, it was the single most unforgivable thing he'd ever done. The day after, he'd found the corner of the barn where Katie must have gone when she fled from him. There in the small impression left by her weight in the straw, he found a metal clip, the kind she wore in her hair. It caught his eye, glittering persistently several feet away, beneath light coming through a narrow crack in the hayloft. He still carried it.

The thing to do now was put all this aside and look to the future. No one knew that better than he did. First he'd buy her the gift, maybe a watch or ring or some nice perfume. Perfume was probably not a good idea, it had connotations. The watch would be best. Gift buying was something Pearl had always taken care of and it stressed him to deal with all the choices, the possibilities. When he got to town he paced the Basin Trading Company for twenty minutes before choosing a white gold Lady Bulova. Old Mrs. Grady wrapped it quickly, as if to get his pain over with all the faster, lest he bolt empty-handed. "Katie will love this," she assured him.

Buck stopped at the service station down the street and put the tire on his bill.

"Bucky, old boy," said the man who owned the station. "What do you got out there at the place so good you can't get to town anymore?"

"Been busy."

"Heard you had a little bad luck."

"Sure did," Buck said and backed out of the station. Everyone in town knew about his bad luck. Buck attributed the beginning of it to the day Charlie left, his own fault for fooling around with Maggie. That was the first of it. Then Pearl said she could never forgive him for getting involved with his best friend's wife. That's how she put it and it struck Buck as odd. He could have understood had she worried about herself and her friend. Wasn't Maggie her friend? It was hard to figure but that was Pearl. Always contrary to what he thought.

Soon after that, Pearl and Katie left, and the rest of the year was just more trouble. Crops were lousy and he had great losses to his herd. The last year had been a hard winter, starting with rain that froze on top of the ground so solid the cattle couldn't get to the grass. Then it snowed. He spent months hauling hay as best he could through one blizzard after another. Many a cold morning, he'd start up the pickup and let it run while he threw bales into the truck bed. They were eerie, white kind of mornings with whiteness in every direction, whiteness so dense he couldn't tell horizon from fence or sky or snow. And the wind was bitter and blew the snow in huge drifts against the house and barn so he had to knock it away from the doorways. When he'd return to the house, the fire more than likely had gone out, and the house, besides being empty, was cold. On top of all that, it was a late spring and he hadn't gotten the crops in until June, which meant he was still harvesting in September.

His problems hadn't ended there. Yesterday, he found many of his fat cattle missing and seven yearlings dead. He guessed that Maggie's boys had left a gate open by the barn the night before. The yearlings got into the rich, concentrated feed and bloated big as elephants and died in the night. Some of the fat cattle wandered off and he had to take the dogs and go out on horse-back to find them all. He'd spent the rest of the day dragging out the swollen carcasses with the truck and had come home tired and discouraged.

Maggie didn't visit often but sometimes, like the other night, she stopped by to see how he was doing. Folks probably thought he and Maggie had a cozy thing going out here with everyone out of the way. But they were all wrong. Things turned sour quick enough and Maggie wouldn't let him near her. She said she felt too guilty about Charlie and about her boys having no father now. And she was right about that, those boys needed a strong hand around. One night Maggie cried because she said she'd broken up his home and hurt Katie and Pearl. No, it was no good between them.

Buck would give anything to have Katie around again, coming along with him on this trip or that, sitting up on the tractor to eat lunch beside him, or flying across the fields on horseback like she used to. She had been something to see all right, those black eyes like her mother's against hair the color of biscuit dough, a combination he liked. Katie had loved him, he saw that now. It was only the last few years that she'd gotten so close to Charlie and it had made him think she liked Charlie more. Once toward the end, he'd asked Charlie straight out why that was, why Katie seemed to like him better.

"Damned if I know," Charlie said. "Why the hell does Maggie like you better?" That had come as quite a surprise to Buck. He had thought he and Maggie were a secret. He hadn't planned to bring up any of it, had in fact gone down to Charlie's to see if he wanted to do a little fishing that day. Charlie had stood on the porch steps with his arms folded on his chest, one foot chipping at a splinter in the floorboards. He didn't ask Buck to come up, but stood there in that position staring off across the fields, twice leaning over the steps to spit.

"What rankles me most," Charlie finally said, "is that you can't seem to see the difference. Your nose is out of joint because I'm a friend of your kid's. Yet no telling how long you've been messing around with my wife."

But they were the same thing, Buck believed that still. Giving Katie attention, wooing her away was the same. Only it didn't do a kid any good at all to look up to some neighbor instead of her own father. He told Charlie that. "For Chrissake!" Charlie had yelled. "You don't give a shit about anyone but yourself!" But evidently Charlie didn't either because he'd left the next day.

Buck could see what a bastard he'd been—taking Katie around to bars, sometimes forgetting all about her, making her wait for hours or letting her work like a man around the cattle. He knew they terrified her but he'd thought she'd grow out of it. She sure as hell wasn't afraid of machinery, though, and could drive anything on the place by the time she was ten, even the Caterpillar.

Buck stopped at Stanford for a beer. He'd have just one. He had cut his drinking down to nearly nothing since that night and hadn't touched a drop of hard stuff. Only once in a while did he allow himself a beer or two. Buck avoided the familiar end of the bar where he used to sit and stood near the door behind a chrome stool with a torn oilcloth seat. He hadn't ever noticed that the place was so dismal.

"Hey, Buck! Long time. Where you been?"

"Hell, Eddy," Buck told the bartender. "You know how it is."

"Sit down, sit down. Let me buy you a drink." He extended a hand over the bar, forcing Buck to move forward to shake it.

"No, can't stay. Just a cold beer for the road." Buck was uneasy. The place had become a dump. The linoleum was ripped and the place looked like it hadn't been scrubbed in days. The air was oppressive with old smoke that had stained the walls and woodwork. He and Charlie had often come here after cattle auctions. Sometimes he'd even stopped here to get beer while Maggie or some other friend waited for him in the truck. Then, like now, he stood behind the stools, eager to hurry out.

It was 5:30 when he left the tavern, and he had another forty minutes or so to go. He passed a sedan, then a semi. He finished the beer. He certainly didn't want to smell like liquor when he got to Etta's. God only knew how much that woman hated him. She hadn't liked him from the first. Etta always acted more like Pearl's mother than her younger sister and as if it was her business to protect Pearl and Katie. Now they even lived with her in that old house that had been their parents' home, cloistered like nuns, and him shut out.

But hadn't he paid enough, goddamn it? He had his rights as Katie's father and he wanted to spend time with her. A man's a fool when he risks everything he's ever had for a few tumbles in the sack and a complete idiot when he doesn't even know it's a risk. He knew all that now. Hell, if he hadn't had plenty of time to figure it out. Lots of time. One of the problems Buck had the most trouble with now was the amount of time on his hands. Add up all the hours he usually spent at the bars or with friends drinking and all related activity such as fooling around, then hand those hours to a man suddenly—that's what he'd done—and the man goes crazy trying to find things to do. He had puttered around fixing this and that, tried making furniture and set up a shop in the garage. Weekends he usually drove into Lewistown for a movie or just walked around town. Buck had hunted and fished last fall but since there was no one at home to eat the meat but him, he gave most of it away. And everyone he gave it to knew why and pitied him and said kindly that he should stay for supper. The fishing, and more especially the hunting, weren't the same as in former days when he had his old friends. Nothing was.

Once a few years ago, Buck had taken Katie hunting. She might have been twelve at the time. They went up into the Snowies to a lucky spot he knew. There were just the two of them, of course. The men he knew didn't hunt with women period, would have considered it bad luck. Pearl packed them a lunch, which they ate sitting on a fallen log after several hours breaking trail through one ravine after another of deep wood and brush. They tracked one deer all day. Buck was sure it was large by the size of the imprints and the droppings it left from time to time in the soft earth.

Finally they split up. Buck told Katie to follow his directions exactly. He told her to walk slowly and quietly up the mountain on an animal trail that skirted around where he was sure the deer was. He walked up from the other side, and just as he had planned, they moved the animal out into the open. He was right—it was a beautiful large five-point buck and Katie was glowing with joy as she pointed him out from across the clearing. He aimed and shot, as perfect a kill as he'd ever made, clean, instant, right through the neck. He hollered to Katie to come look and to his surprise she was motionless, stunned, horrified. "Goddamn it, Katie," he'd said. "What'd ya expect?"

Buck spotted a highway patrolman at the crest of the next hill and slowed down. He considered it a good omen. He was antic-ipating a good evening and felt, in general, new hope.

It had been a while since he'd gotten away from the ranch. Damn if he didn't hate the place sometimes. The whole of his life and all of his father's too had been tied up to a piece of land and what had it meant? Nothing. Well, it amounted to no more and no less than anyone else's life did, he supposed, and it was all he knew anymore. As a boy he'd loved this land, hunted every acre and fished every creek—the only thing he'd been good at as a kid. God knows he had never lived up to anything his old man ever wanted for him. Yet there was only the one time the old man ever beat him for anything. That was the time his two cousins, Ruth and Margaret, got him to go with them into the granary. There, on sacks of chicken feed, they had examined and stroked him and then pulled up their skirts. And then, then the door burst open on them and Uncle Harry dragged him out into the sunlight and told him if he ever came near his daughters again he'd kill him. Buck didn't doubt it for a minute. His pa beat him until he cried.

Girls always liked Buck. A certain type, that is. The kind of girl who gets a big kick out of what a man and a woman can do together. The other kind always avoided him, except to stare at him when they thought no one was watching, curious, as if he were danger. Pearl had looked at him like that. She made no move toward him but no move to avoid him either. It puzzled him and he was struck by her softness, her vulnerability, the pain he saw in her eyes. She was the first person he had ever wanted to do anything for. He wanted to take away her pain. He guessed he never had.

When he got to Great Falls, he realized how hungry he was. Buck decided to go immediately to Etta's and surprise Katie. By the time he got through town and to the house, he felt undecided and drove around the block. If he stopped for a cup of coffee, he could call to make sure it was all right. He wouldn't eat anything so he'd have a good appetite when he and Katie went out. And while he drank the coffee, Katie could get ready.

Buck went into a diner but it had no phone so he drove down the block. He found a café and got some dimes from the waitress

who cracked her gum while she counted out change for a five. He
didn't remember the number and looked it up. He knew what he
was going to say. He would ask for Katie and when she got on
he'd ask her to dinner. He dialed carefully. His fingers were too
big for the holes, and he had to press. It began to ring but by then
he had reconsidered and hung up, figuring that if Etta or Pearl
answered they might put him off, say Katie didn't want to talk.
And what if she didn't? If he just showed up, she'd be too
softhearted to tell him no.

Buck drove back to the house. Of course he didn't want to take
the other chance either, that Etta might hear his pickup and
answer the door and say no one else was home. To avoid that he
parked a few blocks away and waited for it to get dark before
walking to the house.

The ground and streets were full of leaves and the air was hazy.
Buck felt like sneezing. When he got there, he stood in the front
yard. This was crazy and he knew it. He would just go up to the
door, damn it anyway. Wasn't it his family in there?

At the top of the porch steps he hesitated again and finally sat
down out of sight of the door on the porch railing to the far left
so he could decide what to do. Through the window he could see
a light from the kitchen. The living room was dark. Buck wondered if Katie was even home but when the hall light came on, he
couldn't make himself get up, couldn't make himself move to go
ring the bell. He knew all he'd have to say was hello, he was in
town for the evening and hoped she'd join him for dinner. He
could have her home by ten, early enough for a Friday night,
didn't they think so? Who could object to that, for chrissake? If
they did, they could all come.

When Buck stood up to do it, a light in the living room went
on. Etta came in and rummaged around in a large sewing basket.
Then Katie and Pearl entered the room. Pearl sat on the couch
with a magazine and Katie stood on a short stool while Etta knelt
beside her and proceeded to poke and pin the dress Katie wore.

They weren't a dozen feet away, yet he couldn't make out what was being said. From time to time they burst out laughing and then Pearl would put the magazine down on her lap. He wondered if it could be the lighting that made Pearl's face look gay. Had she ever looked like that for him? He suspected that he and Pearl were never good together, not from the start. She always held back from him, was never there with him. Had she been somewhere inside or off somewhere else? He still hadn't figured that out but in any case he hadn't been able to draw her out or hold her there, either one, whichever was needed. He felt lonely around her and blamed her as much as he blamed himself for the running around. That it became a way he looked at things, a habit, menacing and destructive, was inevitable as far as he could see.

Katie was singing or acting out some little drama, Buck couldn't tell which. It surprised him to see it because she'd always been so quiet, never one to cut up. Wasn't it possible that it had been more than just drunkenness that drove him that night? A need to understand her, to penetrate the barriers Katie, like her mother, put up against him? He couldn't be sure.

Buck felt choked by the scene before him and knew he could not knock on that door. Nor could he leave until they left the room because they would hear him or see him run by the window. There he was, trapped on their porch, compelled to stare in at them like a Peeping Tom. The only thing to do was climb over the railing and jump the hedges, but he continued just the same to stare into the living room. He couldn't stop.

When Etta got up suddenly to close the drapes, he jumped as clear of the bushes as he could, but still broke a few branches that cut and scratched his hands and face. Just the thought of Etta discovering him there had startled him. That woman had always been the unnerving sort, but damn it, he was not afraid of her. Buck was sure he had dropped the watch, and he searched his pockets, then the hedge. He felt something with his foot. It was his hat, and he kicked it into the next yard where moonlight flickered against it. It was dark on the ground and he felt around on the grass. He couldn't see a thing. The leaves were soggy with dew and thick near the flower beds. He pulled out one of the rocks that bordered the shrubs. It was the size of his fist. He hurled it over the porch railing and through the window. He couldn't see what happened but there was a tremendous echo in his ears of splattering glass and the light in the living room went out.

He imagined their surprise, then their fear. It made him feel like bawling to think about them huddling in the kitchen in fear of an enemy outside in the night. And then Etta taking charge, no doubt praying under her breath while she phoned the sheriff. She probably thought they were in danger.

But that wasn't it.

What they weren't going to understand—Buck saw this clearly—what they would never understand, was that he didn't do it to hurt them and he didn't do it to scare them. He was sorry that he couldn't help doing it. Buck always regretted his inability to get things under some kind of control. And he didn't understand that, either. But it wasn't malicious, nothing he did was malicious. He just knew in that one moment he would have done anything to get in there. Anything. That was all there was to it, just a need to get in. Nothing more than that.

Buck walked down the block toward the pickup. He could hear traffic and sirens in the distance and he walked slowly, thoughtfully, the way any man might when he had a lot on his mind.

CHAPTER
THIRTY

———◆———

Etta hadn't needed to spot Buck's hat blowing about the yard to know who'd thrown the rock through the window the night before. She pulled her robe tighter and retied the sash before slipping quietly out the front door into barely dawning light. She picked up the hat, which was now resting against the hedge. It was a shame to just throw it away. God only knew what that man paid for his hats.

Etta opened the gate to the backyard carefully so as not to make noise. The last thing she wanted was for Katie to look out from an upstairs window and see her putting her father's Stetson in a garbage can. There was no need for Katie or Pearl to know it had been him. It was Etta's opinion that Buck had never quite known the difference between a good time and disorderly conduct anyway but this certainly surpassed any quirky behavior to date.

It was well known that any party Buck attended could get rowdy, especially if things didn't go his way. But he could have tantrums sober as well. Etta recalled that once he had become frustrated because he couldn't get his pickup to start. It was at the top of the lane above the dam. After working on it for a couple of hours without success, he put it into neutral, took off the brake, and let it roll down into the dam. As far as she knew it was still there.

It had always distressed Buck to find that some things, most things, could not be managed just by the force of charm or unyielding will, the two ways he pushed for what he wanted. Was she too hard on him, Etta wondered, too critical and unfeeling because she disliked him? Even if that were so, he made life bewildering for everyone, and she didn't want him coming here. She feared for damages that couldn't be repaired.

Etta walked down the alley, preferring to put the hat in some-one else's can—as though it were magnetic and likely to draw him back before it could be lifted with all the other throwaways into the garbage truck to be crushed and dumped. The morning was chilly and she hurried back unnoticed into the house. It was time for her morning prayers.

She arranged herself in the chair, tried calming herself. She was flushed from the task she had just completed in the cold air. She felt hot. Prayer, meditation, whatever you wanted to call what she tried to do, was never the same for her. Sometimes she sat in panic, pleading a special case to God, explaining its salient points in worried monologue. Other times she merely—no merely wasn't the word, it suggested belittlement and that wasn't it, effortlessly was more what she meant—she sat effortlessly in reception of something peaceful and reassuring and came away rested and restored. Sometimes she argued with herself about her beliefs, seeking to clarify and define what it was exactly she prayed to. Sometimes her mind caught the very core of some concept previously hidden to her and ran with it wildly, taking it from one gamut of possibility to something quite opposite and contrary. Then, just as suddenly, its illumined aspects might disappear and she couldn't have explained what she had just thought to anyone.

Occasionally she even fell asleep and woke up feeling guilty and a little disoriented. But now she just wanted to calm herself down. Not only had she not gotten much sleep after the rock throwing but when she finally did she'd had the nightmare—the nightmare that made her wake up in a cold sweat, afraid and sorrowful over something she could never recall. But this time, she remembered a child. There was the faint and briefest memory of a child. And nothing more.

Etta tried to meditate. She wanted to enter a stillness and surrender, not only herself but Katie and Pearl too. She wanted to remind herself that she must trust to some higher plan than her own, to some better will than hers.

When she was sure she had at least for the moment relinquished all fear, she got up from the chair, folded the lap robe she always put around her shoulders, and went to the kitchen. She opened the shutters in the dining room on the way to dispel the gloom she could still feel from the night before. She decided to have something more elaborate than toast and fruit for breakfast, maybe waffles and bacon as a special treat. She called up the staircase to wake her sister and niece, then looked up the phone number of the nearest glass repair.

When they were at last all sitting down—Katie had taken twice as long as usual in the shower and Pearl had decided to gather up all the laundry—it was Etta who fidgeted and rattled her coffee cup and played with her food. There she went, taking back all the worry she'd just thought she'd let go. Thinking about the child in her dream had brought up all the fears she had ever had for Katie. Will she survive mumps? Will she need braces? Will the scar on her face ever heal? (It had.) Will other kids appreciate her? Will there ever be a man good enough for her? The last was a little premature but still on Etta's mind. And ones worse: She'll fall off that tractor; she'll get hit by a car; she'll get pregnant; her own father might hurt her. That had been a persistent worry, that something had happened to Katie that involved Buck.

"Anything you want to talk about?" she'd say to Katie whenever she had that absentminded look of disappointment or its alternate, puzzlement and fear. But Katie always declined or changed the subject. And sometimes at the mention of Buck's letters or calls—he'd never come around until now—Katie flinched. Imperceptible to her mother, perhaps, but Etta caught it and was convinced something had happened. Buck had either lashed out at her in that mean way he had or maybe slapped her for being sassy. Sometimes she could be sassy. Maybe he told her the separation was her fault and Katie believed him. Something. There was something.

"I think it was Cameron," Etta heard Katie say.

"Cameron?" She hadn't been paying much attention.

"Who threw the rock. He's such a brat."

"I feel sorry for him," Pearl said. "His mother always goes out nights and leaves him alone."

"That's not surprising. She probably doesn't like him either," Katie said and the three laughed.

"Shame on us," Etta said. "Making fun of that poor boy." She could picture Cameron, the neighborhood bully, awkward, tall, and chubby, with no waist she could discern, unliked and mean, taking the blame for something Buck had done.

"If you want me I'll be at Jenny's," Katie said, getting up and clearing all the dishes she could carry to the kitchen. Katie was only good for one load when she was in a hurry as she was now. She was helping Jenny paint her bedroom.

Katie passed through the dining room again and waved good-bye to them. Etta marveled at the effect Katie had on her. Some days she couldn't imagine life without Katie and feared the day she would leave the house and never return. Off to college or marriage or a faraway city. Etta was sometimes jarred by the painfulness of her love for that child, it was too intense, too smothery, too afraid. It couldn't be healthy to feel so strongly for someone, to fear in advance the loss of her. Katie was an obsession with her and it was frightening. Etta poured more coffee and tried to explain it to Pearl.

"Pearl, I worry sick over that child sometimes."

"Well then quit," Pearl said, annoyed. "Where's all that faith you say we should have? God knows you do enough praying."

"When it comes to her, I don't know." Etta could admit that.

Pearl turned back to the newspaper.

"Do you think it's natural? I swear I worry more about her than you do."

Pearl glared at her but made no comment. These conversations never went anywhere. Etta always ended up irritating Pearl instead of getting her point across. Etta always blurted out something that sounded like something else. What she should have said was that her fear was not for Katie, but for herself—that someday, in the same way she had lost Harold, she would lose Katie. Not that Katie would die, of course not. She just wanted to explain to Pearl what she thought—that it must be a lesson for her, Etta, to learn that loved ones must be allowed to come and to go unfettered and free of charge. Moreover, she had to accept that Katie would have lessons too, ones that neither Etta nor Pearl could alter, soften, or anticipate.

Etta was sorry she'd brought the subject up; she'd only put Pearl in a bad mood. Pearl thought Etta had an unnatural need to define and prescribe, to give everything designations. She was probably right. Besides, Pearl had her own problems. She was trying to find another job so she could give up waitressing and get off her feet. She was trying to sort out the past, make sense of her failed marriage, her anger at Buck. Of course, like Etta, like Katie, she didn't talk about any of this. Not in so many words. It was just something Etta surmised, that people usually made a secret of their deepest grief.

Now Pearl slammed down the newspaper. "So if all that prayer doesn't make you feel better, why do it?" Obviously she had been stewing instead of reading. Etta didn't answer.

"You're devoting your life to this religion or whatever it is and still you're no better off than I am. Why don't you just go to church on Sundays like everyone else?"

It was a good question. Because Etta didn't like church, and
for the silliest of reasons. She didn't like how the minister or the
old ladies and pink-faced men who passed out the order of
service at the door smiled at her and kept smiling at her. Good
morning or welcome, they said between teeth clasped rigidly
with goodwill, as if to indicate some mastery over life as well as
the jaw.

But why did she devote so much time to prayer? What was she
trying to prove there? She didn't know.

The doorbell was ringing and Pearl got up to answer it. "Your
turn to do the dishes," she said. Actually it was Katie's but Etta
didn't mind and she gathered up the remains of breakfast.

"Etta, it's George," Pearl called from the living room.

"What happened to the window?" she heard George ask as she
entered the room.

"Someone threw a rock through it," Pearl explained. George
was agitated and seemed not to notice anything remarkable in
that. "Leona didn't come home again last night," he said. "I
can't stand it any longer. How many wives go around disappearing every time they take a notion?" Etta had to agree—not many,
especially at her age.

Leona had always been a predictable woman who did laundry
on Mondays, floors on Tuesdays, baking on Fridays, and so
forth. But an unusual pattern had taken over Leona's routine for
the past six months, a pattern that kept George speculating and
worrying. When she'd return, Leona would tell them where she'd
been but George never believed her. He checked on her a few
times, but only a few. He felt guilty, he said, not trusting his own
wife. He discovered, however, that in June she really had spent
the weekend at a Catholic retreat at the Ursuline Academy.

"But you're not Catholic," he had said as she unpacked.

"I know that," was all he got her to say.

What's more, in August Leona really had taken the new passenger coach across the highline, picking it up at Havre for the

ride west through Missoula, Plains, Sand Point, and then to
Spokane. She stayed in Spokane to shop, then took the train back
two days later. All she'd said that time was that the area between
Sand Point and Missoula was once a huge glacial lake, and then
waved a book of geology at them.

"Why don't you tell George your plans before you leave?" Etta
asked her once.

"Right. Then he wouldn't worry," Pearl added.

"You're badgering me," Leona said. "Shame. Two against
one. Shame."

There were other trips too: Virginia City, the museum in
Helena, a drive to Big Fork to sit beside the lake. Etta had heard it
all from George. She and Pearl hadn't taken any of it too seriously, were in fact sort of proud of Leona, had noticed a new
energy in her. Even joy.

"But why are we sitting here?" Etta now asked Pearl and
George. The living room was dark because of the blanket they
had tacked up around the window frame to cover the broken
glass. "Come on, George," Pearl said. "We'll make you some
lunch." She pulled him by the arm to the kitchen. He sat at the
small table while Pearl toasted sandwiches and Etta made fresh
coffee.

"I knew I should have taken away her car keys," George said.
"Since she inherited that money from her mother, she's been
crazy."

"Mustard, George?" Pearl asked.

"Anything," he said. "This time I'm calling the police."

"But if she has always come home on her own before, why not
now?" Etta asked him.

"Because it's been four days. She's never stayed longer than
two nights away. This time I have a feeling there's more to it than
a shopping trip."

"Okay. Eat and we'll call the bus and train stations," Etta
promised.

"And the police," he said. "I'm giving her description and license number to the police."

No one had seen a woman of Leona's description—forty-one, five foot one, 102 pounds, short, wavy hair (a touch of gray, no yellow), blue eyes—a woman who liked to wear herringbone wool slacks and sweaters in pastel shades of pinks and blues and who was probably wearing a navy coat, as it was missing from the hall closet and had recently come back from the dry cleaner's.

The police sounded concerned. Then, after hearing a history of Leona's recent bizarre behavior, they sounded less so. Etta sent George home and Pearl got ready for work. Today she was working the three-to-eleven shift.

"I'll go to the market after the window is fixed," Etta told Pearl. The repair man still hadn't come and she'd have to call him again. "And maybe Katie and I'll come for dinner." Usually once a week or so she and Katie went to the restaurant and sat in Pearl's station and chatted with her when she had a minute.

Tonight they invited Jenny to come along. Etta suspected she could stand to get away from the house, from the wet paint, from her nervous sister Shirley, from her brother Jim, who probably wasn't home, but who'd be quarrelsome if he were, and from George, who was likely drunk by now.

The girls were quiet in the car, so quiet Etta wondered if the music on the radio wasn't something special, though it sounded like the same stuff to her.

"Where do you think my mother is?" Jenny asked her.

"It's hard to guess," Etta said. "So far your mother's been pretty innovative." Jenny laughed at that and Etta thought there was less tension in the air. "I have a feeling she's fine, though," Etta added. That seemed to reassure Jenny further. Etta knew her feelings had a reputation for accuracy.

When they got to the restaurant it was crowded and Pearl

found them a small table at the rear. The girls ordered spaghetti and Etta, ravioli. Pearl managed only to grin at them as she ran by. When they were through, she brought them spumoni and little wafers and said that there was a party of thirty or so coming and she had to go to the back and fill baskets with breadsticks.

The girls went up to Katie's room when they got home, and Etta decided to read a while. She shut the drapes on the new window but didn't feel like sitting there alone. She took her book upstairs. It was about 11:30 when Pearl came running in. "I saw Leona's car," she said excitedly. "A couple of busboys and I were just leaving work when this guy walked out just ahead of us and got into Leona's car. I called the police and one of the boys followed him. We better go tell George."

When they got next door George was watching television in his undershirt, amazingly sober. He was alarmed to see them that late.

"What's wrong?" he said and waved them in. The phone was ringing and all of this at once seemed too much for him and he shook his way to the phone.

The police had found Leona. The officer told George that she was alive and well, though a little tipsy, in a motel by the river. The gentleman with her had been spotted pulling out of a parking lot driving Leona's car, he said. Etta felt sorry for George. All color drained from his face and he shook with anger and desperation as he listened and then related the conversation to them.

"This time she's gone too far. I don't want her back."

Etta offered to go get her. She left Pearl with George. She hoped Pearl could calm him down, convince him to forgive Leona. It was more likely she'd remind him that he'd been no prince himself all these years and that Leona could have thrown him out a long time ago with everyone's blessing—including his own kids'. Luckily, none of those kids were home tonight, at least not yet.

When Etta got to the motel, the stranger was explaining for the third time, he said, that he'd met Leona at a bar several days ago—no, he couldn't say how many exactly—and they hit it off and they'd been staying here and that was all there was to it. He had driven her car to get food and more to drink and, of course, that was okay with her. Etta could not quit looking at the man. He wasn't what she expected, though she hardly knew what that would be. He was neat appearing, sat erect in his chair, and looked directly at the officer asking the questions.

Leona came out of the bathroom finally, walking as steadily as she could, and matter-of-factly said, "Good-bye Phillip, my friend is here," as if she were going on an errand. Without looking at all surprised to see Etta, Leona walked to the door.

Etta didn't know what to say, and Leona, smelling of alcohol and cigarette smoke, refused to talk.

"Are you all right?" Etta asked. A policeman followed them in Leona's car and another followed behind him. Etta looked back at their lights in the silence. "Weren't you planning to come home this time?" she asked next. There was still no answer. The car was cold and Etta shivered. "Leona," she tried again, "aren't you glad to see me?"

"Yes, of course, dear," Leona said and burst out laughing. Etta was so startled that she laughed nervously too. Etta knew it wasn't funny, though the whole episode had definite elements of comedy.

When they got to the house, Etta thanked the police officers and helped Leona, who would not give them even a glance, up the porch steps. Inside, George still sat on the couch and did not acknowledge their homecoming. Etta then helped Leona up the stairs to the bathroom and Pearl stayed down with George.

In the bathroom, Leona began arguing with Etta and refused to cooperate as Etta tried to undress her. Etta finally got her stripped and persuaded her to get into the shower.

"You're not supposed to wash your hair before going to bed," Leona said.

"Wash it anyway," Etta told her.

Etta gathered up all the smelly clothes, including the navy blue coat and stuffed them down the laundry chute. There was no sense in George coming upstairs to these. She found a clean nightgown in a drawer.

When Leona was out and dried off, she lay limp on the bed. Etta saw it was useless to try to get the nightgown on her and pulled up the covers around her. She went downstairs where George and Pearl were having a drink.

"She's asleep, George," Etta said. "Deal with this in the morning, okay?"

He nodded. He appeared broken. This loud and bullying man appeared to have no fight left, not enough energy to finish his drink. Etta found him a pillow and blanket and she and Pearl turned off the lights for him and went home.

The house was quiet and the lights in Katie's room were off. Etta was glad Jenny was staying the night and had missed out on all that. Pearl said she was tired and they both climbed the stairs to their rooms. Etta lay on top of the covers of her bed for what must have been hours. She tried to pray but couldn't get everyone off her mind.

First Buck, then George and Leona. What was wrong with people? Maybe Pearl was right. What good did it do to pray? She couldn't say. All Etta knew at this moment was that she didn't want to think that people were what they appeared to be or that life was what everyone agreed it was: a war zone of good versus evil, heaven against hell or worse—a survival of the ablest, the healthiest, the smartest, the youngest, and most perfectly formed. Rather, Etta liked to think of life more or less as a series of vignettes and dramatic scenes, a part for everyone, prearranged, of course. (This life, you be the villain and I'll be the princess. Then you will understand ugliness in the world and I will know beauty. Or, I'll be the drunk and comprehend addiction and you can choose sainthood and learn obedience and commitment.) Then after the final scene, when a person stepped from the costume and took off the mask, Etta liked to think souls not otherwise engaged on stages elsewhere had a big party and said, Not bad, not bad, to each other, or My goodness, but you took that role seriously. Etta couldn't help wondering too if it didn't take more of something special to agree to some roles than others — Judas, for instance.

Etta understood how illogical and absurd what she liked to think would sound to Pearl, how it might upset her, and for these reasons would never bring it up.

Nevertheless, it was what she liked to think.

Sometime before dawn Etta awakened horrified. Once again she'd had the nightmare. Only this time, she knew every detail and she went over each one so that she would never, ever forget.

There was a child in a dark room, surrounded by tools of some sort. The room reminded Etta of a garage and there was only a small window at one end of the room, high up, almost to the ceiling. The child was frightened because a man had come in. He stood over her threatening her in some way. He seemed to be holding a tool of some sort. The child turned and Etta saw that it was Pearl. The child ran and the man chased her but they were still in the room even though they seemed to run very far across what she thought was grass. Then the man caught the child, and the child, she saw, was now herself. The child struggled and stumbled and finally began to fall, only the drop to the floor seemed to be miles away and the child was falling slowly and floating. And Etta saw all this happening to someone she knew to be her, but like an observer and not as a participant. But then the child was no longer her or Pearl but Katie. And still the man came in pursuit and Etta could see his face now. It was the man at the park with the blank face that Etta had seen when she was a kid. But as he came closer and closer to the child, she saw that it was not the stranger. It was her father. And he grabbed at the child, who had now fallen to the floor and was trying to get up. Now the man was Buck, and he suddenly fell on the tool he still held in his hand and disappeared into the floor or grass. Then Harold was there and he held the child. Etta could no longer see the child's face, it was lost in Harold's chest.

It was then that she woke up.

Etta went downstairs and made some coffee and sat with it at the kitchen table. The sun was coming up through the leafless boughs of trees outside the window, and Etta watched the light reach across the various branches, now brittle and shiny with frost. Etta tried to breathe through all the emotions she was feeling so that she could think. If she could do that, go past the emotions, she would get to the truth.

Unspeakable as that truth might be, she was ready to face it.

CHAPTER

THIRTY ONE

Sunday at work Pearl was tired and distracted. She hadn't slept well either Friday or Saturday night. Friday, after the rock hit the window, she had run to the dining-room window to look out. She didn't see much, just a man or maybe a boy, walking down the street. She tried to place him because there was something familiar about him. A neighbor? Or Cameron, as Katie had suggested? Maybe. Cameron was certainly as big as the figure she'd seen. No, whoever it was hadn't looked blocky enough to be Cameron.

Had this person seen the rock thrower? Or was he the rock thrower? It didn't seem likely, as whoever had, surely, would have run. She guessed it had been kids who threw it, then hid in bushes or in a backyard when they saw the man she saw walk by.

"Wake up, girl," Beto said. "You have an order out and table seven wants their check."

Saturday, as soon as George came over, Pearl had forgotten the man, and of course in all the ensuing fuss over Leona, had never gotten back to thinking about him. Not until this morning, that is. Now that brief glimpse of not much more than a shadow in the dark kept returning to mind.

"I know who it was," she told Rita.

"Who?"

"I mean I know but I can't place him."

Rita, of course, looked at her suspiciously. Rita had a certain look of suspicion she gave anyone who appeared confused. To her way of thinking, thoughts did not jump around, good minds did not change course, and the greatest dummy ought to know what he wanted to eat — a thing she told customers dawdling over a menu.

"Well, I do," Pearl said and went on trying to fit a name to the person.

It was probably just George, she told herself, George, absent-mindedly walking around the block looking for Leona. But he was too short. Or was he? How did you gauge height in the dark from that distance and under trying circumstances?

After Beto yelled at her the third time, she gave it up. But on her way home that night, the identity of the person she had seen in the window came to her.

"Buck!" she cried out loud.

It made absolutely no sense to her. Why would he be in their neighborhood walking by? Or more to the point, why would he throw a rock through their window? There was no reason but she knew it was him, though the man she'd seen was as dim and fleeting a figure as ever.

Before falling asleep Sunday night she decided what to do about it. She would drive to the ranch in the morning and confront him. Not only would she ask him about this but she would ask him what was going on between him and Katie, what had made Katie so upset with him, or him with her, that he hadn't tried to see her in more than a year. Or did he just not give a damn? At first she had been glad to have him out of her hair. Then after several months had gone by without a word from him, she had become concerned. Now she was mad.

After breakfast Pearl told Etta she had some shopping to do

and that she would go from shopping directly to work. She told Katie the same thing. She did not want them knowing about any trip to see Buck. But their minds were not on her. They were distracted by an article in the paper and hadn't even asked why Pearl had on jeans and a sweater. A teacher Katie had had the year before had been killed by a train. Evidently, she had jumped into its path. Suicide.

Pearl knew the road to Winslow by heart. After more than a year, she still knew where beyond the next hill to expect a tar patch or curve or straight stretch. Every fading landmark was as familiar to her as if she'd just passed by the day before.

She took her time. The roads were clear though a recent rain still lay frozen along the shoulders. There was little traffic but she was in no hurry. When she got to the last twenty miles after turning off at Winslow, all gravel now, she slowed down further, driving in the paths of other tires in the recently graded and regraveled roadbed.

She passed by Charlie's place, now Maggie's place. There didn't seem to be much activity there.

The ranch was not unlike the first time she had seen it. Nothing changed here. The barn and old buildings still defied neglect and despite wind, storms, and gravity, continued to stand.

She had expected to have trouble getting up the lane and had worn boots in case she had to walk it. Rainfall this late in the year could stay frozen until spring, in layer after layer under snow that would fall soon. But there were only patches of ice and sticky salt and her tires easily gripped tracks Buck must have made earlier.

There was no vehicle around except for the Cat and the cattle truck. She decided to wait. Buck, more than likely, would return soon from some errand to the pastures.

It was cold in the car and she walked to the house. She hesitated before entering but thought of no good reason not to. As she went in, a number of memories came to mind, all connected to sensory stimuli—the way light fell across the kitchen in the mornings, woodsmoke and the snap of a fire, the sound of a key in the door latch, the give in the floor at the entrance to the living room. It was though she herself had just come back from some errand at the barn to check a pie or roast in the oven. It was warm and clean inside. There was an order here she hadn't expected.

There were fruit and vegetables in the refrigerator and a carton of milk, everything organized in rows, presumably for the convenience of whoever was cooking dinner. There was no beer in the refrigerator she realized after she'd closed the door. Nor in the pantry. Gone were the usual cases Buck always kept there alongside enough hard liquor to stock a small nightclub. That was missing too.

A log fell in the woodstove and she jumped. The ironing board was up in the dining room and a shirt hung down from one end of it. Did Buck iron his own shirts? It hadn't dawned on her that he might ever do anything like that for himself. No, likely a woman lived here who would be upset to find Pearl snooping around like this. Pearl would not have been surprised had one come through the door and yelled at her. But there were no signs of any woman about the house. One dirty coffee mug was on the table, one plate and bowl in the sink, Buck's things only in the bedroom and bath. Only male smells here, of shaving things, cigarette smoke, Lava hand soap, leather boots.

Wherever Buck was, he had the dogs with him. She didn't see any signs of them but a half-empty tray of food outside the back door. She walked down to the barn and feedlot. The barn was colder than the outside air and smelled faintly of hay and feed. She didn't bother with a light there and quickly went back out into the sun. Cattle were chewing alfalfa from the bales thrown them that morning, curiously looking at her but undisturbed as she walked among them.

She sat on the fence. The countryside was covered with frozen dew that twinkled in the early winter sun. It was all too peaceful, too quiet; not even a breeze moved across the hills. The cattle looked tired and ragged, appreciative of peace. The calm before the storm and they knew it too.

She went to the garage then and turned on the light. She couldn't believe it. It was organized and all the old machinery parts were stacked neatly in one corner. There was the pleasant smell of wood and sawdust and the tools were arranged along new wooden shelves. In the center next to a bench was a cedar chest, complete but for the top that leaned against the wall. The chest was sanded and held together by furniture clamps, a finished product but for hinges and a finish. What an unusual thing to find here. Buck or someone had taken up woodworking.

She turned off the light and closed the door. Pearl walked up the hill above the barn to a spot where she and Katie used to sit summer mornings. Though it was cold, she sat down on the ground. She half expected to see ghosts here—that of the young mother, Buck's mother, killed by fire not a hundred yards away from where she sat, or of old August, Buck's father, or of Norman, the man struck by lightning just over the next hill. But there was nothing, not even the feuding spirits of father and son; nor was there evidence of a more recent history having taken place, that of a child running across the yard below with a pack of dogs. There was nothing but old buildings and a little smoke to suggest anyone lived here at all, that and a few ruts from tire tracks on the frozen lane.

Pearl had come here as a bride, hopeful and eager. She'd left mourning something between them that had never quite worked. She'd gone on with her life haltingly, troubled by memories, worn down by regrets. And though the place was his, she had loved it more than he had. She knew that, he knew that.

Pearl saw now that Buck, in his own way, had loved her. She had known him better than anyone ever had, maybe better than he knew himself. But the man she thought she knew so well had evidently changed over the year. He had become someone else. They had all changed and there was nothing here now to regret.

Pearl heard the pickup long before she saw it. It came down the road past Charlie and Maggie's old place and disappeared from view. She could hear it getting close and it suddenly swung over the bend by the dam and came up the hill and stopped. Barney Johnson's boy. She had forgotten his first name. He got out and walked over.

"Hello, Mrs. Buckman," he said, not showing the slightest surprise to find her there sitting on the frozen hillside.

"Saw your car go by a while ago."

"Yes," she said. "I came out to see Buck."

"He's been gone for a few days. Hunting, I guess. I'm looking after the place for him."

"Oh," she said. "There's a fire in the stove. . . ." She pointed to the house, to the chimney smoke fading into the cold air above it.

"Yeah, I lit it earlier. Don't want everything to freeze up."

"No," she said.

"Well, he'll likely be back in the next few days. Wasn't too specific about when."

"I suppose not. Well, I guess I won't wait then," she said, and the boy laughed shyly.

"Looks like a storm coming," he said.

"Yes, I guess I should get home before it starts."

"Well, I'll be off now," he said. "Nice talking to you."

"Yes, good-bye," she said but remained sitting there.

She watched his vehicle retrace its path down out of sight, visible again across the flat land by Charlie's place and then out of sight.

There was something sad about watching the only sign of life disappear like that. In the long run man had not made much impact across the face of this country and probably never would. Besides a few buildings, a line of fence, a few arrowheads, and ancient tepee rings, little change had taken place. When everyone on Squatter Creek was dead and gone, the wind would still blow across these same arid hills and jagged buttes. Snow would continue to pile each year into its lime-stained gulches and that dam and, come spring, nothing but wild things would ever flower.

The land would outlast everything.

Etta would say that it didn't matter, that life itself exceeded boundaries of birth and death and landscape. She would say too that love and attachments went broader and deeper than the surface of one foolish life. Pearl hoped Etta was right because as far as she knew, here on earth, intimacy usually failed. Like old rope, it frayed and broke at its weakest point. And she didn't want to lose Katie or Etta, as she had Buck, to weakened strands.

It was starting to snow and Pearl, conscious suddenly of how cold she was, hurried to leave. She had a life to get on with, a different but better life. And, what's more, she had to get to work.

CHAPTER
THIRTY TWO

———————◆———————

Buck was still hung over.

After leaving Katie's Friday night, hatless and despairing, having failed miserably, he had driven up to Neihart, rented a cabin next to a bar he knew, and gotten stinking drunk. The next night, not having had enough, he did it again.

Buck knew a guy named Mickey who had a cabin across the creek and a half-mile up the canyon. Buck knew that most evenings, at least at one time, his friend could be found at the bar. And a drinker's habits didn't change much. But Mickey hadn't shown up, and Buck decided that if by Sunday he still hadn't, he would go up and see for himself what was going on. Buck wasn't in any real hurry, he just wanted to do some hunting and spend a little time in the mountains. There was no rush, he decided, after he met a woman at the bar who was pretty good company.

Saturday morning Buck had awakened beside her and for a minute he was back at the ranch with Pearl, curled in the contours of Pearl's body, his chest to her back, his legs bending as hers did. Then he remembered that this was Marynell and that his head and his heart ached, and that, after a year of sobriety, he had fallen off the wagon.

Marynell was thirty-five, widowed, and lived off her husband's railroad pension. She picked up extra money by working in the area bartending or cooking at Kings Hill during the ski season. There was something about her that was attractive, a kind smile maybe, and golden eyes.

She made him breakfast that morning over at the bar and they sat on stools because all the chairs were stacked on the tables and the floor was still wet from where it had been washed not long before. Then they drove into town so Buck could buy some clothes and arrange for someone to do his chores.

He called Barney Johnson's boy. "Donny," he said. "Can you handle the watering over to the place for a few days?" At present all the cattle were on full feed and he had just rolled a week's worth of grain. He'd sold the cow too, as there didn't seem to be much need for one now and he didn't like messing with the milk. "Thanks," he said. "I'll make it worth your while."

Next he bought a couple of shirts, a pair of pants, and some underwear. After he had cleaned up back at Marynell's place, a small log house in Neihart, they decided to take a ride, then go over to Cub's Den for dinner and dancing.

"So how come you never remarried?" he asked her. She had been a widow now for six years.

"Oh . . . ," she said, tapping the table with her long fingernails as she considered the question. "I guess the right guy never asked. Why did you get divorced?"

It was a straightforward question and Buck saw no reason not to answer. "My wife got smart," he said honestly. "She left. I made a lot of mistakes," he said, drawing on the cigarette she had handed him.

"No law says you can't change," she said.

"I have changed some. But I don't know that it's enough." That's what he told her sober, but no telling what he'd said the night before. He couldn't remember.

The next morning was Sunday, and he decided it was time to square himself. About noon he crossed the creek and drove up the canyon to see his friend Mickey.

Mickey was splitting wood when Buck arrived. He put down the axe when he saw Buck at the gate. "Decided to do some hunting, did you?" Mickey said, shaking his hand. "Good to see you."

They went inside and Mickey made coffee. He took a fifth of whiskey from the cupboard and poured some into his mug and then hesitated over Buck's. "A shot?" he asked.

"No, no," Buck said. "Had too much last night."

"Heard a rumor you quit drinking."

"I did but the last couple days I got carried away. Hey, how come I haven't seen you at the bar?"

"Aw," Mickey said, "I only go down there nowadays when I run out of things to read."

Buck nodded. "So how's the hunting this year?"

"Good, good. The damn fly-boys are still coming up to the area but otherwise it's fine."

"And they still don't know a deer from a mule?"

"That's right. They ought to hang pictures from a zoo up in the barracks," Mickey said and Buck laughed.

"Don't laugh. Last week they shot a cow. Instead of telling anyone so they could save the meat, the bastards left it to rot. And you remember a few years ago when that fly-boy—some kid from New Jersey—shot a horse out from under old John Bailey."

"Yeah, I remember that," Buck said.

"Listen, tomorrow we'll take the horses and go up to a place the jetbutts don't know about. You can hardly get a jeep in up there."

"Sounds good," Buck said.

"So what say we have some dinner. I'm one hell of a cook. We'll play a few hands of rummy, go to bed early, and take off at dawn."

"Fine," Buck said. "While you cook, I'll split that wood."

Buck must have worked for an hour before Mickey rang an old dinner bell on the porch. The exercise, Buck felt, had done him good. After dinner, beef stew and biscuits, Buck fell asleep in the chair. Mickey woke him and directed him to a bed.

Mickey shook Buck awake about four the next morning. He pointed out a washrag, soap, and a porcelain pan full of hot water. "Breakfast in five minutes," he said. They quickly ate bacon and eggs and leftover biscuits and got their hunting gear together. "It's damn cold. Take this hat," Mickey said, taking down a red plaid wool hunting cap from a shelf of assorted sweaters, hats, and worn-out boots. They gathered up sandwiches, two pints of whiskey and a thermos of coffee and saddled two horses.

It was still dark but they could see light beginning its climb over the east ridge of mountain and they rode to meet it. It was beginning to snow. Mickey led the way to an animal trail that circled around and up one fairly forested area. When it was light enough to see, they checked the tracks they found in the crusted snow. They decided that they had been made by a doe and fawn but followed anyway to see what else might be in the vicinity. Finally, they stopped for coffee and lit cigarettes, standing quietly beneath trees that dropped small clumps of snow on them from branches burdened recently by heavy snowfall. The morning light struck the snow-covered ground around them in random and dazzling patches through the trees. They could have heard a man spit over the next range of mountains it was so quiet.

After they had finished the coffee and smoked a couple more cigarettes, Mickey put the thermos away and they mounted the horses again. The next tracks they saw were sizable and many, indicating the movement of a herd, not ambling or stopping to graze, but moving fast as if something had alerted it. Mickey thought the tracks might be as fresh as minutes old, judging by steam coming from assorted droppings and by how fast the falling snow concealed them. Not ten minutes farther along Mickey spotted something red in the snow and got off his horse to check.

"I'll be damned," he said. It was an empty cigarette pack, discarded over an hour ago, he guessed. The hunter, or hunters, were on foot, as there were no signs of horses or pack mules. They had probably left a vehicle parked somewhere down below the line of dense timber and hiked in. "That's what was pushing that herd," Buck said. Only the herd had apparently circled back recently and was probably behind the hunters. They continued.

Not more than fifteen minutes later, Buck was sure he heard the deer in the thick brush and timber up ahead. It sounded as if they were beginning to run and Buck guessed they had heard the horses. The two men pushed on now, though it was impossible to go very fast. Mickey was bending under low-hanging branches in front of Buck when they heard the first shot. It was followed by two more. There was nowhere to go but forward.

"Son of a bitch!" Mickey yelled and Buck shot into the air to let the bastards who were firing know that they were shooting at men. Mickey's horse reared suddenly, threw its rider, and then took off through the trees. Mickey lay on the ground. Buck dismounted quickly and pulled his own horse securely by the reins. Mickey had a bullet in his right thigh, and his blood was melting a circle of snow around his leg.

"There's a first-aid kit in your saddlebag," Mickey said, grinning. "What do you want to bet it was some eighteen-year-old fly-boy from Philadelphia?" Buck bandaged the wound as best he could and wrapped a tourniquet above it.

"Can you sit up?" Buck asked him.

"Sure," Mickey said. "Hand me that medicine." He pointed to where the pint was. "And help me up." Buck pulled him up to his left leg and mounted. Mickey was able to swing his right leg over the saddle behind him but Buck felt him wince as he did. Buck turned the horse around and they began the descent, Mickey drinking now and then from the pint and whistling under his breath in pain, his head leaning against Buck's back. Buck was cold and knew Mickey must be too. The runaway horse had carried their thermos, sandwiches, Mickey's rifle and binoculars, and the second pint.

When they got to the cabin, Buck carried Mickey from the horse to the pickup, which he started and left running with Mickey inside. Buck took the saddle off the horse, dried him quickly, and threw a dry blanket on him. He led him to the horse shelter beside the cabin and left him grain and water. Buck ran into the cabin for blankets, a pillow, and more whiskey. He locked up behind him. He had to drive to the gate, get out, open it, drive through, close it. He went as fast as he could down the rocky road and crossed the creek, coming up behind the deserted bar. It was five after ten in the morning.

By the time he got to the highway, it had quit snowing and was clear and sunny. Buck took the highway out of the mountains as fast as snowpack would allow onto the dry roads of wheat country and into Great Falls to the hospital. He arrived at the emergency room door and honked. Without waiting for help, he carried his friend inside. He was shown to a room with a surgery table where he carefully placed Mickey on his back. How Buck hated these places. Mickey opened his eyes, not drunk enough and in pain.

A doctor appeared from somewhere with a needle and gave Mickey a shot, undid his bandage, and went to work extracting the bullet. Because it was a gunshot wound, Buck had to sign a statement explaining what had happened. Mickey would be all right, the doctor said. Buck asked the nurse for paper, pen, and a safety pin.

"I'm going back to find your horse and anything else in the area," he wrote. "See you tomorrow. I'll bring more medicine." He pinned the note to the nightshirt Mickey now wore and went to find a phone.

When Buck got back up to the bar he stopped to tell Marynell, who was bartending, what had happened. "I called the sheriff and they're sending someone out to check on it," he explained.

She made him a sandwich and he drank a beer. She promised to put out the word in the Neihart and Monarch areas for any nervous hunters who might have quit early in the day.

"I'll be back tonight," he told her.

"If you're not, I'll send a posse," she said, smiling.

It was two o'clock by the time he got to Mickey's. He had only three hours or so of daylight left to find the runaway horse or to see if the hunters were still in the area. He doubted they were. He put the saddle on the horse he'd ridden that morning, checked his ammunition and rifle, and started up at a trot. It had started snowing again and the sky was a dark gray. It took him about an hour to get to the place where Mickey had bled, though snow had covered every sign but the new-fallen branches the horse and rider had broken. It was snowing harder now and the wind was coming up. Buck knew he'd have to find Mickey's horse fast or leave it because it was getting harder to see all the time. He still could make out where the horse had disturbed the underbrush and broken its own trail. He followed carefully.

The wind knocked snow from treetops and it swirled in the air around him and stung his face. He continued for a short distance until any signs of a frightened horse running through timber had disappeared into the bluish haze of blowing snow. Buck decided to forget the runaway and return the way he had come, pick up either the old logging road or the creek, and follow one or the other down to the cabin.

He turned his horse around, trying to find the way he'd just come. Buck finally dismounted and led the horse, which was getting jumpy in the blowing wind, wind that began now to whine eerily through the trees. The nervous horse reared and pulled back on the reins as the whine gave way to a low howling; Buck knew it would be dark soon. He thought he had picked up the animal trail they'd been on that morning, as he was having to fight fewer and fewer branches with his face. Often a branch was inches from him before he saw it, too late to avoid it smacking him. But the trail seemed clearer now, less dense, and he considered mounting his horse again when at that moment the earth dropped away beneath him and he landed on his belly in what was left of the creek — enough icy water to soak him. The horse shied and reared behind him, and he heard the animal pounding through the woods.

Buck tried to walk the banks — the creek bed was safer but too cold. He kept falling and sliding down the slipping bank, but he knew he must keep moving. It was dark now and he could feel the cold piercing as deep as his bones. He wished he'd thought to bring a pint of whiskey along and would have liked a cigarette but they were wet as were his matches and his hands, now too brittle to hold one to his mouth. His frozen jeans cut his legs through his long underwear and he knew they must be making a scratchy, clapping sound if he could only hear it above the wind.

Buck kept moving, groping from tree to tree, exhausted and wanting to rest but daring not. He thought he was losing his sense of time and distance and sometimes had the sensation he had been hypnotized by the unreality of the angry, swaying woods, the ghostlike snow that hurled itself again and again with a force of attack sufficient to knock him to his knees. This alternated with a peculiar knowledge of warmth, as if he had found a warm pocket of air and was sailing on it like a weightless balloon, watching himself moving ponderously through the storm in slow and solitary motion. Then suddenly he'd be thrown back into his own pain, his own exhaustion, his own terror.

But even the fear passed at some transparent and untroubled point, one lucid moment when he knew he'd either live or die and one seemed no more preferable than the other, neither way better or worse. When he was thrown down again, he was without resistance and leaned gratefully against a tree for a minute's rest. He recalled what an old man had told him once: that there was a difference between the men from the prairie and ones from the mountains.

The plainsman looks outward—at the weather, politics, the marketplace—because his crops and his animals depend on it. But the highlander can't see anything for mountains and trees, and for that reason, the old man said, spends his life looking inward.

Buck, both because he couldn't see anything period, and because he considered the whole idea a crock of shit, laughed. He thought he heard the sound of that laughter despite the wind.

Soon he had that same sense of disorientation he'd had earlier, that sense of calm and weightlessness, there above himself, but aware of himself. This time, however, the wind seemed to stop its tirade against him and even the sun had come out to warm him.

Like earlier that morning, it was quiet. He could have heard a man spitting over the next ridge.

CHAPTER
THIRTY THREE

Katie looked over her last few journal entries for October in the spiral datebook she kept on her dresser.

FRIDAY
Broke up with Billy. He's a jerk.
SATURDAY
I couldn't sleep last night. It was creepy to have someone throw a rock through the window. The more I thought about it, the more I knew it was meant for me. Then this morning, I was looking out my window and saw Aunt Etta putting Pa's hat into a garbage can down the alley.
SUNDAY
I still haven't figured out why Pa would throw the rock. Has he gone crazy? Does he hate us? Why is Aunt Etta keeping it a secret? Is it to hide it from Mama or just from me?

Katie turned the page and wrote under "Monday":

Leona came home sometime over the weekend, and she and George are not speaking. Jenny wonders what's going on. I said I didn't know.

She closed the notebook and went down for breakfast. Etta was pouring coffee and her mother was scrambling eggs. In the mornings, the two carried mugs around as they cooked, moving them as they moved, from counter to sink to stove. Often one asked, "Where'd I leave my coffee?" and the other said, "That's mine, yours is there," and pointed. Katie tried to solve that problem once by buying them each a special mug. But it hadn't worked, as they had a set of mugs already that they preferred — because a proper mug is not so wide that it cools coffee fast, nor is it that thick kind that gets porous, or that thin glass kind that clicks against your teeth.

What they told Katie was that they didn't want to risk breaking her gifts. The new mugs ended up on the counter on display. The red flowered one of Etta's gathered coins, assorted nails and screws, and paper clips. Her mother's, a blue striped one, held receipts from the milkman and grocer.

Katie poured herself some juice and sat down. On school days they didn't bother setting the table in the dining room and the kitchen was warmer anyway. Her mother went to the front porch for the newspaper and Etta dished up the eggs and placed hot buttered toast on the table.

"Listen to this," her mother said, bringing in the paper. "Remember that social studies teacher you disliked so much? She jumped in front of a train in Seattle. Killed herself."

"Mrs. Martin?" Katie asked.

"That's the one."

"How awful," Etta said.

Katie remembered Mrs. Martin well. She was the one teacher who'd never missed a day of class all year and the one teacher the kids prayed would. She addressed the class not by names, but by numbers handed out according to the seat assigned and the row it was in. Katie, who sat in the first row by the window in the third seat behind Johnny Polutnick, was A-3. Jenny, in the corner, was F-8.

"Put your numbers and the date on your papers," Mrs. Martin would say. Or "C-2, explain the Boston Tea Party." Katie had never seen Mrs. Martin smile. If she could have given her a number, it would have been 0-8. Mrs. Martin's puffy head of hair made a tidy 0, and her round glasses lay across her rather long face like a reclining eight. Her tall, large-boned body, cinched in as it always was—usually with a narrow patent-leather belt—gave an eight shape to round buttocks and a generous, buxom chest that arched in a slow C-curve to the belt.

"What a shame," Etta said, looking over Katie's shoulder at the paper. "She was only thirty-four."

The newspaper article had no more information on Mrs. Martin than Katie did. Just that "a Great Falls resident who taught ninth grade social studies at a local school was reported to have jumped in front of a train Sunday morning while visiting in Seattle, according to authorities there." The article went on to say more about the train than about Mrs. Martin, except that she had stayed in a transient hotel near the piers.

Katie couldn't get Mrs. Martin off her mind that day. The death gave new dimensions to the woman, tragic, puzzling ones that made Katie feel strange and sad. She wondered if Mrs. Martin had had a luckless life, burdened in some way, and if that were to blame. Or had she no life whatsoever and so had done it for that reason? She told Jenny about it at lunch and neither could recall Mrs. Martin ever talking to other teachers in the halls, or discussing anything with a student not incidental to the curriculum.

After school that day Katie walked through Gibson Park. The autumn leaves, once crisp and colored, had all turned a wet, earth brown and lay in soggy matting along the ground. The park was almost empty. One wino stumbled by, clutching a hat he should have been wearing in one hand and a brown bag in the other, and a young boy threw balls for his dog. She had never seen the park so stripped, exposed meanly to the wind while it waited for a cloak of snow or shiny frost. The last time here, she'd come with Billy. It was peculiar then too, sort of hushed and empty that day and only one swan had been on the glassy pond.

"What happened to the other swan?" she asked a man raking leaves around empty flower beds.

"Died," he said.

"Why don't they get another one?"

"It's not that easy," he said and shrugged.

The single swan was gone now too and so were the ducks, though the pond wasn't frozen yet. Even the birds and squirrels had already left for better winter locations.

When she got home, she threw off her coat and lay on the couch. She liked looking at the room upside down and imagining life taking place this way. She pictured Etta carrying teacups on a tray, stepping over the now high threshold and sitting down beside the chandelier, which would be erect and rather like a huge Christmas ornament and just the thing to gather around. They would need a ladder to get to the bookcase and if someone threw a rock through the window the glass would rain down upon their heads and probably get in their tea.

What if life was like her upside-down version of this room, simply something she saw from a certain perspective, not necessarily real? Was it even possible her life went on only in her mind, so though it appeared she might be sharing experiences with others, she wasn't at all? And similarly, did others live exclusive, solitary lives too, that went on only in their minds? It was even likely she was the only person alive and the others all something she made up. Or what if it were all a dream she might awake from to find herself not herself but a boy in Africa say, or an old woman in China.

Katie went to the kitchen and made a peanut butter and jelly sandwich. Then she found her army surplus sleeping bag in the basement, got a pillow off her bed, and put on her coat. With the sandwich in a pocket, she took everything out to the backyard.

She put the pillow and bag down in the middle of the yard, arranged them, got into the bag and zipped it up. The grass was brown and the ground felt frozen. The sky held no definite clouds but was gray overall. The wind had gone down and she thought it was a little warmer. It was going to snow.

Why, she wondered, had Mrs. Martin been in Seattle? It hadn't been a long weekend or holiday and, after all, they had trains in Great Falls. Was she running away or about to disappear for good? Katie finished the sandwich. Next time she would add more jelly. Jenny's mother disappeared too, but she always returned. Jenny couldn't understand it. Well, she could. That one was simple. Leona was sick and tired of her boring life. Being married to a fat, crabby man and having three sloppy kids couldn't be a lot of fun.

It was her own father that Katie couldn't figure out. Why was he outside their house Friday night in the first place? Why would he drive all that way just to throw a rock? He never sounded angry in his letters or when he called. He'd even told her once that he'd visit soon.

Katie would like to be able to talk over things with her mother and aunt but it was just about impossible. Their embarrassment was too great if they knew the answer and their silences too long if they didn't, as if she had asked them to tell about their sex lives or explain the cause of World War II. They were too anxious for Katie to see things just right or to see that they saw things just right—with understanding but maybe not approval. Of course, they didn't know what to think of their own confusion, either, over the predicaments others got themselves into.

Katie heard Etta's car coming down the alley. She barely managed to get out of the bag, run it and the pillow to the basement stairs where she flung them, and get back to the garage to help Etta with the groceries.

"Your mother left for work early today. Did you see the note?" Etta asked as they entered the kitchen. "Katie, you didn't clean up after yourself," she said, seeing the peanut butter and jelly and bread still out on the counter where she was attempting to put down the bags she carried. She slid the offending clutter over with her elbows. "I hope you didn't spoil your appetite." Why Etta and her mother always said that, Katie didn't know. But they did, one of the two, every afternoon. Totally predictable.

"It's going to snow," Katie said.

"Oh, how do you know?"

Aunt Etta never paid attention to weather until what was going to happen happened. Then she'd say absentmindedly, "It's raining," or "The sun's shining," as if the person walking with her hadn't noticed it too. Katie's mother, though, liked reading the sky and often complained to Etta's horror that they should cut down the big cottonwoods, both so they could see something and to allow more sunlight in.

"I can tell by the air," Katie said. Actually, she didn't know how she knew. There was just a smell to the air that to her preceded snow.

She went to her room, put on the Peter Gunn album that she loved, and danced before the mirror. She moved in long, exaggerated movements, shoeless and as quietly as possible so that Etta wouldn't yell up the staircase. She spent the rest of the afternoon dancing to both sides of the album until she collapsed, exhausted, on her bed. A five-by-seven framed picture of Billy was still on her night table. Katie pulled out the picture, marked a large X across it with a ballpoint, and put it back in the frame.

She had broken off with him for two reasons. The first one hadn't really bothered her for a long time. Billy lied—he lied about little things, big things, things of consequence as well as those that as far as she could see did not matter one way or another, so much so that on the rare occasions she discovered him telling the truth she was surprised, suspicious, and on the alert for a trick. He once told her his father owned the apartment building he lived in but she had inadvertently seen a rent receipt on the cluttered kitchen table. He said he had a brother off at reform school. He didn't. He was an only child. He lied about the cost of his clothes—he always paid more—when everyone knew the price of Levi's or Jantzen sweaters. He would even lie in the morning that he hadn't brought a lunch, only to have it tumble from his locker that afternoon. Most everyone forgave him his lying to some extent. They all liked him anyway; he was fun, and they excused it as a form of teasing and a need for attention. In the long run, though, it got on Katie's nerves. Add to that his newly acquired fault and Katie decided she'd had all she wanted of him.

The past few months, Billy tried to put his hands on Katie's breasts every chance he got. He preferred trying to put them up her shirt but would consider any approach—leaning against her breasts with the outside of his arm, covertly dropping his hand from her shoulder, dancing in a new crushing embrace, or trying to tweak her nipples.

"Is it romantic?" Jenny once asked her, clearly impressed.

"Perverted's more like it," Katie said.

"Katie, dinner is ready," Aunt Etta now called.

That evening after she did the dinner dishes, Katie returned to her room to study. She had twenty plane geometry problems that she concentrated on and finished. After that she felt restless and couldn't read the assigned chapter in her text. She started "Democracy in the New World" three times. She looked out the window. It was snowing and the wind was starting to blow.

Maybe Mrs. Martin killed herself over an illicit affair with a student's father. He came to her to discuss Bobby Jr.'s F and they fell into an embrace on the desk. No, she wasn't exactly attractive enough for that. But how attractive did you need to be? Ugly people got married and pregnant and all that anyway, so perhaps it was something of that kind. Or maybe she had a husband— they called her Mrs., after all—whom she adored and he ran off with his secretary or nurse just as happened so often according to

Jenny's mother. Katie stared at the James Dean poster on the wall opposite. What if Mrs. Martin killed the husband over that and later felt unbearable remorse? But no doubt she would have heard about a murdered husband before this, had that been the case. No, Mrs. Martin probably just went insane. She obviously wasn't too stable, going around numbering people like she did. Another possibility was that she was so lonely she wanted to die.

Could she have been murdered? Of course! Mrs. Martin met someone at the pier or a real transient at the hotel or maybe someone followed her from Montana to where she had gone to hide. The murderer or murderers discovered her trying to board a train and, unseen, had pushed her off the platform. That would account for her being in Seattle on a weekend during the school year.

Oh dear, she wondered. On Monday morning was there a ninth grade class of numbers greeted for the first time by a substitute who wanted to know their real names? Katie sighed. This wasn't getting anywhere.

"What is Mrs. Martin's real story? There is sure to be one," she wrote in her datebook under the morning's entry and went to the kitchen for a piece of cake.

"Isn't Mom home yet?" she asked Etta, who was reading.

"Not yet," Etta said.

"I think I'll go to bed."

"Good night, dear. Don't forget you have a dental appointment tomorrow."

"Cripes," Katie said and went back to the kitchen to put away the cake.

Katie showered, brushed her teeth, and took a few snips off her bangs with Etta's sewing scissors. She had forgotten to retrieve her pillow from the bottom of the basement stairs and knew if her mother or aunt saw it, she would be asked to explain. She ran down in the dark and brought it up, hung up her clothes, and was at last ready to turn off the light.

*   *   *

That was the last thing she remembered before awakening from her dream. She couldn't recall it exactly—it was something about knowing two guys were coming to the back door but she beat them to it, locking the doors in terror that they might get in and harm her. But then, remembering that the front door was unlocked, she ran through the house only to find short little walls that anyone could step over. She locked the short little door anyway, knowing it was no use. Then she either woke up or dreamed that she woke up.

Everything was all right. She was in her room. There were the same posters over her desk, the same pom-poms in the corner, the usual drooping banner with a large blue bison overhead. It was still snowing but quietly, without wind. She lay back down but she couldn't sleep. She thought she might read but all she had was a book Jenny had lent her, a mystery, and she wasn't in the mood for that.

Katie remembered more about her dream—that when she ran from the back door to the front she passed a woman reclining on a couchlike bed who seemed to know that Katie was in trouble but did nothing to help. She didn't even bother to look alarmed as Katie recalled. Who was she? She was familiar but Katie could not place her.

She decided to include the dream woman in her notes where she kept track of all the woman stories she'd ever heard. She was writing a book. There were stories in there her mother and aunt had told her and ones she knew herself. What had happened to all those women? It was anybody's guess. She turned on the lamp and began to write on the back of an old term paper:

Mavis and Darlene, retired madams, moved to the Catholic hospital, where the nuns gave them a private room, the reason being their large contributions over the years to the sisters of mercy. The young nurses in training, to their never-ending disgust, had to wash and iron Mavis' and Darlene's laundry and run down three flights for milkshakes.

Grandma Buckman: To this day no one will admit what secret persuaded her to return to the burning house but a young detective named Katherine Rose will someday determine what it was with help from certain close friends.

Etta's friend Helen Engle became the first woman disciple in heaven and was put in charge of guardian angels in the western hemisphere—except Montana, where none were appointed. Helen felt people there should figure things out for themselves. It was never clear why.

The goat lady sold all her sand dunes to the College of Great Falls and retired to luxury. When she died she left a sizable fortune to a nephew who promised to take care of her goats and reopen the Tumbleweed Tavern.

At this writing, no one knows why a woman as against nonsense as Mrs. Martin was would jump into the path of a train.

Katie: Katie moved to the coast, where she tangled with—well encountered in a big way—both a young sea captain and an Oregon lumberjack. On holidays, however, it was her habit to return home to Montana, where rain or shine her aunt and her mother sat waiting on the porch to welcome her, a wreath of lilacs beside them and a bottle of champagne. Imagine finding lilacs at Christmastime, but they did. It was good champagne that was hard to come by.

Katie turned off the light again and tried to sleep. But then she was certain she heard something or felt something, and she lunged forward in some collision with herself, as she sometimes did when half-asleep and startled by a noise.

She was afraid. Someone was there. But who? Instantly, her

mind locked, fixed now on pain, a grim and sharp flash of horror and danger that struck even her bones. She kept her eyes shut tightly, her body still, her breathing quiet so that she might be overlooked by the intruder.

Then she thought she heard her father's voice, though not words exactly. It was more an impression she had, an impression of sound, more a feeling of a voice than any actual voice. When she dared open her eyes to look, he was there at the foot of her bed, just standing there. He didn't have his hat. Of course not, she remembered. It was in the garbage can. She wondered if he'd come for that and if she should tell him where it was. She was sure he wanted to say something but he just stood there. All of a sudden without thinking about it, Katie was aware that she felt no fear, that she didn't have to be afraid, that for whatever reason he came this time, it was not to harm her. All that in one instant. She thought to ask him why he threw the rock but he was trying to tell her something.

"Forgive me, Katie," she thought he said. "Please forgive me."

"I do," she cried. "I do." She knew he didn't mean for throwing the rock, just as she knew there was nothing she didn't forgive him for. "I do," she cried again because he was going.

"I love you, Katie," she heard him say though she couldn't see him any longer. "I love you too, Pa," she said, hoping he could still hear her. She sat up in bed now, wide awake from the sound of her own voice in the dark. She waited in the darkness for some time, not wanting to sleep in case he came back.

Katie awakened late. There was sunlight at the window and her mother was calling to her as she came up the stairs.

"Katie, you're going to be late." She came in carrying a soggy, faded gift-wrapped box. The bow was limp and frayed and much of the wrapping paper was gone. There was a small gift card attached, soiled and hanging.

"The boy threw the paper into the hedge again. Look what I found. It says 'To Katie with my love.'"

Katie peeled away the wrap and inside the box was a velvet case containing a white gold watch with tiny diamonds around the face. She knew it was from her father. She took it out of the box and tried to put it on her wrist, struggling with the clasp.

"It's just a wonder I found it," her mother said, apparently puzzled, maybe wondering why it was in the hedge.

Katie's hand shook clumsily and the watch fell to her lap. She began to cry.

"What's got into you?" her mother said and embraced her awkwardly. She held her gently for some time and Katie knew she was crying too. They wept in silence.

"Well," her mother said finally, pulling away and wiping her eyes. "Let's try that again," she said, and Katie handed her the watch.

"It's beautiful," Pearl said and held Katie's wrist up to the window. Katie could see the diamonds like little points of light through her tears, moving as her hand moved, and bright like the crystals sunlight makes on snow.

ABOUT THE AUTHOR

Toni Volk was raised in Butte, Montana. She dropped out of school at the age of sixteen, had two children and one divorce, and then passed her GED test to obtain a high school diploma. She moved to Missoula, majored in Journalism and graduated from the University of Montana. She then studied at the Iowa Writers Workshop, and received a James A. Michener Fellowship from the Copernicus Society of America which enabled her to complete this novel. She now lives in San Diego, California.